The Ecology Club
A Cozy Mystery
(and How to Save the Planet)

I0687074

The Ecology Club
A Cozy Mystery
(and How to Save the Planet)

Mr. Szilard Substitute Teacher Mystery #1

D.R. Oestreicher, PhD

Omega Cat Press — California

Omega Cat Press, independent publishing since 1990

Paperback ISBN: 978-1-954225-21-3
Electronic Book ISBN: 978-1-954225-03-9
Hardcover ISBN: 978-1-954225-05-3

7 8 9

"Simplex sigillum veri"
Simplicity is the sign of the truth.
Herman Boerhaave, Dutch Hippocrates, (1668-1738)

"Teaching occurs at the boundary between creative chaos and attentive order."
Ms. Lucinda Salas

"You never learn anything when your mouth is open."
Zarand Szilard

"When you hear hoof beats, don't expect to see a zebra."
Dr. Gwendolyn Curie, MD, PhD

"Evil is evil. Do not compare."
Fitch

Dedicated to strong women of all ages

By J. Oestreicher and D. R. Oestreicher

Pandemic Mysteries #1: Darwin's Paradox
#2: Plague of Equals
#3: The Two Pearls

Suramarti Saga #1: Kitane, Bull Jumper
#2: The Murders, The Mosque

By Joy Oestreicher

Legends of Azureign #1: Dragon and Oracle
#2: Raka and Secrets
#3: The Pirate Queen
#4: The Compact Shatters

https://amzn.to/2SpaDMN

Blurb for The Ecology Club

When substitute teacher Zarand Szilard is awakened by a last-minute call to cover Ms. Salas's classes at Stony Estancia High School, his gut alerts him to expect trouble. By the first period, his worst fear materializes: a student discovers Ms. Salas's lifeless body.

Zarand's intuition tells him it's murder.

As a substitute, he has no standing with the school or the police. Regardless, he uncovers plenty of motives. Ms. Salas investigated college admission fraud at the high school. She solicited harassment complaints against the principal. She knew about the infant grave discovered on school grounds. She distributed condoms.

While investigating her death, he discovers she is not Ms. Salas. To find her killer, he also must uncover her true identity.

How can Mr. Szilard unravel these mysteries within mysteries when the school and the police want to close the case before someone sues?

See **Help Is Available** at the end of the book.

Table of Contents

1. NOT YOUR TYPICAL DAY: MONDAY AM

The rear door burst open. Everyone turned to see what had disturbed our classroom. Brooklynn staggered in and dropped her backpack with a thump. Something was wrong.

Earlier that morning, when the substitute call came late and I missed breakfast, my gut told me this wasn't going to be an ordinary assignment.

The day began in a typical way. I handed out donuts in homeroom. The tardy buzzer gently reminded Ms. Salas's first-period AP Biology students to finish greeting each other. I allowed them a few minutes to settle.

Following the school district's policy and my intuition, I locked the hallway door. At Stony Estancia High, safety came first, even though this privileged suburban campus only made the news to celebrate student awards and accomplishments, never for trouble.

This school was an example of Stony Estancia's understated opulence. While it appeared ordinary, the cafeteria had an on-site bakery and a chef who prepared organic specialties. The library had current best sellers and subscriptions to academic journals. They donated shelf-worn books to other schools. The PTA provided each teacher with a stipend for enrichment materials and field trips.

Not expecting Brooklyn, I raised Ms. Salas's bell to signal the start of class. When they saw my hand go up, the chatter died down and the few students remaining in the aisles headed for their seats. Classroom management was not an issue with these well-behaved kids. I could focus on teaching.

But before I rang the bell, that rear door burst open.

I stared over the lab bench that served as Ms. Salas's desk and watched the girl charging across the room. She jostled a boy who was standing in the aisle. She bumped into a table knocking a laptop to the floor with a crash. Nothing slowed her progress. Tears pooled in her green eyes. Her black ponytail whipped back and forth.

Something was very wrong.

I braced my hands against that cold black countertop and leaned forward willing her to deliver the unwelcome news that I was sure she had.

Instead of approaching me across that barrier, she dodged around it, stood on her toes, and placed a hand on my shoulder.

I tensed up. *Here it comes.*

She whispered, "Ms. Salas is dead."

Impossible, I thought. Just this morning, Ms. Salas called me to sub for her.

The class stared at Brooklynn. Their blank faces confirmed they hadn't heard the whispered message. They looked at us expectantly.

The room was silent. Brooklynn and I froze. I faced her and touched my finger to my lips. When I didn't make an announcement, the class lost interest. The buzz of teenage socialization resumed.

I moved closer to Brooklynn and asked, "Whassup?" Surely, I misheard.

"Murdered," she reiterated even softer than before.

I didn't believe her. What could a teenager from Stony Estancia know about murder? How could she be so calm? Was this some new adolescent slang? She was mistaken, confused.

I checked the class. Their chatter continued unabated. Heads looked down as fingers tapped on cell phones. The students were blissfully unaware. To maintain our secrecy, I turned my back to them before I silently mouthed, "Murdered? Where?"

She looked at her backpack sitting alone on the other side of the room, and in her regular voice, she said, "In the Ecology Club workroom."

All prospects of a normal day evaporated.

My eyes followed Brooklynn's gaze. Rachel Carson's penetrating sage-green eyes stared at me from that closed door. The larger-than-life photograph said, "In nature, nothing exists alone."

I thanked my lucky stars that the computer selected me for this sub assignment. I was uniquely qualified as a retired

LAPD detective to respond to whatever was on the other side of that picture of Rachel Carson.

'You're welcome,' replied Fitch.

Fitch is my spirit guide—protector, advisor, and critic. Unfortunately, my intuition often disagreed with Fitch. Sometimes he was a timeless Buddha, and other times a teenage Loki.

My gut told me that everything beyond that closed door had its genesis on the previous Friday. Detectives prayed at the altar of cause and effect—no coincidences. Everything had to have a reason.

Friday had been uneventful until I received a text from Ms. Salas. U TEACHING TODAY?

The rules prohibited cell phone use during school hours, but we were between periods. I texted back, PHYSICS [SMILEY FACE].

I NEED A FAVOR.

NO PROB. WHASSUP?

SCIENCE GARDEN DURING LUNCH. [FROWNY FACE] PLEASE.

I'M ON IT. EASY PEASY. [ANOTHER SMILEY FACE].

The science garden was an Ecology Club project, and she was the club sponsor. I'd stood in for Ms. Salas before. That Friday lunch break should have been routine, but it wasn't.

2. SCIENCE GARDEN: PREVIOUS FRIDAY

When the lunch buzzer sounded, I went into the courtyard. Waving a green and white Ecology flag, I recruited students to prepare the new science garden. I offered them extra credit, but the gratification of clearing the land would have been sufficient, harking back to those primeval farmers who abandoned their hunter-gatherer ways. They stampeded across the field, eager to flex their muscles and tame that wild environment. Those enthusiastic teens attacked that last stand of chaparral with shovels, saws, and raw adolescent energy.

The satisfaction of our lunchtime activity was interrupted when my nemesis, Principal Kapitsa, hiked across the football field. He glanced at me and shook his head with disdain before addressing the students in a stern voice, "What are you doing on the wrong side of the yellow line?" He tapped his pen on a pad of referral slips. "And why are you digging up the native vegetation? You're all getting detention. If you're written up again, you'll be banned from prom."

Fitch sneered, *'He never goes to prom, so he's going to ban everyone else.'*

Prom was in two weeks and the principal had recently been using it as his go-to threat. As we neared the end of the year, detention had lost its effectiveness. The Ecology Club looked to me with questioning faces. Why was Kapitsa threatening them—after I gave them permission to clear this strip of land—more like I bribed them with extra credit to give up their lunch break. They were my adopted grandchildren. The ones that brought me back day after day and made putting up with Mr. Kapitsa worthwhile.

The principal was the last person I wanted to see mixed up in our activities. I backed out of the future garden to lure him away from the group. Once he followed, I closed in—until my chin practically rested on his bald spot—poorly disguised by a brown combover. He stepped back but I kept close enough to see the tracks of sweat dripping across his pallid cheeks. The short man reminded me of a steamed pork bun.

I was decades his senior, but I could still be intimidating—even without a uniform. My hair might be gray, but my buzzcut covered the territory. My face might have creases, but regular exercise kept my shoulders strong and my abs firm. Growing old is not for the weak.

He retreated further. With one long stride, I reentered his personal space. In a voice only the two of us could hear, I asked, "Principal Kapitsa, why don't you leave them alone?" I resisted adding, '*you petty tyrant.*'

He startled and dropped his pad, not expecting anyone to question him, particularly not me. I was a substitute teacher, the bottom of the pecking order. However, I was also a retired detective and not intimidated by self-important bureaucrats.

I reached down to retrieve his fallen referral slips before he could react, returning them to him with a flourish. He snatched the pad. When he began writing, I explained in a calm voice, but loud enough for my students to hear, "I told the Ecology Club that they could work here."

The kids turned to each other with approving expressions. I relished the role of defender, one of the things that drew me to law enforcement.

The principal fumed, "Blast, it's you again, Mr. Szilard. Whenever there's trouble, you're in the middle of it. Those plants are historic."

With the principal's ire directed at me, the students returned to hacking away at the stubborn foliage.

He didn't upset my balance. I continued in an even tone with just a tinge of sarcasm, "Did you forget the school board directed us to create a science garden here?"

He pursed his lips and stuck out his chin. His lack of any other response signaled that he recollected the board's decision. Showing him no mercy, I added, "I thought the project needed to be accelerated. The school year is almost over. It will soon be too late to plant our seeds." He should have known this, and I was delighted to see that it disturbed him even further.

He thrust an accusing finger in my direction. "You-you-you're just a substitute teacher. Stop thinking and just do what you're told."

I didn't pass up another opportunity to tweak the arrogant administrator. Clasping my hands and bowing my head in mock contrition, I retorted, "Ms. Salas asked me to do this while she was in an IEP meeting."

The students acknowledged my poke at the principal with suppressed laughter.

"Blast," he responded. Unable to rebut me, he redirected his frustration to Annie, a shy girl wearing a loose embroidered top. "Straighten out your skirt, young lady." He scribbled a detention slip and handed it to her. "Remember the dress code. Cover up."

Annie crumpled the paper and shoved it into her pocket. She wore her natural hair in box braids, each finished with an ebony bead. Those beads complemented her bronze complexion. True to her unassuming nature, her face didn't show any emotion. However, when the principal turned away, she shook her head and the beads clacked angrily.

Kapitsa smacked the pad of unused referrals against his palm and retreated to the courtyard, in search of others to harass.

As soon as he was out of sight, the Ecology Club's animated chatter resumed. I grabbed a pitchfork and joined in, stacking the gray-green plants. Later the maintenance crew would grind them up and compost them.

That composting operation had been an Ecology Club initiative. They had raised funds for the woodchipper that never found its way into any budget.

Annie pulled up a stump attached to a web of roots, spraying sandy soil over her skirt and blouse. In a surprisingly brazen move, she exclaimed, "Look at this! Look what I found!" She picked up something entangled in a stray root. The other students turned in her direction as she placed a bracelet of earth-colored disks on her wrist.

That artifact transformed our routine gardening into a celebration. There were shouts of "You go, girl," and applause. Some of them dropped their tools and moved closer to appreciate her find. Unaccustomed to being the center of attention, Annie covered her face. Her nose and cheeks darkened with a barely perceptible blush.

Charlie clasped his freckled hands behind his back like a small child whose parents had warned him, "Don't touch." He leaned over for a closer look and stuttered, "Th-th-that's from the S-S-Serrano Indians."

When I studied for my teaching credential, I'd read everything I could find on local history and never missed an opportunity to share this knowledge. "A Serrano relic would be big news. They haven't lived here for a long time. This was their land, but the Spanish, and then the Mexicans, and ultimately the Californios, drove them from Stony Estancia to make way for rancheros, which grew into villages, vineyards, and cities."

Brooklynn, always ready to show off, countered with, "Yes, but I agree with Charlie. That looks like a Yuhaviatam bracelet to me. I've seen similar ones in the county museum and—"

Richie, who had been leaning against the fence with his hands shoved into his pockets, snarled, "Yuha what?"

She flipped her ponytail and faced his acne-covered forehead, "Yuha-*vi*-atam. That's their name in their language—people of the pines." She pointed, "Notice the colors from light tan to deep brown, some even brick red. These shell disks came from the Chumash on the coast and were used for trading long before any Europeans arrived."

Richie stepped toward Brooklynn and the bracelet. He scoffed, "Okay, nerd, how do you know this isn't a copy?"

Knowing Brooklynn as I did, I wasn't shocked when she held her ground. "It's not. It is just like one in the museum labeled as *discolored by cremation rites*." A few of the students voiced disgust with this grisly detail. However, she ignored them and continued to berate Richie, "Use your eyes. Look how each disk is different and how they all fit together. This is obviously—"

Richie sprung at Annie, snarling, "That's mine. I saw it first!" He grabbed the relic destroying the twine that held the bracelet together. The disks exploded into the air and fell to the ground.

Annie looked straight into his brown eyes, "Not yours!" She moved swiftly to collect the tiny disks buried in the dirt between them.

They transformed into a pair of toddlers fighting over blocks or toy cars. "Mine." "No mine." Ineffectual grabs and slaps.

That assertive response was out of character for Annie.

Fitch gasped, *"Um, when did that puppy become a rabid hyena?"* In his overly dramatic way, he went on to suggest that she stood up to Richie because she was itching for a fight—because she was suicidal. That seemed a bit much, but Fitch was often closer to the truth than it appeared.

I had a history with Richie. He was a frightened child. I recalled the first day back after winter break.

He limped into the classroom wearing sunglasses and a hat, both prohibited by the dress code.

I walked over to where he sat, "Remove the hat and sunglasses."

He ignored me, surprisingly without any attitude or backtalk. He silently opened his laptop.

His subdued affect had me concerned. I knelt beside him and whispered, "Are you okay?"

"Fine, thank you. Please let me wear my hat."

Richie never said please or thank you.

"Are you sure you're okay?"

"Just fine. New Year's Eve party at my house. I fell down the stairs."

And Richie never explained himself.

Now that I was close to him, I saw his black eye, not something from falling down the stairs. I let him wear his hat and sunglasses. My grandfatherly compassion outweighed Kapitsa's dress code.

As a mandated reporter, I was legally required to notify Children and Family Services. That felt like a solution, but Richie's behavior hadn't improved. CFS never told me the results of their investigation. I suspected that they just ignored any report from a substitute. I kept a watch on him waiting for the next opportunity to help. Regardless of his behavior, he was still one of my surrogate grandchildren. I would support him.

"Richard Fowler," I warned, "Back off."

He continued to collect the shell disks.

Charlie looked up from sawing a sagebrush trunk, "Richie, you h-h-heard Mr. S. G-g-give those back to Annie. You know you c-c-can't keep them. They belong to the Serrano community."

That should have ended it. But instead of relinquishing the disks, Richie ranted, "Stay out of this. You can't stop me. I have a collection of old stuff that I sell at swap meets. Finders, keepers."

Then, he stomped on Charlie's saw blade making a loud twang. Richie's foot just missed Charlie's fingers. I pulled him away. "Drop those. They aren't yours."

The moment my fingers reached his shoulder, he howled as if shocked by a Taser and collapsed to the ground. "You can't touch me," he taunted, adding, "I don't *pose a clear and present danger of serious physical harm.*"

The reaction was so fake that I couldn't help smiling. That was privilege for you. He lay there with a smirk on his face and his arms crossed while quoting California's Education Code. Despite his defiant façade, he was still just a kid with acne and an abusive parent.

When he rose and advanced in the direction of the other students, I blocked him. We had a standoff, and his mini reign of terror was over.

I didn't need to arrest him. I was no longer a cop. I left that life in Los Angeles. In Stony Estancia, I was an honorary grandpa. The situation called for understanding. I let him strut around kicking piles of soil and crowing, "Everyone dig. Let's see if there is any more hidden treasure."

The others ignored him. They continued cutting down sagebrush and clearing the stumps. I took a cleansing breath giving him a respite to cool down. In my peripheral vision, Brooklynn approached.

Richie also noticed her. He kicked the bush Charlie was sawing. Charlie moved out of the way when the gray-green leaves sprang back. Richie taunted, "Oh Ch-ch-charlie. Look who's here, a girl to fight your battles."

Brooklynn approached Richie with fists clenched weaving around the students and chaparral in her path. Teenagers are a volatile lot, but usually good-hearted and harmless. There was no *clear and present danger*. I positioned myself between Richie and everyone else, isolating him for a timeout.

Then Brooklynn caught me off guard. She feinted to the left and cut to the right sidestepping my position like a pro running back. She invaded Richie's personal space. Her green eyes locked onto his brown ones. "Drop the disks. Apologize to Annie and Charlie." She paused and added in a threatening voice, "Then I might forget this."

With a disgusted look, he hissed, "Leave me alone." Like someone in a badly acted video, he stormed away. He tripped over a stump, regained his balance, and kept going. I imagined his exit surrounded by laughing emojis. He still had a few shell disks, but the audience had logged off from his viral moment.

Charlie resumed sawing. Annie returned to sifting through the soil to recover her spilled disks. A couple of girls joined her, and someone found a paper bag to hold the treasures.

Unfortunately for Richie, Brooklynn didn't subscribe to a forgive-and-forget philosophy.

Fitch chuckled, *'This is going to be good.'*

She took her phone out and called to his back, "Richard Fowler. Let's see what this says." She tapped a few times and then grinned, "Look at this. You have an arrest record."

He stopped and gave her a puzzled look.

"Oh no. My bad. That's your father. The apple doesn't fall far from the tree."

She tapped her phone a few more times.

"Here you are. Amen, Richie, you're old. An adult."

He turned around. His anger diminished to wariness.

Poor Richie. I didn't feel sorry for him. He'd started this and Brooklynn was the wrong person to cross.

She berated him in a sing-song voice. "Selling artifacts is a federal crime. The Native American Graves Protection and Repatriation Act—NAGPRA—is older than you." She wagged her finger at him. "But you're old enough to go to jail."

He took a couple of steps in her direction and shook his fist. "Yeah? So what? No one will do anything about it."

He was right. The Stony Police Department didn't enter the campus unless invited and Mr. Kapitsa would never do that.

All activity ceased. The Ecology Club watched the players on our garden stage. Brooklynn stayed focused on Richie, but his eyes flitted back and forth checking out the crowd. Someone had their phone raised and was making a video.

"Well look at this. The FBI has an online tips form." She held her phone pointed at his face. "Smile for your mug shot." Her phone clicked.

Richie looked like a trapped animal, backing away, but the audience's attention held him like a leash.

Now I felt sorry for him, but not enough to interfere.

Her fingers danced over her screen. "F O W L E R. Amen, look at that. The FBI autofilled your contact info. Shall I tap send?"

Richie wilted. The other students smiled at each other. When he looked at me, I just raised my shoulders and palms to show that I wasn't getting involved. He threw the shell disks in front of Annie and mumbled, "Sorry."

It didn't end there. Brooklynn said, "Another thing. Our state assemblywoman is a member of the Serrano band. I'll be checking with her next week. You better have turned in your stash."

"That old stuff isn't worth anything. It's random bits and pieces I found in the hills. I doubt any of it is even Serrano."

"Just turn it in."

"I heard you." He walked away. "I didn't want to be here anyway. I'm just going to community college, so I don't need any extra credit."

After Richie disappeared across the football field, everyone resumed work.

What about the bracelet? Why were we finding artifacts in an area settled so long ago?

Fitch said, '*The evidence doesn't add up. You missed something. You're not seeing the whole picture, how everything fits together.*'

I filed away Fitch's enigmatic comments for later. His anxiety was no reason to upset my day.

Charlie paused from cutting a tough sage bush trunk, "Mr. Szilard, why are we clearing away the chaparral? Doesn't it sequester carbon and prevent erosion?"

I took off my slouch hat and ran my hand over my gray buzzcut, doing my best imitation of a dashing archeology professor. "True, but this little patch between the fence and the path is just a fire hazard and can be put to better use as a garden for Biology classes." I pointed north. "There are the San Gabriel Mountains, as much wild space as Yosemite National Park. Plenty of chaparral there, a vibrant ecosystem, including deer, cougars, bobcats, coyotes, and even bears—our school mascot."

Another student struggling with a tenacious stump wondered, "How old do you think these bushes are?"

I grabbed the stump and together we pulled it out with a shower of dirt. "These plants can live longer than people. This strip of chaparral grew here before the school was built and long before that."

"What about this basket?" Annie asked shaking the ebony beads woven into her dark braids.

We all watched her hands scoop dirt from the indentation where she'd found the bracelet.

"What basket?" several voices asked.

She continued to scatter the dry dirt until we all could make out an arc of coils nestled between the sage plants. Her fingertips danced around the tightly woven grasses until she'd uncovered a full circle.

Basket! Fitch was right. Here was the missing piece. The shell disks were unexpected. But this basket was larger and more ephemeral. What had Annie uncovered? Even though I was no longer a detective, I still loved a mystery.

Immediately I formulated a plan—solving puzzles was in my DNA. First, we'd notify the county museum and then we'd post pictures on social media.

'What about the principal?' Fitch reminded me.

I had no intention of involving Kapitsa.

Everyone knelt around the basket, as Annie carefully scooped out the contents. The hole grew as we all watched.

"Eww. Bones!" Annie squealed and jumped up so quickly that she lost her balance.

Had we uncovered a Serrano burial site? But how old could it be if the basket hadn't decayed?

Everyone retreated from the bones, except Brooklynn. I admired her curiosity and fearlessness. She picked up what looked like a femur.

Charlie said, "My, my, a ch-ch-chicken bone."

Someone suggested, "Or a rabbit."

I'd been a homicide detective. I knew something about skeletons. "Brooklynn, it would be best if you didn't touch that."

She replaced the bone where she'd found it. "Do you think these might be human remains?"

Annie exclaimed, "No. No. Don't tell me that's a baby!"

I leaned forward and took a closer look. The bone was a femur, not much bigger than my hand. If it was from a human skeleton, the size meant we'd discovered a newborn. I buried my face in my palms and said a little prayer. I'd seen plenty of death with the LAPD, but I never hardened to it. And I didn't expect it here at the high school.

The reaction of the students ranged from laughter to fear. Everyone moved away, especially Annie who pressed against the fence—the ebony beads adorning her natural braids ringing against the chain links.

Charlie put his freckled arm around her shoulders. "Look how it was placed in that basket. This was a sacred burial for a loved family member."

That calmed Annie, but I hoped that he just had an overactive imagination. I'd be happy for this to be the remains of a picnic.

Fitch nudged me, *'Don't count on it.'*

No one moved. We could hear the crowd in the distant courtyard. A few small brown birds landed on our pile of debris feasting on the bugs we'd stirred up. They discussed their providential bounty with high-pitched chirps.

Slowly and silently, the students moved forward for a closer look. Each child viewed the still-buried skeleton and retreated. Death was foreign to Stony Estancia High School. Charlie collected a few students in a prayer circle. I saw sad faces and closed eyes as we all instinctively honored the dead.

As suddenly as it started, the memorial finished. The ever-practical Brooklynn ended our solemn interlude, "What should we do?"

That was adolescents for you. Shock, anger, mourning, and acceptance, all in a few minutes.

This wasn't a police matter. "We need a Native American archeologist. I'll call the county museum. They'll know who to contact on the reservation. In the interim, let's get something to protect our excavation."

This grisly discovery cut short our project to clear the science garden. The Ecology Club headed back to the courtyard to reclaim what remained of their lunch recess.

Charlie found a piece of plywood to cover our find. It would be safe over the weekend inside the locked perimeter of the school.

I tromped across the gridiron to join the others. While I enjoyed my lunch of leftover barbeque ribs—supplemented with oatmeal cookies and milk from the cafeteria, I considered these new mysteries—Annie's assertiveness, Richie's senseless aggression, and an archeology site that appeared from nowhere. All puzzles worthy of my detective skills.

I was most concerned about Annie and her sudden fierceness. What triggered this personality change? Fitch was convinced she was suicidal.

Stony Estancia might not be the bucolic small town I'd imagined, but it still wasn't Los Angeles. It was impossible to keep a secret here and I knew exactly where to go to learn the truth about Annie. Ms. Salas.

When the final buzzer sounded, I went to Ms. Salas's classroom, close by in the Science building where I was teaching Physics for the absent Dr. Chandrasekhar.

She revealed so much more than I expected.

3. WARNINGS: FRIDAY AFTER SCHOOL

Stony Estancia was the epitome of a thriving suburb.
Wide boulevards lined with palm trees and maintained by
city gardeners. No graffiti or homeless people. Well-kept
yards (more gardeners) and late-model cars. It supported a
flourishing community of mobile pet groomers and auto
detailers. Upscale retail and a prosperous commercial
district of clean warehouses—no smokestacks or oil wells.
Regardless, this shiny suburban lifestyle didn't guarantee
perfect lives for the adolescents.

Annie wasn't in the red folder that warned substitutes of
health issues—asthma, diabetes, allergies, or seizure
disorders. Some things weren't documented. Even though it
should have been confidential, I knew Annie was at risk for
self-harm.

*On my first assignment of the school year, Annie was
sobbing, hiccupping, and blowing her nose. The class
whispered and busied themselves on their laptops. I offered
to let her wait in the teacher's workroom until she calmed
down. She refused. Charlie sat next to her, but he was
unable to console her. Ultimately Brooklynn escorted her to
the health office.*

*The next day I visited my mentor, Ms. Salas. I was
pleased when she told me that I'd done well. Then, she
counseled me, "Don't get emotionally involved. You never
know the full story."*

"You forget my years as a detective."

Ms. Salas said, "But—"

*I protested, "I'm good at reading people. I know Annie.
She may be quiet, but she's happy...except for today."*

*Lucy pursed her lips as if debating whether to say more.
Then, she took a deep breath. "On Prom night, last year, she
accelerated her car against traffic up the Van Vleck off-*

ramp of the Desert Freeway. The police report said quick thinking by the oncoming drivers prevented fatalities."

I'd seen my share of head-on collisions. Even with airbags, seatbelts, and crumple zones—the impacts were painful to recall.

My heart raced reliving Annie's brush with death. "I'd never have guessed. I'll keep my emotional distance."

Ms. Salas said, "That's for the best."

After a good dinner, I reconsidered that promise. I never shirked responsibility. I stayed up late researching teen suicide.

The warning that one of my students might hurt themselves never left me. That was the lesson I took from Ms. Salas's disclosure. I set up alerts for the latest studies on teen suicide and self-harm. Risk factors included previous attempts and unusual behavioral changes. Annie ticked both those boxes.

Annie was shy and reserved. I took her confrontation with Richie in the science garden seriously. I would not court catastrophe by ignoring the warning signs.

Fitch agreed, *'Either her parents are getting divorced, or her mother is dying of cancer.'*

I didn't know anything about Annie's home life. Ms. Salas had cautioned that I'd never know all the facts, but I didn't accept that as an excuse. Fitch jumped to the worse case. Either way, Annie remained on my suicide watch list.

Fitch said, *'You should be watching Richie. He's itching for a fight.'*

I discounted this. A bully picking on a weaker kid was nothing unusual.

'Do you call yourself a detective? Richie taunted Annie and Charlie just to incite someone stronger—Brooklynn.'

Fitch made a good point. Would Richie continue to escalate? The district had warned the teachers to be on the lookout for signs of violence. Would Annie harm herself? Would Richie bring a weapon to school? Regardless of Ms.

Salas's sound guidance, I wouldn't let 'not getting emotionally involved' invite disaster.

These considerations following the drama in the science garden dominated my afternoon. My classes passed in a blur. Had I monitored an exam or shown a video? I had no idea. I didn't even recall what I had for lunch.

I knew better than to take this anxiety home to my empty apartment. Unresolved student issues could spoil even the finest dinner.

Was Ms. Salas right? Did I care about them too much?

I cleared the science garden with the Ecology Club as a favor to her. These were her students. When the final buzzer sounded, I sought out her advice.

"Come in Zarand. I hear you had an unpleasant encounter with Kapitsa."

Ms. Lucinda Salas, a petite Latina with short black hair, wore a beige linen jacket over a red blouse. She had decorated her room with the AP Biology curriculum. To my left, she'd posted TIMELINE OF CELL BIOLOGY that started with Antonie van Leeuwenhoek and went to Emmanuelle Charpentier and Jennifer Doudna, recent Nobel Prize winners. On the opposite wall was EVOLUTION AND HEREDITY with Charles Darwin and Rosalind Franklin. She dedicated the back wall to CLASSIFICATION AND ANATOMY with Carl Linnaeus and Barbara McClintock. In the center of that wall was the door to the teachers' work area covered with a display for ECOLOGY—Rachel Carson.

I admired Ms. Salas's composure, energy, and ready smile. She was too old to have arrived at Stony Estancia High straight out of college. She always looked relaxed, like teaching was a simple matter compared to whatever she'd done previously. Beyond that hint, those missing years were a mystery—a cold case I hadn't solved but didn't abandon.

'Maybe she was a special forces medic,' Fitch helpfully offered.

Lab tables replaced student desks in the science classrooms. She was straightening out the round stools and picking up trash. I went to the back of the room and worked forward mirroring her activity.

I said, "Don't worry about my run-in with the principal. Did you hear about Annie?"

She greeted this with an enormous smile. "Oh yes. She found a shell bracelet from Santa Catalina."

"Yes, that and—" I paused not certain how to introduce the confrontation between Richie and Annie.

"Or are you thinking about that basket of bones? I heard about that too. There are no secrets here. Isn't it wonderful to have an archeological dig on our campus?"

Ms. Salas didn't have the same view of the events in the science garden as Fitch did. I blamed his paranoia on our time with the LAPD, but what history had Ms. Salas brought to the school? I looked around her workspace for clues. She displayed pictures on the wall behind her desk. Surely, she had pinned a key to her backstory among those snapshots.

None of them included her—no selfies. I narrowed in on one with a young woman holding a baby. I took a wild guess. "Is that your daughter and grandchild?"

Her face lit up with a big smile. I anticipated her revealing some of her story, but she went in a different direction. "Oh no. That's Megan Rainwater. She had that child while taking AP biology in my first year teaching."

"That must have been awful."

"Not really," she responded to the judgment implied by my question. "I integrated her and her baby into several lessons on human sexuality and development. So much better than the textbook."

'Then what happened?' Fitch pondered in his morbid way.

"Did she marry the father?" I queried.

Ms. Salas beamed with pride. "Oh, no. That wasn't a promising idea. He'd already proven himself irresponsible."

"Was that hard on her?" I sighed thinking of all I'd heard about the plight of single mothers.

"You can decide for yourself. Do you want to know where she is today?" she asked rhetorically. "She's not married. She's in medical school, and I understand her little girl is excelling in pre-school, already reading the *Magic Tree House* books."

Lucy's eyes got big, and she stared into the distance. "Those lessons with Megan Rainwater's baby in the classroom remind me how well the students respond to learning without a textbook. This weekend I'm going to write a lesson about how archeologists use Biology. I might even get some of those bones to have the classes examine them."

I doubted the County Museum would release them for a high school science class. I was more concerned about Annie than the bones. "Did you hear that Annie stood up to Richie?

"Oh yes. Isn't that great?"

"Is it? That's not like her. I've read that behavior changes are indications of deeper issues. Do you think she is considering another suicide attempt?"

"Once a cop, always a cop. You shouldn't jump to conclusions. I can tell you what's going on with her."

"Yes. Please." I was ready for something to balance Fitch's pessimism.

"Annie had found herself increasingly isolated as her middle school girlfriends became high school couples. That loneliness weighed heavily on her."

"Is that why she was so upset at the beginning of the year?" I asked remembering that day when Brooklynn escorted her to the health office.

"No. That was something else."

'She's not telling you everything,' warned Fitch.

I trusted Ms. Salas to fill in the details. I waited.

"Annie has a boyfriend. Someone she met at church. His name is Jackson."

"How do you know this? Do you attend her church?"

"No, but she introduced him to me."

"That was nice."

"Even better, his family is taking him out of private school, and he'll start here at Stony Estancia High School on Monday."

"Are you saying that all Annie required was a partner?"

"Oh no. There's much more to it, but that is the gist of it."

"So, the opposite of depression. I'll stop worrying about her." Silently, I stuck my tongue out at Fitch, *'You must stop being so suspicious.'*

On each table, she stacked, aligned, and centered the biology books. I picked up papers scattered on the floor that had missed the recycling bins.

With the room prepared for class on Monday, she stopped smiling, checked the doors, and lowered her voice, "I could use your investigative skills."

Why did she require police assistance? "Sure. What do you need?"

"I've been doing a little detective work. It all started when the MIT admissions office called to follow up on my recommendation letter for Richie."

"Richie applied to MIT? He told the Ecology Club he was going to community college. Did you write him a good letter?"

"I might have if he'd asked, but he didn't. During my awkward conversation, I learned that in addition to the forged recommendation letter, someone had falsified Richie's transcript. I recalled him as an average student, usually earning a B, sometimes a B-, and rarely a B+. I checked my grade books—the backup copy I keep on my personal laptop—just to be sure. My memory was correct. However, on the transcript MIT received, each B had magically become an A."

"Did you report this to Kapitsa?"

"Oh, certainly, but he didn't believe me. 'Nobody can hack into the district's computers,' he said."

I agreed with the principal. Security was one of the annual training modules required by everyone, including substitute teachers, even though we never had access to anything. For example, the teachers entered attendance online, but substitutes took roll on paper. We weren't even trusted with attendance records. Still, I wasn't ready to blame this on a hacker. "Could his grades have just been entered wrong? Typos?"

"Don't you listen? She tapped her screen and spun her personal laptop around. Look at that. Check for yourself."

I countered with, "Hackers are less common than shown in the media, so they are an unlikely explanation."

"Whatever," she said shaking her head, treating me like a student who wasted class time debating evolution versus intelligent design. "You can believe whatever you want but that recommendation letter wasn't a typo. It came from my school email account." She paused.

I didn't expect what came next.

She slapped the table and raised her voice, "Whether you like it or not, it was hackers! You would have realized that had you stopped mansplaining and listened."

Whoops. She was more disturbed than I realized. No problem. I knew just what to do. "You're right. I don't doubt you. I just double-check everything. An old detective's habit."

And that didn't help. Timeout. I noticed a few more papers that had missed the recycle bin and went across the room to collect them. I straightened out some biology books and admired Megan Rainwater's child.

Lucy's neck muscles were still twitching when I offered, "This is your investigation. I shouldn't have said anything until you'd finished."

"That's right," she said softly.

She was still frustrated. She shook her head, "You didn't give me a chance to show you the threatening notes I received."

She slid a sheet of paper across the table. It could have been from any of the printers scattered throughout the school. Everyone, even substitutes, had access to the printers.

She explained, "After I reported the forgeries to Mr. Kapitsa, I received this warning." The note read, MIND YOUR OWN BUSINESS OR YOU'LL REGRET IT.

'How did the hackers know she'd reported them?' Fitch queried.

"Did you notify Kapitsa about the forgeries with an email?" I asked seeking an answer to Fitch's question.

She slapped the table again. "Of course not. I'm not stupid!" She continued in a condescending voice, "We have hackers. They can see emails." She picked up another page and looked at it before pushing it in my direction.

That page said WE ARE NOT FOOLING AROUND. STOP OR WE WILL DOX YOU ON THE DARK WEB. After I read that, she handed me a printout of her personnel record including her Social Security number, banking details—everything. I no longer doubted that serious hackers were involved, but fortunately, hackers were rarely violent.

Then she passed me a final page. DON'T GO TO THE POLICE. WE KNOW ABOUT YOUR DAUGHTER.

"Daughter?" I blurted out. "Do you have a daughter? I didn't even know you were married."

"Oh, what does *married* have to do with *daughter*?" she spat back. Then, in a voice so soft that I felt like she was talking to herself, and I was eavesdropping, "I shouldn't have shown you that page. Don't worry about it."

She closed her eyes as if she were holding back tears. "You want to know the cruel irony? I don't know where my daughter lives or even her name."

I didn't follow up on this new mystery. There would be time to pursue her daughter when she'd calmed down. Experienced detectives knew the importance of asking the right question at the right time. "I'll find the hackers. I'll commence my investigation immediately and see Vicki tomorrow morning. We'll make those hackers sorry."

"Vicki? She's your girlfriend in the Stony Police Department? Right?"

I nodded.

"Still not listening," she said shaking her head. "You can't go to the police."

"I won't get the Stony Estancia PD involved. It will just be Vicki."

"Can you trust her?"

"Yes," I assured her.

'She's in over her head,' Fitch warned in his not-helpful way.

I easily fell back into the role of detective. Familiar synapses fired in my brain. New energy flowed through me, and I felt years younger. I asked, "Is that the whole story?"

She leaned back in her chair, exhausted. "Yes. You can interrogate me now. Go ahead."

I dove in, "Do you think Richie could have done this? It was his application."

"No. he doesn't have the tech skills. Besides, he doesn't care about education. He just plans to slide into a local community college, not to apply to a competitive out-of-state school."

"Do you have any suspects in mind?"

"His parents. His father. That's the place to start."

"Why his father?"

"Mr. Fowler travels overseas."

"Good point. We know that hackers could just as well be far away as around the corner."

After a shiver, she asked, "Am I safe?"

"Hackers never show up in person." I wondered about the daughter but didn't bring it up. "You're fine."

"Thank you," she said, appearing relieved.

"We'll run some background checks on Richie's parents for starters."

Fitch was concerned, 'You're retired and now you're also in over your head.'

I didn't want to leave her alone. "I was planning a microwaved dinner-for-one tonight, but it can stay in the freezer. Would you like some company? This has been a difficult afternoon."

She nodded consent and headed for her car looking a bit like a sleepwalker.

We went to Cocina de Cetto, a popular hole-in-the-wall Mexican eatery. It had been a burger drive-up in the prosperous post-World War II years before corporate fast food took over. Here in So Cal, we supported our independent Mexican restaurants. No one cared that they hadn't updated the décor. We ate at a rustic picnic table covered with a thick layer of polyurethane.

After a couple of Carta Blancas and a pleasant debrief about Annie's new boyfriend and Richie's aspirations to leave home without leaving Stony Estancia, we went our separate ways.

I had so many questions, but I mistakenly believed there would be time for them next week.

Fitch woke me in the middle of the night to alert me that I should have taken Lucy's threatening letters more seriously. *'Did you consider that those notes were printed, not emails?'*

I ignored Fitch while constructing a midnight sundae— scoops of vanilla ice cream with fudge sauce heated in the microwave, whipped cream, and a maraschino cherry. The fudge wasn't hot enough and I ended up with brain freeze.

Fitch took advantage of my temporary incapacity. He harangued, *'Someone had to be on-site to deliver those threats—on paper, not email. The hackers are in Stony Estancia with access to the high school. Not just hackers. Domestic terrorists.'*

He made a good point in his paranoid way. Monday would be soon enough to warn Ms. Salas, but I didn't dare wait before involving the police. Fitch's conclusions demanded action. However, without a specific threat, I couldn't call nine-one-one or walk into the station and speak to a desk sergeant. Besides, Ms. Salas didn't want the police involved.

No problem. I'd go straight to the top.

Senior Detective Victoria Yukawa.

Unfortunately, Detective Yukawa had her own agenda, introducing another mystery before investigating mine.

4. Mysteries: Saturday AM

When I escaped Los Angeles, I required a car. I sentimentally chose a black-and-white one, but I didn't want it mistaken for a cop car. I selected an electric Mini—too small for any confusion. The Ecology Club loved it and it compensated for the lack of public transportation.

Saturday morning, I parked at Heisenberg Park, the recreation center of Stony Estancia. It housed the community center and adjoined the Pacific Electric Trail, named for the defunct Pacific Electric Railway—a missed public transit opportunity. I stretched while waiting for Vicki.

Victoria Yukawa, several years my junior, was the reason I retired to Stony. We'd met when she joined the LAPD. I remember that first encounter. Her uniform had military creases and her straight black hair had a white part across the center of her skull without a single hair crossing to the wrong side. Her black eyes sparkled with intelligence and if she was wearing makeup, I couldn't tell. I thought, this lady has strong attention to detail and will make an excellent detective.

I recruited her into my squad. She learned fast and eventually moved to the Stony Estancia Police Department for a nice promotion. We kept in touch.

When I retired, I asked her to turn in her badge and join me to cruise the world. But she had other ideas, like a promotion to Chief of Detectives. Our compromise was short cruises. We had tickets for an excursion to Baja California to embark in two weeks. Only if Stony Estancia wasn't hit by a crime spree.

'*Um, small chance of that,*' scoffed Fitch. He missed the action of the big city.

Vicki arrived at Heisenberg Park before I finished stretching. She took off shouting, "Let's go."

I went up on my toes for a burst of speed and soon was running beside her. But before I caught my breath to alert

26

her about the terrorists, she said, "Are you going to tell me about your federal case?"

Still panting, I gasped, "Federal case? What federal case?"

"Tish and César are featuring a story about a Serrano burial at the high school."

César and Tish were our hyperlocal news team. If it happened in Stony, they covered it on their website—STONY ESTANCIA SURFS. Anything from school activities, youth sports, and library news to politics and business.

"They interviewed Brooklynn Curie. Isn't she your friend?"

We'd settled into a comfortable pace, and I recovered enough breath to respond, "Absolutely. She's an honor student and was there when the Ecology Club uncovered a skeleton interred in a coil basket."

"Gosh, she's calling for a federal investigation of NAGPRA violations. You should have heard her schooling everyone about the Native American Graves Protection and Repatriation Act."

I picked up my pace and smiled imagining Brooklynn giving that lecture.

"Can't you control your students?"

No one, not even Vicki, was going to disparage my grandkids. "My job is to encourage, not control. I'm proud that Brooklynn spoke out."

Vicki stopped. "We're not going to board that cruise if we have to host a NAGPRA investigation."

"S'cuse me, this is not a federal case yet. The Serrano band is sending an archeologist."

"Good. That bone posted on Brooklynn's social media looked like a chicken bone to me. I think you just can't stand being retired."

I resumed jogging while protesting, "I love retirement. My surrogate grandkids need me."

I must not have sounded convincing, because she beat her favorite drum, "Instead of stirring up trouble at the high school, you should join the Stony PD. I'm sure we can find a case to take advantage of your old-fashioned skills."

I said, "Even though I love mysteries, I also like teaching. I can do both."

"Do you crave a mystery? Instead of calling in the National Park Service, I can recommend a cold case involving your school."

I couldn't refuse. The baby-in-the-basket puzzle was good; another one would be even better. "Really? Tell me," I said. My legs warmed up as we coasted along shoulder-to-shoulder.

"We call him the graduation ghost. When they announced Alex Marconi's diploma, no one stood up."

That didn't seem as interesting as the basket. "So? Who cares?"

"The parents cared, and the case continued all summer with volunteers combing the mountain trails and reviewing CCTV videos from San Diego to San Francisco. They thought they spotted him on the UC campus in La Jolla, but that lead was a dead end like so many others. The Marconis had Alex late in life and both parents passed away without any resolution."

"S'cuse me, didn't you say the case was still open?"

"Yes. Mr. and Mrs. Marconi were long-time Stony Estancia residents and had burial plots at the Bragg Vineyard Memorial Cemetery. The county coroner, my friend Persey, raised money to buy the space next to the parents and erected a headstone for Alex. That empty grave kept the case open. The department assigns each new detective to the graduation ghost until they can add something to the file. Sort of an initiation."

"Seems gruesome, but I'm game. I'll look for him too. But that doesn't mean I'll join your police department."

The path narrowed where the sage grew to shoulder height, and the chaparral encroached on both sides. The jogging trail was recent, but the regrowth looked like those ancient shrubs at the school. The sagebrush in the science garden wasn't as old as I'd assumed. If the plants were recent, then the infant's grave could be also.

We jogged along with a silent camaraderie. As we loosened up, Vicki gradually picked up the pace.

I took deep breaths and stopped talking as I struggled to match her speed.

"I'm looking forward to our cruise to the Mexican Riviera. I even bought a new bathing suit."

I took a long breath before responding. "A new bathing suit sounds—" I stopped myself before saying *sexy*. Vicki was in good shape, but not a sex object. She hadn't selected that suit to attract a male gaze. I started again, "What color is it?"

"Violet rose and periwinkle."

"Sounds lovely," I replied wondering what those colors were and what happened to purple and blue? I returned to my initial topic, "I don't want to be the one to delay our cruise, but there is a problem at the high school. Ms. Salas—"

"Isn't she the one that helps you with all the teenage angst?"

"That's her." I told Vicki about the hacked email, the tampered transcripts, Lucy's daughter, and the desire to not involve the police.

She slowed down. "No worries. Computer crime is outside of the PD. We refer those cases to a consultancy that the city has on retainer."

"Is that legal? Do you deputize them? Can you trust them to interrogate suspects? Will judges issue them search warrants?" My head was spinning. "Why would you do that?"

"Gosh, no. They don't have any contact with people," she lectured me like I was a confused child. "I don't think they are even in Stony. They have experts and do all their investigating over the internet. When they find the culprits, they email us, and we make the arrests."

"The internet," I scoffed. "So-called scientific crime-fighting never works, and certainly won't in this case." I explained how someone had delivered paper notes to Ms. Salas. "The people we're looking for have been to the high school. They're in Stony Estancia. Local terrorists. A case for real detectives. How can you contract policing to some distant office?"

"You've been retired too long to understand how much can be done over the internet. It is so much more efficient. You'll see."

"I doubt it. Is that your plan? Well, don't worry. I'll keep my eyes and ears open. That's the only way this case is going to be cracked."

Vicki shook her head. "Whatever. Remember that you said that Lucy wants a low-profile investigation. She's concerned about her daughter. Nothing is more low-profile than these computer nerds who never leave their cubicles. Don't mess it up."

"I'll be careful. I won't jeopardize her child." Lucy's daughter brought me back to the infant buried in the science garden. Charlie's description of the basket as a sacred burial resonated in my mind.

I said, "I couldn't sleep last night, so I did a bit of research."

"Don't tell me you're looking for another cruise. When I agreed to Mexico, I'd figured we were set."

"No, nothing to do with cruises."

"That's good. We're embarking in two weeks and I'm working to clear my caseload. A senior detective can't just disappear."

'Um, especially one who wants to be Chief,' Fitch interjected.

"Yes. I know. I've been there. No time off year after year." I stopped running. My glasses had slid down my nose. "Wait up." I pushed them back and turned to her. "Not another cruise. I was researching that grave at the high school." I winked at her, "See? I can use the internet too. You don't need that secret consultancy."

"Gosh, what did your internet wizardry reveal?"

I started with the background. "The California Environmental Quality Act requires a survey for cultural resources before any project is approved."

"What does that have to do with your basket of chicken bones?"

"Not chicken bones," I corrected her. "Those surveys locate tribal remains before construction starts. They use the latest technology—GPR—ground-penetrating radar. No one should discover anything afterward, especially not a basket so close to the surface. Don't you find that suspicious?"

She dismissed me, "I'm not convinced you haven't uncovered chicken bones."

The trail ran through a neighborhood where the houses backed tight against the abandoned railroad right-of-way. Friendly dogs cheered us along—amid the aromas of Saturday morning—frying bacon and warm maple syrup.

While we waited to cross Bohr Boulevard, the two-mile mark, she said, "Until Persey determines that you have uncovered human remains, I'll stay with the real crimes—especially if you want to embark on that cruise."

The light turned green, and she raced ahead.

When I caught up with her, puffing loudly, she joked, "You're getting old. Are you sure you have the energy to solve this chicken-in-a-basket mystery?"

I laughed, "Don't underestimate us. Fitch and I will solve the case of the unwanted infant."

"Unwanted infant? That's a bit dramatic but let me know when you need my help."

"Same to you. I'm also available to pitch in with any of those real crimes."

My phone vibrated. It wasn't a school day. Vicki was right there. "Who can be calling me on Saturday?"

"Let me see. Do you have another girlfriend?"

I passed Vicki my phone without looking at the notification screen.

"It's a text from your buddy Brooklynn. It says ARCHEOLOGIST HAS ARRIVED."

I stopped running. "That's going to be the answer to our chicken-bones-or-human-remains question. I'm going to the school."

We turned around and headed back to Heisenberg Park.

"For a retired guy, you're awfully busy."

"Sure am," I said proudly and sprinted ahead of her with a second wind.

As we jogged side by side, I reflected on my retirement. I had acclimated myself to the tranquil suburbs, exchanging my urban high-rise with its elevator for Higgs Haven where I carried my groceries up a single flight. Instead of urban sidewalks, the Higgs Haven grounds were landscaped like a resort with palm trees wrapped in fairy lights and serpentine pathways of decomposed granite.

Recently this idyllic environment had taken on a sinister turn with the graduation ghost, the unexplained burial at the high school, and hackers threatening Ms. Salas and her daughter.

Fitch told me that there were more mysteries to come.

Before I parked my car at the high school, I spotted the signs of trouble. A crowd had collected. They were shouting and someone was beating on a drum. High school students and a group from the Serrano community had gathered in the parking lot. As I exited my car, I identified the difficulty. It wasn't hard and I wasn't surprised.

5. Bare Bones: Weekend

Kapitsa was blocking the gate, flanked by security guards—tough-looking off-duty cops. They wore gray twill shirts with oversized chrome badges and embroidered district patches on the sleeves. Instead of guns and Tasers, flashlights and the cutest canisters of pepper spray hung off their belts.

I recognized one of the cops—his badge read Tsui. I pointed to the tiny container hanging where he normally carried his sidearm and gave him an exaggerated grin.

He covered his mouth and pretended to be embarrassed.

The principal placed himself in my path with his arms crossed. Sweat dripped from his brow, again recalling the unflattering impression of a steamed pork bun. It was a warm April day, and he'd foolishly worn a coat and tie. He barked, "It's you again, Mr. Szilard! Wherever there's trouble, you're in the middle of it."

I ignored him and greeted a stocky man with a video camera and a large press pass hanging around his neck. "Whassup, César, *mi amigo*?"

I turned to his *esposa*, Leticia, "*Hola*, Tish."

He was the camera person, and she was the sound engineer. She had a microphone covered with a neon-blue windscreen suspended from a broomstick. They didn't look like much, but Stony Estancia Surfs was the place to go to keep up to date on local news.

Tish explained, "Once Brooklynn posted that an infant was discovered, this story moved to the top of our list,"

"You can't film here!" fumed Mr. Kapitsa.

"*Sí, se puede*," quoted César, "Yes, we can."

The principal turned to the off-duty cops, "Make him stop. Confiscate his camera."

César pointed his lens at the guards and Leticia held the blue microphone over their heads.

Officer Tsui gave me a salute. "Say hello to Senior Detective Yukawa next time you see her."

"Will do. We had a nice run along the Pacific Electric Trail this morning."

It was clear that the men with badges weren't going to attack the press, so César stopped filming, saving his batteries for something more newsworthy.

Just beyond the film crew was a group attired in a modern representation of Serrano dress. A couple of women in long embroidered skirts danced in a circle, surrounded by several others clapping. A teen girl kept the rhythm on a drum. I knew her from the high school—her name was Flora.

"Stop making that noise," Mr. Kapitsa fumed. "I can't think." He pointed to Flora. "I'm going to give you detention."

She ignored him, not missing a beat.

I appreciated his frustration. Here he was working on his day off. Volunteering. Unpaid overtime. His effort was taken for granted, and he didn't get the cooperation he deserved.

As much as I understood Kapitsa's predicament, I didn't care. During school hours or not, he was just a grumpy old guy, mad with his power over so many teenagers.

Brooklynn noticed me and waved, "Hey there, Mr. S. You got my text."

I nodded.

She chanted, "Open the gate. Open the gate." The other students joined in. César raised his camera and Tish positioned her mic.

The principal stood firmly planted blocking the way. He pointed to a placard proclaiming: AUTHORIZED PERSONNEL ONLY. *SOLO PERSONAL AUTORIZADO*.

Brooklynn's group responded by moving closer and chanting louder.

The archeologist could settle my argument with Vicki—chicken bones or human skeleton—but Kapitsa and the crowd were at an impasse. It was up to me to break open this traffic jam. I grinned to myself, formulating another opportunity to tweak the rigid principal. I knew just what to do and approached the beleaguered administrator with an evil grin. "S'cuse me."

The group went quiet. I could hear the lazy Saturday traffic driving by on Blackett Street and Flora's drum gently marking time.

"Please, can you let us in?" I asked the principal, giving him one last chance before I sprang my trap.

He called to the guards, "Make sure no one gets through this gate." Then he tilted his head in my direction. "Especially him. He's nothing but trouble."

The cop who knew Vicki gave me a friendly wave.

I turned to César and Leticia, "Are you ready?"

I faced the camera. Tish positioned the microphone with its fuzzy cover. I smiled at the principal and mouthed, "My apologies, but—"

My plan was simple. I'd escalate the rumors until he gave us access to the archeologist, fearing our fake news more than anything she might let slip. Looking directly into the camera, I began, "I am Zarand Szilard, a teacher at the high school. I was with the Ecology Club when we uncovered an old grave."

A woman with a long gray plait and a shell necklace that reminded me of the bracelet that Annie had discovered asked, "Was it a Serrano burial?"

I grinned at that perfect setup. "Hard to say." I rubbed my chin in an exaggerated manner, stalling to build suspense. What was the most outrageous story I could concoct?

"We uncovered a murdered child—"

The dancing women ululated.

The drummer and the other students approached Mr. Kapitsa shaking their fists, "Baby murderer! Baby murderer!"

I turned to César. "Are you getting all this video?

Tish gave me a thumbs up. "Great sound quality too."

This was protest theater at its best. I almost felt bad for Kapitsa out here in the hot sun on his day off. Almost.

"Stop! Stop!" The principal raved and stood in front of the camera. "He's just a substitute teacher. He doesn't know anything." He yelled to his guards. "Enough of this circus. It can't get any worse. Let them in."

Everyone cheered as Officer Tsui opened the gate.

With a pained grimace, the principal announced, "Follow me. I'll take you to Dr. Alvarez. She's an archeologist and can give you the real story. Don't listen to him."

Before he could say anything else, I entered the school yard and was leading the crowd to the football field. Brooklynn joined me, "Well done, Mr. S." Tish and César ran ahead to video the procession climbing the hill and marching across the field.

The Ecology Club's gray-green patch of sage was bursting with rainbow colors. Dr. Alvarez had brought a team of archeology students from the local Cal State University—all wearing bright shirts and caps printed with their motto, WE DIG THE PAST. The student closest to me wore an orange T-shirt with a purple hat. Beside her was a yellow sample tray. She'd been hard at work. Dirt covered her pants, but her tray was empty.

Like the other university students, she dug beside a small blue flag. I watched her break up an area with her rock pick. Once the soil was prepared, she swept it into a shovel and transferred it to a sifting screen. Carefully she shook the screen until all the finest material passed through onto a waste pile. I leaned over to see what she was looking for. With her gloved hand, she inspected all that remained. I didn't see anything of interest, and she agreed, dumping everything onto the waste pile. She repeated the process, digging deeper each time.

She looked up at me. "Welcome to archeology—hours of tedium anticipating the elation of discovery." Then she asked in a gentle voice, "Do you want to know the secret?"

"Yes, please," I answered in a conspiratorial whisper.

She picked up her empty sample tray and turned it upside down. "Sometimes we only find the tedium."

"That's like being a detective," I observed.

"Sure," she answered, "We are detectives. Investigators of the past."

I walked around to see how the others were doing. They all were repeating the same process beside their individual blue flags. I found the symphony—the gentle percussion of rock picks punctuated the susurrations of brushes and screens—relaxing but couldn't help but notice the futility of this archeological orchestra. All the student sample trays were empty.

Only Dr. Alvarez had something. Her red tray had bones and the orange tray had fragments of the basket.

While the archeology ensemble buzzed, the tribal delegation collected sage leaves. They had come prepared with knapsacks which they filled.

Mr. Kapitsa visited with the young women from the university to check whether they considered a teaching career. When one student expressed an interest, he stayed with her extolling the virtues of Stony Estancia High School.

César and Leticia took B-roll footage. The woman with the gray plait explained the ceremonial uses for sage. César filmed my friend with the purple hat digging, screening, and discarding. Tish interviewed her and she repeated her archeological secret. César shot close-ups of Dr. Alvarez's sample trays and wide-angle panoramas. Tish even cajoled the costumed Serrano folks to burn some sage.

After an hour of tedium, César announced. "If nothing else is happening, we'll be on our way. We don't want to miss the first pitch of the girls' softball game at Heisenberg Park."

Dr. Alvarez looked up. "I can't say anything conclusive until we take everything back to the lab, but I can make a bare-bones statement."

'Bare bones,' Fitch echoed with a giggle.

Mr. Kapitsa broke away from his recruiting activities and interrupted. "You should clear that with the district office first."

She thought for a moment. "Not necessary. The Serrano council sent me here, and they're always happy for me to talk to the media."

The costumed Serrano observers protectively gathered around her.

Once again, events had outmaneuvered our petty dictator. Nothing was going his way.

Leticia switched to a hand-held mic. "I'm going to pause between questions, so we can edit this later."

Dr. Alvarez frowned. Fitch laughed, *'I'll bet she's been quoted out of context.'*

Leticia clarified. "We always include a link to the unedited interview—ums, stutters, dead air—everything."

With that, the archeologist agreed.

"Please introduce yourself."

The professor described her education and her experience throughout San Bernardino County, ending with, "Our county is the largest in the country, bigger than the states of Connecticut and Rhode Island combined."

'Um, that's only because Alaska doesn't have counties,' Fitch muttered.

"What can you tell us about what you unearthed?"

She pointed to the red tray. "These are human remains. A newborn."

"Can you tell us how long ago the child was murdered?"

"No, I can't. With our dry climate and alkaline soils, bones can survive for a long time. These could be recent or back before the Great Depression or even older." Dr. Alvarez paused. "Just to be clear, we don't know that the infant was murdered. That determination would come from Persey, the county coroner."

Fitch nudged me. I said, "I'd like to ask a question."

Before the principal could protest, Tish moved her microphone.

I explained the Ecology Club project. I didn't mention my friendship with Vicki or my former life as a detective. "I notice all the other sample trays are empty. Is that common?"

The professor paused to think. "Now that you mention it, no."

'Score one point for Fitch.'

"We'd expect a burial to be associated with others. Most cultures have communal areas where bodies are interred—a cemetery. For some reason, this grave was isolated, secret. I can't say more until we have some dates and a DNA analysis."

At the end of the interview, Dr. Alvarez returned to the dig. Beyond confirming that we'd unearthed a human skeleton, not chicken bones, she'd offered little additional information.

As I left the university team to complete their work, the major unknown was the date of the burial. That would require laboratory results.

Fitch asked, *'Homicide or stillborn? Police case or museum exhibit?'*

My intuition told me there'd be more surprises before we solved this puzzle.

Regardless, an infant had died and whether it was recent or historic, murder or medical, it was still sad. I walked away from the crowd to mourn this infant in private, promising I'd uncover his or her story.

Sunday afternoon, that infant was still on my mind when I stopped at the market to pick up comfort foods for dinner— prepared broccoli-cheese soup, microwave turkey tetrazzini, and a bake-at-home sourdough baguette. I watched *Midsomer Murders* until I was ready for bed.

Before I went to sleep, I left a voicemail for Ms. Salas arranging to meet her after school on Monday. I planned to update her on the baby-in-the-basket and brainstorm with her about the hackers.

With no job scheduled, I didn't set an alarm and looked forward to a lazy morning with a special breakfast. I fell asleep weighing the alternatives of French toast made from the leftover baguette or eggs Florentine with broccoli-cheese soup instead of Mornay.

Chuck Berry woke me with School Days, my ringtone for the substitute notification system. My fingers explored the night table searching for that rock-n-roll disturbance. Once located, my thumb tapped ACCEPT.

There was an assignment for me, but not one that I could have foreseen.

6. HOMEROOM: FIRST THING MONDAY

"We have an assignment for *Mr. Szilard*." A computer enunciated the first part and my voice eerily spoke my name.

An assignment.

I tapped in my ID and passcode while the last remnant of a Mexican Riviera dream faded from my consciousness. Bright sunlight streamed across my room alerting me that the school day started soon. Why was the call so late?

The system announced in staccato, each phrase spoken with a unique voice, "Ms. Salas. AP Biology. Monday. This is a same-day job."

I met with Ms. Salas on Friday. Had she said anything that suggested she might be out today?

No!

Exactly the opposite. She'd been excited about a lesson to supplant the boring textbook—the grave just beyond the football field, the science of archeology.

With some uneasiness, I accepted the job.

While I threw on my clothes, I thought about Ms. Salas. She was hyper-organized. I'd never received a last-minute call from her. What caused her plans to change? Now that I knew the hackers were local, I feared that she confronted them. Had my assurance of her safety inspired her to go off on her own?

Fitch, burst to life, *'No time for breakfast. Bad omen. I told you she was in over her head.'*

I shoved an orange and a granola bar into my pockets, gripped the banisters with both hands, and raced down to the garage where my Mini was plugged in.

The little black-and-white car sped past the swimming pool and palm trees to Higgs Road and then made a right on Blackett Street heading for Stony Estancia High School. Along the way, I finished the granola bar and stopped at the Blackett Bakery. Even though it was late, I craved something to supplement the orange remaining in my pocket.

I prided myself as one of the popular substitutes. Stationed at the classroom door with a box of fresh donuts, I high-fived and shook hands while distributing the sweets. Everyone took a fried treat except Richie who snuck by with his head down and wearing dark sunglasses. This reminded me of our encounter back in January when he *fell down the stairs*. I let him pass without notice, thinking he might still be upset about Brooklynn and the Serrano bracelet.

The class gossiped about the day's baseball game and a party at a new kid's house—his name was Jake, or Jackie, or Jackson. Jackson! This must have been the new boy Ms. Salas had told me about—Annie's boyfriend.

No one mentioned the Ecology Club.

I showed my school spirit with a Bruin-green polo. Green and gold jerseys distinguished the baseball players. The cheerleaders wore matching skirts, an anachronism from their parents' generation. Aside from game days, few girls wore skirts.

Once everyone had entered the room, I followed the Stony High safety protocol and locked the door. I wrote MR. S. on the whiteboard. While they milled around finding their seats at the black lab tables, I went over to Richie and offered him one of the last donuts. He took a powdered sugar one and said, "Please can I keep my glasses on?"

I took a chocolate glazed one.

While we ate our sweets together, I caught a glimpse of another black eye.

I'd already reported Richie's situation to Children and Family Services back in January. There was no sense in calling again as Richie was now an adult and not under their jurisdiction. Did Brooklynn's online tip lead to his bruise? I made a mental note to ask her to give him some slack.

I weighed alternatives such as a stern talk with his parents. Confrontation with perpetrators, acting as judge and jury, was like those boxes of my guilty pleasure—mac and cheese. Once I got started, I couldn't stop. I'd eat one box while cooking the next—instant gratification followed by regret and remorse. It was the same with perps—if I let myself get started, they might end up in the emergency room or worse. Just like I never let those tempting cartons into my apartment, I wasn't going to give into the temptation to visit Richie's parents.

I slipped Richie a card for the Domestic Violence Hotline and wrote a note granting him permission to wear those dark glasses.

He returned the card, shaking his head, "No," and looking scared. It hurt my heart to see this reaction. After reading the note, he said, "Thank you," and took a second donut. That was encouraging—every note and donut helped.

When the buzzer sounded for the start of homeroom, I stood behind the massive lab bench that served as the teacher's desk and took a bite from the last donut—plain cinnamon, not one of my favorites, but worse if it got stale.

I searched for Ms. Salas's bell. It wasn't in the sink that held a model of the human torso. I searched among orderly stacks of marked and unmarked papers. I finally found it in the last place I looked, behind a large jar of candies. Her bell was ceramic, decorated with hand-painted wild cats and "San Diego Zoo" written in script.

I rang the bell. The sound was delicate, but it worked its magic. The classroom noise level dropped, but they had questions, so many questions.

"Where's Ms. Salas?"

"She didn't tell us that she'd be out."

"When will she return?"

I raised the bell, and, like Pavlov's dogs, they chilled. "I was called late this morning for one day. Now, quiet down for attendance."

I wasn't concerned when a few continued talking. These were good kids and would listen just enough to hear their names.

I called the first one. "Brooklynn."

Without looking up from her phone, she mumbled, "Present."

I ignored the fact that the school rules prohibited using a phone during class. This was just homeroom, and I didn't write a lot of referrals. I abdicated that honor to Mr. Kapitsa. Certainly, this minor transgression didn't require a disciplinary response, a trick I learned on the big city streets. Looking the other way for small violations often paid off when investigating major ones.

However, I didn't let the inmates run the asylum. I gave them the illusion of autonomy, just the illusion. I was the adult in the room. I managed with an iron fist in a velvet glove. In a well-behaved school like this, they rarely saw the iron fist.

Attendance went smoothly until I came to Jackson, the new kid. I looked around for an unfamiliar face, but there were too many. I called, "Jackson," twice. When there was no answer, I rang Ms. Salas's bell. The room quieted down, and I said, "Jackson Siegbahn."

Finally, a boy responded, "Sorry." He paused to check where I'd printed my name on the whiteboard. "Sorry, Mr. S. I didn't hear you."

Fitch was suspicious. *'Has this boy already answered? Is he covering for someone who is tardy?'* Fitch noticed a group in the back laughing. *'They're mocking you. That boy isn't Jackson.'*

I studied the boy who responded. I saw several other boys with brown eyes and fuzzy almost-mustaches. Jackson was the only one with an earring. I'd recognize him next time. Analogous to cell phone use, this was something else to ignore. I could demand to see his school ID, but in the case that he was new, he might not have it yet.

The roll continued without further irregularities. I relaxed and scored this homeroom as a success. The secret to substitute teaching was not to expect perfection. Today was good enough.

When the buzzer ended homeroom, the students streamed past me to the hallway. Out of the corner of my eye, I spied Brooklynn approaching the backdoor decorated with the picture of Rachel Carson. She was taking a shortcut through the teachers' inner sanctum—a narrow space separating the back-to-back classrooms. At the ends were doors to the hall. This multipurpose room served for storage, preparation, lunch, and whatever the teachers preferred to do without student interference. It was also a secret passage between rooms or an escape to the hall.

Brooklynn was a good student, so I ignored this minor transgression.

When the ECOLOGY door slammed, Fitch needled me. He warned that I'd missed something. Fitch was like the ancient oracles, prescient in retrospect but incomprehensible in the present.

I pondered, *Should I have blocked the entrance to the teachers' space? Should I have checked Jackson's student ID? Should I have forbidden phone use? Should I have made Richie remove his dark glasses?* Of course, this was Stony Estancia High, not a big-city crime scene. I finished the cinnamon donut and these questions faded.

I looked forward to Ms. Salas's archeology lesson.

I'd read about Ötzi, recently discovered in a melting glacier in the Italian Alps—thanks to climate change. Surely, Brooklynn and the Ecology Club would have something to say about that.

He lived over five millennia ago, yet, incredibly, using science, we knew he was forty-five when he was killed in a knife fight after a mountain goat sandwich for breakfast. I anticipated teaching the science behind the determination of age and diet.

Ötzi and I believed in a good breakfast. Unfortunately, we both discovered that it didn't assure a good day. I was soon to learn how bad a day could be.

7. MURDER! MONDAY 1ST PERIOD

The purple folder, labeled in large black letters: EMERGENCY LESSON PLAN, replaced my anticipation with disappointment. No archeology lesson. It held a video on weather forecasting. This was for the generic substitute. Ms. Salas wouldn't have known whether her sub knew any Biology or could even spell *mitosis* or *meiosis*. This was doubly true because she'd requested a sub in the morning—always a risky venture.

Lucy had told me she was going to write an archeology lesson. It had to be here. If I could find that plan, I had the background to use it. Archaeology wasn't that far from forensic anthropology. I searched the papers on her desk, leafing through the stacks page by page. I found old sub plans, late homework, makeup tests, and takeout menus. The lesson wasn't there. The printer tray was another good place to look, but it was empty.

The last place to examine was her classroom computer.

She was still signed on.

'That's not like her to leave her machine logged in,' Fitch observed with his characteristic paranoia.

I was more concerned about a better lesson plan than whatever conspiracy theory Fitch had. I searched for documents with the terms: ARCHEOLOGY, BURIAL, and DIG. I found a saved news story about Ötzi and her proposal for the science garden, but nothing else. Nada.

I resigned myself to teaching weather. I was disappointed, but my job was to engage the students even though I was hobbled with a lesson that wouldn't be on a chapter test or the AP Bio exam. I accepted that—and more—when I signed up to be a sub.

She'd prepared a worksheet that I would collect, and she would grade. That helped. I might not be Bill Nye the Science Guy, but I could bring this thinly veiled time-filler to life with my enthusiasm for all things scientific.

The tardy buzzer sounded. I gave them a few minutes to settle. While they socialized, I followed safety protocols and locked the door to the hallway.

I raised Ms. Salas's bell to signal the start of class. The chatter died down. The few students remaining in the aisles headed for their seats.

Before I had a chance to ring the bell, the rear door burst open, upsetting our routine. Everyone turned around to see what had happened. Brooklynn staggered into the room and dropped her backpack with a thump.

'Why did she come back? This can't be good,' Fitch declared.

I stared over Ms. Salas's lab bench and studied this girl charging across the room. Tears pooled in her green eyes.

I didn't need Fitch's prognostications. I knew something was wrong.

I leaned forward willing Brooklynn to hurry up and deliver the unwelcome news that I was sure she had.

She dodged around the lab bench, stood on her toes, and placed a hand on my shoulder.

I tensed up. *Here it comes.*

She whispered, "Ms. Salas is dead."

Impossible, I thought. Just this morning, Ms. Salas called for a substitute.

The silent room stared at Brooklynn. Their blank faces confirmed they hadn't heard the whispered message.

"What?" I asked. Surely, I'd misheard.

"Murdered," she hissed even softer than before.

I didn't believe her. What could a teenager in Stony Estancia know about death and murder? And she was so calm and composed. She was mistaken, confused.

I again checked the other students. Their puzzled faces confirmed that they were still in the dark. To maintain our secrecy, I leaned in close to Brooklynn and asked, "Murdered? Where?"

She turned back to where she'd dropped her backpack, and in a normal voice, she said, "In the Ecology Club workroom."

'When did the teachers' inner sanctum become the Ecology Club workroom?' Fitch asked.

Any death at Stony High was hard to imagine. My brain swirled with different courses of action. I didn't want to leave my class unsupervised. A call for backup over my PD walkie-talkie would have been prudent, but I was retired. No walkie-talkie. No backup.

I considered calling the office, but supposing Ms. Salas was in fact dead, Mr. Kapitsa was the last person to involve. I had to improvise. Brooklynn stood next to me wiping her eyes with a cloth hankie. She would be my backup.

I turned away from the class. "I will go look. Are you okay?"

She nodded.

I waited a moment, watching her breathing. She was remarkably calm for someone who'd just seen a dead person. I didn't want to further burden her, but she was my only option.

"I need you to take charge while I am gone."

She nodded again.

I gave her the weather forecasting questionnaires. "Please hand these out."

She blew her nose, cleaned her hands with a bottle of sanitizer from Ms. Salas's table, and accepted the papers.

I thanked my lucky stars that she was there. I could count on her.

As I walked to the door decorated with Rachel Carson's picture, I announced, "Today we're watching a video. Brooklynn will distribute the quiz."

I stopped at the door. "Write your name and number on the top of the page. These will be collected and graded." That was the last normal thing that happened.

I opened the door to investigate whatever Brooklynn had seen. As I entered the room, I smelled Ms. Salas's lavender-scented shampoo mixed with a hint of something rotten, something foul—death. I closed the door behind me to prevent the odors from escaping into the classroom.

Ms. Salas sat motionless in a desk chair with her phone held in her lap. She could have been reading. "Don't be dead," I repeated over and over as I approached her.

I placed my index and middle fingers against her windpipe. I could feel my neck throbbing as I checked for Lucy's pulse, but my fingers found nothing. I checked the other side. I held my breath and checked with the other hand. Still nothing.

I picked up her limp arm and checked her cold wrist. *She was dead!*

The universe collapsed to just the two of us. My fists tightened into two black holes that were prepared to flatten whoever did this. My frustrated fingers fought to escape, to search her clothes for clues. Before I put any of these impulses into action, my brain alarmed, "STOP!"

My vengeance and grief surrendered to my detective instincts: Preserve the scene. Collect the evidence. Don't get emotionally involved.

I felt the familiar exhilaration of being first to a crime scene.

That euphoria was short-lived when I flashed back to the previous Friday.

A frightened Ms. Salas had reached out to me for help. The same Ms. Salas who'd been there for me when I thought Annie was suicidal. When I'd gone to her, she didn't laugh. She didn't demean my concerns. She listened.

Did I return the favor? No! I discounted Lucy's story about the hackers. I assured her that she was safe.

Now she was dead. A cold chill shook my body. The past couldn't be changed, but I could find the person who killed her.

Another deep breath. I was a detective—keeping my emotional distance from the victim. I had a job to do— observing and analyzing. I was the right person to identify her killer.

Ms. Salas's lifeless body sat in a desk chair. I noticed her purple ankles. Lividity had set in—evidence that she had died before school started, before the other teachers arrived, before sunrise.

At that point, I could have made the calls to nine-one-one and the school office, but my investigation expanded to a pool of blood on the floor. I noticed that the yellow serum had separated from the red center. That supported my conclusion about the time of death. She died before the campus opening time.

'We are too late,' Fitch bemoaned, 'The bad guys are long gone.'

As much as I regretted not capturing the murderers, the time gap assured my students' safety.

I reverted to my detective training—witnessing and evaluating. I walked around the corpse, careful not to touch anything or step in the blood. I searched for signs of a gunshot. The corpse had no visible wounds or bruises. The floor was clear of empty shells and the walls and cabinets had not stopped a bullet. This comforted me. We had regular drills for school shooter scenarios. Fortunately, that was not part of today's tragedy.

This was unquestionably Ms. Salas, dressed professionally, in nice jeans, a Bruin-green blouse buttoned to the neck, and black leather shoes with slight heels. Her attire suggested that she had expected to teach today.

Fitch interrupted my train of thought, 'So, who requested a sub for her?'

There weren't any signs of a struggle. Her black wool blazer lay neatly folded on a nearby counter. Her hands were holding her phone and her clothes were clean except for some minor blood spatter. Did that blood belong to her or her assailant?

'But why was there so much blood without a struggle?' Fitch asked pointing to the puddle on the floor.

I took pictures. The puddle. Ms. Salas from so many angles. The water splashed around the sink. The remains of someone's lunch. A stack of old calendars from conservation groups. Some blood spatter on a cabinet door. The plastic wrapper from an ice pop. I reached for my field kit to collect evidence, but I didn't have one. I was retired.

A familiar surge of adrenaline filled me with energy. I was eager to track down Ms. Salas's attacker. I'd be tempted to be judge and jury when I found out who did this.

I took a deep cleansing breath and centered. This was as far as I was going with this mystery. I reverted to being a substitute teacher. I had a class, not a case. On the other side of the wall were high school students waiting to learn about weather forecasting.

'You hope,' snickered Fitch.

I cracked open the classroom door. Brooklynn stood guard while the class was chatting and tapping on their phones.

She gave me a questioning look.

Since she was my backup, I took her into my confidence, "You were right."

She collapsed to the floor and took out her phone. This time her phone was a problem. I didn't want her spreading news of Ms. Salas's demise. I held out my hand. "You're not allowed to use that during class."

She pointed to the other students.

"They don't know what you do."

She frowned but surrendered her phone before reaching into her backpack for a book to read, a college text, the size of an old LA phonebook.

I didn't want to leave the class to Brooklynn again, but I still didn't have an alternative. I returned to the workroom, closing the door for privacy. I didn't call nine-one-one or the school office. Vicki held the place of honor at the top of my favorite contacts.

She answered, "Zarand. Whassup?"

"Mornin' Vicki. This is your early warning. It's going to hit the fan in a few minutes. A teacher has died at the high school, murdered."

Her jovial tone disappeared. She was all cop. "Are you certain?"

This was a strange question to ask a former detective. I was no longer an old friend, but a witness. I'd be a good one. This was what she needed from me. "Yes. A student found the body."

"Oh no!" she exclaimed. "Is it too late to secure the scene and avoid panic?"

"Nothing like that," I assured her. "The body is in a teachers' workspace, not open to students."

'Um, what was Brooklynn doing back there?' Fitch teased me.

Before Vicki could ask more questions, I added, "Ms. Salas is dead."

"Your friend? That Ms. Salas?"

I could hear Vicki's detective wheels whirring. I was moving from witness to suspect. "I'm here to substitute in her classes. Someone entered her absence into the system. They would be my top suspect."

"Have you called nine-one-one?" she asked.

"Not yet, but I'm going to call the office next, and they'll do that."

Vicki paused for a breath. "Okay. I am on my way. Secure the scene and avoid panic."

"Yes, Detective," I responded crisply, expecting the Stony PD would solve this case quickly both for Ms. Salas's sake and our cruise.

'Twelve more days,' Fitch calculated.

She added, "Don't touch anything and stay in your classroom when we arrive."

"Yes, Detective," I reiterated with a virtual salute.

As I turned back to the classroom, I spied a box of disposable gloves. I took this as a sign from the detective gods awarding me permission to perform a more detailed survey. I knew what I was doing, and Vickie would never find out. I put the gloves on before I locked the doors to the classrooms on each side and the exits to the hallways on both ends.

Secure the scene. Check.

Properly gloved, I opened drawers and cabinets—taking more photographs. Reams of printer paper. Extra textbooks. Colored pencils. Markers. Old Halloween candy. Hand sanitizer. Art supplies.

Every murderer removed something from the scene and left something else in exchange. I hadn't found the smoking gun, but I knew it was there.

I returned to the countertop and examined the folded blazer. The inside pockets were empty. The right outside one held a green whiteboard marker—Go Bruins—and the left one brought forth some condoms.

'What was she doing with those condoms?' Fitch queried.

I considered collecting them as evidence, before recalling Vicki's admonition not to disturb the scene. I returned the blazer to where I found it, replacing the evidence into the proper pockets. Remembering my role, I made a quick call to the office and took the used gloves with me to leave the scene undisturbed.

I felt like a cat watching a bird feeder, eager for action. I yearned to collect evidence, read the coroner's report, and interview witnesses. I took a deep cleansing breath and centered myself before I left the crime scene. The word *crime scene* caused my heart to race. Whether I was working for the police or the school, I was still a detective.

Back in the classroom, I dove into weather forecasting as if nothing had happened.

Avoid panic. Check.

I didn't retreat behind the teacher's lab bench but walked up and down the aisles while I addressed the class. The more I moved, the more likely they were to pay attention.

"How many of you checked the weather forecast this morning?" Most of the class raised their hands. Some responded with, "Doesn't everyone?" or "Why wouldn't we?"

I leaped up on a stool. The chatter stopped and all eyes were on me, even Brooklynn's. The theatrics took my mind off the dead body just beyond the wall.

"Your grandparents rarely checked," I exclaimed. "Back then, they didn't have satellites. They were blind. Even when the data were available, they didn't have computers, so they couldn't figure out what it meant anyway. Weather predictions were a gamble that the forecasters often lost."

I turned off a bank of lights and started the video. I continued my banter over the opening credits to hold their attention. "Note how often they mention satellites and computers." We hadn't finished the introductory clips of tidal waves and tornadoes, when the classroom speakers announced, "Lockdown. The school is under lockdown. Be safe. This is not a drill."

The lockdown announcement was the end of their attention to my weather forecasting theatrics. I'd lost them. The class went wild. I just let them go. Iron fist in a velvet glove. They had to burn off the excitement before they'd be ready to settle down.

Following our well-practiced protocol, I covered the windows with black cardboard. Despite the pandemonium, students remembered to slide their tables to block the doors as regular drills had taught them. With their practiced tasks completed, they sat tightly against the cabinets that circled the room.

There was nothing else to do. Everything was happening outside our sanctuary. My opportunity for action would come later.

The students took out their phones. The room filled with mutterings about no signals. I laughed. These tech-savvy teens hadn't imagined that the cell towers wouldn't support the entire school requesting service simultaneously.

I sat on the floor next to Brooklynn.

She leaned against me and asked, "Do you think Ms. Salas was murdered?"

I silently mouthed, "Yes."

She confided to me, "I've never seen a *real-life* dead person even though my mother has shown me pictures—heart attacks, strokes, trauma, cancer, stuff like that."

That seemed like a strange topic for discussion around the dinner table until I recalled that her mother was a professor at the medical school. This explained why Brooklynn was able to report Ms. Salas's demise without breaking down.

I had my own reasons for not panicking. "Well, I've seen enough death for both of us."

Just then my phone vibrated. Vicki texted, I'M HERE. REMAIN IN PLACE.

I replied, KK.

Senior Detective Victoria Yukawa would deal with the corpse. I would comfort my surrogate grandchildren. As Brooklynn had reminded me, this would be the first exposure to death for many of them. With time, the school and the community would supply counseling and support, but for the moment, I was on the mental health frontline. I dedicated myself to my students and let Vicki be the detective.

The class, unaware of the unfolding drama, questioned the need for a lockdown. They took out their phones. Most texted their friends, compared notes, and exchanged theories. A few checked STONY ESTANCIA SURFS. Others texted their parents—reminding me that for all their independence, they were still children.

With a lockdown declared, I could no longer use weather forecasting to occupy them. I picked up Ms. Salas's candy jar and offered a piece to each student. Annie shook her head no, but Charlie took two, "The extra one is for Annie, for later." She gave him a small smile. Richie also took two, without any explanation. I let it pass. Ms. Salas wouldn't need the candies. Anything to distract them from the police activity on the other side of the wall. Avoid panic.

Xuan Hua crossed the room to sit next to Brooklynn, who guarded the door to Ms. Salas's death chamber. They appeared to be studying that college text, but I suspected they were discussing their absent teacher. Xuan Hua reached for the phone tucked into her back pocket, but Brooklynn stopped her. As long as Xuan Hua didn't take out her phone, I'd let them be. This was the beauty of Stony High—explicit discipline was unnecessary.

Richie's behavior was unforeseen. After his confrontation with Annie in the science garden, I didn't expect they'd have anything to do with each other, but today they sat together. He hadn't eaten any candy and offered her a choice of chocolate or caramel. What had changed?

Charlie moved around the room, pausing to chat with different students. Vicki had the investigation under control and my grandkids weren't in jeopardy. I took out my phone to follow the action on STONY ESTANCIA SURFS. Tish and César reported the police activity as routine, just another day in our peaceful suburb.

My stomach wondered if the lockdown would disrupt the cafeteria. Lunchtime was approaching and in my morning rush, I hadn't packed anything.

Fitch scolded, *'Ms. Salas is dead and you're thinking about lunch?'*

The discordant clanging of the wall phone interrupted my reverie. I picked up the old-fashioned handset attached to a coiled cord. "Mr. Szilard, substitute teacher."

"Good morning, Mr. S. This is Mrs. Wilson from the office."

'From the office? Is there another Mrs. Wilson?' Fitch mocked her.

She was the substitute coordinator and Mr. Kapitsa's lieutenant. I signed in with her every morning. She could only be calling with some administrative nonsense.

"Yes, Mrs. W. What can I do for you?" I replied with a thinly disguised tone of annoyance.

"You should know!" she snapped. She often acted like she was in charge, not just a clerical assistant. "I'm calling for the attendance report."

I shielded my mouth to muffle my voice and prevent the class from overhearing. "Don't tell me Kapitsa has everyone compiling lists of students. There's no need for that." I lowered my voice further. "They told you that there's no intruder, didn't they?"

"Well...maybe," she stammered, "Why do you make everything a battle? Just give me your report."

With the death of Ms. Salas and the possibility of missing lunch, I hadn't had time to think about mundane things like attendance. Besides, this roll check was just a procedural formality. I dismissed her with, "I have all my students, plus Brooklynn Curie."

But she wasn't that easy to get rid of.

"That's first period. What about homeroom?"

Homeroom seemed so long ago and irrelevant. O.B.E. Overcome by events. B.S. Before Salas. But the bureaucracy marched to a different drummer, so I stood at attention and saluted like a good soldier, "All present and accounted for, sir."

"That's better," she said ignoring my sarcasm and adding, "Stay on the line for Mr. Kapitsa. He wants to speak with you."

Kapitsa was yelling, so I put my hand over the earpiece to prevent the class from overhearing. "You called the police before calling the office, didn't you?"

I broke the lockdown protocol—pushed the table barricade out of the way, unlocked the classroom door, and extended the cord into the hall. In a stern whisper, I said, "Do you realize there is a dead body outside my room?"

This was incredible. Someone had died and he was talking about who I notified first. This was the petty bureaucratic behavior that drove me crazy and the reason I called the office last. I had little patience for him. "Listen to me," I said closing the door on the phone wire, "Murder. Is. A. Police. Matter. Stay out of the way." This echoed the instructions Senior Detective Yukawa had given me.

No surprise. He missed the point. "This is my school. I am in charge. You should have informed me first. When you find out something, make sure you call me before your cop girlfriend."

"Yes sir, Mr. Kapitsa," I said with no intention of enabling him to wheedle himself into the middle of the police investigation.

Like his assistant, he ignored my mockery. "I know the students like you. You're a clown. On the day that you mess up, it will be your last day teaching."

He handed me back to his faithful assistant.

"Be reasonable Mr. S. He has a stressful job and is under a lot of pressure. Panicked parents are calling the office wanting to know where their children are."

"That's nice Mrs. W. Did you forget Ms. Salas has been murdered? She takes priority over a nervous principal."

Now Mrs. Wilson got huffy. "You should remember Mr. Szilard that you are just a substitute teacher. If you are not respectful, you can be replaced."

I whispered, "W T H. What the heck? There is no shooter, no intruder. Both of you should calm down."

I returned to the classroom, not even bothering to secure the door—another violation of the lockdown protocol and an indulgence to my frustration. I hung up and took a moment to enjoy Mr. Kapitsa's distress. My guilty pleasure—*schadenfreude.*

Next, my cell phone rang. VICKI.

"Listen Zarand. My forensic team will enter the scene from the hallway. Is the witness, Brooklynn Curie, with you?"

"Yes."

"Okay. I'll interview her once her parents arrive. Stay put and stay safe."

That was it. Vicki dismissed me. She had a job to do.

Fitch reassured me, *'They'll be thankful when you solve the case.'*

As I surveyed the room, I was glad to see that the class hadn't taken notice of my phone calls. They were enjoying their unplanned holiday from classes, while I was solving a murder.

Every Stony Estancia detective and forensic tech had shown up. It sounded like a small army just beyond our wall. They were examining every drawer and cabinet. I heard the zips from the opening and closing of evidence kits as they searched for clues.

The class noticed the noise. They asked, "Mr. S., what's going on?"

'Avoid panic,' Vicki had said.

I did my best to downplay everything—the lockdown, my phone calls, and the activity beyond our classroom. I shrugged my shoulders. I offered a typical teen response, "No idea. Not my problem."

This didn't satisfy them. They turned to Brooklynn, sitting in front of the door that led to all the commotion. "Whassup?"

I looked to the back of the room confident I could count on her.

She copied me, "Not my problem."

They invented crazy theories. "Did someone steal the answers to the chapter tests again?"

The truth—*your teacher was murdered*—was harsh. A half-truth was better. "I doubt there's any danger. The police are searching for an intruder."

Richie's voice dripped with teenage sarcasm when he opined, "That's a lot of people checking to see if someone is hiding in the teachers' workroom."

Annie hugged him and sobbed.

This outburst silenced the others. In addition to the disturbance beyond the wall, the inconsolable Annie presented another mystery. She was so aggressive on Friday and now she was all in tears.

Ms. Salas had ascribed her behavior to her boyfriend Jackson. He was here. He'd answered roll call in homeroom. Why was she still upset?

'Are you certain that was Jackson?' Fitch questioned recalling the earlier confusion. That was just like him to worry about details even when something like Ms. Salas's death had overshadowed them.

Charlie patted Annie's shoulder and said, "Can I help you?"

She just bawled louder.

This was like a replay of the original lockdown announcement—another round of nervous gossip and overuse of the cellular network.

Vicki's investigation was in progress, but that didn't prevent Fitch from constructing his own plan.

First, how did Ms. Salas die?

Second, whose blood was pooled on the floor?

Finally, find the witnesses. There were always witnesses.

Those were Fitch's detective priorities.

I had my teaching responsibilities. With a room of students with no interest in weather forecasting, what was I going to do? They would soon get bored and classroom management would become a challenge. Idle teenagers were volatile and unpredictable. Eventually, someone would take it upon themselves to investigate the commotion on the other side of the wall. I wouldn't let it go that far.

Before I explored my options for an emergency emergency-lesson-plan, I reviewed the facts. There was no intruder, and no reason to keep the students locked down. Even Kapitsa would figure out that they should be dismissed. They weren't in danger and the police required the immediate area for the investigation. Vacating my classroom would come first. I decided to do nothing.

That gamble paid off when the PA system crackled to life. "The campus has been secured." I smiled at this bit of misdirection. The announcement continued, "Uniformed officers will collect each class and escort you to the theater where you'll await your parents."

Immediately, there was a knock on our door. I removed the black cardboard from the window. Officers from neighboring San Amano stood back displaying their identification. Stony Estancia must have called for reinforcements. I went out to double-check their credentials.

Once everything was in order, I invited them into the room and made introductions. "Officer Karl and Officer Susan will escort you to the theater. Please give them your cooperation."

Richie and Charlie helped Annie to her feet. Someone else picked up her backpack. The rest of the class collected their belongings.

While I organized the class for dismissal, I was glad to see Brooklynn and Xuan Hua guarding the door to the teacher's workspace. Curious students looked in their direction, but no one approached.

When the class had packed up and collected at the front door, Brooklynn and Xuan Hua joined the crowd.

I returned Brooklynn's cell and told her to wait in the theater for the detectives to interview her.

"No problem," she replied, "My mother's teaching. I'm not going anywhere until she finishes her lecture."

Since the escorts weren't Stony cops, they needed a guide to navigate our sprawling campus. "This is Brooklynn. She will show you where to go."

A student said, "Our parents have been called. My mom just texted that she's on her way."

Another whined, "That's great for you. My parents work downtown. They're not coming to get me. I'm always on my own until they arrive home with dinner."

What was Kapitsa going to do with the normally unsupervised teenagers? He'd need to improvise some way to release them on their own recognizance.

I laughed. *Schadenfreude* again. If he hadn't been such a control freak, he could have declared a minimum day and dismissed them. This was a problem of his own making.

I said goodbye to my grandkids. They followed Officer Susan with Brooklynn in the lead. Officer Karl waited and marched with the last students as rearguard.

Just like that, my school day was over. I collapsed onto a student stool and took a cleansing breath.

The halls reverberated with adolescent chitchat as uniformed officers evacuated the other classrooms. The noise rose as each group passed my open door and fell when they exited to the courtyard. When the last group headed for the theater, the place was eerily quiet.

I had free time on my hands.

What about the baby-in-the-basket? With the campus deserted, this was an opportune time to revisit the science garden. I had my best insights when free from distractions.

Or the graduation ghost? All the teachers had the afternoon off—a perfect opportunity to reminisce and casually interrogate the people who'd been there.

The sounds of Vicki's investigation interrupted my reveries. Standing beside the picture of Rachel Carson with my eyes closed, I visualized the activity. Forensic techs opening cabinets. Door latches clicking. Drawers sliding open with a swoosh. Every now and then a forensic tech zipped open an evidence bag, dropped something in, and a squeaky marker labeled it with the collection location, date, and time. Next in the evidence parade were the photographers adding electronic beeps to the soundscape. The cabinets remained open for the shush-shush of luminol spray bottles checking for blood. Finally, a trainee slid the drawers back in place and clicked the doors closed.

One thing was missing. They worked in silence. Nobody from Vicki's squad excitedly called, "Come look at this." They were going through the motions but hadn't found anything useful. This was going to be a tough case and they could use someone with my experience and intuition. Their fancy forensics weren't going to be enough.

They needed me. Eventually, they'd realize this. For the moment, I had other mysteries to keep me busy. I was heading out the door to visit the baby-in-the-basket's final resting place when a familiar noise stopped me.

A jarring noise came from the back workroom. Only one thing could have made that racket—a gurney bouncing over the threshold. The coroner had arrived to collect Ms. Salas. This was my last chance to examine the scene with the corpse in situ. I pushed the student table out of the way—lockdown was over—and swung the door open.

Crime scene tape blocked my way—Vicki's not-so-subtle reminder not to interfere with her investigation.

Instead of crashing through, I jerked to a stop. Staring between the yellow ribbons, the workroom was just as I recalled it. Ms. Salas's purple ankles. Her serene repose in that desk chair with no signs of a struggle. The pool of blood.

The coroner's assistants dressed in white protective suits rolled Ms. Salas's chair away from that solitary red puddle. They wrapped her hands in paper and carefully lowered her into a cadaver bag stretched out on the floor. Rigor mortis had not set in. Lividity and lack of rigor mortis reconfirmed that she'd died shortly before school opened.

While they closed her up in the bag, I saw black spots on the bottoms of her shoes. *Blood!* She'd stepped in the blood spatter.

Fitch deduced, *'That pool of blood doesn't belong to her.'*

I agreed with his logic. She'd been ambulatory. Lucy was alive and walking around while someone else bled on the floor.

That didn't explain all the evidence. If she'd stepped in blood spatter, the floor should have had flattened spots that mirrored the ones on her shoes. None were visible. Every contradiction leads to a deeper understanding.

'Simple,' laughed Fitch, *'They were interrupted in the middle of cleaning up.'*

Vicki noticed me and tore away the yellow tape. "Welcome." She gave me a brief hug. "I shouldn't let you back here, but an extra pair of eyes can't hurt. Look around. What do you see?"

The crime scene techs had already bagged the evidence. That plastic wrapper from an ice pop was gone. "Nothing out of the ordinary."

"Right!" she exclaimed. "Therefore?" she challenged me. Without waiting, she answered her own question, "The scene was cleaned up before we arrived."

I didn't mention that Fitch agreed with her. She went on, thinking aloud as good detectives do, "Someone staged the corpse in that chair."

'Um, obviously,' Fitch guffawed.

Then she added, "We haven't found Ms. Salas's personal laptop. Did she have one?"

Lucy's laptop. Vicki was right. Ms. Salas was rarely without that laptop. "Oh yes. She carried it with her."

'Whoops,' squeaked an embarrassed Fitch, *'We missed that.'*

I assured Vicki that the laptop wasn't in Ms. Salas's classroom. I would have seen it when I searched for the nonexistent archeology lesson.

"We'll check her residence," Vicki said.

"I doubt you'll find it there. I've never seen her without it close by."

"So, you're saying the killer took it?" Vicki queried.

I stated the obvious inference, "Yes. It contained incriminating evidence."

Vicki nodded before adding, "We'll check her home just to be thorough."

Fitch contributed his discouraging commentary, *'It's been destroyed. They'll never find it.'*

"I wish we had a better idea of what happened," Vicki said with a sigh.

"What do you mean?" I asked. "She was murdered by the hackers."

"The evidence is contradictory. The blood suggests violence, therefore murder. While Ms. Salas's appearance suggests a natural death. It can't be both."

"Ms. Salas's death and the blood are unrelated. The evidence points to two different crimes."

She wasn't convinced, "You're always so sure...until new evidence proves you wrong. Then you spin a new story with the same conviction."

"Not this time. Did you notice the blood spots on her shoes?"

She asked incredulously, "What blood?" Before I could respond, she called over one of the techs, "Show him the photos of her shoes, blood free."

I gently corrected her, "Not the uppers. The soles."

Her eyes shifted to the empty space where Ms. Salas's chair had been. Her gloved hand examined the floor. "I don't see anything but that single pool of blood."

She called the techs. "Check for blood spatter over here."

Shush-shush of luminol spray bottles. Click-click of switches turning off the lights. Beep-beep of cameras recording the transient blue radiance.

Vicki addressed her people, "Ms. Salas stepped in that blood spatter. You'll find matching blood stains on her shoes."

Everyone gathered around Senior Detective Yukawa except one crime scene tech who ran out the door. When she returned, she said, "You're right. Here are the pictures of the bottoms of her shoes."

"Very good," she praised the photographer, before pointing to me, "Mr. Szilard discovered that evidence. He's retired from the LAPD and is assisting us."

That was a welcomed pronouncement. Vicki accepted me onto her team. I was no longer a suspect.

"Follow me," she ordered as she left the workroom and entered my classroom. She pointed to the nearest student lab bench. "Take a seat."

I sat down and waited.

"What do you always tell me?" she asked.

"*Simplex sigillum veri*. In simplicity is truth," I replied—preempting Fitch.

"Exactly. We have a pool of blood and a body. The blood came from that body. Isn't that the simplest explanation?"

She changed topics when I didn't answer. "We haven't started interviewing witnesses. You can be the first." She placed her phone on a table. "I'll be recording this."

I nodded. When she seemed to be waiting for more, I identified myself for the record.

She looked at her cell. "11:34 A.M. Monday. Stony Estancia High School. Senior Detective Victoria Yukawa, interviewer." She slid the phone closer to me. "What can you tell me about the deceased?"

As formally as she behaved, she was still Vicki to me. "Well," I responded casually, "You know, subs rarely see the teachers, we're always here when the teachers are not."

She scoffed, "This isn't a joke. Don't give me that nonsense. You're a detective, or at least you once were. You told me more than that on Saturday."

I reiterated my last conversation with Lucy and the warning notes she'd received. "Those threats seem more serious in retrospect."

'Um, duh, she's dead, isn't she?' ridiculed Fitch.

"That's a good start, now give me some background on Ms. Salas as a person."

I straightened up, doing my best to play the role of a good witness to her tough cop. "I've been visiting this school for a long time. Here's the low down. Ms. Salas—Lucinda—Lucy was well-liked by both the students and the teachers. She started working here in—"

"Yes, yes. I can get her employment details from the principal's assistant, Mrs.—" She tapped her phone. "Mrs. Wilson. She already contacted me to offer her help and asked me not to bother the principal. What else can you tell me, *Detective?*"

That felt like a challenge, so I got more creative and crossed over into hearsay territory. "Mr. Kapitsa didn't like Lucy. Philosophical differences. He viewed everyone as children, while she treated them all as adults."

"I see. My experience is that teenagers are a little of each."

I rambled on, "Furthermore, Lucy wasn't some young woman who became a teacher right out of college. She had another career before coming to Stony High."

"I see. You said she had a daughter. Was she divorced?"

"I can't say anything about her personal life. She kept to herself. I first heard about this daughter on Friday." I pointed to Ms. Salas's rogues' gallery pinned to the wall. "That girl with the child is Megan Rainwater. I recognize other faces, all students. None of those pictures show Lucy's daughter. The other teachers might have more information."

I stopped to think about what I knew about Ms. Salas's life outside of school or before teaching. "She has no history. Beyond this classroom, she is a blank page."

Vicki stopped the recording and gave me a grin, abandoning her tough cop persona. "I see, so maybe a retired spy or witness protection."

I responded nervously. "That escalated quickly."

"Got you. That was a joke," she laughed and resumed recording.

I smiled but also accepted that she might be on to something. What had Lucy done before she joined the faculty? She certainly knew her subject matter. She exuded that real-world confidence that didn't come from books. Spy was the wrong direction, but something to do with science or technology could be promising.

"Did she get along with the kids?"

"Oh, yes. She coached girl's football and sponsored the Ecology Club."

Vickie jumped in another direction. "I've already received some background on our witness. Brooklynn Curie's mom is a doctor. Right?" She checked something on her phone. "Does she spell her name with a double n?"

"Yes, and yes."

Vickie abruptly switched topics again. I smiled because I'd taught her this technique to keep witnesses off balance. "Do you think she was supplying the students with condoms? Is that why she was so popular?" She added as an afterthought, "Of course, anyone in California can buy condoms, but for the embarrassment factor."

Even though I knew what she was doing—good cop, bad cop, and changing topics—the techniques still threw me off. Aggravating this was the topic of condoms. Each year the kids got younger and younger. I'd seen stolen kisses and embraces, but I found it uncomfortable to imagine more. Intellectually I knew some were going farther, but I couldn't visualize it and didn't try. "No idea," was my response to her condom question hoping she'd switch topics again.

"For a big city detective, you're certainly an innocent." She leaned across the table and kissed my forehead. "That's what I love about you."

As much as I wanted to move the interrogation along, I had to ask, "What about condoms? Why are you asking about them?" I knew the answer. Somehow, she'd caught me with my fingers in the evidence.

"We found some in her suit jacket pocket." She stared as if waiting for me to say something. When I didn't speak up, she said, "You are getting rusty my friend. My forensic people noticed the condoms had not settled to the bottom of the pocket. Someone had removed and replaced them while the jacket lay folded on the counter. That had to be you."

"You got me," I confessed and change the subject, "Did your team discover anything else?"

"We'll check that whiteboard marker for fingerprints, but I'm not holding out any hope for a breakthrough there. About fingerprints...my technicians are discouraging. They collected enough unique impressions for a full baseball team."

I walked over to the wall of photographs. "We know so little about Ms. Salas. Look at all these pictures. Not a single adult. Not even a selfie of Ms. Salas herself. Take this one of Megan Rainwater with her baby. She had that child while in Ms. Salas's class. I know Lucy kept in touch. Megan is in medical school now. Why isn't there something newer? It's like Lucy didn't want to entertain a discussion about anything that happened outside of school."

Vicki examined the wall. "I see what you're saying. Look at the low-rise jeans, miniskirts, and Uggs. They bring back memories. The ones over here are more recent—ripped jeans, crop tops, and cold shoulders. All high school students. What do you think she was avoiding?"

"I've known Lucy for years, but I haven't learned anything except pedagogy and classroom management. I didn't even know she had a daughter."

Vicki was still looking at the photos. "I'm glad those low-rise jeans are gone."

I agreed. "They drove Kapitsa crazy, even more than the crop tops. I can still see him in the courtyard writing out detention slips and demanding that they cover their bare skin."

Vicki shook her head. "How are we going to find the motive for her murder given that we don't even know who she is."

"We know she was investigating the hackers. That's the place to start," I offered to be encouraging.

"Yes, but I'm still not convinced hackers and murderers mix." She went back to the table, sat down, and turned off her phone. "Let's begin with the means instead. How was she killed?"

"You're right. The key to this case is the cause of death. I see a pristine corpse beside a pool of blood as the most important mystery."

She leaned back and folded her arms. "Oh, wise man, what do you conclude?"

I mirrored her posture. "Ms. Salas knew her assailant. Her clothes show no sign of a struggle. The medical examiner will find a severe chest or abdominal trauma. Broken ribs. Punctured lung. Ruptured spleen. Internal hemorrhaging. Something like that. Killing body blows." I waited for this to sink in.

She gave me a smug smile, "Like I was saying. You're so assured and so wrong."

"S'cuse me?" I could tell she was toying with me. Enjoying that she found something that I'd missed. Payback for my discovery of blood on Lucy's shoes.

"When we examined the body in preparation for transferring custody to the coroner, we noticed a lump on her head and a cut beneath her hair."

"Sharp-force trauma," I mused. "Did you also find the weapon?"

"No, but we did find a bloody tarp stuffed into a cupboard."

"Interesting," I said pondering all the blood and the missing weapon.

Someone could have struck Ms. Salas from behind. That would explain the lack of a struggle. But how did I miss a killing head wound? I reviewed the scene in my mind. Ms. Salas sat in a chair. I had walked around looking down on her from every side. Could I have missed a lethal head injury? *No way!* That hidden head trauma didn't leave that pool of blood and it certainly didn't kill her.

Just then my phone interrupted with my substitute teaching ringtone.

The substitute notification system announced, "We have an assignment for Mr. Szilard. AP Biology. Tuesday. This is a vacancy."

By the time I'd tapped through all the menus to accept the job, Vicki was gone. I was on my own for lunch. I stopped at a farm-to-table salad bar on the way home, followed by a welcomed nap.

I woke up in the late afternoon and logged into the substitute system. I indeed had the assignment for Ms. Salas. Mr. Kapitsa hadn't fired me. Was I the only sub willing to cover for the murdered teacher? Regardless, I'd be returning to the crime scene tomorrow. Evidence alone didn't solve crimes. It took logic and intuition to piece together the story. Tomorrow would give me a second look. One without the Stony PD watching over my shoulder.

I anticipated a quiet dinner followed by an uninterrupted night and an orderly start to Tuesday—plenty of time for a good breakfast.

It didn't turn out like that. Lucy returned from the dead.

COVERUP: TUESDAY

A supernatural presence cocooned me in yellow crime-scene tape. The harder I fought, the tighter the tape confined me. Just out of reach was a ghostly Lucy, wearing her black blazer. I cried out, "Who killed you?"

"Where did the blood come from?"

"Why were you in school so early?"

"What about the hackers?"

The yellow tape evaporated when a phantom Ms. Salas reached into her pocket and pulled out an endless strip of condoms. "Take them," she said. Approaching me like a zombie, she moaned, "Condoms, condoms."

Detective Yukawa floated beside her whispering, "Don't be such a prude."

They drifted towards me with gold and silver strips of foil circles. I screamed into the night, "Forget the condoms! They don't matter!"

They wailed, "That's right," while wrapping me like a mummy. I gasped for air and awoke. Then like a bubble bursting, the specters were gone.

The subdued light of an overcast morning suggested that it was early, and I could bury my head under the covers, but a one-eyed peek at my phone confirmed that it was time for school. Only a faint echo of my sleep remained. The foggy wind whispered in Ms. Salas's voice, "Take care of my students, your honorary grandkids."

All my stomach would accept was dry toast and coffee which was mostly milk. After that meager breakfast, I opened my closet. What was I going to wear on the day following Lucy's death? When I was with the LAPD, my dress uniform honored those who passed away. I wasn't on the force anymore. My search for solemn attire turned up a pair of black slacks, black shoes that I'd worn as a police officer, and a navy shirt with buttons and a collar. They'd have to do.

At the school gate, a parent with flaming red hair wore a little black dress and a short veil that didn't hide her smile. She handed out black T-shirts printed with Ms. SALAS, WE LOVE YOU, and yesterday's date. Clearly, no one knew her birthdate. In death, as in life, her past remained a mystery.

I accepted a size 2XL and put it on over my dress shirt. The courtyard was an expanse of black. The diverse population of Stony High, the popular kids, the athletes, the geeks and nerds, and the ethnic and racial cliques, had all become a homogeneous community of mourners. Ms. Salas's misfortune had brought us together.

The cheery glow of the cafeteria spilled out onto the crowd. The fluorescents had recently been upgraded to LED lights—the consequence of a multi-year Ecology Club campaign. None of the black-clad teenagers moved in that direction. Lonely trees, each circled by a low brick wall, dotted the courtyard. On sunnier days, they offered seating and shade to boisterous groups. Today those walls only collected dew. I was surrounded by awkwardness. How could I instruct these traumatized children?

The advice from my dream returned, *'Take care of my students, your honorary grandkids.'*

I wouldn't teach. I'd commit the biggest substitute sin— throwing out the lesson plan. They'd want to share their feelings about Ms. Salas and her death. Giving them a safe place to do this was more important than any state-mandated curriculum. I was on the frontline of mental health until the district's postvention plan brought in professional counselors.

Once the buzzer rang for homeroom, I took my position at the door and silently greeted the students. They arrived alone or in small groups. I didn't shake hands or high-five anyone. I greeted the ones who looked up with a nod. By the time they finished trickling into the silent room, the buzzer sounded again, and homeroom was over.

Mrs. Wilson would be unhappy that I hadn't taken attendance, but I just wouldn't tell her.

First period. I didn't bother locking the door. A hospitable room outweighed the security protocols. It was too late for precautions. Lucy was already dead.

I rang Ms. Salas's bell. Blank faces looked up without interest. "Today is a distressing day. I'm thankful that you're all here." I looked around the room—black shirts at black tables. I offered, "Would you care to share your feelings?" This is what they wanted. They'd come to school to be with their friends.

I scanned the room expecting raised hands, but nobody moved.

Did they need me to call on them? Certainly, if someone began the discussion, they'd all join in. But where should I start?

I approached Annie, encouraged that she wasn't crying today. She'd been close to Ms. Salas and was an ideal candidate to get the ball rolling. She returned my stare, pursed her lips, and crossed her arms. Her body language was as clear as if she had shouted, "No. No Way."

Charlie was my next choice. While most students had their heads hung down with inward thoughts, he was alert. He'd comforted the others during the lockdown. I said, "Charlie—," but he cut me off repeatedly mouthing, "No."

I turn to Richie. He liked having an audience. But not today.

Third strike. I was out. Even though they rejected my invitation, I refused to revert to weather forecasting.

Fitch whispered, *'They need to express their grief, but not aloud, not in public.'*

I slowly rang the bell three times. After a pause, I repeated this time-honored death knell. After another pause, I gently announced, "You can use this time to write your remembrances of Ms. Salas."

When no one opened their laptop or took out their phone, I clarified, "These will not be shared or collected. If you want to text someone confidentially, the 9-8-8 Suicide and Crisis Lifeline is available 24/7."

Some students started typing. Slowly they came to life. Tears ran down the cheeks of a few of them while others just closed their eyes.

I usually walked around the classroom but not today. Some would journal their emotions, while others might be on social media or playing games. I left them free to process their sorrow however they wished—without oversight, without adult intervention.

The remaining periods were the same—not a single person shared aloud. Senior Detective Yukawa was waiting in the hall after the last class. "I have a meeting with the principal. I'd like you to join me."

I had planned to reexamine the crime scene, but after spending the day with uncommonly quiet students, I was glad for some conversation, even if it included Mr. Kapitsa. "My pleasure," I replied honestly.

Mrs. Wilson wore a long green calico dress covered with small pink flowers. Her blonde hair was pulled back in a tight bun. She was short, even shorter than Kapitsa. With long sleeves and a high collar, she could have been Tom Sawyer's Aunt Polly. She stood between us and the principal's office with her arms akimbo, "Stay here. I'll announce you."

We waited—like penitents seeking an audience with the high priest—while she entered his office and closed the door.

After a few minutes, she emerged. "Mr. Kapitsa will see you now."

I gave Vicki a who-does-he-think-he-is smirk. I'd never been inside his office and was not prepared for the scene that greeted me. A carved desk—massive, dark wood, curved lines, something from another time—and matching armchairs dominated the center of the room. The chairs had chocolate leather upholstery and nailhead trim. A man wearing a dark suit with a blue and gold striped necktie occupied one of the chairs.

Everything looked regal on a burgundy Persian carpet patterned with dragons and lilies. Incongruously, behind the desk sat a high-tech chair, a marvel in black leather and chrome with more controls than a Japanese toilet. To the right hung an oil painting of the principal standing beside a greyhound in a gilt frame and on the left he had a bookcase in the same over-the-top style as the desk. None of this came from the district's warehouse and emphasized that we were guests in his domain.

"Come in. Senior Detective Yukawa, you can sit here." He pointed to the other chocolate leather chair in front of his desk.

Vicki had worn her dress uniform with all her insignias and ribbons. I often joked that she looked like a parody of a general from some third-world country. With the principal playing the role of a despot, Vicki's costume reflected her astute understanding of the meeting, another sign of her political awareness and destiny to become Chief of Detectives.

Kapitsa introduced the man in the suit, "You all know Mr. Jensen, Chief Counsel for the district."

Fitch laughed, *'I've never met him, never even heard of him.'*

The lawyer stood and shook Vicki's hand.

At this point, I expected a parlor maid to appear with tea, and a three-tier tray of crustless cucumber sandwiches, scones with clotted cream, and sweet biscuits. Unfortunately, Kapitsa's hospitality didn't even include water.

The principal sat behind his desk. "The first order of business is the abysmal mismanagement of our community outreach. Parents and reporters are all over my campus. Rumors are rampant." He leaned back and examined his fingernails. "Totally unacceptable."

His monologue continued, "I don't blame the police or the district, but starting today, we need to speak with a unified voice, a single message."

From my position, standing in the doorway and underdressed for this formal occasion, I asked, "Shouldn't our priority be to follow the district's postvention plan and take care of the students?"

'Or find out who murdered Ms. Salas?' Fitch chimed in.

The principal scowled and looked at Vicki, "What's he doing here? Did he sneak in with you? Should I call security?"

I'd lost interest in this meeting. With the students gone, this was my opportunity to reexamine the crime scene. I was wasting time with Mr. Kapitsa. I wanted to absorb the entirety of the space where Lucy died—to fit the pieces together. I turned to go.

"Stop. Stay here," Vicki spoke in a calm voice. She turned to the principal, "Mr. Szilard is an experienced homicide detective. I invited him."

"That's nice, but this is my school, and I don't want him here. He's part of our problem. I wouldn't be surprised if he leaked the story about the condoms."

Fitch laughed, *'Not you. Each time someone mentions condoms, you get embarrassed and shut up.'*

"The Stony Estancia PD recognizes your concern, but—" Vicki paused.

I doubted she cared what Mr. Kapitsa thought any more than I did, but the Police Commissioner wouldn't promote her to Chief of Detectives if she got into a fight with every petty bureaucrat.

She began again, "This is your school, but someone was murdered here. We must balance those needs."

I was glad she didn't engage him on the topic of condoms. Murders and dead babies in baskets took precedent, and I still didn't want to think about what high school students might be doing in private.

The principal turned to the lawyer who had been noticeably silent. Kapitsa spat out, "He is an employee." As if I was something dirty that had stuck to the bottom of his shoe, he added, "A substitute teacher. Must I allow him to be here?"

I had no interest in this bureaucratic tussle and again turned to leave.

Vicki jumped up, pushed me aside, and closed the door. "Go sit in my seat." She stood blocking the exit and stared obstinately at the principal.

His face turned red. "Do something, Jensen!"

I stood behind the chair, not willing to advance the battle by occupying Mr. Kapitsa's personal furniture.

Jenson responded, "Detective Yukawa has a valid point. In a murder investigation, the police can employ anyone they wish. Of course, he doesn't have to teach at your school."

"Can you at least get a gag order? Someone leaked that horrible story about Ms. Salas handing out condoms. Can't we sue for libel?"

The lawyer muttered under his breath, "It is only libel in the case that it isn't true."

"Can't we classify all of this? Confidentiality or something? You know I already have an angry parent committee complaining about the Family Life courses. If they weren't state-mandated, I'd cancel those salacious lessons." Kapitsa let out an extended sigh. "The rumor mill has exploded that condom story into sex parties—students having sex together in the mountains. This has even been reported on that awful news site."

Vicki maintained the equanimity that would propel her to be Chief of Detectives. "Forget about condoms. The real issue is murder."

Mr. Jenson spoke slowly, as if to a small child, "As Chief Counsel, I'd also advise you to move beyond condoms and do everything in your power to solve this murder." He straightened his tie and moved closer to the principal, "The Williams Act tasks the school board with keeping the schools safe. Any reasonable court would agree that murder is *prima facie* evidence to the contrary. I am sure lawyers are preparing to sue. The board will be displeased if they receive those summonses before the police make an arrest."

The lawyer pointed to Mr. Kapitsa and raised his voice, "You will be in serious trouble if it appears that you didn't give Senior Detective Yukawa your full cooperation."

The principal looked down and closed his eyes. He hadn't been thinking about the school board. Gone was his position as lord of the manor. The threat from the board reminded him that he was a vassal to the king. I enjoyed his discomfort—*schadenfreude* again. Every petty tyrant reported to a larger one.

I hadn't considered the district's liability for dangerous schools. They were so safety conscious—locking doors, active shooter drills, anti-bullying seminars—that I never considered someone might sue them for unsafe conditions. A lawsuit would certainly complicate Vicki's investigation. How stupid could those lawyers be?

While I was regretting our litigious society, Mr. Kapitsa's face expanded into an uncharacteristic expression of glee. "I know how the stop those lawsuits. Announce that Ms. Salas died of natural causes. Heart attack or stroke or something."

He turned to me. "Here Szilard, you can make yourself useful. Detective Yukawa says you're a homicide expert. You've seen lots of people die. Ms. Salas could have just dropped dead, right?"

We didn't have conclusive evidence for murder, but my gut told me that was the case. I didn't want to join this discussion which struck me as bureaucratic chicanery.

'Nonsense. It was murder,' asserted Fitch.

Vicki must have liked the idea because she replied, "We found her dressed for teaching and sitting in a chair—no obvious signs of violence."

Like a good bureaucrat, the principal added, "That's a good point. We can use that. Let's not be too specific. The key to a believable story is not to include too many details."

The lawyer also went along with the coverup. He looked up at the portrait of the principal's dog and mused, "I'm just thinking aloud. Until we hear from the coroner, Kapitsa could be right. It doesn't have to be murder, does it, not just yet?"

The lawyer added, "Remember to add that this is preliminary, awaiting the autopsy."

Vicki agreed.

Using some language that I didn't understand, they'd decided to sweep the murder under Kapitsa's Persian carpet. I figured that this was their business and Ms. Salas wouldn't care as long as we found the culprit—which I intended to do.

Mr. Kapitsa stood, "Here's what we'll do. Zarand, you'll give aw-shucks grandpa interviews to the media."

I didn't respond. I just scowled at the three coconspirators.

The principal changed his mind. "Blast! You are always trouble. I should just fire you. Never mind. You don't need to do anything. Just keep your trap shut."

I could do that.

"Mr. Jensen, arrange a commemoration ceremony for poor Ms. Salas. Try to keep it from becoming a circus." He turned to Vicki, still standing by the door. "Detective Yukawa, do what you can to delay the autopsy report. I know the county coroner. Persephone is a Bruin, a proud alum. Appeal to her loyalty to the old alma mater."

And so, the coverup coalesced, and this strange committee cleared the Bruins of anything suspicious. It had been too easy. Starting with the flimsy possibility of a natural death, the principal's desire to control everything, and the Chief Counsel's fear of lawsuits, our little group agreed to downplay the obvious. I doubted that César and Tish, or the parents, and especially the students, would buy this new line.

Fitch also had his doubts. *'There is more to this coverup than is being said. We need to find the bigger story here.'*

When I left that meeting, Chuck Berry's music was on my phone. Tomorrow would be my third day subbing in AP Biology. I took that as a positive omen.

I didn't look forward to any ceremony thrown together to support Kapitsa's conspiracy theory. How could a lawyer, who didn't know our school, arrange something to commemorate Ms. Salas?

In the end, I'd owe Jenson an apology. He accomplished what I hadn't. Students shared their grief and honored Ms. Salas. The event added names to my witness list and clues about Ms. Salas's shadowy past.

Fitch wondered, *'How can there be so many suspects for the murder of a high school teacher?'*

11. THE REMEMBRANCE: WEDNESDAY

I knew better than to try group therapy again, but it was still too soon to revert to business as usual. I considered showing a movie but none of the approved ones fit. Ms. Salas had an extensive collection of videos featuring the frenetic Bill Nye the Science Guy, but they were too upbeat for our solemn situation. I considered sneaking in one of the many television shows about forensics, a mixture of science and current events. They matched Ms. Salas's approach to education—a fitting tribute—but they all seemed ghoulish considering our current circumstances.

I checked the web for inspiration and discovered that STONY ESTANCIA SURFS offered a memorial documentary about Ms. Lucinda Salas's life, *Science Teacher for the Future.* I had to give Tish and César credit for having their fingers on the pulse of the community and for a rapid production cycle. It was conveniently the same length as a class period, solving my lesson plan dilemma. We could all be respectful without anyone sharing their feelings.

The video opened with students streaming into the school to a cheery major key soundtrack, followed by her empty classroom and a somber minor key. After the briefest mention of an ongoing police investigation and no mention of murder, it featured different students and teachers. I took down all the names for later interrogation.

The most memorable was a segment with Megan Rainwater. "With her support, I raised my daughter as a single parent and continued my education."

The camera zoomed out to reveal a girl hugging Megan Rainwater's leg, wearing jeans with muddy knees and a shirt that quoted, THOUGH SHE BE BUT LITTLE SHE BE FIERCE. The small girl carried a big book.

Tish asked Ms. Rainwater, "Is this your daughter?

"Yes." She pulled the girl closer. "This is Lucy."

"That's a lovely name. Did you name her after your high school teacher?"

The mother smiled, "Yes, Ms. Lucinda Salas."

Tish lowered the blue boom mic into the frame, positioning it for young Lucy. César asked, "What are you reading?"

The girl proudly held up her picture book. "Biographies. Women scientists." She turned the cover to face the camera. "That's Marie Curie and her daughter." She gave the reporter a huge grin like she'd done this trick before and knew she amazed her interviewer.

César paused. He didn't have a follow-up question about scientists. I expect he would have had an immediate response for princesses or furry animals.

Little Lucy rescued him from dead air. "Seven of them won Nobel Prizes."

After that, the video ended with Tish saying something about Ms. Salas and feminism.

Fitch summarized, *'So, they don't know anything about her life before teaching either.'*

I didn't show *Science Teacher for the Future* as many times as I expected. Mr. Kapitsa dismissed school early with the announcement, "Today is a minimum day. Please join us on the football bleachers to remember Ms. Salas."

Outside the gym, on the way up to the football field, the same parent in a black dress and a veil that distributed black T-shirts yesterday was handing out *In Memoriam* cards today. The reverse side, in small print, read THIS PAPER IS PLANTABLE AND WILL CREATE A LASTING WILDFLOWER TRIBUTE. I still didn't know who the lady was, but I was sure the Ecology Club had something to do with those cards.

Students and parents gathered on the wooden benches. A life-size cardboard standee of Ms. Salas coaching the Lady Bruins football team stood beside the podium. She looked small surrounded by the girls in shoulder pads.

In front of the picture were flowers, balloons, and stuffed animals. Mr. Jenson stood behind a portable podium with two microphones—one for the PA system and the other belonging to our ubiquitous reporters from STONY ESTANCIA

SURFS. In a row of folding chairs sat Mr. Kapitsa and several teachers, all wearing black armbands.

The first speaker, introduced by Mr. Jensen, was Dr. Rudra—call me Chandra—Chandrasekhar, the chairperson of the science department. I made a mental note to place Chandra at the head of my interview list. He put a teddy bear dressed in a white lab coat and holding a stethoscope with the other memorial gifts. "We're here today to remember Ms. Salas. She arrived at Stony High after a full career in health services. She was always ready to share her experience. I am sure many of our students went on to be scientists and doctors because of her."

'Health services isn't specific,' Fitch whined. *'But that's more information than we had.'*

I pondered. She could have been an EMT or an oncologist. With her interest in science, she might have been in research like Brooklynn's mom. I'd discover more when I interviewed the department chair.

The boys' football coach followed Chandra. "Lucy came to our school with medical experience. Let me give you my favorite memory."

'Now we're getting somewhere,' Fitch cheered.

"During practice, one of my boys got dizzy and passed out. Fortunately for everyone, the girls were practicing nearby. Lucy took one look at him, shouted, 'Call nine-one-one,' and raced for the locker room."

He paused to let the suspense build.

"She returned with a small orange container. Later I learned that it was his Glucagon Emergency Kit—glucagon is the hormone that raises sugar levels, the opposite of insulin. If he had been conscious, he would have self-administered the glucagon, but he wasn't."

There was sweat on the coach's brow and his breathing became shallow and rapid. He was reliving the panic of the incident. After taking a deep breath, he continued.

"When it was all over, the EMT told me that Lucy had saved the boy's life. She injected the glucagon directly into his vein. That extra speed had made the difference."

He coughed and wiped his eyes. "Just to be clear. If she hadn't known how to administer the medication intravenously, he could have suffered brain damage or even died."

He bowed his head. "We'll all miss her."

I still didn't know exactly what she did prior to coming to Stony High, but it was clear that she knew how to respond to an emergency and had more than a passing familiarity with medical procedures. I had years of first aid and emergency training, but I never attempted an IV injection.

Mr. Kapitsa was the last faculty representative. "Thank you for coming today to commemorate the amazing life of Ms. Salas. She was a devoted friend and counselor." He followed by reading a potpourri of clichés and inspirational quotes from a stack of index cards, undoubtedly prepared by Mrs. Wilson.

Heads bobbed in agreement but not mine. His suggestion that Lucy was his "friend and counselor" offended me. Mr. Kapitsa never went for advice to Ms. Salas or anyone else. The teachers scared him.

Next came the student speakers.

There was none of the reticence that I had experienced in my classroom. The adults speaking first made the difference. I'd remember this for the next time, though I hoped there wouldn't be one.

The captain of the football team walked to the microphone in uniform, including pads and cleats, and a helmet under her arm. "I place this helmet on Ms. Salas's memorial to protect her on her next journey as she protected us."

Xuan Hua Tuy stood for the Ecology Club. "I will never forget Ms. Salas saying that science without compassion is as bad as no science. I am sure her life lessons will last longer than the answers we memorized for the chapter tests."

After the scheduled speakers, Mr. Jensen opened the mic.

Many students were like Annie who said, "I'm not a football player and I'll never be a scientist, but Ms. Salas was my friend and I'm going to miss her." Annie prophetically added, "We had a special bond."

A tear rolled down her cheek, but by this point, many students and adults had wet eyes.

After a dozen students spoke, many mentioning the Ecology Club, Mr. Jensen asked, "Would anyone else like to say a few words before we move to the gym for refreshments?"

A final person approached. He wore a gray twill shirt with an embroidered district patch above the right pocket. "I'm Adamah Mbacke. I recognize all of you. I clean when the school is empty. You come when I go. We are like ships in the night. *Señorita* Lucinda spoke with me often. I'll miss her. *Vaya con Dios.*"

Some people touched a few lives, and some touched many. Adamah showed that Ms. Salas touched more than most. I'd been to many of these ceremonies and my reaction was always the same. The victim deserved justice, and I wasn't going to rest until we found the culprit. Even though I was retired, I committed myself to tracking down the men who ended her life.

I joined the crowd sampling the assortment of sweets in the gym. After a few cookies and a glass of punch, I was ready to sneak away to the workspace behind Ms. Salas's room where this all began, but an early exit seemed disrespectful.

Detective Yukawa appeared and preempted my quandary. She waved and called, "Zarand, I must talk to you." I grabbed a brownie to-go and followed her to the deserted courtyard. We sat on a low brick wall encircling a California pepper tree.

"Zarand, I have Persey's preliminary autopsy report. Kapitsa's wish for a natural death may have come true."

I'd been waiting for this.

"The sharp-force trauma was superficial. It had nothing to do with her death." She waited a moment before adding, "Her torso was uninjured. Your theory of broken ribs didn't pan out either. I don't know how you can be so confident when your intuition is so often wrong?"

Fitch answered, *'Indecision never helps.'*

I ignored Vicki's skepticism. I trusted my gut. Regardless of the *preliminary* post-mortem, Lucy was too young and healthy to just drop dead. I didn't care who thought it was a natural death—something awful had happened here. "That can't be right. Fitch is sure that she was murdered."

"Not Fitch again. Aren't you too old for an imaginary friend?"

"Fitch is more than a childish imaginary friend. My spirit guide solves difficult cases and keeps me safe. You ignore him at your peril. Just because Persey hasn't determined the cause of death, that doesn't mean Lucy wasn't murdered."

Vicki said in a half-hearted agreement, "Persey is still investigating cardiac arrest, stroke, and asphyxia."

"What about poisoning?"

"That too. Her initial toxicology screen was negative, but she sent out samples for gas chromatography and colorimetric analysis."

"So, the autopsy could still go either way," I pondered aloud.

"Forensic science is powerful, but it takes time."

"Did Stony High alumna Persey check the hyoid bone for signs of strangulation?"

"I know you don't think much of us in the suburbs, but of course, she examined the hyoid, and it was intact."

Vicki raised her index finger signaling she'd remembered something else. "The autopsy did offer one clarification."

I waited for her to continue.

"When I checked with Mrs. Wilson, she told me that Ms. Salas was a new college graduate. Her personnel file said that she was not old enough to have had an earlier career. However—"

Nothing about this case was easy. We were going to miss our cruise and those spectacular buffets.

'You can rebook that cruise after we find Lucy's killer,' said Fitch who never ate or got hungry.

I jumped in, "New college grad? That's in direct contradiction to all the talk about her medical experience. I just heard eulogies extolling her abilities. Those records are wrong, but why?"

"Calm down. I was about to explain. The autopsy agrees with you. Her pubic symphysis proves she is older than her personnel file attests."

My head was spinning, so many paths to visit to unravel this mess. "Did someone question the district office?"

She shook her head, frustrated with me, "Again, calm down and give me a chance to explain. This was the easiest mystery to solve. The school was desperate for science teachers. Ms. Salas had an ideal transcript, and her Social Security Number checked out."

"S'cuse me. That's the work of witness protection. Someone from her past discovered her identity and murdered her. A professional."

"Gosh, I hope not. I might as well return my bathing suit today. Witness protection would confound the investigation. If that is the case, we should cancel our cruise."

Now it was my turn to counsel calm. "Don't return it yet. It wasn't witness protection. They wouldn't be clumsy enough to change her chronological age."

"Witness protection. Not witness protection. I admire your conviction, but you remind me of a snake."

"S'cuse me? A snake? Are you calling me deceitful and evil?"

Vicki laughed, "Gosh, no. That's the serpent. A snake has no long-term memory. Each moment is new. First, it's witness protection, then it's not. Do you even listen to what you're saying?"

There was nothing wrong with my memory, except for those senior moments when I forgot why I'd gone to the kitchen.

Fitch laughed at this. *'You always just want a snack.'*

Vicki was just jealous of my intuition. She hissed out a long breath between her teeth. She sounded like a snake.

I elaborated, "This is an amateur case of something like witness protection—identity theft. What did you discover about that pool of blood?"

"The pool? All that blood? The bloody tarp? The forensic techs even found some in the sink drain."

I recalled a picture of the scene. "S'cuse me. Someone cleaned up, but not very well. Again, not professionals. Did your forensics techs find Lucy's blood?"

"No. As Persey said, the head wound was superficial. Lucy might have been dazed, but it wasn't a killing blow, and none of the blood at the scene belonged to her."

"I see. Did you find the weapon?"

"No."

I considered the implications. So much blood. A protective tarp. A cleanup. Several people were involved.

'That would be good,' Fitch declared, *'The more perpetrators, the better chance someone will slip up and be discovered.'*

I asked, "How many blood types?"

"Just one—not Ms. Salas's. We're doing DNA testing. With so much blood loss, I expect we'll find another corpse."

That might be, but I only cared about Ms. Salas. I and my chosen grandchildren missed her, and we wouldn't let a second victim distract us.

While Vicki and I had been solving crimes, everyone else had been attending Mr. Jensen's punch-and-cookies wake. Knots of students streamed out of the gym talking.

I divided my brownie in half and offered both sections to Vicki, "Take your pick."

She took the smaller one, broke off a bite-sized piece, popped it into her mouth, and returned the rest to me with a smile.

I savored the chocolatey goodness while we observed the shenanigans of the spirited mob.

"Look at that. I remember when my kids were teenagers. Their moods changed as quickly as they could scroll. These students were somber as they entered the gym and now, they're full of life."

I could overhear the boys and girls.

"I hope they don't cancel prom."

"They wouldn't do that. It's next week."

"What about the state tests? I'd be happy to skip them."

"No. Not that either."

"Minimum day today. That was it."

"School is back in session."

That was easy for some of these students, but Ms. Salas's classes wouldn't be ready to return to academics just yet. It had been their teacher who'd been murdered. Principal Kapitsa and Coroner Persey might be on the fence, but Fitch said murder. I trusted Fitch.

Murder or not, school went on.

"Yeah. I have a book report due Friday. It wasn't even delayed to over the weekend."

"Bummer. No respect for the dead."

They all laughed.

By this time, the gym had emptied, and students had filled the courtyard. Vicki raised a finger to her lips and whispered, "Let's get out of here."

When we reached her unmarked police car, she opened the passenger door. It took a moment for her to remove her laptop and snacks from the seat. "Get in. I'll bring you back to your car later."

"No problem," I replied. "Do you mind if I take one of these?" I asked grabbing a bag of chips from her cache of snacks.

"Go ahead. I can't believe you're still hungry after that brownie."

Vicki didn't say anything more until she'd driven out of the parking lot. "Are you still teaching?"

Why did she need secrecy for that question? "As far as I know. No one is eager to take the dead teacher's classes."

"Gosh, that's good. Law enforcement has limited access to the schools, but teachers are free to go anywhere and talk to anyone. On your own, you can discover evidence that would be unavailable to me."

Now I understood her caution. "I can look around and keep my ears open, but none of that will be admissible in court."

"No problem. I can uncover legal evidence when I know what I'm looking for. We need a breakthrough, some direction. Find it."

I understood her predicament. I worked with many confidential informants during my years in the big city.

She pulled to the curb and let me out. "Thanks. We haven't gone far. You can walk back."

"No problem," I said shoving the empty chips bag into my pocket and picking up another to-go. As I watched Vicki drive away, I was grateful my role in her investigation had changed. At first, I was a combination of annoyance and suspect. Now I was her consultant and CI. Through all this, I'd been steadfast in my promise to Ms. Salas to uncover the truth of her demise.

Vicki had dropped me on Blackett Street, in front of the bakery. I had parked my car on the other side of the school. Rather than walk around, I cut through the courtyard where a cacophony of adolescent excitement bombarded me. After a few days of muted voices, the campus again reverberated with activity. Bright So Cal sunshine illuminated the courtyard. The monochrome of black T-shirts was gone, and the full color of Stony High's diverse population had returned. The campus echoed once again with multiple languages. School was back in session.

The immediacy of tomorrow's classes demanded I think of a lesson plan. I still had the weather forecasting video, but that time filler assumed that Ms. Salas was returning, which she wasn't.

I was more interested in Lucy's murder and the baby-in-the-basket, but I didn't worry. I ordered a pizza for dinner and after a good night's sleep, a plan would appear. It always did.

Gone was yesterday's morning overcast. The glow of the sun peeking over the San Bernardino Mountains bathed my bedroom with light. An AP Biology lesson plan had not manifested, but the early morning gifted me with an opportunity to take advantage of Higgs Haven Garden Apartments. The lawns and palm trees imitated a private club. From my balcony, I saw rabbits and house finches—small brown birds with red heads. I had time to go to the fitness center for a workout. Sets and reps would inspire that required lesson plan.

'*Um, not so fast!*' interrupted Fitch. '*Notice the clock. This is the time Ms. Salas was murdered.*'

Fitch was old school. A crime scene wasn't just a place. It was also a time. He'd solved cases questioning delivery drivers and joggers whose schedules coincided with the timeline. I could take a hint. I quickly showered, dressed, and grabbed an orange from the fridge and an energy bar from the cupboard. I ran down the stairs, opened the fire door to the garage, and was soon speeding down the deserted Blackett Street on my way to school. My only regret was the CLOSED sign on the bakery. Bright lights revealed that the bakers were preparing the day's fresh breads and cakes even though the display cases were still dark.

As Fitch had predicted, my early arrival uncovered clues that had disappeared each morning once the campus was invaded by students and teachers.

12. WITNESSES: THURSDAY

With my Mini tucked into a far corner of the parking lot, I staked out the early morning activity. I listened to oldies and ate my breakfast—waiting outside the locked fence, staring at the placard AUTHORIZED PERSONNEL ONLY. *SOLO PERSONAL AUTORIZADO.* The school didn't look like a murder scene.

I heard a chain rattle. A gate opened. Someone was wheeling a bin piled high with black plastic bags. It was good that Brooklynn wasn't with me. She hated those bags. I recognized Adamah Mbacke from the remembrance ceremony.

Fitch had pointed me in the right direction. Here was the witness that had been overlooked.

I got out of my car and called, "Good morning, Mr. Mbacke." I waved with both hands to show that I wasn't a threat.

"*Buenos días,*" He replied, cautiously adding, "You're one of the teachers, aren't you?"

I reached out to shake his hand. "That's right. I'm the substitute for Ms. Salas. I heard you speak at her memorial."

His guarded expression became a broad smile. "*Sí.* I recognize you. What are you doing here...so early?" he asked while removing his glove and offering his hand.

We shook hands.

"I'm with the police, looking for her killer."

"How can I help?"

"First, can you tell me who has keys to the gates?"

"*Todo el mundo,*" he laughed. "The maintenance staff. Mr. Kapitsa. Mrs. Wilson. The teachers." He paused to think. "Some people from the district office. The police. The fire department. The Ecology Club—"

I interrupted, "The Ecology Club?"

"Yes, sir. They come early to clean the solar panels."

"That's a lot of keys," I said with a shocked tone.

He found my reaction funny. "Don't forget the captain of the swim team. They practice before the sun comes up. I'm sure there're more."

"Do you remember seeing Ms. Salas last Monday?"

His friendly smile disappeared. "You mean the day she died?"

"Yes."

He looked around the parking lot like he was searching for her. "Ms. Salas was my friend. I'll never forget that morning. I was collecting trash when her car rolled into the parking lot." His eyes moved side to side as he recalled the details. "I didn't hear anything, but her headlights lit up the courtyard. I knew it was Ms. Salas because she drives a van. It's quiet like your car, electric." He pointed to my black-and-white Mini.

"Are you sure it was her?"

His hands gripped the bin of trash bags. He looked nervous like he was trying to give me the answer I wanted, but he didn't want to lie. Honesty won out. "I was too far away, but I don't know anyone else who drives a car like that."

I encouraged him, "Good. Good. That's helpful."

"No, it's not," he said sadly. "I should have gone over to say, *buenos días*. I usually did. Perhaps if I had, she'd still be alive."

I waited for his fingers to relax their death grip on the rolling bin before I asked, "Did you notice anyone with her?"

"*Sí.*" he replied with confidence. "A couple of cars followed her—small like yours and also electric."

What luck. Here were my suspects and my witness. We'd close this case long before that cruise embarkation. "What happened next?"

"I watched them. They parked next to Ms. Salas in the teacher's lot. They weren't teachers. They didn't belong there. She walked into the science building with them gathered around her." He took a deep breath and sighed. "Why didn't I shout, *buenos días?*"

I rhetorically asked, "Would you recognize those people if you saw them again?"

With that question, Mr. Mbacke's shoulders slumped, and my optimism evaporated.

"No, sir. I was far away. I couldn't tell if they were adults or students, *niñas o niños*. They could have been trained monkeys." He laughed when he said *monkeys*.

I laughed too. "Monkeys. That's a good one. *Gracias*. One more favor, *por favor*. Could you let me in?"

"*Solo un minuto*." He pushed his bin to the dumpsters where I helped toss the trash bags before we went to the gate. I entered alongside him and his cart. He locked the gate behind us.

I wandered around the campus as the school came to life. This case was a worthy challenge. Every time I learned something, it added to the mystery. The morning was going so well that I considered a hike to the science garden to look for more baby-in-the-basket clues, but I had AP Biology classes starting soon. I still was searching for a lesson plan.

The thick texts stacked on the tables were inviting, but I recalled Ms. Salas's disdain for those books. I searched through the materials stored around the room, a bounty that Ms. Salas had accumulated—supplies she'd intended to use for many years to come. Supplies that sadly outlived her.

One cabinet held a class set of dissection kits, but no frogs. The diffusion experiment had all the necessary materials, but Ms. Salas had written herself a sticky note to remember that she'd taught that lab a few months ago.

In the back of a drawer, I found a plastic box of prepared microscope slides: ONION MITOSIS, ROOT TIPS. These were perfect. I'd teach about cell division. Even if it was a repeat, its importance justified the review, and it would certainly be featured on the upcoming AP exams.

I had my lesson. It was the winning combination of hands-on science and art.

The class arrived for homeroom with no delays. I still wasn't taking attendance. After Ms. Salas, it didn't seem important. I put the homeroom class to work. "We are setting up for AP Biology. Everyone on the TIMELINE side of the room please get a microscope. One per table."

They collected the laboratory-grade microscopes—more evidence of the suburban privilege that permeated Stony High—under the watchful eye of Leeuwenhoek, inventor of the first practical one. I let them chat as they completed this task.

After the microscope setup, I said, "Now, those of you on the EVOLUTION side please get the colored pencils." In a few minutes, each table had a microscope and a pencil box. At this point, the end-of-homeroom buzzer sounded.

I completed the preparation by distributing an onion root-tip slide beside each microscope. Root tips were perfect for this experiment because they grew quickly and showed all stages of mitosis.

When first period started, the microscopes on the tables signaled a hands-on science activity. The students' anticipation guaranteed that I had everyone's attention. "Do not uncover the microscopes," I announced. Not everyone cooperated. Richie put his hand under the plastic dust cover and adjusted the microscope body up and down. He turned to the girl sitting next to him and leered, "Do you like that?"

She smacked his arm, "Shut up."

Xuan Hua stared into her lap where I assumed she was doing something on her phone.

I ignored these minor transgressions.

"What is rule number one?" I asked as I circled the room.

I stopped beside Xuan Hua who slipped her phone into her pocket. "Never touch the lenses," she answered in a strong voice.

Everyone was engaged even though we were just reviewing the rules. All eyes were on me. I had achieved substitute teacher nirvana—the class was paying attention.

"Now, how to load the slide." I uncovered Xuan Hua's microscope. "First, lower the stage and clip the slide in, label up."

I scanned the room to check that I still had their attention. Happily, all eyes were on me.

"Next raise the stage and focus using the lowest resolution. What do we watch out for when focusing?"

I stopped at Charlie's table.

"D-d-don't cr-crash the lens into the slide."

"Exactly."

It was time for me to stop talking. "You can all load your slides and see what's on them."

These slides showed the various stages of mitosis. I visited the tables and made sure that everyone could see the cells. Once the novelty wore off, they were ready to learn, and I continued my lecture.

"Today we're not interested in any technical jargon or scientific vocabulary. I just want you to observe the different cell configurations. All science begins with careful observation. Tomorrow we'll identify these differences and how they help cells divide."

After a brief period of unstructured exploration, I asked, "What do you see? Discuss this with your partners."

"Some cells look like regular fried eggs and others look like double-yolk eggs."

"Is this what sex looks like?"

"Look at this cell. It has a spider inside it."

"Maybe spider sex."

"And this one is full of worms."

When the patter died down, I gave them their assignment. "Sketch as many different cell types as you can find. Tomorrow we'll label each picture."

They continued drawing until the end-of-period buzzer. Art projects were always a crowd-pleaser.

When the final period's students had vacated the room, I went to each table to collect the slides into their storage box. I put away the microscopes, but the pencils stayed for tomorrow's lesson.

Then I locked my room and meandered down the hall in search of science department chair Dr. Rudra Chandrasekhar who had delivered that nice remembrance of Ms. Salas yesterday.

I spotted him in his classroom staring at his computer. "S'cuse me, Chandra. Can I come in? I'm not interrupting something, am I?"

"No worries. I know you're always interested in the latest tech." He turned his large computer screen towards me. All the teachers had touchscreens. Chandra's had no fingerprints. Only the younger teachers poked the screens with their fingers. He moved the cursor with his mouse and said, "Look at this."

He was in charge. I was prepared to be fascinated by his technology. I was undercover for the Stony PD, waiting for an opening to ask my questions. His computer screen had a list of statements color-coded green, yellow, and red. 'Energy and momentum are the same,' was colored red.

"What am I looking at?" I queried.

"This is *teaching with data*. I'm testing it. At the end of every class, they take a short online quiz. It's all automatically tabulated, and I have immediate feedback. You're looking at today's lesson."

I pointed to the red statement careful not to touch his pristine display. "So, this is something you'll reteach tomorrow?"

"Exactly. Isn't this great? No waiting until the chapter test to discover where the class is confused."

"I'm surprised. After all your years, I expected that you had your lectures honed to perfection." When he stepped back, I feared I might have said the wrong thing. I needed him in a good mood for the furtive interrogation I was planning.

His answer wiped away all my concerns. "I always repeat that lesson. This was a distinction that baffled Newton. His contemporary Leibniz had to straighten him out."

"Well, you have good company there."

He moved forward. We were still friends. "I'll follow today's lecture based on my pal Newton with my buddy Leibniz tomorrow."

I laughed at his joke. "Wow. Newton and Leibniz. I didn't think you were that old."

He laughed.

Now that we laughed at each other's jokes, I asked, "Tell me. Do you remember the graduation ghost? Senior Detective Yukawa tells me this is still an open case with the Stony PD."

"No wonder. When that goth girl Persephone erected a tombstone over his empty grave, I knew the case would never close."

"Is that goth girl the coroner?"

He smiled. "Oh yes. I remember when she was just a student—one of the smartest, but always dressed in black, with all that black makeup. Still, they can't expect to solve that case after all these years."

"Pretty foolish," I agreed. "Is it indeed hopeless?"

"I doubt anyone ever thinks about it." He pursed his lips and closed his eyes as if trying to remember. "Alex something. They called his name, but nobody walked up to the podium. The crowd fidgeted with an embarrassed silence. Finally, a young Mrs. Wilson called the next name."

"Mrs. Wilson was there?"

"Sure. Mr. Kapitsa wasn't hired until later. She and I are the only survivors from back then. Of course, she's a lot younger than I am. The teachers were baby boomers. They're retired now."

"Do you recall anything else about this guy Alex?"

"He's more of a myth now. We've told his story so many times as a cautionary tale to warn seniors to order their caps and gowns, I doubt any of the truth remains."

"So, mythology. Alex went off on an enchanted quest and will someday return with magic beans," I said keeping the conversation light.

"Sure, something like that, but he better hurry before I retire."

"What about those students? Surely, they haven't all left town."

"I can remember a few. Dick Fowler is a successful marketing guy. He was so skinny, that they called him Dick the Stickman. I don't remember what he sells, but he travels a lot and makes bushels of money. Some people think he's involved in smuggling. He married Charlene Bragg—"

"Is she related to the Bragg Vineyard Memorial Cemetery?"

"That is not what she was known for in high school. She was a hot number—everyone called her Cha Cha. They were a cute couple—Dick the Stickman and Cha Cha, king and queen of the prom."

"Are they the parents of Richie Fowler? He's in one of my classes." I didn't say anything about him being a bully or an abused child—not wanting to spook Chandra. Keeping someone talking is a delicate skill, but I had plenty of practice.

"Yes. Richie is a second-generation Bruin. The other alum I remember was Jackie Siegbahn. She's some sort of artist and she had a terrible accident. I don't recall the details."

This seemed like an opportune time to ask about Ms. Salas. "Was Lucy at that graduation?"

"No. Of course not. It was longer ago than that."

I took a risk since there was no clever way to disguise my real intent. "Can you think of anyone who would have wanted to murder her?"

He stepped back. "Are you asking as a teacher or a cop?"

Whoops. I'd raised his suspicion. "Cop? No. I'm retired."

"Yes, but you're friends with Detective Yukawa, aren't you?"

This school was even a smaller town than Stony Estancia—absolutely no secrets. That would play in my favor to track down Ms. Salas's murderer. "Yes, but I'm just a substitute teacher. I'm curious because I'm teaching in her room. Do you think I'm in danger?"

That little half-truth did the trick.

"I can't think of anyone who didn't like her."

I prompted him. "I heard you speak at her memorial. All those people liked her, but she was murdered anyway."

He backed away again. "Didn't Kapitsa say that she died of natural causes?"

This line of questioning made him uncomfortable, but I pressed the query—even at the risk of him shutting down. I took a chance. "You don't believe everything he says, do you? I certainly don't."

Chandra gave an involuntary smirk. My gamble had paid off. I remembered his PhD and pressed forward. "You're a scientist. Do you have a hypothesis?"

He looked around to confirm his room was still empty, shut the door, and moved in close. "She was a big advocate of birth control for teenagers. I think some parents objected, but there wasn't much they could do about it."

I pressed him for details. "I heard some rumors about condoms. Do you think someone would murder her over that?"

He shook his head. "I hope not."

I agreed and we were back on a friendly track. I took advantage of my good standing to ask about my most promising line of investigation. "She told me about forged recommendation letters and faked transcripts. Do you think she ran afoul of those people?"

That was the wrong question.

He spat out angrily, "If you want to play cop, don't include me." He sat down in front of his computer. "I must get working on that lecture for tomorrow."

Something had touched a raw nerve.

Fitch was ready with an explanation, '*He knows about the college entrance fraud. He's scared of the hackers.*'

One thing was clear: Chandra had dismissed me. Our discussion was over. His reaction suggested the hackers were active throughout the school. They must be stopped before we had another murder.

By speaking to Mr. Mbacke and Chandra, I had made several steps forward—the list of suspects had grown. Also, the urgency to solve this case had increased—before someone else died.

As soon as I got in my little black-and-white car, I called Vicki. "I interviewed a teacher and another witness who both knew Ms. Salas. Let's have dinner. If we put our heads together, I expect we can crack this case wide open."

Vicki didn't see it that way and my sloppy attendance reporting proved to be more troublesome than I expected.

I met Vicki at Cocina de Cetto to brag about my successful interviews. "You'll be impressed with what I learned at the high school." While we snacked on chips and salsa, I reported my talks with Mr. Mbacke— "You won't believe how many people have keys to the schoolyard." —and with Chandra— "He was frightened when I brought up the college application forgeries."

She leaned back and drained her bottle of Dos Equis. "That's interesting, but not enough to crack the case."

When our food arrived, she poured the remaining salsa over the rice and beans that came with her enchiladas. I unwrapped the corn husks from my tamales as quickly as I could to spare my fingers from the escaping steam.

"Even if the case isn't cracked wide open, you must admit it's opened a crack. I discovered Mr. Mbacke, an important witness. Two cars accompanied Ms. Salas. Don't you see how everything fits together?"

"Really? I'm saving the receipt from my bathing suit if you're counting on that night maintenance guy to solve the case."

'Don't be bashful. Tell her how you reconstructed what happened,' Fitch encouraged me.

I took a bite of my tamales. The corn was sweet, and the filling was perfectly spiced. I explained, "We know several people arrived with her. That tells me two things."

Vicki ate in silence.

"First, Lucy didn't come to school that morning on her own. The people in those other cars coerced her. Second, they came here to get something. If we can figure out what is missing from her classroom, we'll know their motive."

"That's quite a story you put together," she said in a tone of disbelief.

I didn't let her discourage me. "There's more. From speaking to Chandra, I know those people were part of the college entrance fraud gang."

She stirred up a mixture of rice, bean, and salsa, and scooped it into her mouth. I cut a bite-size piece of tamale. We both chewed our dinners while she considered my conjecture.

I had taken another portion when she replied, "Don't you feel that you're making a big leap—from two cars to conspiracy and abduction?" She took a mouthful of enchilada and sipped her beer before leaning back and clasping her hands behind her head. "Police work hasn't stopped evolving just because you retired. Do you know what the biggest change is?"

I ate a morsel of tender carnitas covered in masa, chewing slowly while pondering her question. After swallowing the tasty mixture, I answered, "Absolutely. Civilian oversight. Review committees. Miranda warnings. Nobody trusts us anymore."

Fitch laughed at me, *'That's all so last century.'*

After another bite, I added, "I can remember a time when lost children were told to look for a policeman. I don't think that happens anymore."

"I doubt it ever happened. You're confusing early television, all whitewashed fantasies, with reality."

"Whitewashed? Do you think the change is about diversity? More women, people of color?" The police had been under so much pressure recently. "How about, education? More officers with college degrees?"

"Those are all good points." She took a swallow of beer, realizing that this game could go on for a long time. "You can stop guessing. I was thinking of forensic science. Both mysteries at the high school are going to come down to lab reports."

"Lab reports?" I asked incredulously.

"Yes," she replied. "When we board that cruise ship, it will be thanks to scientific tests. Right now, we want to know the cause of death. Modern post-mortem techniques will solve that riddle."

"So, we just sit around and wait? You expect this case to be solved by your friend Persey, not the detectives?" I asked rhetorically, not believing it for a moment.

"Absolutely," she smiled. "More than the police have changed. People are wary of eyewitness recollections. Prosecutors and juries expect lab results, not *witnesses*. They believe forensic science more than anyone's recollections."

"That's crazy. Look how much I've learned from just two interviews."

"Really? Your witnesses didn't help. They just let you conjure up a conspiracy theory that should be in a novel, not a police investigation. What are the important questions? Who is Ms. Salas? What is her history? And that pool of blood? Rest assured that the DNA and data scientists will uncover those answers."

"DNA?" I asked not disguising my disbelief. "We need to know more about Ms. Salas. I want to know everything—her feelings, her likes, her fears, and her hopes. DNA won't answer these questions. I'll put my money on good detective work over forensic wizardry."

"You're just not familiar with the recent technology." She took a forkful of my tamales and smiled. "I think you're afraid of it."

"Not true," I protested. "I just read a DoJ study on the impact of forensic evidence. They found that there were higher clearance rates when the forensic evidence was ignored. Ignored!"

"You can think what you like. For a case like this where we have no witnesses—"

"What about Mr. Mbacke?"

"Mr. Mbacke? Didn't he say he could have seen trained monkeys? I wouldn't call that a witness."

"He's a witness and you'll see that he's important."

"I doubt it. It's going to be the DNA."

"Well don't expect me to just sit around waiting for those magical lab results."

"No sense arguing about that now. We'll have plenty of time while on board our ship drinking margaritas and enjoying endless guacamole. That will be thanks to the forensic evidence, not your fantastical stories."

The next morning, I awoke full of energy and optimism, I went to the fitness center for a morning workout—arms, abs, and legs, followed by a swim and a shower.

The sun was bright and scratch buckwheat pancakes with Vermont maple syrup were on the menu for breakfast.

I sang along with the music while my Mini headed to school. TGIF for sure.

I checked in with Mrs. Wilson. She wore a severe bun and her typical prim and proper dress—calico, long sleeves, white cuffs and collar. This one was blue with yellow wheat. "Good morning, I'm here for Ms. Salas again," I chirped in my most cheerful voice. She didn't look up from whatever she was doing. Common for many low-level functionaries, she exercised her small modicum of power by not acknowledging my arrival. I signed the log and waited.

While she typed on her computer, I offered some pleasant chit-chat. "Is this going to be a long-term position? The AP exams are coming up. Should I be thinking about test prep?"

She just typed faster and harder. Something was upsetting her. Before she destroyed her keyboard, she stopped and said, "Mr. Kapitsa wants to see you. I'm warning you to be careful. He has a stressful job and is under a lot of pressure."

Purposely not acknowledging poor Kapitsa's plight, I changed the subject, "Do you want to give me my key card now, so I don't interrupt you again?"

"No— No— Just see him. Immediately."

As I turned around, she added, "And don't upset him this time."

Mr. Kapitsa met me outside his office. He was having a heated discussion with a red-faced man—taller and in better shape than the doughy principal. Kapitsa kept saying, "Mr. Purcell, getting upset is not going to help." That was ironic coming from the excitable principal.

I assumed this Mr. Purcell was a parent, though I didn't recall any students with that name. The principal wore a suit and tie, and the father wore a coordinated workout outfit with logos that matched his shoes, accessorized with a black-faced electronic watch. He didn't look lean like a jogger, but brawnier like a midlife-crisis bodybuilder.

The would-be sports-apparel model shook his phone at Mr. Kapitsa, "I'm beyond upset! A week has passed and still nothing."

This had been a week of surprises. First, the Ecology Club unearthed the baby-in-the-basket.

'Strictly speaking, that was last week,' Fitch chimed in for no obvious reason.

Then Brooklynn found Ms. Salas dead. And all that blood without a body. What would be next? I interrupted, "S'cuse me. Should I come back later?"

Kapitsa seemed relieved by my appearance and turned to the irate parent, "Here is the answer," he said pointing to me. "Tell Mr. Szilard when you last saw your son?"

"Church Sunday morning. We went together. I sat in a front pew to video the service for my wife. She's an artist and keeps crazy hours, so we let her sleep in on Sunday. Jackson joined the other teenagers. After services, he went off with his friends."

I relaxed. Kapitsa had summoned me as a detective, not a teacher. I slipped right into my familiar role, "Mr. Purcell. Are you saying your son has been missing since Sunday? Almost a week?"

"Yes and no. I didn't receive a call from the school. Jackson could have been staying with a friend. As long as the school didn't report him absent, I wasn't worried."

The principal poked his finger at my chest. "You! Your primary job as a substitute teacher is taking attendance. You *signed* the attendance sheet every day."

It took all my restraint not to grab his finger. The jerk didn't want my help. He was looking for a scapegoat.

The upset father resumed his tirade, "Yesterday I spoke to his friend Toby Wigner. He hasn't been in school all week."

From the principal's reference to my attendance reports, I deduced that the missing son was the same Jackson who had been added to Ms. Salas's homeroom on Monday. However, that Jackson wasn't named Purcell. How could this man be the father? "S'cuse me, Mr. Purcell—"

"You can call me Vinnie," he interrupted.

I faced Vinnie, ignoring Kapitsa, "Is your son Jackson Siegbahn?"

"Absolutely!" he stammered.

"S'cuse me, Vinnie," I started again. "Do you have a picture of your son?"

He grunted and scrolled through the photos on his phone. "Here he is."

I was looking at a pale boy with a square chin, white hair, and sapphire blue eyes. No fuzzy almost-mustache. No earring. Certainly not the boy who answered for Jackson Siegbahn on Monday. "I haven't seen him. Just to confirm, your son is Siegbahn, not Purcell."

"Righto, but none of your business."

I was ready to let it go at that, but he continued, "Unwed mother, raised the boy on her own, brilliant artist, didn't change her name when we married."

I wasn't concerned about the mother. I needed to track down the boy with the earring who had been covering for Jackson all week—to get to him before the principal did. Kapitsa would just frighten him, and we'd learn nothing.

Fitch jumped in. *'No coincidences here. Jackson, or the overwrought Mr. Purcell, had something to do with the murder.'*

I addressed the angry stepfather directly, "Someone has been answering for your son each morning." That was a lie. After Ms. Salas's death, I just blindly signed the attendance. I had more important things to think about—a murder, a class full of grieving teenagers, an unidentified baby in a basket.

My explanation didn't satisfy Mr. Purcell. It just got him more upset. "Are you saying a group of teenagers fooled you all week?" He shook his head. "What kind of teacher are you?"

In my best monotone, I answered, "I am a substitute. I can't know all the students."

Kapitsa was eager to blame me. "Mr. Szilard signed the attendance forms. This is his fault. I will hold an inquiry and until then I won't let him teach." He puffed out his pudgy chest. "My school takes its responsibilities very seriously."

Fitch summed up my feelings with, *'Good riddance. We have more pressing things to do with our time.'*

I turned around so the principal wouldn't see my involuntary grin at this ludicrous idea. An investigation was beyond Kapitsa's capabilities. He couldn't even discover who was stealing the chapter tests.

Looking across the lobby, I noticed Mrs. Wilson scowling. In the case that he fired me, it would fall to her to find a replacement. Realizing this, I tweaked Mr. Kapitsa. With a straight face and my hands clasped in a mock pose of supplication, I asked with all the innocence I could muster, "No problem. Do you have someone else to take Ms. Salas's classes today? I can tell Mrs. Wilson who it is."

I glanced in her direction. If looks could kill, I would have been another victim for the Stony PD to investigate.

He gasped when he realized his predicament. "No. You take her classes as you agreed. I'm not letting you off the hook. Your suspension will be effective on Monday."

I resisted smiling when Jackson's father gave Kapitsa a puzzled look. I could tell he'd given up on the school. I expected him to call the police and his lawyer when he finished with the principal.

I followed him out. His wife—Jackie Siegbahn, unwed mother, brilliant artist—was on Chandra's list of alums. "S'cuse me, Vinnie. I'm Mr. Szilard, Zarand. I may be able to help you."

He kept walking. "I may be new to this school, but I've heard of you."

"Don't believe everything Kapitsa says."

"Forget him. He's just a petty tyrant, a low-level administrator. I own an IT consulting company—Purcell and Associates. I'm plugged into Stony politics. You have a reputation."

"A good one?"

"Mixed, I'd say, but I admire someone who gets things done." He offered his hand. "Especially someone prepared to ruffle feathers along the way."

I shook his hand. "I also recognize you. You manage the city's network, don't you?"

"Righto, that's me."

His hand was calloused. He was management, not blue-collar, so I deduced those callouses came from his athletic club—gym hands.

"I see you're out of work. Come by my office on Monday. I'll hire you to find my son."

I reached around his shoulders with a friendly man hug. Hard muscles. They were real, as was the holster he wore under his tracksuit. "Monday it is. In the meantime, you can help the police by giving them DNA samples to help identify Jackson—both you and your wife."

"You'll only need my wife. Remember, I'm Jackson's stepfather."

"Okay. They're open around the clock. The sooner the better."

"No problem. I'll bring her by tomorrow. I'm not busy on Saturday."

As he walked away, Fitch wondered what computer-guy Mr. Purcell with hard hands and a gun had to do with the growing list of puzzles. And where was his stepson, Jackson?

As this was my last day on campus, I sought to learn as much as I could. If I was going to show Vicki the value of traditional detective work over forensics, today was my last chance.

Instead of going directly to Ms. Salas's room, I hung out in front of the cafeteria. Lucy's memorial standee had been moved from the football field to the courtyard. The balloons had deflated, and the flowers wilted.

A few teachers wore black armbands. All other traces of Ms. Salas's demise had faded. The students welcomed summer with shorts and tank tops. I watched Kapitsa policing student dress. *No short shorts. No visible undergarments. And, especially, no spaghetti straps.* After his uncomfortable meeting with Vinnie Purcell, he looked positively elated to be writing detention slips and making students put on jackets. Of course, as soon as he returned to the office, those cover-ups would disappear.

Students packed the courtyard. I scanned the crowd looking for clues. That's when I caught sight of Brooklynn and the boy who I now knew wasn't Jackson. He marched at her side carrying the Ecology flag on a long aluminum pole like a military honor guard. They were too far away to hear, but they were walking toward the cafeteria, and I could read their lips.

Fitch mocked me, *'Your surveillance skills are out of practice. She made you.'*

For the briefest moment, our eyes met. I turned away from her and studied a group chatting about the upcoming prom. By that time, she was close enough for me to hear what she was saying.

"Four days!" she shouted. "I'm sure he's had enough time to escape. He should be in Canada by now."

They entered the cafeteria and I followed.

The boy waved the flag and yelled, "Join the Eco Club. Clean up the upper field today."

The cafeteria lady pushed a rolling cart from the kitchen and waved to Brooklynn. The scent of freshly baked cookies followed her. On the top shelf was a green rectangular coffee dispenser, colloquially called a coffee cub. The warm chocolate-chip cookies served on a baking pan were on the lower shelf accompanied by a stack of single-use cups, cardboard containers of coffee whitener, packets of sweeteners, and plastic stirrers.

Brooklynn grabbed the flag. "Toby, you can carry the cub."

So, the boy masquerading as Jackson was Toby.

Annie had just finished her breakfast, so Brooklynn enlisted her, "Can you take the cookies?"

Brooklynn left everything else on the rolling cart. "We don't need that stuff. Ecology Club members carry reusable cups and drink their coffee black. Sugar cane plantations exploit workers. And don't get me started on whiteners."

I caught up to her. "Good morning, Brooklynn."

She startled. "I didn't see you, Mr. S."

'Small chance,' quipped an unbelieving Fitch.

I just smiled, "Can you introduce me to your friend?" I lowered my voice. "I know he's not Jackson."

Brooklynn, to her credit, didn't flinch. "This is Toby, Tobias Wigner. Sorry about fooling you with the attendance. I hope you didn't get into any trouble."

The attendance had upset Mr. Kapitsa and gotten me fired, but none of that concerned Brooklynn and her friend. "No problem. Good morning, Toby."

"Mornin'," he said just like my ringtone.

We walked across the courtyard together.

By the time we reached the gymnasium, they'd collected a crowd. Charlie volunteered to help Toby with the cub. They carried the heavy container between them as they climbed the hill.

Brooklynn said, "Thank you Mr. Mbacke," pointing to the trash containers, blue for recycling, green for composting, and black for landfill. She turned to me, "We collaborate with the night maintenance crew. Together we're reducing the number of trash bags sent to landfills contributing to the toxic leachate."

She directed a group to work under the bleachers. Flora, wearing blue examination gloves, picked up a used condom. "Gross, what should I do with this?"

Annie said, "In memory of Ms. Salas call it by its name: *condom*."

Flora asked again, "What should I do with this *condom*?"

Brooklynn replied, "Put it in the black bin."

Charlie called, "Someone's been partying over here." He kicked the remains of a campfire.

Brooklynn picked up a stick and poked the ashes. "There's nothing dangerous here. Put it in the green bin. Wood ash is a valuable source of lime, potassium, and other trace elements."

Charlie ran to the nearby maintenance shed. "I'll get a rake and a shovel."

Someone found the remains of a joint and held it up. "Some party."

Brooklynn, ever on task, said, "Compost."

"C-c-come here. H-h-hurry!" Charlie yelled from inside the shed.

Toby was the first to reach him, closely followed by Brooklynn. He grabbed something from Charlie's hand and handed it to her.

She studied it briefly and slipped it into her back pocket.

"What did you find?" I queried.

Charlie looked at me with wide eyes, as if he'd forgotten that I was there. We all backed out of his way, as he awkwardly juggled a rake and a long-handled shovel out the door.

I turned to Brooklynn and Toby who were sharing secret looks. "What did you find?"

"Nothing," they both said in unison.

Fitch guessed, *'More marijuana? The missing chapter tests?'*

I didn't care about any of that. Besides, the first buzzer had just sounded. "It's time to open my classroom. I'll see you all later."

On my last day of teaching, my goals were to interview Brooklynn about the missing Jackson and revisit the murder scene. I'd been trying to investigate the teachers' workroom all week, but something always got in the way. Nothing was going to sidetrack me today.

My persistence paid off. Even though the crime scene had been thoroughly searched, it still held some surprises.

14. URGENT CARE: FRIDAY

As the students entered homeroom, I shook some hands and high-fived others. These were my surrogate grandkids. Now that Kapitsa had fired me, I was going to miss them. Regardless, I was here to spy on them on my final day.

Fitch predicted that my suspension was temporary. *'After you find Lucy's attacker, they'll welcome you back.'*

I knew the truth. Kapitsa was glad to see me go and wouldn't waste this opportunity to be rid of me. When the buzzer sounded, Brooklynn and Toby hadn't arrived. I had plans for them. They'd better not cut class.

I gave the attendance a cursory glance—just marked Jackson as absent and signed it. Halfway through homeroom, Brooklynn and her sidekick swaggered in.

She offered an excuse, "We had to return the coffee cub and the baking pan."

After shuffling through the growing piles of papers on Ms. Salas's table, I found the detention slips—small multipart forms. I wrote BROOKLYNN C and TOBY W and handed each of them their copies. "You have lunchtime detention. Report here."

When the buzzer sounded, they dramatically tossed their detention slips into the recycling. I ignored this small act of defiance. Brooklynn would show up. I didn't know about her buddy, but I expected he'd appear wherever she did.

"Yesterday was the mitosis art project. Today will be the science." I wrote CANCER on the whiteboard and the AP Biology class dutifully keyboarded it into their electronic notebooks. That was a start, but I wanted them to think, not just copy.

"Who knows someone who had cancer?"

Hands popped up and several students called out.

"My grandfather died."

"My aunt lost her hair after having chemo."

The scourge of cancer had touched many of their lives. I gave them time to share. The class wouldn't settle down to critical thinking until they'd voiced their fears and mourned their losses.

"Cancer is so many different things. What is the common thread? Discuss this in your table groups."

The room hummed with ideas about cancer, hospitals, and dying relatives. Some students got serious, while others made nervous jokes.

"Can anyone tell us the common thread?"

Charlie said, "P-p-people die."

I waited for the nervous laughter to die down before asking, "Something else?"

The room went silent. I called on Annie.

She said, "Cancer cells multiply like crazy—beyond the control of the host."

That was a textbook answer. I had a question to shock them out of memorize-and-regurgitate mode. "Good. What else has cells that multiply like crazy beyond the control of the host?"

This answer wasn't in their reading. Annie was in the hot seat. The others looked away, distancing themselves.

I gave them a hint. "A tumor is an unwanted growth. I'm thinking of something else, something loved."

Annie's eyes got wide, and she whispered, "A fetus?"

Yes, I cheered. Now they were thinking.

Someone in the front row said, "They thought my cousin was pregnant, but she was just fat."

The class defended the cousin.

"That's body shaming."

"You shouldn't say that."

"That's mean."

I chose my next example to distract them from pregnancy and obesity. "Another case is that growth spurt you experienced, usually in middle school for the girls and high school for the boys."

Richie cracked a joke about growth *spurts*, obviously thinking of something else.

A few children laughed, until Charlie scolded him, "N-n-not nice. Always thinking with your—" He stopped before finishing, having said enough.

I ignored them and pushed ahead. "All growth is from dividing cells, but cancer cells divide more than others. One way to slow cancer is to slow cell division."

I wrote SLOW CELL DIVISION = SLOW CANCER on the board, and they all entered this into their notebooks. Ms. Salas said, "Teaching occurs at the boundary between creative chaos and attentive order." In her memory, I was balancing on that edge.

I asked, "How do cells divide?"

First, a few hands went up. Those students helpfully nudged their friends and pointed to their notes from yesterday. One by one, more students raised their hands.

"Everyone, how do cells multiply?"

"Mitosis!" they shouted, except for Richie who said, "Sex."

This time the class ignored him, looking to Charlie who expressed his disapproval with crossed arms

I cleared my throat, giving the room a steely-eyed glare. I turned to the whiteboard and wrote MITOSIS. I circled the word in red and drew a slash through it.

"That's how taxanes, a popular form of chemotherapy, work—interfering with mitosis."

The class lit up with that *aha* moment. They knew how to control cancer. They got it, even Richie who was making ejaculation jokes.

I walked around the class as they sketched artistic slashed circles in their notes. They'd learned something today.

I let them color and animate their artwork before explaining the four phases of mitosis: prophase, metaphase, anaphase, and telophase which they matched up with their drawings from yesterday.

After more classes of the same, I put out my lunch of an organic peanut butter sandwich, an orange, and a thermos of green tea flavored with fresh ginger. I scrutinized my meal through Brooklynn's Ecology Club eyes. The sandwich was in a reusable container and vegetarian. A lucky choice for today.

Yesterday I purchased a cheeseburger from the cafeteria which came on a landfill-bound disposable plate.

Brooklynn also showed up with an environmentally friendly lunch. "I grew these tomatoes and the lettuce in our greenhouse. Fresh veggies all year round."

Toby carried a tray with that same cheeseburger that I'd bought yesterday. I watched her cringe as grease dribbled down his chin and he wiped it off with a stack of paper napkins, also destined for a landfill. I had to wonder what she saw in him.

'Um, he's headed for the landfill,' joked Fitch.

Toby and Brooklynn whispered to each other as we all ate. I played the role of the warden, and they were the detainees. I weighed starting my interrogation with Brooklynn—she knew more—or Toby—a more vulnerable target. Fitch cast the deciding vote, *'Go for the weak kid.'*

I didn't have anything on Toby. I'd just learned his name, but Fitch prompted, *'Make something up. None of this is going to court and you're not even a cop anymore.'*

"Tobias, you answered for Jackson on Monday and today he is missing. The police found a lot of blood. They think it belonged to Jackson, and that you murdered him."

A frightened boy exclaimed, "Jackson wasn't murdered. He's not dead." He looked to Brooklynn before saying, "He ran away."

Brooklynn looked at poor Toby with disgust. "I told you to keep your mouth shut."

He gave her a half-smile and shrugged his shoulders. He dipped his fries in a puddle of catsup that reminded me of the blood at the crime scene. I was done with him. He served his purpose. Without antagonizing Brooklynn, I let her see what was at stake.

I turned to her. "Can you tell me what happened?"

She took a big bite of her sandwich releasing the pungent basil and garlic aroma of the pesto. She chewed slowly composing her response. I sipped my ginger tea and waited.

"Jackson's mother is a sculptor, not famous, but you can see some of her pieces for sale around town."

I checked my list of students. "Her surname is Siegbahn, right?"

"Yes."

"But his father's name is Purcell," I added remembering the angry stepfather.

"Yes," she agreed. "That's the origin of the problem. She kept her maiden name, Siegbahn, Jackie Siegbahn."

I was confused. Jackson was new to our school. How did Brooklynn know these details? "S'cuse me. Where did you hear this?"

Toby spoke up, "We all go to the same church, Stony Community Church at the intersection of Higgs and Bridgman. Annie and Charlie also attend."

Brooklynn gave him another stern look.

I repeated "Jackie Siegbahn," several times until I recalled seeing her work displayed in the city library. Her round and restful figures looked like Inuit art. *Siegbahn* sounded like *autobahn*, German. Inuit and German weren't close.

'Not German, dummkopf,' Fitch chuckled, *'Swedish, like the father-son Nobel prize winners.'*

Brooklynn continued with her story. "Jackson's stepfather demanded that his wife stayed at home, but she traveled up and down the California coast to art festivals. That is until she drove off the road in Big Sur."

I played innocent even though I'd heard this from Vinnie. "Did she die?"

"Amen, no. It was touch and go for a while. Our church held prayer vigils while she was in the hospital. Ultimately, she was fine."

Toby looked to Brooklynn. When she didn't scowl at him, he added in a quiet voice, "Physically."

I waited for Brooklynn to elaborate.

"Jackson's stepfather got his wish. She doesn't travel anymore. She rarely leaves the house—agoraphobia—fear of the agora—the marketplace. That was the turning point for Jackson."

"What happened to him?"

"He blamed his father."

Toby again added something, "He was named after his mother."

"He decided he'd be a writer, even though his father pushed him to be an engineer."

Toby again interrupted. "He was never going to be an engineer. He and I struggled in Integrated Math. We just couldn't do it."

"Toby's right. Jackson's father got him tutors and punished him when he didn't complete his math homework or got low scores on tests."

I took a bite of my sandwich with more tea. "Do you know where Jackson is?"

Toby looked nervously to Brooklynn, this time heeding her warning.

She answered. "He met some Canadian writers online. He was headed for Vancouver."

That was the same thing I'd overheard in the courtyard.

Toby went back to his cheeseburger and fries.

Brooklynn looked thoughtful. Fitch told me she knew more than she was saying. I finished my lunch in silence waiting for her to complete her chronicle. The slower she chewed, the more Fitch screamed, *'Half-truths. Half-truths.'*

I broke the impasse by changing the subject. "What did Charlie find in the maintenance shed this morning?"

Toby collected the greasy scraps of his lunch and carried them to the recycling containers.

Brooklynn called after him. "Don't throw that in the recycling. That's trash, landfill." The way she said it, the last word sounded like the nastiest thing ever. After a final mouthful of her sandwich, she stowed the reusable container into her backpack, wiped her mouth with a cloth napkin, and pointedly zipped away all traces of her meal.

I mirrored her actions, putting away my thermos. "S'cuse me. What did Charlie find?"

She reached into her back pocket. I expected to see her phone, instead, she flipped some plastic cards onto the table.

Following years of training, I leaned forward to examine them without touching them. On the table, under the energy-efficient LED lights, were a California driver's license and an image of a California brown bear—a Stony High student ID. I recognized the pale boy with white hair from the photo Mr. Purcell had shown me: Jackson Siegbahn.

"If he went to Canada, why are these here? He can't cross the border without them."

'Don't you listen? I've been telling you that Canada is just a distraction.'

The two of them had no response.

I examined the driver's license. "Look at this. Do you see that?" I asked pointing to a dark spot.

They both looked closer but didn't say anything.

"That's blood. His blood," I said in my most serious voice. "Where is he?"

Both children responded in unison, "No idea."

I gave them a scare to grab their attention. "He didn't go to Canada without his IDs." I paused to let them consider the alternatives. "That's Jackson's blood. He's bleeding somewhere waiting to be rescued."

They looked suitably concerned.

"Do you know anyone who might want to harm Jackson?"

They both shook their heads. Brooklynn said, "Nope. Nobody."

I went back to Ms. Salas's desk and found an envelope to keep the IDs safe. "I'll keep these. Are you sure you don't know where he is?"

"Yes, sure," they both murmured over and over.

The frightened looks on their faces told me they were telling the truth this time.

'That pool of blood could belong to Jackson. He could be the second victim,' Fitch mused.

During my prep period, I entered the teachers' workroom—the inanimate witness I'd been pursuing all week. The room had seen the crime and if I gave it my full attention, it would reveal its secrets. Every detective lived by Locard's principle—with every contact, there will be an exchange. There was more to be discovered.

The Stony PD had taken Ms. Salas's chair and the maintenance crew had removed all traces of blood. I was sure they did a thorough job because we all took the state-mandated Bloodborne Pathogen Training. Since the HIV epidemic, California took blood very seriously.

No hint of Ms. Salas's lavender shampoo remained, but a faint smell of death still hung in the air.

What had I missed? Fitch insisted there was more.

I took an energy bar from my sling and savored the chocolaty goodness. I examined the room. In the old buildings of Los Angeles, we tore up floorboards and inspected inside walls to search for hidden caches of money, drugs, or weapons. This was a modern building. The construction rested on a concrete slab, so no floorboards, and the walls were cinder blocks, so no hidden caches. The forensic team couldn't have missed anything in the simple cabinets that lined the walls.

Fitch conjured up a chair and smugly sat precisely where Ms. Salas had been found, *'Don't give up.'*

I closed my eyes, searching up and down in my mind. *I have it!*

While the wall and floors were solid, the ceiling was suspended tiles. I scrambled up onto the counter. With the light from my cellphone, I searched above the ceiling. All I found were dusty fingerprints left by gloved hands. The forensic team had beat me to it.

I again searched the room. This time with my eyes open. I examined everything—found nothing. It had been days since the murder and too many people had visited the crime scene.

'Do you see that?' Fitch exclaimed.

"What?"

'Those two doorknobs are shinier than the others.'

Fitch was right. I put on gloves and opened those cabinets. Stacks of printer paper filled the space. This didn't explain the lustrous patina. There had to be another reason for the frequent opening and closing of those doors.

I unpacked the paper and piled it on the floor. Scratches marred the bottom shelf. I was able to pry it up with my pocket knife.

There it was.

Neat rows of condoms, so many condoms, plus emergency contraceptive packets, home pregnancy tests, and jars of prenatal vitamins—soft chewables.

Ms. Salas was running an urgent care pharmacy from her classroom. Even though these were all OTC medicines, she was just a teacher. Mr. Kapitsa could have had her arrested for practicing medicine without a license and who knows what else.

The hidey-hole also had a small notebook, the flimsy kind with a blue paper cover. Back when I was in school, we called them blue books and used them for essay questions on exams. Everything was computer-based these days, so why did she have them?

Ms. Salas's book had neat entries—each with a date, what I guessed were coded names, and a small sketch. There were four different sketches.

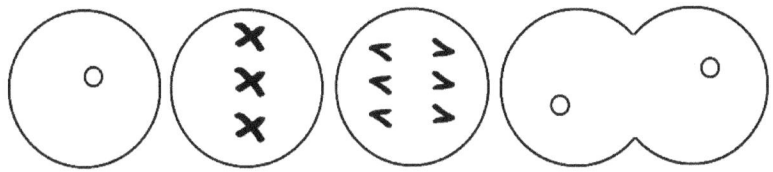

I examined the booklet for other clues. I didn't find any. I flipped through the pages to confirm that all the sketches were of the four types I found on the most recent page. They were.

I called the first one an eyeball. Most of the entries were eyeballs. I called the last one a double eyeball. There were very few of those. The drawings must have had a meaning for Ms. Salas, but I had no idea what.

Fitch recognized the drawings immediately, *'Um, were you sleeping through your own lecture? Mitosis!'*

Once he said that, I realized that the sketches were the stages of mitosis I'd just taught to the AP Biology students—prophase, metaphase, anaphase, and telophase. I still didn't know what events they signified.

She had packed the book with single-line entries in block letters. The dates were in order and went back years—still only part of Ms. Salas's tenure at Stony High.

I removed the neat rows of drug store boxes to be sure I hadn't missed anything, hoping to uncover Lucy's missing laptop. The Stony PD had not found it when they'd searched her apartment. Under the pink and blue boxes, I discovered older booklets but no laptop. This was a long-running operation. I understood the dates, but that didn't bring me any closer to explaining Lucy's demise.

I considered the names—not names—just jumbles of letters. I compared them to the class lists. There were no obvious patterns. I went back to the classroom and searched through the drawers of her worktable until I found an Ecology Club list. Again, there were no correspondences.

The last entry was the date of Lucy's murder with the name BOOJF and a telophase drawing with its distinctive figure-eight, double-eyeball, shape. Quickly leafing through the pages, I verified that there were few telophase drawings, one or two per year. Most of the drawings were plain circles—eyeballs, which I recognized to be prophase. I was sure this was important, but—

'It's a code. I'll figure it out. I always do,' Fitch confidently predicted.

I folded the flimsy booklet and stuck it in my pocket.

I returned the boxes of emergency contraceptives, home pregnancy kits, and vitamins to their places, took photos of everything, reinstalled the false bottom, and restacked the printer paper.

The mystery about Ms. Salas's life before teaching took on a new urgency. Why was she running an unlicensed clinic? Senior Detective Yukawa's computer wizards could help here. There had to be some digital record of those hidden years.

I thought forward to Saturday. Vicki and I would jog in the mountains. She'd share what her team had found about Ms. Salas's history. I'd show her Jackson's IDs and surprise her with Ms. Salas's urgent care. Together we'd solve the mystery without needing to decode the blue books.

'Um, it's not going to be that easy,' said the ever-pessimistic Fitch.

Vicki showed up with her own evidence—not something I could have foreseen.

When I sat on a boulder to adjust my trekking poles, I frightened a lizard. It disappeared into the chaparral. The poles offered additional stability and a nice workout for my upper body, but I could manage on my own. I leaned forward on them to check that they were clamped properly.

A familiar voice announced Vicki's arrival. "I have lab results. Let's jog up to Pauli Falls. That way we'll have plenty of time to discuss them."

She didn't have to ask me twice. I opened the lock levers, collapsed my poles, and stowed them in my car. After tightening my trail shoes and pulling on a pair of climbing gloves, I returned to the trail head and bounced on my toes. "I didn't expect results so soon. You said science takes time."

"We got lucky."

We sprinted the flat stretch of the path before settling into a comfortable climbing pace. Our slower jog still overtook the casual families on Saturday morning hikes.

"I also have some new evidence," I said thinking of Ms. Salas's drug store. I'd left Jackson's IDs in the car with the trekking poles.

"Excellent. This has been a productive week. My lab reports are complicated, so why don't you go first?"

That was the problem with scientific results. They were difficult to apply—impeding as often as aiding—explaining why clearance rates were better when the forensic evidence was ignored.

The rugged trail rose above the valley. I lunged to the side to avoid a large rock embedded into the middle of our track.

Vicki laughed, "Careful there, old man."

Air-conditioned houses and gleaming solar arrays receded like toys in the distance. The cloudless sky and burning sun slowed the families—children demanded water and dogs panted with their tongues hanging out. We had privacy to talk.

I explained how Friday had been my last day on campus. "Kapitsa has been looking for an excuse to get rid of me. He finally found it and suspended me."

Vicki laughed, "Remember you always have a place with the Stony PD."

"I'm not thinking of anything beyond Ms. Salas and our cruise."

I then told her about my new evidence. "I revisited the teacher's workroom. Fitch noticed that a set of doorknobs were shinier than the others." Without making a big deal of the success of my traditional methods, I said, "We found coded logbooks and a cache of medical supplies."

"That was unexpected. Your discovery increases the priority of investigating Ms. Salas's background. I will tell the team to put more effort into that."

When I turned to check that she wasn't mocking me, I tripped on a rock—instinctively adjusting my footing to regain my balance but quickly I realized that I was going down. I put my arms out to prepare for a hard landing, grateful that I'd worn my gloves. I flexed my elbows to absorb the impact.

That quick thinking didn't help when one hand slipped on the uneven terrain. I collapsed onto my shoulder. That landing wouldn't have won a gymnastic award, but I avoided serious trauma.

Vicki retrieved my glasses and reached out a hand to help me up. "That was impressive. Are you alright?"

I jogged in place. My shoulder had a slight twinge. "Good as new," I said. "On to the falls. Pun intended."

After running in silence for a while, she said, "This reminds me of that time we went sky diving. Didn't you have your arm in a sling for months after that?"

"I'm fine. Thanks for the assist."

To my amazement, we were greeted by a crowd when we reached the falls. Children and dogs splashed in the creek. Everyone enjoyed the respite from the harsh sun under the only trees for miles around. Beyond this mountain oasis was chaparral—sage and spiky yucca—reminiscent of the small patch the Ecology Club was demolishing for the science garden.

The popularity of the falls forced a choice between seclusion and shade. We chose seclusion and climbed over moss-covered boulders until we were out of range of the bubbling falls and any eavesdroppers. We rested on a fallen tree.

The creek flowed into the broad valley below. "This must have been a welcome sight to the pioneers who crossed Death Valley and the Mojave Desert to reach this point."

"Yes," Vicki agreed, "We live in a verdant valley compared to what lies beyond." She took a drink from her water bottle and opened an energy bar. "I'm sure you want half."

I accepted the sweet offering. "What are your complicated lab results? Are they going to set us back?"

She began, "Do you remember the welfare agency that denied a mother's application for the WIC Supplemental Nutrition Program because DNA tests showed that her children weren't actually hers?"

This was a digression from Ms. Salas, but I went along. "Really? Isn't it mean-spirited to demand DNA tests for her children?"

Vicki shook her head and said with a sigh. "It was during a time when *welfare mother* was a dirty word. Anyway, they were her natural children."

I was confused. "Was it a case of babies switched in the hospital?"

"Nothing like that." She seemed to be enjoying my quandary.

This was a perfect example of why I preferred traditional detective work. I reviewed what I knew of the science. The mom only contributed half the DNA. Still, Vicki was saying that children hadn't received their share of the mother's genetic material. How could that happen?

Instead of enlightening me, she gulped some water and stood up. "Let's start back before it gets too hot."

I accepted that I'd have to wait until she was ready to answer the riddle. "Let's walk back," I suggested. I didn't want to risk jogging downhill without my trekking poles.

"You have no idea, right?"

"Yeah. I give up. What happened?"

"The mother was a chimera."

"Do you mean a mythical lion that's part fire-breathing goat and part snake?"

"That's the idea, but this is the real version. The woman had multiple DNA profiles. The cells in her body were from two different eggs that fused shortly after fertilization."

I got it. Two fertilized eggs, but instead of twins, the two eggs merged. Some of the mother's cells grew from one egg and some from the other. I smiled with understanding, "So her right arm belonged to one twin and her left arm belonged to the other."

"Close enough. Fraternal twins sharing one body."

Vicki continued, "The DNA they found when they did the initial maternity test was from one of those twins, but the other twin had provided the eggs for her children. When they retested her, they found DNA from the other twin, and the mystery was solved." She jumped down a steep section to the trail below. We were back amid the crowd.

I cautiously reversed and backed down on all fours, again feeling that spasm in my shoulder. "Wow. That confounds DNA testing, doesn't it? If a chimera committed a crime, they might escape by leaving DNA that didn't match the FBI records."

'Um, or the forensic wizards might declare there were two perpetrators when there was only one,' Fitch laughed. *'Would each DNA profile be sentenced separately?'* Fitch found this hilarious and went on with crazy examples for a while.

She walked in silence until we were out of earshot of the families. "Not really. Human chimeras are exceedingly rare."

I kicked a big rock out of the path as a service to the next jogger. "I'm guessing the lab results reminded you of this scientific curiosity."

"Correct. Twice actually. Do you want to hear about the baby-in-the-basket or Ms. Salas?"

"Baby."

"The county museum and the Serrano community have determined preliminary dates for those relics."

"I gather the dates don't match. That's the chimera analogy."

"Right again. The style of the basket is from the Gold Rush period while those shell disks date much earlier—before the Spanish missionaries. The curators figure out these dates by comparison with artifacts of known dates, so the results are approximate. Still, they are confident that the bracelet and the basket don't go together."

What could this mean? Fitch jumped to his typically paranoid conclusion, 'Scam. Piltdown man. Calaveras skull.' I ignored him, having little interest in archeological hoaxes. "What about the child?"

"A little history first. The cold war nuclear testing raised carbon-14 levels and the later test ban treaty abruptly ended this contribution. This *bomb pulse* assures that carbon-14 dating for the present period is highly precise and distinctive."

"I'm glad some good came from the cold war. Are you saying that the baby was born after the test ban treaty?"

"Gosh, yes, way after. They assured me the second George Bush was in the White House."

"S'cuse me. Are you saying this is a Stony Estancia murder case?"

"Absolutely," she whispered.

"Do you think the baby had anything to do with the graduation ghost?"

"The ghost has a thick case file, but I can assure you there is nothing about a baby in it."

I could hear a family with two arguing children approaching us. I stepped to the side to let them pass. When they disappeared around a curve in the trail, I said, "Still, it sounds like a child of one of the Stony High students."

"That is one scenario."

"I wonder what happened to the mother. Do you think we'll have to delay our cruise?"

"I'm not returning my bathing suit yet, but I have the package ready to mail."

Now I was sorry I'd let Kapitsa suspend me. I could have used access to the science garden.

We rejoined the lower loop trail. Casual walkers crowded this gentle path. She had promised two chimeras, but the area had become too busy for that conversation. "I'm hungry. Let's get lunch," I suggested.

"You're always hungry," she responded with a good-natured laugh.

I remembered the envelope of IDs that I had in my car. "I'll meet you at Cocina de Cetto and show you what I discovered about Jackson."

Jackson's IDs made for an interesting lunchtime discussion, but her second chimera changed everything.

Vicki arrived at the restaurant first. I dipped my tortilla chips into the mild salsa verde she had put at my place, saving the spicy salsa roja for herself.

"Shall we order?" she suggested when we finished our Modelos.

"Sure. I'll get it," I responded.

But before I could stand up, she was on her way to the window. "You got it last time. My turn." She let her arm go limp and shook it. "Rest your shoulder."

I pulled my arm across my chest, mimicking a sling. "Got it. Are you going to spoon-feed me?"

She smiled before she turned around and resumed her quest for food. She returned with another round of cold beers.

While we waited, I told her about Jackson, his angry father, his agoraphobic mother, and his planned escape to Canada.

"Gosh, do you want me to follow up with the RCMP?"

'Um, dead or alive, he's still in Stony Estancia.'

"Not so fast. He didn't go to Canada."

"Why do you say that?"

I reached into my pocket and passed the envelope across the table.

She slid the IDs out without touching them. "I see. His school ID." She put it back into the envelope. "And his driver's license." She turned the license over and scanned the 2D barcode with her phone. "This is his REAL ID license. He can't cross the border without it."

I nodded. "Here comes our food."

Before the boy carrying our meals arrived, she dug out a plastic evidence bag from her black satchel embossed with the Stony Estancia seal. After securing the evidence, she returned it to her official case for safe keeping.

The waiter handed me my carnitas burrito with rice and beans. Vicki received chili rellenos with fries.

She picked up a fry and said, "I'll have the forensics folks look at the IDs, but we won't start a missing person investigation until we hear from the parents."

"I'm shocked that Mr. Purcell hasn't contacted you. He sounded like he was going straight to the police when he exited Kapitsa's office yesterday."

"He might have gone the PI route. The law doesn't require him to get the police involved. I'm happy for him to DIY his missing son, we have our hands full with the suspicious deaths of the baby-in-the-basket and Ms. Salas."

"Right. You had something to tell me about a second chimera."

"Of course, you remember that the blood pool didn't belong to Ms. Salas."

"Yes. Have you identified the source?"

She shook her head. "No. But further testing has shown that a small amount of that blood had a different DNA profile."

"Perfect. So, the unidentified victim is a chimera, someone with multiple DNA profiles. That should help, shouldn't it?"

When she didn't immediately respond, I added, "Didn't you say that human chimeras were rare?"

"Most chimeras go undetected, so not as useful as you might imagine. However, we did learn something helpful."

That astonished me. Helpful DNA was an oxymoron in my book.

She continued, "The blood is from a female and shares DNA with Ms. Salas. The computer suggested her sister—yet another reason to find out more about Ms. Salas and her family."

"Wow! The missing victim is her sister. Do you think she's a twin and there are two Ms. Salases? The body we found belongs to her twin sister?"

Vicki scoffed, "There you go again, making up crazy stories. The real world isn't like those mystery novels you read."

"S'cuse me. Twins or not, we need to figure out who she is," I said as I reached across the table to swipe some of Vicki's fries.

She playfully slapped my hand. "Those aren't good for you."

My shoulder froze in pain.

"Puppies, puppies, puppies," I exclaimed. That was the word I used so I didn't embarrass myself with inappropriate interjections in school. I grabbed my injured arm and pulled it against my body. I continued to repeat, "Puppies," while I moaned and rocked back and forth with my eyes squeezed shut. I leaned over and rested my forehead on the table. I was still panting when Vicki sat down next to me.

She opened her satchel and took out her radio. "Senior Detective Yukawa calling for an ambulance. Paramedics. Cocina de Cetto."

She wrapped her arms around my shoulder and hugged me. The pressure forced something back in place. The pain subsided but didn't go away.

By then we'd attracted a crowd. Vicki reached into her satchel to retrieve her ID. "I'm Victoria Yukawa, Stony Estancia Police. The paramedics will be here soon. In the interim, do you have a first aid kit?"

I made a joke. "I won't steal any more fries."

"Don't move," she said. She opened the first aid kit and wrapped an elastic bandage tightly around my shoulder.

"That helps. Thanks."

When the paramedics arrived, they strapped me to a gurney. They had a hard job—so often dealing with cranky people. I swore I wouldn't be one of those. I didn't need to go to the emergency room but knew better than to argue. I simply said, "Thanks for getting here so quickly."

A paramedic complimented Vicki. "Nice bandaging."

"Stony PD. I've had practice. Can you resupply the restaurant's first aid kit?"

"No problem. We'll get resupplied when we deliver your friend."

"Puppies, puppies!" I studied the ambulance, cursing my fate. This was taking time away from tracking down Lucy's killer.

Who was I to complain? Less than a week ago Ms. Salas had also been in an ambulance, but she didn't have EMTs monitoring her blood pressure, respiration, and pulse. She was dead. I was alive and I owed her my full attention. My responsibility was to solve this case.

I reviewed the new evidence—chimeras, sisters, murdered babies, and missing teenagers—until the gentle rocking of the ambulance and the hum of medical equipment overtook me.

After jogging in the hills, I welcomed a pleasant nap, but my   sleep   was   interrupted.

The ambulance driver announced, "Here we are." The paramedics tightened their seat belts. The siren sounded and we took a fast left turn. An orange bottle fell to the floor and clattered into a corner. In the twilight of my nap, I sensed a force holding me safely in place. It took all my befuddled concentration to identify my guardian.

A spectral Lucy sat beside me, dressed professionally, in nice jeans, a green blouse buttoned to her neck, and ready to teach her classes.

"Tell me who murdered you." I implored.

'I can't say. You must solve that mystery yourself. I'm depending on you. My life ended too soon.'

"Don't despair," I encouraged. I recounted her accomplishments, "Megan Rainwater is in medical school and living with her daughter. That diabetic football player is alive. Fewer unwanted pregnancies. More healthy babies."

'Oh, that's it? I had planned so much more.'

"You will do more through the students you inspired to study science and medicine."

'Not the same.'

And with that, Lucy's ghost faded. I pleaded, "Wait. Help me solve your murder. What did you do before teaching? Did you watch your sister bleed to death?"

But instead, a bright light flashed, and she was gone. Her words echoed in my brain—*I'm depending on you.*

"You had a bad dream. Wake up, buddy. We're here."

I opened my eyes, stretched, and took a deep breath. The high ceiling glowed with fluorescent lights. A swarm of people in blue scrubs and white lab coats moved with urgency, questioning patients, and escorting the lucky ones through one of the many doors. A lone cleaner pushed a polisher across the tile floor navigating through the chaotic crowd.

I was in Stony Estancia Hospital. One EMT was exchanging papers with the admitting nurse. The other transferred me to a hospital gurney. He called for help when my foot became entangled in the side rail.

My nap had rejuvenated me. I surveyed the waiting room—performing triage. A well-dress woman with ash blonde hair shuttled between her balding husband and the nurses' station. I waved to Officer Tsui who was with a handcuffed teen. Her thigh was wrapped with an improvised bandage, soaked through with blood. Many people had more urgent needs than mine. I resigned myself to a long wait. I took advantage of the delay by going back to sleep—hoping to meet Lucy again, but she was gone.

The doctor's broad shoulders filled the doorway as he entered the examination room, reminding me of a wide receiver. His name tag read, DR. MBACKE—same as the night custodian. With no preliminary chit-chat, he said, "Stand up."

He pointed to the computer, "It says right shoulder pain. What happened?"

I recounted jogging to the falls, tripping, and Vicki slapping me when I swiped her fries. It felt good to tell my story, but he circled his hand, signaling me to hurry up—I was wasting his time. He didn't need to hear the entire narrative.

I rushed through Vicki bandaging my shoulder and the arrival of the paramedics. Before I had a chance to tell him about seeing Lucy in my dream, he cut me off. "You tripped. Stand still."

He placed one hand on my shoulder and the other on my elbow. Gently he moved my arm, rotating it forward and back while slowly elevating it. His touch was so smooth that it felt like my arm was moving on its own until my elbow rose above my shoulder. "Puppies! Stop! That hurts!"

He lowered my arm. "You going to faint?"

I gave him the short answer he preferred, "No, just sore."

"At your age, could be arthritis, tendinosis, torn rotator cuff. The MRI will tell."

That was the most I'd hear from him. I had so many questions. Had I done serious damage? Would he restrict my activity? But mostly, how soon could I return to searching for Ms. Salas's killer?

Before I could say anything, he was gone, and a nurse handed me a couple of hospital gowns. "Put one on backward." I also received a plastic bag labeled PATIENT BELONGINGS in bold letters. "Stow this under the gurney."

Modestly covered and with belongings stowed, I climbed back onto the gurney in time for a patient transporter to roll me out of the examination room. She looked like a child dressed in her mom's scrubs, too large and rolled up at the cuffs. She maneuvered me through the hospital maze with a speed and agility that made me wish I were young again.

She was the opposite of Dr. Mbacke—talking non-stop.

"MRI," she said. "Don't worry, it doesn't hurt. But you go through a metal detector. You're not carrying a gun, are you? No, not you. You look too nice. Any bullet fragments? You'd be amazed."

Her patter continued nonstop until she dropped me off. She never paused for me to answer any of her rapid-fire questions. I didn't mind. As a detective, I'd been trained to let everyone ramble on. They drilled us over and over, "You never learn anything when your mouth is open."

The MRI technician transferred me onto a narrow pad that slid into a huge white donut.

Fitch cut in, *'Are you always thinking of food?'*

The tech handed me a button. "Lie still. Don't speak. That's the panic alarm."

Speaking would never have occurred to me. The huge machine moved with a series of loud clicks. There was no way to talk over that racket. I was glad they gave me earplugs.

When a different patient transporter deposited me into a different room, he said, "You're waiting..." He paused moving his arm back and forth like a metronome and going *tick, tick, tick* with his tongue—his attempt at humor. "...for your MRI results and the orthopedist." With that, he was gone.

Sooner than I expected, there was a knock on the door.

Though it wasn't necessary, I responded, "Come in."

"It took me a while to find you, and I had to show my badge and tell a few half-truths to get in here," Vicki explained.

She was still in her hiking clothes. She must have come directly from Cocina de Cetto. "I'm glad to see you. Just so we can keep our stories straight, am I your domestic partner or prisoner?"

"Gosh, those are both clever ideas. I told them you were my uncle."

"Uncle? I'm not that old. Couldn't you have gone for brother?"

She squinted her dark eyes at me. "Yukawa and Szilard? We hardly look to be related."

"Half-brother?"

"I'm here and you're complaining. You sound just like your cynical friend Fitch."

I changed the subject. "Lucy visited me in the ambulance."

"Did you learn anything," she asked in an incredulous tone.

"Just that there is a mystery to be discovered." When I voiced this aloud, I laughed. That was not a revelation.

Vicki sat down in a plastic chair and countered my vision with her investigation, "We completed the background search on Ms. Lucinda Salas. It matched the personnel records that Mrs. Wilson had shared with me. She attended Stony High, followed by CSU, and then returned to Stony High as a teacher."

This fake background made me think of witness protection again—or identity theft. Fitch might have declared, 'Nonsense,' but I gave a more measured response, "That's an interesting paper trail, but you said that her autopsy revealed she was older than that. Also, everyone thinks she had a medical career before coming to teaching."

Vicki didn't argue. She changed the subject, "I can give you another mystery. Ms. Salas has an older brother—Pedro Salas. We can't find him. He just disappeared."

As much as I liked a good puzzle, this case was spinning out of control. My senior brain struggled to hold all the details. I wouldn't disappoint Lucy. She was counting on me.

I encouraged Vicki with, "We need to start solving mysteries faster than we uncover new ones. Keep in mind, that we have reservations to embark in one week. Lucy's murderer must be in custody by then."

Vicki's phone sounded a siren ringtone. "That's the office." After listening to her phone, she turned to me, "I can thank you for that. Mr. Purcell brought in his wife, and we've collected her DNA sample."

"Good," I said to be agreeable, though I doubted that more DNA would be of any use.

Vicki added, "On a side note, when we interview her, we should do it at her home. When her husband brought her in, she was trembling and had difficulty breathing. She has agoraphobia."

"I knew that. If I realized it was that serious, I would have gone to her house myself."

"I'm Dr. Curie, the orthopedic specialist, here to discuss your shoulder." She pointed at Vicki. "Do you consent for your..." She checked the computer. "...niece to be here?"

I smiled and reached out my good arm to Vicki. "No problem. She's my favorite niece. If I become bedridden, she'll take care of me." I was glad for a light diversion, so I continued the joke, "I changed her nappies when she was a wee one. Turnaround is fair play."

She stood up and gave me a peck on my cheek, "Thank ye, Uncle."

The doctor ignored our silliness, "Your shoulder is nothing special for someone your age. From the MRI, it looks like you've led an active life. You'll just need some rest and physical therapy."

Vicki continued our little charade, "Gosh, Uncle Zarand has been very active."

Following my favorite interrogation technique, I went off in a new direction. "I work at Stony Estancia High. Are you Brooklynn's mother?"

Dr. Curie was startled for a moment. "Yes, that's my brilliant daughter," she said proudly. She pointed to her name tag, "Formally, Dr. Gwendolyn Curie, MD, PhD, but you can call me Wendy." She went back to look at the computer. "And you're the substitute teacher for poor Ms. Salas. Brooklynn loved her."

Now that we'd exchanged names and Wendy had mentioned Ms. Salas, I was more interested in pumping her for information about the murder than hearing about my shoulder. I jumped at the opportunity to question someone with medical training about the different DNA profiles. "Do you know anything about chimeras?"

"I assume you don't mean the mythical lion that's part fire-breathing goat and part snake."

Vicki jumped in. "No. We're concerned about someone with multiple DNA fingerprints."

"Sure, I teach that at UC. Sometimes they're called mosaics. Bone marrow transplants create them. Recently a few have been created in China using genetic modification with CRISPR, but that procedure is frowned upon. I've never seen one occur naturally. Only about 100 or so cases of chimerism have been recorded in the modern medical literature."

"Maybe you can help us." I told her about the pool of blood. "The computer told us that the blood matched a DNA profile for Ms. Salas's sister, plus there was a small amount of blood with a different, but also related, profile."

Vicki jumped in. "That would be good, except she doesn't have a sister, just a brother. Could her brother have a female DNA profile?"

Wendy just nodded and let us ramble on. She would've been a good detective.

Vicki repeated that the second DNA profile seemed related to the predominant one. "Is that common with chimerism? Also, there was so little of that second sample that the techs missed it the first time they looked."

Wendy laughed.

Had we made some rookie mistake? I looked to Vicki. She raised her eyebrows and shoulders. We both waited in silence.

"Do you know what we tell medical students? We say, 'When you hear hoofbeats, don't expect to see a zebra.' We don't want them jumping off in some exotic direction when a perfectly ordinary explanation is available."

'Simplex sigillum veri,' Fitch reminded me. In simplicity is truth.

Vicki's jaw dropped and she said, "Oh, gosh. I get it. Chimerism is like a zebra. So, tell us, what is the ordinary farm horse in this case?"

Dr. Curie's voice became deeper as if she were lecturing to a full hall. She raised a finger. "First of all, the DNA profile that your computer identified as her sister—" She interrupted herself. "You said she didn't have a sister, didn't you?"

She paused to let that sink in.

"Her brother could have a female genotype—XX male syndrome or de la Chapelle syndrome, but that would be another of those zebras. More likely, that profile could just as well have been her mother or her daughter."

I volunteered, "She did say something about a daughter."

Vicki asked for clarification, "So the blood could have belonged to Ms. Salas's daughter, instead of her mother or non-existent sister?

Dr. Curie concurred, "That would be the most likely conclusion." In a quieter voice as if she was sharing a secret, she added, "Especially since the evidence is against it being her mother."

"Why not her mother?" I questioned. Wendy was an MD, PhD, and everything, but I couldn't imagine how she concluded that from the DNA. She'd just told us the DNA could be from Lucy's mother, or sister, or daughter. Now she was excluding the mother. We hadn't even shown her the test results.

Wendy smiled, "I'm getting to that."

That was a step forward, but we still didn't know where the blood came from or why there were two different DNA profiles. "So, we still have a chimera?"

Dr. Curie shook her head. "Forget chimeras. Stop looking for zebras." She raised another finger. "In cases where you see blood with a small amount of related blood, the most likely explanation is a birth."

"Baby?" Vicki and I said together.

"Nature is like that, taking better care of the new child, the future generations, than the mom. During a delivery, the mom loses more blood than the child."

'Why didn't you think of that?' Fitch taunted me.

I put a cheerful face on it. "S'cuse me. There was no second victim. The mother and newborn just walked away. This case finally got easier." I turned to Vicki and offered a celebratory high-five. "Off to Mexico, we go. Dessert buffets and endless guacamole."

That high-five was a mistake. "My shoulder," I screamed in pain, followed by, "Puppies, puppies, puppies!"

Dr. Curie put her head outside the door to order a sling.

The introduction of a daughter confounded the murder scene.

Like a good detective, Vicki asked for clarification, "So, that blood means we should be looking for a mother and infant, not a corpse."

Dr. Curie nodded while she adjusted the sling to my arm. "You'll need to wear this shoulder immobilizer all day and night until you've had a chance to mend."

I was glad there wasn't a second murder. I had seen enough and looked forward to a baby instead. On the other hand, I had no idea how to find a baby. In my years as a detective, my suspects were adults and occasionally teenagers. Babies don't rob or murder or do drugs.

While Vicki drove me to retrieve my car from Cocina de Cetto, she discussed the next steps. "Our best clue is that the baby's mother is Ms. Salas's daughter."

I echoed, "The baby's mother is Ms. Salas's daughter? She told me she didn't know where her daughter was." We had to find Lucy's estranged daughter. "Do you think you can get a judge to issue warrants to collect DNA samples from all the girls at Stony High?"

"Why just the girls?" she protested. "We have the infant's DNA. Any grounds to identify the mother, also apply to the father."

She was right. I considered a new possibility, "Do you think the baby could be connected to Jackson's disappearance?"

Vicki responded, "Why don't you and I go to church tomorrow?"

I didn't remember the last time I'd been to a Sunday service, certainly never with Vicki. "Why the sudden interest in church?"

"Jackson's friends all attend Stony Community Church. We should go there."

"Right." I checked my phone. "They have two Sunday celebrations. One at eight and the other at eleven."

"We're looking for teenagers. They'll be at the later service."

That night I slept sitting up to protect my shoulder.

Lucy's ghost returned to thank me for finding out about her daughter. 'I desired to tell you, but there are rules. I didn't know she was my daughter when I was alive. I'm not allowed to tell you something I only learned after I passed. Find her.'

I felt sad for Lucy's daughter. How awful to lose your mother on the day you become a mother yourself. How regrettable to lose your mother before you even know who she is.

Still, learning about Lucy's daughter and her daughter's daughter answered all our questions about the pool of blood—our first real progress. Unfortunately, our visit to Stony Community Church would set us back introducing additional complications.

Stony Community Church didn't have a steeple or stained-glass windows, but the full parking lot attested to an active congregation. The repurposed supermarket wasn't much from the outside. Once inside, lofty ceilings, white satin drapery, and brightly colored pennants inspired awe. As a member of the procession arriving for Sunday services, I took smaller steps and lowered my voice in respect for its solemnity.

I spotted Mr. Purcell in the first row. He was adjusting his phone mounted on a tripod to record the service for his agoraphobic wife. "That's Jackson's stepdad. I have an appointment with him on Monday. He wants to hire me to find his son. There's a space beside him. Why don't you talk to him before everything starts?"

Vicki shook her head, "No."

When I gave her a puzzled look, she pointed to the dais. The minister, in a conservative yellow dress, with matching nails and heels, was coming across the stage. Her natural black hair was adorned with gold beads reminding me of Annie.

We arrived too late. Our interrogations had to wait until after the service.

Also late, a group of teens ambled down a side aisle. Sure enough, there was Brooklyn, her minion Toby, Charlie, and some others. Annie was absent, as was the albinism-appearing Jackson.

We sat in the back pews to surveil the congregation and be near the exit. "If those kids leave, I'll rush out to intercept them."

After the first hymn, a family joined our pew and I found myself sitting next to a young girl in a Hawaiian dress with a matching floral hair tie. Her father handed her his program and a small box of colored pencils. He said, "Don't bother that nice man."

She replied, "Yes, daddy," while looking at me with her big brown eyes.

I winked.

She settled down to drawing military robots. I tapped Vicki's shoulder and whispered. "Look at that. She's a good artist."

I wasn't as quiet as I thought. The girl overheard. She proudly held up her pictures for Vicki's appreciation. We waggled our fingers at her.

After the welcoming prayer, my buddy put down her artwork and ran to the stage to sit on the minister's lap for children's time. The minister graced the little ones with a story of Moses floating down the Nile in a basket.

During the time that the kids scrambled through the large sanctuary returning to their parents, the choir led us in a hymn about baby Moses. Charlie had joined the choir. The service continued uneventfully until the sermon, which was based on the adult rendition of the baby Moses story, Exodus 2:1-10.

I was having difficulty keeping my eyes open until my little friend waved the PUZZLE PAGE at me. She said, "Do you know how to do this?" From her impish grin, I took this as a challenge, rather than a request for help.

I read the BRAIN TEASER. It said: HOW IS MOSES RESCUED? [HINT: CAESAR CIPHER] RJCTCQJ'U FCWIJVGT UGGU VJG DCUMGV CCOQPI VJG TGGFU.

I nodded, "Yes."

She said, a little louder, for sure challenging me, "Show me."

I whispered back to her the tried-and-true teachers' response, "I'm not going to do it for you, but I'll help."

She was okay with that.

"Count all the letters. Which one is used the most?"

She settled down to numbering the letters.

When I got back to the sermon, the minister was saying, "Think of Jochebed's neighbors, how they judged the new mother who put her baby in a basket and floated him down the river. What would you have thought of her? Would you have gossiped about her? Would you have judged her?" She pointed into the congregation. "You. You. You."

She lowered her voice to an intimate whisper, "Let's be honest with ourselves. Most would."

With that, her sermon about leaving censure to God and loving all our neighbors captured my interest. Not what I expected.

My attention to the sermon was interrupted by my friend with the Hawaiian hair tie. She tapped my arm. "G. There are eight Gs."

I suspected she'd solved cryptograms before. "Good. What is the most popular letter in English?"

"E." She pointed to the hint, CAESAR CIPHER, and said, "I know what that is. I can do this. Easy peasy. E to G is two steps."

When I returned to the sermon, the minister had left Moses and leaped forward to the infant exhumed at the high school. She admonished her flock not to condemn that teen mother. "She might be sitting next to you today."

She made a good point. I turned to Vicki, "We should be looking for the baby-in-the-basket's parents."

In the final twist, the minister praised the good people in her congregation who had campaigned for the Safe Surrender program. Thanks to their activism, a new mother could surrender her child, anonymously and without fear of prosecution.

The congregation responded to her praise of the California legislature with a solid, "Amen."

My buddy showed me the clear text, PHARAOH'S DAUGHTER SEES THE BASKET AMONG THE REEDS.

I gave her a thumbs-up, thinking that Moses was the first Safe Surrender.

If I could depend on all sermons being so uplifting, I'd consider attending regularly. I didn't know when I'd return, so when the collection plate came by, I emptied my wallet.

When I looked up from my money, I realized Brooklynn and her friends had left. I waved goodbye to the code breaker in the Hawaiian dress and ran for the exit.

There had been no need to rush. The teenagers were just hanging out in the parking lot. I waved. They waved back.

"Any more ideas about Jackson?"

They looked at each other before shaking their heads, "No."

'They know something, but they're not talking.'

Rather than upset them by pressing the question of Jackson, I switched subjects. "Any idea who might have hurt Ms. Salas?"

Charlie answered, "N-n-not any of the students. We all loved her."

Flora, the girl I remembered playing the drum with the Serrano dancers, added, "You know she handed out condoms, don't you?"

I responded with a noncommittal, "I heard that."

She continued, "Did you also know Mr. Kapitsa harassed us girls?"

I prided myself on being observant, but this was a shock.

Charlie added with contempt, "He's stared at them. He loved to go on d-d-dress-code patrol."

A girl said, "Yuck, He stalked me—giving me detention every day for a whole week."

'A creepy surprise,' remarked Fitch.

Flora added, "I was sent to his office where he lectured me, like forever. I was late to band practice."

Brooklynn added, "Listen to Flora. Kapitsa is out of control. He must be stopped."

Flora clapped her hands and led the group in a rhythmic chant, "Stopped, stopped, stopped NOW!"

I didn't like the principal, but in this case, was it the students who were out of control? How was something like this happening? Was Kapitsa harassing these girls without any adult knowledge or action? Their story was unbelievable.

Charlie answered my unspoken questions, "M-M-Ms. Salas called him an invasive sp-sp-species but advised that we should be patient. She assured us that the Ecology Club would eradicate him."

"Did she say how?"

Brooklynn explained with a tinge of anger in her voice, "Ms. Salas required testimony—she called them affidavits. She requested that we send statements to her personal e-mail. She promised to present them to the school board."

Flora added in a frustrated tone, "Never happened."

I saw both sides, but I trusted Ms. Salas's judgment. The question of harassment could wait until we solved the murder.

'That's why the killer destroyed Lucy's personal laptop. It held all that evidence against Kapitsa,' concluded Fitch.

I silently countered, *'We don't know that the alleged harassment and the murder are even related.'*

I didn't want them running off on their own. I echoed Lucy's call for moderation with, "Let's not forget Ms. Salas's plan to have proof before going after Kapitsa."

Whatever the principal was doing, this was something for the adults to deal with. DNA from these kids could lead to Lucy's granddaughter's parents and back to Lucy's killer, but I didn't want to explain all of that. I made up a story. "Can you all give me DNA samples? It will help stop Mr. Kapitsa."

"Like spit in a bottle?" Toby asked with a laugh.

Brooklynn scowled at him.

"Exactly," I said, racing back to retrieve collection kits from my car.

This struck them as fun.

"You'll get that lecherous Mr. Kapitsa, right?"

"No problem," I assured them, and soon I had my sling packed full of samples.

Before I returned to my car, I reminded them, "Just wait as Ms. Salas advised." I trusted my suburban friends to follow their teacher's directions even though Brooklynn's green eyes expressed determination and urgency.

"Anything else about Ms. Salas's enemies?" I prompted.

I waited. Every detective used silence to drive the suspects to talk.

Charlie finally broke, "Sh-she knew a lot of s-s-secrets."

What secrets? Could I uncover them by decoding the blue books?

Before I could interrogate Charlie further, Brooklynn shut down the discussion, "We're leaving." As she walked away, she added sarcastically, "We'll let you know if we think of anything else."

I was going to tell them that the principal had fired me and give them my contact details, but they disappeared too soon.

When I returned to where Vicki and I had parked, she was waiting for me. I asked, "Did you talk to Mr. Purcell?"

She frowned. "I introduced myself as Detective Yukawa from the Stony PD. He was happy to chat with me, but I didn't learn anything useful, he didn't even mention his missing son."

"So, a waste of time," I commiserated.

"Yes, except—for a professional guy, he had hard hands—calloused like a laborer."

"Yes. He's a gym rat."

"And he carries a gun."

"I also noticed that, but I have no idea what it means." I displayed my collection of DNA samples. "I had better luck with Brooklynn and her friends."

She looked at the tubes of spit tucked into my sling. "Some of those kids are minors and I don't see any release forms from their parents. Have you gone rogue? I still need to disturb a judge on Sunday to get DNA search warrants."

"Not exactly rogue. I just want to solve the mystery. I'm sure you can figure out how to get a conviction afterward."

"Gosh, you're cavalier about making my job harder."

"The more I learn about this case, the angrier I get. I'm going to get justice for Lucy, even if I must administer it myself. For Ms. Salas, I'd be judge and jury."

Vicki diverted me from vigilante justice with a suggestion, "That sermon gave me an idea. You should check the Safe Surrender sites for Lucy's daughter's child."

I agreed. And with that, I had my Sunday afternoon planned for me. I was happy to be of use. My intuition told me we were on the right track. The Safe Surrendered girl would lead to her mother—Lucy's daughter—and Lucy's daughter would lead to Lucy's killer.

The fire station was directly across Higgs Road from the church—a red brick building, little more than an enormous garage. An ambulance was in the driveway and the EMTs were polishing its red and gold finish. I walked over.

I had no idea how many Safe Surrender locations there were in Stony Estancia, but I had all afternoon. I'd go to as many as I could—hoping to get lucky.

"Good morning. I'm Zarand Szilard."

"Mornin'," they all replied.

I pointed to the blue and white Safe Surrender logo attached to the wall. It glowed in the bright sunlight, like the windows and firetrucks. Everything was sparkling clean.

I casually asked, "Do you receive many babies?"

"What?" a woman with brown wavy hair, who seemed to be in charge, asked. "Babies?"

A man, who had been polishing the headlights, answered. "We don't perform many prehospital deliveries. Our goal is to get them there in time."

The woman added, "But we're trained, and can assist when the child's in a rush."

I walked over and tapped the blue and white plaque. "Safe Surrender babies. Do you receive many of those? Did you receive one last week?"

"No. Whenever a fire station receives a Safe Surrender, César and Tish are all over it. We'd be the top post on STONY ESTANCIA SURFS if we had one."

"A prehospital delivery is already big news."

"Would they also report a Safe Surrender at a hospital?"

"Absolutely."

The woman tapped on her phone. "Across the entire state, Safe Surrenders happen less than weekly. That's for all of California. I don't recall the last time we had a Safe Surrender in Stony."

This was discouraging news. I had been sure we were going to find the baby girl. That infant was my best lead.

The EMTs were so helpful, that I decided to take a different tack. "Would you hear about a home birth?"

"We hope not. We're only called when something goes wrong. Those, and cardiac arrests, are the worst. Fortunately, most of our patients arrive at the hospital with a pulse."

I ignored their dark humor.

When I was back in my car, I checked the web. There hadn't been a Safe Surrender. I had no reason to visit the other locations. I was disappointed that I hadn't found the child, but I took advantage of the free time to pick up a whole roast duck from the Chinese market.

"Chop?" the lady asked.

"*Shi. Shi,*" I replied and watched her wield her Chinese cleaver to reduce the duck to so many tasty morsels.

I pointed to the steamed bao buns to balance the rich and crispy duck skin.

At home, I ate my fill and settled down for an afternoon nap. Surely, I'd wake up with new ideas and new directions.

While I slept, the FBI contributed to the investigation, a twist that shocked even Fitch.

That evening I went to Vicki's house. It was one of those expansive suburban residences—an open design with the kitchen, dining room, and living room all flowing one into the other. The walls were white, decorated with an eclectic variety of concert posters, and the carpet was tan. Vaulted ceilings and so many bedrooms. She had originally shared it with roommates. Most of the furniture was of the ready-to-assemble type from when the house resembled a dormitory. Over the years, she'd bought those roommates out without bothering to redecorate. We lounged beside the pool—bigger than the one at Higgs Haven.

When her cell announced the pizza delivery, she went to the front door, and I got a six-pack of Tecates from the fridge. As we dug into the Margherita pizza, I asked, "Good news or bad news?"

"Good news. Always the good news first."

"A Safe Surrender baby is a big deal. I didn't need to visit every fire station and hospital."

"If that's the case, I know the bad news. There were no Safe Surrenders."

"You're right. Lucy's granddaughter is somewhere else."

Vicki shook her head. "I hope the infant is well cared for. I have some ordinary news and extraordinary news."

"What's the ordinary news?"

She brought out her black satchel, the one embossed with the Stony Estancia seal. "Look at this. I have DNA search warrants for all our people of interest."

"Good work."

"I also have a search warrant for Ms. Salas's personal computer files."

"Great! Do you have her laptop? I checked for it when I uncovered her private pharmacy. No luck. Where did you find it?"

"It's still missing, but when it turns up, I have legal authorization to search its contents."

"That's thinking ahead. And what is the extraordinary news?"

Vicki took a bite of her pizza and sipped her cerveza.

"At soon as we realized someone had murdered Ms. Salas, we sent her DNA and fingerprints to the FBI. They found a match in CODIS, their DNA index system—not as Lucinda Salas, but Dorothea Ghez."

"Dorothea Ghez? Who's that?"

I grabbed another slice of pizza, folded it in half lengthwise, and took a big chomp out of the point.

"Long before she was Lucinda Salas, a student at CSU, she attended the Institute of Midwifery, eventually receiving a CNM license—Certified Nurse-Midwife. She was entered into the FBI databases as part of her licensure."

This disclosure boggled my mind. I had so many questions. The one at the top of my list was, "Is that license still active?"

Vicki scrolled through the CODIS report. "Yes."

"Well, that makes me feel better. Her private dispensary of OTC treatments is legal. She was licensed to practice medicine."

Vicki grinned, "That was your biggest concern? No one is likely to arrest a corpse. Why is that important?"

"I have been trying to understand what kind of person she was."

"And what have you concluded?"

"I figured her as someone who followed the rules. No cutting corners. No exceptions."

"How did you decide that?"

"Small things. For example, the time-off policy tells all teachers to have an emergency sub plan, but few bother. Ms. Salas's plan was the most complete I've encountered."

"What else?"

"In the same way, the IT group warns teachers to keep backup copies of their grades. I suspect most teachers ignore this advice. Lucy had those backups."

"I see."

"I was concerned when it looked like she was running an illegal health clinic—a teacher dispensing medical care. But your CODIS search shows she was licensed."

'Midwife! She delivered the baby,' Fitch blurted out.

It all made sense. I excitedly shared my epiphany with Vicki, "That's why no one called the EMTs when her daughter was ready to deliver. Lucy delivered the baby herself."

"So, your witness, Mr. Mbacke, didn't see a mob of thugs with Ms. Salas. Those cars held her pregnant daughter."

"Yes. I can see it all. The hackers had been waiting for her. When she arrived with the others, their plans were interrupted. They waited until the new parents left before surprising Ms. Salas."

"Oh, Mr. Snake Memory," she sneered, "Are you certain this time or will the story change again tomorrow? So, Mr. Mbacke's trained monkeys are now students, including her pregnant daughter, not kidnappers?"

I saw no reason to respond. I trusted my intuition.

"This certainly sounds like one of those mystery novels you read." Vicki became sad, "So, you're saying she didn't know the baby was her granddaughter?"

"Right. And she never figured it out."

'But now that she's passed, her spirit knows,' Fitch unexpectedly put a positive spin on the circumstances.

Vicki helped herself to another slice of pizza. "If she was such a straight arrow, why did someone murder her?"

"That's exactly why she was murdered. She didn't compromise. The hackers couldn't make a deal with her."

"I wish I could be as confident as you are."

I didn't let Vicki's doubts discourage me. I moved on to the implications of Lucy's high school medical practice, her *licensed* dispensary. "Everything fits together. Her experience as a midwife motivated her to distribute condoms."

I took a long swallow of my Tecate. I was in a self-congratulatory mood as I returned the extra bottles to the refrigerator, "This has been a good weekend. We solved the mystery of Ms. Salas's background and figured out the blood pool came when Dorothea Ghez, a licensed midwife, delivered her own granddaughter. I'm optimistic we'll embark on that cruise next weekend."

"You're retired. You'll be on board. I still have a murdered teacher, a runaway boy, a missing baby, and a mystery infant in a basket on my plate."

"That's all? What about the forged transcripts and graduation ghost?" I teased her.

"I can't worry about everything. I told you the hackers are not a concern of the PD, and no one cares about the graduation ghost."

I concurred, "I spoke to Chandra. He attended the graduation where Alex Marconi didn't show up. He agrees with you. Let's forget the graduation ghost."

I wasn't willing to forget Lucy or her granddaughter, and I was sure Jackson was part of that case. Still, her list was too long. "I'm happy to also defer the baby-in-the-basket."

Vicki agreed, "That's good. Someone buried that child in the school field long ago and no one noticed. I don't see any urgency."

"Puppies! I forgot to tell you that the principal has been harassing the girls," I exclaimed. "Ms. Salas called him an *invasive species* and had a plan to *eradicate* him."

"Gosh, that is a dreadful wrinkle to our puzzle. I've been considering Mr. Kapitsa as an ally. That makes him a suspect. I have no tolerance for men who take advantage of their positions, especially with underage girls." Vicki thought for a minute, "Some of these young women are over eighteen. That doesn't excuse Kapitsa, but the law makes a distinction."

I voiced my long-standing discomfort with the principal, "He's a bully. I never trusted him."

"I'll tell my team to check his background." She patted her black satchel. "I have a search warrant with his name on it. We'll get his DNA and check our databases. Modern forensics are perfect to trap this kind of perpetrator. They can't hide, can't escape. Of course, we have a murder to solve first."

"More DNA isn't our answer. There are too many moving parts. We need a detective to step back and see the pattern. Without that, this is a jigsaw puzzle with no picture."

"I hope you find that elusive picture, but I'm not waiting for lightning to strike you. While you're wishing for some mystical intuition or insight from the spirit world, my forensic folks will be in the lab solving our case."

I returned to Higgs Haven with a to-go box of leftover pizza confident I'd see the big picture after a good night's sleep, but I didn't need my sleepy subconscious. The next clue literally knocked on my door.

My shoulder immobilizer made it difficult to sleep. It had too many straps and buckles. I managed a few short catnaps before I gave up. It was still dark when I exchanged my pajamas for gym clothes, climbed down the stairs, and went outside.

The Higgs Haven landscapers wrapped the palm trees in fairy lights. From my balcony, it looked like an alien forest. At ground level, the effect was a perpetual twilight. I could follow the sinuous pathways with no risk of getting lost or bumping into something. Walking cleared my mind.

Years ago, I'd read *The Magical Number Seven* announcing a limit to short-term memory. I laughed at that idea. I had no difficulty remembering. I didn't need to write down shopping lists or carry a daily planner. My memory made me a great detective. I recognized patterns in cases that baffled the others. No level of detail overwhelmed me.

As I got older, I lost my edge. Some days I ignored Jackson and at other times the baby-in-the-basket. I couldn't juggle all the pieces without dropping some.

My first thought was to drag my whiteboard up from the garage. When I was a detective, I used it to help the others keep up. The LAPD gave it to me as a retirement gift, attaching an engraved nameplate: ZARAND'S MEMORY BOARD. I thought of it as a gag gift and forgot it after my retirement party. However, when I moved into Higgs Haven, someone threw it into the back of their pickup truck and brought it out to Stony Estancia. It's been in my garage ever since. I saw no reason to fight the thing up the stairs. I didn't even own any markers.

Walking among the fairy lights, I let my mind wander, searching for a pattern. The perpetrators—Ms. Salas's murderer, Kapitsa, the hackers. Missing people—Ms. Salas's daughter, Jackson, the graduation ghost. Babies—Ms. Salas's granddaughter, the baby-in-the-basket. Witnesses—Mr. Mbacke, Chandra. Parents—Mr. Purcell, Jackie Siegbahn,

Cha Cha, Dick the Stickman. There were too many lists. Each time I reviewed them—they were different.

'It's right in front of you,' taunted Fitch who had no trouble with his memory.

Pshh. Pshht. The sprinklers came on and I ran away before they soaked me. I took that as a sign. My nighttime walk was over. I headed home.

Before I reached my apartment, *Boom!*

An explosion reverberated off the buildings and the surprise knocked me over. I twisted on my way down to protect my injured shoulder, successfully landing on my left side. My glasses went flying. Without them, I couldn't identify the source of the blast. I crawled through the wet grass until I recovered my missing spectacles.

With my eyesight restored, I saw that someone had bombed my apartment entry blowing the door off its hinges. It lay useless on the ground. A fading cloud of gray smoke marked where it had been. When the haze cleared, the circle of light from my video doorbell shone proudly, but cleverly, someone had blocked the camera with a stick-on googly eye.

The entryway was now open to the outside. The explosion had charred the fire door to the garage. I could still open it and the Mini was unscathed. The first few stairs were scorched, but I had no difficulty using them.

As bombs go, this was not much. A quick investigation revealed that the door hinges had been unscrewed from the frame. Between a sparkler and Armageddon, this was like the Fourth of July in the backyard. When I entered my apartment, a sheet of paper on my dining table upset me more than those firecrackers. Even before I read it, I realized that it meant that someone had been inside.

The hackers had been in my apartment. I suppressed the feelings of violation and followed my detective instincts. I searched the bedroom, my closets, under the bed, and even out on the balcony. They were gone. There was no way to secure the entry door at the bottom of my stairs. The intruders had taken care of that, so I closed the apartment door at the top and bolted it.

I put on gloves and reached for an evidence bag, but I was still retired—no evidence bags. I picked up the note by a corner, dropped it in a freezer bag, and examined it through the plastic. THIS IS YOUR WARNING. BE SMARTER THAN LUCY WAS. STOP INVESTIGATING THE ECOLOGY CLUB.

I searched the apartment again, looking for clues this time.

'They see you as a threat,' Fitch said proudly.

He was right. I must be getting close. They'd never frighten me away. The more they tried, the more chances they'd take, and the sooner I'd catch them.

They'd already made their first mistake.

That warning was the key to the puzzle. I ignored the firecrackers and did a little happy dance.

I had my connection. They hadn't warned me away from investigating Lucy's murder. They were concerned about the Ecology Club.

The Ecology Club was my anchor. Around it I organized the jumble of parts and pieces, putting together a coherent pattern.

The Ecology Club was more than recycling and picking up trash. They campaigned to save the planet with composting, reuse, and clean energy—the many ways an individual could contribute—but they did much more. They distributed condoms. If they failed, pregnancy tests, emergency contraception, and prenatal vitamins were available. If the student chose to keep the child, Ms. Salas offered a discreet delivery, like the one she performed shortly before someone killed her.

Fitch and I still didn't know who, how, or why, but we would answer all those questions. If Ms. Salas hadn't died, no one would have known about the new baby. Who knew how many babies she'd delivered?

Mr. Kapitsa's *eradication* as an *invasive species* was another Ecology Club project. How far were they willing to go? If this had played out differently, would Vicki and I have been investigating the principal's death instead?

'It wouldn't have come to that. Ms. Salas called for moderation,' Fitch reminded me.

I reviewed my meeting in the church parking lot. Mr. Kapitsa had upset those students more than I had realized. Who knew what those well-behaved kids from suburbia were capable of? "Patience," Ms. Salas had counseled. Now that she was gone, would they still follow her lead?

'Um, what about the baby-in-the-basket? What kind of project was that?' Fitch asked.

The science garden was also an Ecology Club initiative. Had Ms. Salas planned for us to discover that shallow grave?

Fitch added, *'The students who mentioned the club at Ms. Salas's memorial were speaking in code, not thinking about recycling or even climate change.'*

He was right. The door that led to the teachers' work area, now fit into the pattern. The picture of Rachel Carson and the label ECOLOGY looked like the other AP Biology displays, but to those knowledgeable, it marked the entrance to the Ecology Club. That's why Brooklynn had no hesitation when entering.

Understanding the Ecology Club was the breakthrough. I needed to figure out how Jackson and the hackers fit, but I had a bigger picture and would soon learn where the other pieces belonged. The graduation ghost could wait for another time.

I still couldn't sleep. I'd already taken my nightly painkiller. Rather than take another, I deconstructed my sling, unbuckling the straps and freeing my arm. I examined myself looking for the irritation that was keeping me awake, contorting myself in front of the bathroom mirror—being careful not to reinjure my arm. I noticed red spots where my arm pressed against my side.

Those red spots were the reason I couldn't sleep.

I fell down an internet rabbit hole of red spots. The web lined the tunnel with rashes, hives, and even little hemorrhages. They had strange names like fifth disease and Christmas tree rash.

After my lengthy red-spot education, I applied an internet treatment. I cleaned my arm, placed a dry washcloth in my armpit, and put my sling back in place.

It was too late to go back to sleep, so I scrolled through my crime scene photos hoping to see something that the techs had missed—specifically Lucy's laptop. With each new image, I anticipated discovering the corner of her device hiding at the picture's edge or peeking out from under some innocent object. Alas, that would have been too easy. Lucy's murderer was intent on blocking me at every step.

I didn't find the missing computer, but with my heightened awareness for red spots, I noticed some on her cheek. Surely, the coroner had seen them. I passed them to Fitch, "See what you can make of those."

'On it. The most important clue yet!'

With the rising sun, I remembered my appointment with the gun-toting Vinnie Purcell. Was he an Ecology Club accomplice or adversary? What was his part in this newly discovered pattern? He was at the top of my to-do list, but Vicki had other plans. Someone else jumped to the front of the queue.

From the balcony, I watched an ambulance and a ladder truck pull into my parking lot, sirens wailing and lights flashing. The cheerful crew jumped from their shiny red and gold vehicles and converged on my damaged apartment. My friends from the Higgs Road fire station were upstairs looking around without waiting for an invitation. The lady with brown wavy hair introduced herself this time, "We meet again Mr. Szilard. I'm Lieutenant Mutai."

"Good morning, Lieutenant. I assume my neighbors called you."

"Yes," she said with a good-natured laugh. "The county nine-one-one center is still receiving calls."

"Not unexpected. Not much happens at Higgs Haven."

Vicki walked in, "But when something does, the residents let us know. We regularly get reports of dangerous mountain lions and wolves—that turn out to be frightened bobcats and coyotes who disappear back to the hills when the patrol car arrives."

Lieutenant Mutai turned to Vicki, "We've looked around the apartment. The damage was restricted to that downstairs entryway."

"Will your arson people do the forensic work on the blast?"

The lieutenant made a happy laugh. "Blast is a strong word for this."

"It had to pack a punch to knock the door off," countered Vicki.

Another laugh. "That was just for show. Someone unscrewed the hinges. A strong wind would have been sufficient."

"It's still arson, isn't it?"

"Sure. Arson. We'll take the lead, but it looks to be consumer fireworks. We don't allow them in Stony, but our culprit could have bought them in San Amano. I doubt we'll find anything we can trace."

"Can we quote you on that?" César and Tish had arrived.

"*Hola*, César," Mutai greeted him with a hug. "Sure, go for it." She turned to Tish with her blue microphone. "Do you want to interview me in front of the damaged door?"

"Good idea," I said. "I don't want to break up this fun reunion, but I need to talk to Vicki about—" I stopped myself before leaking information to our internet reporters. "About another case."

"Let's do that interview." Mutai winked at me and led Tish and César downstairs giving Vicki and me some privacy.

Once safe from internet surveillance, I showed Vicki the threatening note from the hacker.

She observed, "This looks like the ones Lucy received. Generic printer paper. Same font."

I handed her my improvised evidence bag. "Your forensic people will want to examine this." I sarcastically added, "It's something else they can check for DNA."

After she placed it in her black leather case, she said, "Now that you mention DNA, I'm off to serve my first search warrants. I'd like you to accompany me."

"Can't. I have an appointment this morning with Purcell and Associates. He's my prime lead for the hacker."

"Are you sure you want to meet him without backup? He's a tough guy, works out, and carries a gun."

After my years in the big city, I wasn't going to be frightened by anything in this jolly suburb. "S'cuse me, I've taken care of myself until now. You don't need to babysit me. Besides, Fitch would warn me if I was in any danger."

'*I would, wouldn't I?*' Fitch said in a sleepy voice as if he'd been lost in other thoughts.

She playfully punched my good arm. "Nothing like that. I'm starting with Richie's parents—Richard Fowler and Charlene Bragg-Fowler. I'd like you to observe and give me your take."

I wanted to see Richie's dad. Children and Family Services were no longer interested in the eighteen-year-old. A home visit would give me some insights and suggest the next steps. Richie required help before he got into real trouble. "Okay. I'll move my appointment with Vinnie to the afternoon."

The Fowler's house was set back from the road. The front yard had rows of grapevines and a playful sign announcing THE LAST BRAGG VINEYARD. The house was mission style—white stucco and red tile roof. Behind the grape vines was a wall with four bells modeled after Mission San Juan Capistrano.

Mrs. Bragg-Fowler answered the door. She wore a sleeveless blouse accented with a brightly colored scarf. Her red hair looked like she'd just had it done. We'd come at an inconvenient time—she was on her way out or expecting company.

Vicki displayed her badge. "I'm Detective Yukawa. We're investigating the murder of Ms. Salas at the high school. Can we come in?"

I expected some resistance since we'd showed up uninvited, but she stepped back from the door and said, "Certainly. That murder was just awful. I organized black commemorative T-shirts for the students and attended her memorial. I'm always ready to pitch in."

With that reminder, I recalled seeing her in a black dress and a veil handing out T-shirts and those plantable *In Memoriam* cards.

The living room looked company-ready with purple and teal throw pillows on a navy sectional and matching armchairs. A large-format book, *Images from African Capital Cities,* sat on the low glass table between them. Beyond this room was a dining area with a suitcase on the table.

The walls were decorated with original paintings from everywhere but Europe. It could have been an international art museum, but it was just another home in the understated Stony Estancia style.

Vicki and I sat on the sofa.

"I just baked shortbread cookies. Would you like tea with them?"

Without waiting for a response, she disappeared.

While she was away, Mr. Fowler joined us. He was tall and slim with a long, gray ponytail. Everything about him was long—long legs, long arms, even long fingers. I understood why they called him Dick the Stickman. He looked more like a concert pianist than a bully. He gave us a half-smile.

We stood up. Vicki displayed her ID and explained the purpose of our visit. She offered her hand.

He ignored her friendly gesture, stepped back, and tensed up. "You never forget. Do you? Am I going to be on every suspect list forever?"

Mrs. Bragg-Fowler returned with a porcelain tray holding a matching tea set and a plate of warm cookies. Each white cup was decorated with a traditional blue flower-bird motif. The room filled with the sweet aromas of oolong and baked butter. "Everyone, please help yourself to tea and shortbread."

I recalled what I knew about Richie's family. He was a bully and had been abused at home. CFS hadn't done anything and now he was no longer a minor. Chandra said Mr. Fowler was in international marketing and made good money. I didn't know anything about him being on "every suspect list."

Vicki took a cup of tea and a warm shortbread. After a polite delay to appreciate Mrs. Bragg-Fowler's hospitality, she opened her leather case and took out two search warrants and DNA sample kits. "We have a complicated case with Ms. Salas, her unidentified daughter, a child burial, and a missing student. The judge agreed we have probable cause to collect DNA." She looked at Mr. Fowler before adding, "This has nothing to do with those arrests during your teen years."

He ripped the search warrants in half and threw them into the air. "Not happening."

I thought to myself, he has a short fuse. I felt sorry for Richie growing up with him and better understood how Richie had become an angry bully.

Mrs. Bragg-Fowler sighed and ran her fingers through her perfectly coifed red hair. She looked to her husband, "Dick, we can't live like this. You're so much better than they think."

He pinched his lips so tight, that they seemed to disappear.

"I'll tell them," she offered.

He crossed his arms.

Vicki waited for Mrs. Bragg-Fowler's next move. I let the two of them work this out.

The room was silent.

Nothing happened.

We all stared at each other.

The only sound was crunching shortbread.

'Change the subject,' Fitch whispered in my ear.

Only the topic of their son remained unexplored. "Can we talk about Richie?"

Mr. Fowler moved aggressively in my direction, chin out, lips pursed, breathing through his nose like a charging bull at a corrida with me as the brave matador. Both Vicki and Mrs. Bragg-Fowler jumped to their feet and stood between us like the picadors.

Mr. Fowler shook his fist. "You're safe, old man. The women will protect you."

I recalled that Richie had said something like that to Charlie when Brooklynn had intervened in the science garden.

Mrs. Bragg-Fowler hugged her husband. "It's going to be okay."

He turned to her. "This substitute-teacher jerk is the one who called Children and Family Services. I don't want him in our house."

This was disturbing because my training had assured me that any report to CFS would be anonymous. They also said they'd fire me if I didn't report. Carrot and stick. How could I help Richie when everything I said upset Mr. Fowler? This was Vicki's meeting to collect DNA and my agenda about Richie was getting in the way.

Mrs. Bragg-Fowler served another round of tea and cookies. Her husband and I dutifully took a drink and nibbled on the no-longer-warm shortbread. I felt like the dormouse at Alice's tea party—ready for a nap.

After everyone had another chance to eat, Mrs. Bragg-Fowler began, "If you are asking about Richie's college application, we were as amazed as you must have been. Richie has no interest in leaving California. We've talked about it and can't imagine where that application came from."

With a pout, Mr. Fowler added, "And we certainly have no idea how his grades were changed. We are not techies. We pay someone to keep our home network working."

That woke me up. "Purcell and Associates?" I asked.

"It's none of your business, but yes."

I made a mental note of this for my meeting with Vinnie. The college application was irrelevant. What Mrs. Bragg-Fowler was doing about her husband? I required an answer to that question. I began the discussion again, more directly this time. "I know Richie has been abused. That's why he's a bully."

Fitch scoffed, *'Um. So now you're a psychologist too?'*

Vicki collected the pieces of the torn court orders, stacked them neatly, and tapped them on the table to align them.

Everyone had a different goal. Vicki wanted to collect DNA samples—forensic evidence for the murder case. Mr. Fowler wanted to protest his arrest record. I wanted to support Richie now that Children and Family Services had cut him loose.

The parents looked at each other. He nodded. She said, "Dick was also a bully in high school. Detective Yukawa has already alluded to his assault and disorderly conduct arrests. I was pretty wild too." She fluffed her hair with an expression that she'd likely learned as a small child, perhaps watching old Shirley Temple movies.

"The red hair, right?" She made a small grin as if recalling some escapade. "I was hot. They still call me Cha Cha." She flashed a big smile. "But they don't arrest the girls, do they?"

Vicki interjected, not impressed by Cha Cha's cuteness, "Do you want to tell me what happened back in high school?"

"What would you expect? I got pregnant. I wasn't the first girlfriend he got pregnant. We were all wild."

Fitch stirred to life, *"Dick the Stickman is the father of the baby-in-the-basket."*

I shushed Fitch and left it to Vicki whether to pursue his wild fantasy.

"And then?" Vicki prompted Mrs. Bragg-Fowler to continue.

"When Richie was born, we got married. For the first few years, Dick was in medical school and our home life was tumultuous. I regret we didn't get counseling and still blame myself for Richie's bullying. He has a therapist now, but it's difficult because we waited so long."

"We're sorry about Richie." Vicki held up her orderly stack of torn papers, "I still have a court order to collect DNA samples."

In an angry, clipped voice, Mr. Fowler asked, "Why do something now? So, what if that baby you dug up at the school is mine? I offered to marry the mother, but she told me the baby died. Who benefits?"

That was unanticipated. We'd come to investigate Lucy's murder, but instead, we discovered the baby-in-the-basket's father.

I agreed with Mr. Fowler. Who benefits? With his confession, I didn't see the need for his DNA.

Mrs. Bragg-Fowler sat up straight. "Dick had nothing to do with Ms. Salas's death. When she died, he was in Mozambique." She looked at me. "Last New Year's Eve Dick was in Brazil. Richie and I were alone for the entire holiday break."

The statement about Brazil didn't relate to Ms. Salas, but I understood what she was saying. She knew that I'd seen Richie's bruises when he'd returned from winter recess. This had to mean that she was the abusive parent, not her husband.

I knew I was being sexist, but I was less concerned knowing that his mother, not his father, had given him that black eye. I understood why CFS just waited out the few months until he became an adult. They didn't want to pursue his mother.

"Do you want to know why he travels so much?" she asked moving beyond her awkward confession.

I jumped in. "Rumors say that he is in international marketing and makes lots of money, maybe from questionable activities."

Mr. Fowler relaxed, and his wife laughed aloud.

With a big grin, she continued, "We've all known each other since elementary school. What do they say? *Familiarity breeds contempt.* Dick and I went our own ways after graduation. They just made up that marketing stuff. Dick went to medical school, not business school. He's a surgeon!"

He held up his long fingers, "Surgeon's hands."

She and her doctor husband looked at each other and laughed again. He pointed to her, signaling for her to proceed with the story.

"He doesn't make any money from his travels. We pay the expenses out of pocket. I inherited a fortune from Bragg Vineyards. He trains young men and women to perform simple operations. Appendectomies. Césarean sections. Compound fractures."

I read about this in the novel *Darwin's Paradox.* These were all life-saving operations that didn't require rigorous medical training. This was an innovation for places with extreme shortages of doctors. For example, in Mozambique, after classes like she described, the government placed *Tecnicos de Cirurgia* in villages with no access to trained medical doctors to deliver babies and set bones.

She continued, "He hasn't been in a fight in many years and never hit Richie."

Vicki responded without any enthusiasm, "I'm glad he is doing good works. He's still a person of interest. I'll need to see some documentation to support his out-of-the-country alibi."

Mrs. Bragg-Fowler jumped up, ran into the dining room, went through the suitcase, and returned with a small blue booklet. She flipped through the pages until she found what she was looking for. She showed it to Vicki.

Vicki examined the passport, checked the calendar on her phone, and took pictures. She said, "Thank you for the refreshments."

"Yes, thank you," I said, thinking about what had just happened. Dr. Fowler was in Africa and had not killed Lucy. Mrs. Bragg-Fowler was the abusive parent. In my quest for closure, I said, "We can forget the DNA." I stood to leave and tucked a couple of to-go shortbreads into my sling.

Cha Cha Bragg-Fowler looked at me with a twinkle in her eye, "Thank you for not asking, but I'll answer the question anyway. Dick, Richie, and I are all in therapy."

That left us with one less suspect, but the same list of mysteries.

When the door closed, Vicki turned to me. "Don't you ever do that again. I am not forgetting his DNA."

"He practically confessed to fathering the baby-in-the-basket. What more could we want? That closed the case."

"How?" she raged. "We still don't know the full story. You think that knowing the father is everything?"

I didn't have an answer. She made a good point. My empathy with Dr. Fowler clouded my judgment.

"His wife's story of the sainted doctor visiting underdeveloped countries paid for with her inheritance is a beautiful fantasy of privilege." She gave me a hard look. "He could have murdered that baby. Did Ms. Salas find out and blackmail him? Did he murder her?"

"Now you're inventing crazy murder mystery plots," I retorted.

"Whatever. You let him go."

I offered, "I can go back and get his DNA."

She snapped, "This is *my* case. His DNA isn't going anywhere. I'll get it after I uncover the mother's side of the story. You undermined me in there. What were you thinking?"

'Not thinking at all,' sneered Fitch.

That was all I could do with Cha Cha and the Stickman. I never let myself get bogged down in the past. Next on my agenda was an appointment with tough-guy Vinnie. I gave

Vicki a moment to cool down while I entered Purcell and Associates into my GPS. When I finished, she was gone.

On that sour note, I abandoned my plan to have lunch with her. The GPS sent me past the Bragg Vineyard Memorial Cemetery and south on Van Vleck Avenue. When I saw Cocina de Cetto, I stopped. I had a quick burrito and took a bag of homemade tortilla chips to go. Back on Van Vleck Avenue, the GPS told me to turn right on Appleton Route. By this time, I was out of the residential area and surrounded by warehouses. "Your destination will be on your left."

I had checked out Vinnie on the internet. His website was just a single page with a background image of a SWAT officer in full riot gear with the slogan LET US PROTECT YOU. In the foreground were a client list and logos for network management and security software. The only clients shown were the school district and the city. I knew he also had residential clients like the Fowlers.

The website didn't display an email or a phone number. I found it suspicious that he wasn't soliciting new customers. I'd never known a tech company that didn't showcase its skills with a fancy website or want to expand.

Now, considering him a suspect, I wondered why he didn't supply DNA samples. He was so fast to drag his agoraphobic wife down to the police station, but when I brought up his DNA, he'd said, "I'm just the stepfather." Did he worry that we'd find him in CODIS?

And none of this explained why he carried a gun.

'He's a front for money laundering or smuggling,' Fitch opined.

Was he running that fraudulent college admission scheme? The skills to hack into a computer were identical to those to guard against intruders. Cyber-security and cyber-hacking have always been in an uneasy alliance. Even the Feds had difficulty differentiating the white hats from the black hats.

Vinnie's interest in finding his son worked to my advantage. Jackson's disappearance was the perfect cover for my investigation of Vinnie. I'd locate his son and collect evidence for Lucy's murder at the same time.

The city was going to subcontract the forged recommendation letters and falsified grades to some third party. My detective instincts told me to track down the hackers myself. Vinnie's expertise was key to locating them. On arriving at Purcell and Associates, I ironically noted that Vinnie was simultaneously my prime suspect and best resource.

Purcell and Associates was in a strip mall on Appleton Route. The row of storefronts was dwarfed by large windowless buildings on either side. San Bernardino County was the distribution hub for Southern California and those warehouses comprised the economic backbone of Stony Estancia.

I stopped my Mini in front of Vinnie's office between the ghosts of two white lines that once delineated the parking spaces on a pot-hole-infested strip of asphalt. The car faced a blacked-out window, a steel door with an electronic lock, and a sign that read TEXT FOR ENTRY with no number provided. Security cameras mounted on the roof ominously whirred as they scanned the perimeter.

Just to the right, along a weed-infested walkway, was a custom swimwear shop. The windows displayed posters of women modeling bikinis. Their door, not as forbidding as Purcell's, read CALL FOR ENTRY and included a number. I considered buying one for Vicki, but I didn't know her size.

On the other side sat a mixed martial arts studio.

The entire strip mall screamed, mainstream businesses need not apply, and supported Fitch's conclusion that Purcell and Associates wasn't entirely legal.

I took out my phone to text Vinnie but before I tapped my contact list, the door opened, and a young man appeared with blond tips, a fade hairstyle, scruff and stubble beard, and blindingly white teeth—looking more like a maître d' or a hair stylist than the technocrat I'd expected. He approached me wearing a welcoming smile, dark slacks, a blue dress shirt with a tie, and a jacket. "Good morning Mr. Szilard. I'm Mr. Purcell's assistant. Please come in. Can I get you some juice or water? We have fresh fruit tartlets today."

This was more upscale than I expected, another example of Stony Estancia's understated opulence. The space contained nicely appointed office furniture in muted colors and natural woods, huge computer monitors, and oil paintings on the walls—California landscapes with crashing waves and giant redwoods.

The cubicles held professionally dressed men and women wearing headsets. The conversations were muted by the padded walls, except for clear greetings of, "Purcell and Associates. Let us protect you."

I said, "Nice paintings," just to be sociable.

Vinnie's assistant replied, "They were collected by his wife before she became confined to the house."

That was a pleasant euphemism for her agoraphobia.

He continued his tour pointing to the stone carvings that stood on pedestals in the aisles. "She is a sculptor. All of these are hers."

When we reached the back of the building, he opened the door to the only office, "Vinnie, your visitor is here."

Inside there was no artwork. Mr. Purcell had replaced the paintings with a variety of pistols, a tactical knife, and, behind his desk, illuminated by a spotlight, an AR-15. Was Purcell ex-military? What services did he offer beyond malware protection and firewalls?

Vinnie stood to greet me. He dressed smartly wearing a black turtleneck.

I shook his hand. It was as strong and calloused as I remembered. The young man bought papaya juice and tartlets. The juice was smooth and not too sweet. My kiwi tartlet, which smelled exquisite, did not disappoint. The crust was flakey, the custard had a pleasant vanilla taste, and the kiwi added an interesting acidity. I finished the first one and reached for another—mixed berries this time.

Vinnie got right down to business, "Where's my missing son?"

"The kids at school think he's running away from you. He doesn't want to be an engineer."

"I'm not surprised. He can't do the math. His mother is brilliant, but the father was several apps short of a smartphone."

When I didn't say anything more, he answered his own question, "My sources say Jackson ran away to Vancouver. Do you have any contacts in Canada?"

I sipped my papaya juice. "Don't worry about Canada. The police found his IDs. He can't get across the border without them."

"He could have made fake ones. He's good with graphic design software," Vinnie said with a superior expression.

Fitch immediately concluded, *'Um, he isn't a smuggler.'*

I had to concur.

Jackson might have forged fake IDs for liquor stores and clubs, but the DHS wasn't that easily fooled. 'Looks genuine' only worked in the movies. If Vinnie imagined his son's 'good with graphic design software' would get him across to Canada, then he didn't know much about border control. Therefore, Fitch was right. Mr. Purcell was not a smuggler or money launderer.

I didn't get into a discussion of international border procedures. I simply held my ground, "My sources say your son hasn't left Stony Estancia."

This reassured him. His face relaxed. He reached for a strawberry tartlet. After brushing crumbs from his black shirt, he said, "You're the pro. Go find him. I can pay you in cash if you prefer."

Even if he wasn't an international criminal, I still considered him a suspect in Ms. Salas's murder and the fraudulent college admissions scheme. His offer to pay in cash increased my suspicions.

I responded, "I don't want to be paid at all."

Big smile. "You must want something," he said confidently.

"Yes, I'm working on a case involving computers and need some technical advice."

"Can do."

"And perhaps some access to school files," I whispered.

He didn't flinch. "You know that's illegal, but I am a network administrator, and things occasionally get printed during routine maintenance," he said with a conspiratorial expression.

I nodded knowingly. His comfort with crossing the line reinforced his position at the top of my suspect list. He had the means and opportunity. His motive could have been the protection of a lucrative college admission scheme.

I didn't want to reveal that I suspected him, so I asked about his son for some misdirection. "Who are Jackson's friends? Where do you think he could be hiding?"

"I don't know. Jackson and I don't talk much. He's much closer to his mother."

"But you knew about his plans to go to Vancouver. How did you know that?"

"Not from talking to him. I installed spyware on his phone."

That contributed more evidence that Vinnie was comfortable with questionable methods. I encouraged him to keep talking wondering what else he might disclose, "That's clever."

He accepted the compliment with a nod.

I prompted him with, "So, that spyware must let you know where he is now."

He frowned. "No. His phone has not been active since he disappeared. He doesn't want to be located." He smiled and his pride was obvious when he added, "He may not be good at math, but my boy understands computers."

I asked, "Can I speak to your wife? She might have useful information."

"No problem. She's home. I'll call to see if she's free."

After a short conversation, he said, "We can drive up later this afternoon, or earlier if we bring lunch."

I took another tartlet—kumquats dusted with powdered sugar—and replied, "Lunch sounds great."

He told his assistant to have sushi delivered.

"While we're waiting, can you educate me about computer security?"

He leaned back in his chair and put his feet up on his desk. "What would you like to know?"

I asked how hard it would be for hackers to break into the student grades or teacher personnel records—being careful to not hint that I suspected him of being the culprit.

He turned to his computer and typed frenetically. Proudly he declared, "Impossible. I've installed the best security software and have just checked the logs. There have been several attacks, but none were successful. No one broke in."

He was a cool operator, giving no sign that this line of questioning made him nervous. I didn't press my luck with any follow-on inquiries.

His assistant soon arrived with a stack of takeout containers. The pleasant odors of ginger and tempura filled the room.

Vinnie said, "I don't live far from here. You can follow me."

I replied, "Let's roll," and tucked a to-go tartlet into my shoulder immobilizer as we headed to our cars.

I followed him up the hill on Van Vleck Avenue. As he'd said, it wasn't far, but it was the most exclusive neighborhood in Stony Estancia.

'Network administration pays better than I expected,' said Fitch with a long whistle.

Once we were through the gates, we continued climbing until we arrived at his modest house landscaped with ornate stonework and exotic desert plants.

On either side of the double doors stood a polished granite owl—massive brown ovals carved with just the essence of an owl. In front of one of these friendly birds was a NO SOLICITING sign reminding me that Ms. Siegbahn rarely left her home and didn't want visitors. I parked in his circular driveway and took a moment to appreciate the panoramic view of the valley—so many red tile roofs dotted with silver solar energy systems.

He walked over to my car and said, "Wait here."

Carrying the containers of sushi, he entered the house. I assumed he was preparing his wife for my visit—warning her what to say and what not to say.

While he was away, I strategized my approach to Ms. Siegbahn. Would she talk to me? How could I interrogate her about her husband's criminal activities without tipping him off? Brooklynn had insinuated that there was friction between Vinnie and his wife. How could I use that to my advantage?

After a few minutes, Vinnie returned. "Jackie's ready to talk to you. She's eager to find Jackson."

The main floor was like Vicki's home—with all the entertaining spaces combined. However, it made that house, down in the flat part of Stony Estancia, look humble. The Purcell-Siegbahn residence was a perfect example of understated opulence. The interior contradicted the unassuming impression from the street. We walked past a marble fireplace, through a dining area suitable for a multi-generation Thanksgiving, and into a home theater that lived up to its name. The expansive interior served as a showcase for Jackie's sculptures. After hiking past the library and Jackie's studio, I spied her through the French doors. She was waiting for us on the patio overlooking a swimming pool with a water slide. Higgs Haven didn't have a water slide.

Having seen Jackson's picture, I wasn't surprised by her pale complexion and long white hair. She wore a loose dress in an orange, yellow, and brown Polynesian print with her toes and fingernails painted to match.

"Good afternoon, Ms. Siegbahn."

We made small talk while eating our sushi and drinking warm saké.

"Can you tell me something about your son?"

She looked to Vinnie. He nervously flexed his iron-pumping biceps. Had I started trouble?

'Um, don't jump to conclusions,' Fitch warned. *'Look at her face—calm and relaxed.'*

Mr. Purcell stood. I also got up, preparing for any eventuality.

Then, in a voice as soft and sweet as I could imagine, he turned to his wife, "Would you be more comfortable if I left you with Mr. Szilard? I have a lot of work and could return to the office."

She looked at him out of the tops of her eyes and blinked.

I felt a tension in the room, punctuated by birds splashing in a puddle on the pool deck and a distant dog barking.

Vinnie broke the silence with, "I'll bring dinner tonight. What do you want?"

"Mu shu pork and Peking duck," she said with a half-smile.

I saw something pass between them in that brief interaction, recognizing an understanding that evolved over a long-term relationship.

After Vinnie departed, Ms. Siegbahn poured herself another saké and swallowed it in one gulp.

I opened with, "You have a beautiful house," to put her at ease.

"Thank you," she said. "Vinnie planned to entertain for business. I imagined I'd host a salon of painters, writers, musicians, and sculptors. But we rarely have guests *now*."

I assumed that *now* referred to after her accident and agoraphobia. I ate some excellent maguro sashimi while waiting for her to continue.

She poured herself another saké, "When we first married, Vinnie was obsessed with my life as an artist. He demanded to know everything that I'd done before we met and worried about what I might be doing when I went to art festivals. He was jealous of every dealer and collector."

She sipped the saké.

"He pestered me for information, but the few things I told him just upset him. I decided it was best to tell him nothing. That didn't help. However, since my accident, I don't leave the house and he has relaxed."

She looked at the saké but ate some plain white rice instead. "He knows I don't like to talk about Jackson with him. That's why he left."

"Very considerate. What can you tell me about your son?"

"Where should I start?" she asked rhetorically.

No reply was necessary, but I'd learned to say, "At the beginning." If witnesses didn't start at the earliest time, they'd keep backing up to prior events. Since most had little practice recounting their activities, this convoluted timeline confused them. Starting at the beginning yielded the clearest narrative.

I imagined her traveling up and down the coast, showing at art festivals, and meeting new people at every stop. Despite her agoraphobia, she was an extrovert. She wanted to talk. I only had to wait.

"For you to understand what's happening with Jackson, you need to know the history. He hasn't always lived in a nice house with two parents."

I didn't see how going this far back would help find her son, but I always let witnesses begin wherever they chose. This background might also help incriminate Mr. Purcell who I still suspected of Lucy's murder.

"Jackson wasn't my first child. I was home-schooled until I entered high school. Stony Estancia High was a shock. There were so many teens, so many different ones. I fell in with the wrong crowd."

She stopped to wipe some sweat off her face with a hankie that matched her colorful dress.

"Not the wrong crowd. That's my parents speaking. The theater kids. We were all close. I painted scenery and designed posters. I even helped build the sets. I was madly in love with my first boyfriend and became pregnant."

"Was that Jackson's father?" I asked while wondering if she was telling me about Dr. Fowler. Cha Cha had said that he'd had other girlfriends.

"No. Jackson was later. When I became pregnant, I didn't know what to do. I didn't tell anyone. I prayed. I never prayed so much before or since. I starved myself and wore loose tops. My only plan was not to show."

Why was she telling me this? Didn't she have a girlfriend or a therapist? However, she stopped drinking saké, so I just listened.

"Then one night I was at a sleepover at a girlfriend's house, and I had terrible stomach cramps. I knew something was wrong because the baby had stopped kicking a week earlier."

'The baby stopped kicking,' Fitch repeated with concern.

I braced myself for what was coming next.

"My girlfriend held me until my body expelled the bloody thing. The two of us wrapped the tiny child in a silk scarf. We named him Tristeza, Spanish for sadness, and held him the rest of the night. By morning, his body had cooled, and we swore each other to secrecy."

In a faint whisper, more to herself than to me, she said, "I still think about Tristeza."

In a normal voice, she continued, "My girlfriend explained the bloody sheets to her mother as a heavy period. We invented a ceremony. The boys dug a grave in the school yard, on the other side of the football field. We buried the child on the night of a full moon. I swore off sex."

Anything I said would have been insufficient, so I kept my mouth shut. She also waited, until she outwaited the detective. I whispered, "It must have been traumatic."

She paused before going on, "Several years later, I was still in high school, and my girlfriend and I had crushes. We fantasized that it would be beautiful to have sex with them side-by-side under a full moon. We packed blankets, took a bottle of warm saké, and hiked up to Pauli Falls.

"That was Jackson. This time I was proud. I wore tight tops, went to the doctor for prenatal care, ate right, and didn't drink. Jackson was perfect and I love him."

She wiped her brow.

"My early years with Jackson were challenging. I drove up and down the coast with a car full of baby things and a trailer of heavy sculptures. The two of us attended art festivals. I built a following. Things improved."

She looked exhausted. I went into the house and found a pitcher of iced tea in the fridge. I brought her a big glass.

"Where do you think Jackson is now?"

"He was going to Canada. He'd met a group of writers online. That was a good opportunity for him."

"The police are confident he is still in Stony Estancia."

She didn't argue with me. "Something happened recently, and he changed."

"How so?"

"We have a comfortable life. He talked to me a lot about my journey to becoming an artist. We researched workshops and colleges with BFAs in creative writing."

I just nodded.

"A few months ago, this changed. He started talking to his stepfather about jobs. Vinnie tried to find him something, but nothing clicked. He also asked about his college fund. How big? What could he spend it on?"

"You're his mother. What do you think caused this?"

"Because I'd lost Tristeza, I was protective of Jackson. I never gave him a reason to worry about money. Even when I was a single mother, we always had enough. You can imagine that I was taken aback when he suddenly turned from his art to careers and money."

"Have you discussed this with your husband?"

She gave me a puzzled look and didn't respond.

Fitch said, *'This is a good time to leave.'*

I'd thanked her, promised to locate Jackson, picked up a tempura shrimp to go, and made my exit.

The afternoon had been full of surprises. The meeting at Purcell and Associates uncovered additional details that strengthened my suspicion that Vinnie was the hacker and the murderer. The guns, cash, withholding his *stepfather* DNA, and his willingness to exploit his computer knowledge—all circumstantial, but adding up.

Ms. Siegbahn's confessions had also been enlightening. Jackson's conflict with his father wasn't the key, his mother was more important. He had been close to her, but something had changed. Why was he hiding and what had caused his interests to move from writing to money and from his mother to his father?

Debriefing both meetings with Fitch, we identified an important pattern. While Vinnie had appeared cooperative, he'd been avoiding me. When I asked for Vinnie's DNA outside Kapitsa's office, he'd quickly agreed to provide his wife's and deflected my request for his. *I'm just the stepfather.* Again, today, when I was interrogating him, he evaded me. My interview was interrupted to order lunch, drive up the hill, and meet his wife. When it should have resumed, he excused himself.

I admired his ability to be agreeable and elusive simultaneously. For all my detective expertise, I'd not managed to question my primary suspect.

'He slipped out of your net,' mocked Fitch.

I was not one to give up. On Tuesday, I returned to that run-down strip mall on Appleton Route to complete what I'd started and was rewarded for my effort.

Over breakfast with Vicki at the Blackett Bakery, I recommended that we divide up the investigation. "For us to have any chance of embarking on our cruise, we must work separately."

She agreed, "My team will collect the remaining DNA samples."

I assumed she was politely referring to my poor behavior on Monday and the missing sample from Dick the Stickman. I apologized again, "I won't repeat that mistake."

"It's not just Dick Fowler, that saintly doctor and reformed bully. Others are on our list. We're also doing background checks, subpoenaing phone and credit card records, and reviewing social media activity."

"That sounds like a lot. Is it all necessary?"

"I have a team to sift through all that data. This is how modern detectives work. We collect gigabytes of data and AI algorithms separate the information from the noise."

I wished them luck. "I'm going to reinterview Vinnie. He got away from me under the pretense that Jackie wouldn't talk with him in the room. I still have questions for him."

"Are you sure that is necessary?" she echoed my question with a sly grin.

"Yes. Did I tell you that in addition to carrying a pistol, he has an AR-15 in his office?"

"I can help there, checking his registration for that AR-15."

"Thank you."

"No problem. That's how we'll allocate the work. You talk to Vinnie, and we'll check his gun registration and investigate everyone else," she said. I was just one detective, and she had a full team, so that was an equitable split.

I texted Vinnie from the Purcell and Associates parking lot. The CCTV cameras scanned me. I waited.

After a while, his assistant opened the door. He was different from my last visit. His hair—the spiky tips were now neon green. His demeanor—no smile. There was no offer of juice and baked goods. I'd arrived at his establishment without a reservation, my name wasn't on the list. With a tone of disdain, he asked, "Do you have an appointment? I didn't see you on the calendar."

Pointing to a utilitarian waiting area, he said, "Have a seat. I will see if Mr. Purcell is available," as if he was a nineteenth-century butler.

I had no recourse and nothing else planned. I took out my phone but discovered that Vinnie had blocked all signals within his offices—zero bars. Purcell and Associates took their security seriously. I resigned myself to reading trade magazines. Waiting for Vinnie, I had time to scan an article on deep learning applications for law enforcement and another blaming DARPA research during the Vietnam War era for today's internet security problems.

When Vinnie arrived, he didn't sit, as if to remind me that he was busy. "Mornin' Zarand. Are you bringing news about my son?"

I had nothing, so I improvised. "Your wife and I chatted about Jackson, and I have some leads to follow up on." I found Vinnie to be a puzzle. One part of him was a tough guy—flexing his muscles and carrying a gun. The other part was a considerate husband—bringing his wife meals and respecting her privacy. Regardless, he was my number one suspect.

I opened my interrogation with a question to misdirect him from the true reason for my visit. "I heard Jackie was upset when you brought her into the police station for her DNA sample, but she was in good humor yesterday. Does she have mood swings?"

"I don't see what this has to do with finding Jackson, but I can explain."

Vinnie, like his wife, was happy to chat. They were both lonely. Since her accident, they didn't socialize or even talk to each other. His tough-guy persona was good for his security business, but it meant he didn't make friends in peaceful Stony Estancia. He scared off the folks in our quiet suburb.

"After her accident, she lost her self-confidence—something critical for artists. As part of her recovery, I've encapsulated her in a positive bubble." He turned around. "Follow me." He led me down the hall.

"Do you see all these sculptures?"

"Yes, your assistant told me they were your wife's."

"That's right. Her sculptures don't sell well since she abandoned the art festival circuit. I buy most of them—without telling her. That is the positive bubble."

This fit with my understanding of his relationship with his wife. With her trapped at home and dependent on him, he was a caring partner. When she toured the California coast on her own, they had problems.

I assigned him culpability for his wife's accident. His efforts to control her led to her driving off the road in Big Sur. Had he tried to control Ms. Salas? That would never have worked. He might have killed her during a disagreement.

"I see. Is that positive bubble working? Is she recovering? Would you like to see her traveling again?"

"Before, I was envious of each admirer. However, after her isolation, I see how those exhibitions made her happy. I would like her to show again."

Now he was a caring husband, not the one that hounded his wife until she almost killed herself. Was this the real Vinnie?

'No way. He trapped his wife in their house and murdered Ms. Salas,' Fitch answered.

I changed the subject, still avoiding Ms. Salas's murder. "Can you help me with the graduation ghost?"

"I've never heard of any ghosts. I don't even believe in that stuff."

Fitch interrupted with, 'Well I've got a surprise for you.'

Vinnie went on, "Does this have anything to do with Jackson?"

"The graduation ghost is a mystery from before you were in Stony. However, it is another boy who disappeared from the high school. The cases could be related."

"That's a long shot, but how can I help?"

He appreciated a friendly conversation and a diversion from his lonely business. I tapped my phone, still in my pocket, to start recording. My years of experience told me he'd go on for a while. "Can you get us entry into the district office to see what we can learn about this graduation ghost?" Was he willing and able to hack into the district computers?

"We don't need to go to the office. I have a VPN connection to the school's network." He opened his laptop. "What can you tell me about this ghost?"

"All I know is that he disappeared before graduation, and everyone calls him Alex."

"That should be plenty. The state tracks graduation rates. The district maintains a database entry for everyone who doesn't receive a diploma."

He connected to the system like it was no big deal. He typed faster than anyone I knew. "No record. I used Alexander, Alejandro, A L E X, and A L E C. Nothing matched."

I didn't know anything about V P N but was amazed by how easily he could get into the school records. Now I was certain that he was the hacker.

I'd just seen him employing the school's secure databases as his private treasure trove. That was a violation of California law and I had it recorded on the phone in my pocket. That would be leverage for Vicki to arrest him and find out what else he knew. An effective interrogator would soon have him confessing. I was more interested in getting him for murder than unauthorized access.

Vinnie's assistant entered the office carrying a tray. It was as if he hadn't snubbed me earlier, hadn't made me wait in the parking lot, and again in the lobby. "Good morning, gentleman, I brought you some refreshments—fresh-squeezed orange juice with a hint of organic raspberry nectar—an enticing balance of sweet and tart. As an accompaniment, we have fresh madeleines from a wonderful pâtisserie just around the corner."

We took a break from our discussion to enjoy the snacks and waited for the assistant/waiter to restore our privacy. The madeleines were a perfect combination of cake and cookie with an almond taste and a hint of lemon. I ate several before his neon-green-spiky-hair assistant left.

Putting on my best humble detective expression I approached Vinnie with, "Ms. Salas's murder has me baffled. You know the people and you have the advantage of being an outsider without preconceived ideas. Who do you think did it?"

He took a handful of the shell-shaped delicacies and placed them at the edge of his desk. He slumped down in his chair, ate one whole, and examined the ceiling.

"Before you consider suspects, you must understand the victim." He mansplained my job to me. "Ms. Salas was conservative and rigid. She noted every tiny infraction. Anyone with a secret is celebrating her departure."

He was so negative. Everyone else had only praise for her. "Why do you say that? Were you close to her?"

"Oh no. I never met her, but she was a troublemaker." He smiled broadly at his cleverness.

'Nonsense,' said Fitch. 'His opinions are too strong.'

I felt like he was challenging me to arrest him each time he confessed to knowing so much about the victim. His wife had told me he had an obsessive personality. He was clearly obsessed with Ms. Salas.

"Who do you think had a motive to murder her?"

He leaned forward and lowered his voice. "The top of my list would be the principal. Mr. Kapitsa didn't get along with her."

"But he spoke about admiring her at her memorial."

Vinnie scoffed, "What did you expect? She was dead."

"I didn't know they fought."

"Everyone knew. She accused him of harassing the girls. He responded by saying she encouraged sexual promiscuity. She came back that he disrupted her classes. He countered that she undermined his authority. STONY ESTANCIA SURFS didn't mention their names, but posts about this ongoing spat appeared regularly."

I was still recording. "Anyone else?"

"Next on my list." He stopped and popped another cookie into his mouth. I followed his lead.

He was enjoying my rapt attention to his every word.

"Have you met Cha Cha Bragg-Fowler, the heiress?"

I nodded.

"Between the PTA meetings and Tish's society postings, I have a good idea about her."

I waited for him to continue.

"Cha Cha is a classic matriarch. She'd do anything to protect her family and position. Did you know her skinny husband was a bully, and she was a child abuser?"

He paused to check my reaction. I gave him my best WTH expression.

"Ms. Salas knew the family's secrets," he said with a smile.

"Really?" I encouraged him to continue.

'Emmy performance,' clapped Fitch.

"Cha Cha expected deference and flexibility, while Ms. Salas saw everything as black and white."

That, at least, matched my observations. Lucy rigidly followed all the rules.

He continued, "Ms. Salas was getting ready to expose the Fowlers. Mrs. Bragg-Fowler did her in to stop her."

This had been a fruitful discussion. Mr. Kapitsa and Charlene Bragg-Fowler moved up my list of suspects.

Fitch was less sanguine, *'He's misdirecting us.'*

Why had Vinnie abused his position as the school district network administrator? If his actions were known, they could destroy his business and mean jail time. Why was he so eager to supply me with leads?

Only one answer made sense. He was the one who murdered Lucy and he'd try anything to deflect me from his trail. Better to be suspected as a hacker than a murderer.

As soon as I left Purcell and Associates, I called Senior Detective Yukawa. "I've solved Lucy's murder. Vinnie did it."

"I love your confidence. Did Mr. Purcell confess?"

"I wish, but my intuition tells me that he's the one."

"Really?"

"The first clue was all his guns. Purcell and Associates has no reason to own a small armory. Fitch says that they're not registered."

"I can't argue with you there. We didn't find any weapons in his name."

"As I expected!" I crowed.

"Next, his business is a front for illegal activities—no advertising, few customers, but successful. He lives in a big house at the top of the hill."

Vicki agreed, "Our financial forensics turned up large payments, untraceable and unrelated to his activities in Stony."

"Finally, he freely admitted breaking into confidential files. I have it all recorded. I'm sending you the sound file. That alone should lock him away."

"I just received the attachment. I'll send it to our surveillance team for analysis."

"He was running a college entrance scam and Lucy threatened to expose him. That was his motive. What's more, he delivered those warning notes to Lucy and placed those fireworks in my apartment entry."

"That's still an enormous leap. How did you get from reading confidential files to a college entrance scam and murder? I don't see the connection."

"Good question. Listen to the sound file. He hacked into school district databases. He accused Mr. Kapitsa and Cha Cha of murder. He's being super helpful because he's the culprit."

"Gosh, that's good, but not enough. Do you have any idea how he murdered her? The autopsy is still baffling Persey. She told me that gas chromatography and colorimetric analyses came back with no evidence of poison. For another clue, her autopsy found traces of aluminum in that trauma wound on Ms. Salas's scalp."

"Are you saying that the coroner supports Kapitsa's fantasy of natural death?"

"No. Absolutely not. She still says it's foul play, but the cause of death eludes her. Did Mr. Purcell say anything that might help the coroner?"

"No, but I'm sure he'll crack under interrogation."

"Let's cover all bases. I'll get a subpoena and search warrant so we can take Mr. Purcell in for questioning while the electronic forensics team searches his office for evidence. We can go in tomorrow morning"

"I'm afraid I might have tipped him off with all my questions. He could already be destroying evidence."

"Good point. I'll put a rush on this, and we'll go in this afternoon."

"Perfect. I'll start packing for the cruise."

"Just to be clear. I am not closing the investigation until we have a solid case. All we now have is hearsay, circumstantial evidence, and your intuition."

Regardless of Vicki's apprehensions, I felt certain we'd soon have Mr. Purcell in custody.

'No one is just waiting around for you to arrest them,' Fitch reminded me.

This was something drilled into all detectives. We were trained not to make the mistake of expecting everyone to passively stand by while we solved the case. Witnesses spoke to their friends and changed their stories. Bystanders became involved. Suspects formed coalitions and erected diversions. The police weren't the only actors on the stage. They weren't even the stars.

I had this forcefully driven home when Brooklynn took center stage.

While I parked the Mini in my garage, a Stony PD officer waved to me. He was the same one I'd seen moonlighting at the high school gate on Saturday. "Any problems, Officer Tsui?"

"None, Mr. Szilard. The forensics techs have gathered all the trace evidence and your condo association has repaired the door."

I doubted the Stony PD normally stationed an officer at a damaged door. The least I could do was be polite. "Thank you for keeping guard."

I was eager to share our breakthrough and the imminent arrest of Vinnie. However, Stony Estancia was a small town, and I didn't want word to get back to him. "I just spoke to Detective Yukawa, and we don't expect any more trouble."

"Wonderful. I'll head back to HQ," he replied while walking to his black and white.

As Officer Tsui drove away, I carried my empty suitcase up from where I stored it in the garage. I had an uninterrupted block of time to pack, longer than usual. This would be a trip where I didn't forget my pajamas or toothbrush.

I opened the fridge searching for lunch. A couple of leftover pizza boxes greeted me. I slid them into the microwave.

I selected clothes to put in my suitcase while repeating "eight days and seven nights."

When the pizza beeped, I sat down for a relaxing lunch.

Pizza is the perfect food. It includes the four food groups of my childhood—milk, meat, fruits and vegetables, and bread. This reflected the four segments of agribusiness. Beyond nutrition, pizza was the pinnacle of eco-friendly fast food. No paper plates. No plastic forks. Our waste disposal company even recycled the boxes. Nothing destined for landfill.

While chewing a tasty mixture of fresh tomatoes, mozzarella cheese, and basil, I tapped my phone to check Stony Estancia High School on social media. Go Bruins. The top story was a spaghetti lunch organized by the Ecology Club. Brooklynn urged everyone to *be prepared*. Why did they choose something like pasta that required dishes and cutlery? Brooklynn would never have allowed paper plates or plastic forks. Did she expect each student to bring a plate and fork from home? Is that what she meant by *be prepared*?

The next Stony High post was about prom. I took another bite of pizza and sipped my cold Corona before following the link to the prom website. This year's theme was Reuse and Reunite reflecting the influence of Brooklynn and the Ecology Club. The prom committee invited all students, alumni, and teachers, encouraging everyone to reuse the prom dresses and suits from previous years—from friends and family. The publicity included pictures—blasts from the past—miniskirts, bell bottoms, disco suits, and big hairdos. It cautioned against hairspray, glitter, and non-biodegradable makeup.

What could I wear?

I went to my closet. It held enough to pack for the cruise but nothing for a reuse prom. Somehow, I'd find something.

The dance was Friday night. After arresting Lucy's murderer and packing for the cruise, Vicki and I could fit it into our schedule. The website advertised "Tickets at the door." I would enjoy seeing the students dressed up.

My phone received an alert from STONY ESTANCIA SURFS, WHO IS SHOWING TOO MUCH SKIN? I ignored this clickbait. It could have been a sale on leather furniture or a feature about adoptable kittens at the Stony animal center.

My next alert was a text from Vicki, GET TO THE HIGH SCHOOL. NOW. with a link to the *too much skin* story. This time I clicked.

César had posted videos from the Stony High courtyard. The first one was a couple of boys with no shirts and NO MORE DRESS CODE! written on their bare chests. The next clip showed a pair of girls wearing cami tops and holding a poster: OUR BODIES. OUR LIVES. Both videos showed a crowd of unruly adolescents in the background. I didn't need to scroll any further. I grabbed a to-go slice of pizza and soon my black-and-white Mini was turning right off Higgs Road and heading to the school.

I was stunned that my well-behaved students had staged a protest. I was torn. One part of me congratulated them for breaking free, but another part was disappointed that they were being so rowdy.

As I pulled into the parking lot, it struck me. I got the joke. The spaghetti lunch had nothing to do with pasta. It was Brooklynn's code for the girls to wear forbidden spaghetti straps to demonstrate against the dress code.

As shown in César's videos, the courtyard was chaotic.

Mr. Kapitsa was moving from one student to the next writing referrals, "You're banned from prom." Every time he approached someone the crowd roared, "Harassment!" Then they gathered around him chanting, "Me too!" and "Lock him up!"

Mrs. Wilson shadowed him like his personal security detail, looking like Aunt Polly chasing so many Tom Sawyers. When someone approached too close, she pulled them from the melee and handed them over to a police officer. Just like with the lockdown, the Stony PD had requested aid from neighboring forces. I recognized Karl and Susan from San Amano.

I jumped up on one of the low brick walls that dotted the courtyard and tried to figure out who was in charge. The students were running amok in the center, and the police were around the edges, avoiding the conflagration. They had no experience with protests and weren't about to use force on these privileged students. This was Stony Estancia, not Los Angeles. If the students weren't in danger, they could do as they pleased.

The police had revealed their weakness—velvet gloves without iron fists. The more they backed away, the more daring the students became. Adding to the chaos were César and Tish with their big camera and microphone that screamed, *See yourself in the news.*

Kapitsa, never known for creativity, wrote detention slips and banned people from prom. A futile effort. I had no sympathy for him. He'd brought this on himself.

Mrs. Wilson was more effective, dragging the most disruptive students away and parking them with uniformed officers. These shirtless students—they were all boys—each paired with a cop from the Stony Estancia or San Amano police departments. I had to smile. I was uncertain which member of these odd couples was more embarrassed.

'Just like Cha Cha said, they don't arrest the girls.'

The students could have walked away from their guard whenever they wished, but it was a game. If Mrs. Wilson tagged you, you stood politely in police custody. Charlie was having a friendly discussion with Officer Susan from San Amano. They were both smiling and might have continued except Brooklynn joined them and sent Charlie back into the action.

That was the game. Mrs. Wilson captured students and Brooklynn freed them. As much as Mrs. Wilson tried, as crazy as she got—running around and screaming, she could never bring calm. Though the scene looked like mayhem, Brooklynn was in charge. She choreographed the whole thing. If the level of energy ebbed, she offered a new chant or got a pretty girl to yell, "Harassment." If Mrs. Wilson put too many students in the penalty box, Brooklynn released them. This was her show.

Something had to be done, but no one was in charge on the side of order. Kapitsa pointlessly wrote referrals and Mrs. Wilson didn't realize she was on a hamster wheel frantically going nowhere. The teachers watched in small groups from beyond the cordon of police, amused by the principal's predicament.

I was ready to take control myself when the fire department pulled up to the school with lights flashing and sirens wailing. They opened the big gates and drove their ladder truck into the courtyard. Finally, Brooklynn's chaos had met its match. The pandemonium ceased.

Lieutenant Mutai spotted me standing on a brick wall. "We meet again Mr. Szilard."

D. R. Oestreicher

"Greetings, Lieutenant. That man in the suit is the principal. If you remove him, this will be over."

A phalanx of people in fire-fighting gear—yellow Nomex suits, full-face masks, and compressed air tanks—marched into the fray. Like when Moses parted the Red Sea, a path opened through the crowd. With the firefighters taking charge, the students reverted to their polite selves, and Lieutenant Mutai's crew escorted Mr. Kapitsa away.

Fitch waved bye-bye and said, '*See ya.*'

Mrs. Wilson dogged the firefighters, "He's the principal. What are you doing with him? Where are you taking him?" While she was upset, Mr. Kapitsa acted like the students were cheering him. He stood up in the ladder truck smiling and waving as they drove him away. His tone-deaf response demonstrated what the Ecology Club was up against. He had no idea how much the students detested him.

The buzzer sounded for the end of lunch, and everyone returned to their next period.

Just like that, Brooklynn's event was over. Had it failed? What was her objective? Had this been a wasted effort? Brooklynn hated waste.

When the courtyard cleared and the students were back in class, I got a call from Vicki and the city attorney. Mr. Kapitsa had contacted them. He pressured them to prosecute the students, especially Brooklynn. Vicki had reports from the police and fire departments. I was the eyewitness.

Vicki said that no one was hurt, and I added that there was no property damage. Thanks to the Ecology Club, there wasn't even any litter. The attorney, who had run on a campaign to keep the city out of court, cut back on jury trials, and save taxpayer money, concluded with, "These are good kids, and the school year is ending. I say we should mark it up to senioritis and forget about it. I remember my senior year at Stony High. I hung out with Dick the Stickman and Cha Cha. We were wild."

With Brooklynn and the rest of the seniors off the hook, I headed for the parking lot. I still had time to finish packing for my cruise. As I approached the gate, Brooklynn ran up to me, "Mr. Szilard, I have something for you."

192

I was still upset by the disgraceful student behavior. Brooklynn was the ringleader. I gave her my opinion, "What was the point of that? You got some front-page coverage on STONY ESTANCIA SURFS, but nothing else. You're not going to get rid of Kapitsa by throwing a tantrum like little children."

"You sound just like Ms. Salas. I'm sorry she's gone, but while she kept saying, 'Be patient,' the principal was harassing the girls. I am tired of waiting. I have a plan."

One part of me supported orderly due process, while another part realized that the adults had let this go on for too long.

"S'cuse me. Should you be the one responsible for finding a solution?"

She stood up tall. "No one else is doing anything, so, yes, I should."

After this lunchtime protest, did she have something worse for a follow-up? "What's your plan?"

She took a deep breath and shook her head whipping her ponytail back and forth. "You're too concerned about order. I won't burden you with the details." She held up a plastic freezer bag. "However, I need your help."

"What's that?"

"Evidence." I saw a cell phone inside. "This is Mr. K's. Check it out. I'm sure you'll find lots of creepy pictures of girls with bare legs and bra straps exposed."

"What happened with Ms. Salas's plan to collect affidavits?"

"She's gone. This will be better. Bring this to your girlfriend. She'll arrest him."

I accepted the plastic bag. I'd deliver it to Vicki. A stolen phone was questionable evidence, but that would be Detective Yukawa's problem.

I unzipped the bag and looked inside. It smelled odd, not plastic, something sweet and floral. "Nice touch, putting it in an evidence bag. Where did you get it? I know you don't use plastic bags."

"You're right. I hate plastic, all destined for landfill despite those fake recycling numbers they print on everything." She wiped her hands with a washing motion as if cleaning off some plastic stink. "I found it in the office, in Mrs. Wilson's desk. It looked clean." With a disgusted look, she added, "Of course, Mrs. Wilson uses plastic bags." Then she paused and momentarily reverted to being a polite honor student, "Is it okay?"

"Great," I said. "I'll give it to Detective Yukawa."

Brooklynn had proven to be more cunning than I expected. The whole protest was a diversion to steal Mr. Kapitsa's phone. Certainly, after all that excitement, he'd have no idea what happened.

I met with Detective Yukawa at the PD headquarters and conveyed Brooklynn's suspicion about the pictures of high school girls. I also told her about my concern that the polite students might spin out of control. "Can you post a few officers on campus until we can figure out what our home-grown terrorists have in mind?"

"Do you think she's dangerous?"

"She's smart. That makes her a credible threat."

"I will assign Tsui and a female officer to patrol the campus and put a couple of cars on alert to stay close by."

"Thank you." I handed her the plastic bag of evidence. "This is Mr. Kapitsa's phone. Brooklynn took it during the protest."

"Please don't tell me that you're giving me stolen property."

'Whoops,' guffawed Fitch.

Vicki wouldn't use Kapitsa's stolen phone, but I felt an obligation to Brooklynn. I offered the bag again. "I found this. Can you investigate it so we can return it to its owner? I'm sure they're missing it."

She smiled and nodded, "That's better. I'll give this to the forensic techs, but I doubt they'll get to it until we solve Ms. Salas's case."

"Done. After the murder is closed will be soon enough. We're going to arrest Vinnie this afternoon before he can destroy the evidence."

"Once again I admire your confidence, but you know that an arrest is just the beginning, and we haven't even arrested him yet."

"When do we nab him?"

She had the subpoena and search warrant. "Soon but remember this is Stony Estancia. We don't send in SWAT officers in combat gear breaking down doors."

"I agree. You and I can go first. I'm working for him, so he won't be suspicious."

"Good. After we arrest him, I can call the others to come in with the search warrant to collect evidence."

That wasn't going to work the way she expected. "He has all signals jammed. You can't call for backup until we leave the building."

"Gosh, he takes his security seriously. Plan B. I'll hold him while you go outside to signal the others."

"Perfect. Between interrogating Vinnie and the evidence collected by your computer forensics team, we'll have this wrapped up by dinner."

She said, "I can already taste the pina coladas and guacamole on the cruise ship."

I had something else I wanted to say, but instead, I listened to the hum of officers typing reports and others speaking softly into microphones for voice dictation. I found this comforting, so much ordinary activity that had nothing to do with murder or student demonstrations.

Finally, like a nervous adolescent, I wiped my sweaty palms on my shirt. I turned to Vicki, "Friday is prom. They invited the teachers. Would you be my date?"

She kissed me lightly on my cheek. "Love to, if I can find something to wear."

I didn't have a chance to explain the strange prom theme or the need for retro costumes because Vicki's team had assembled and was eager to get started.

Like many such ops, it didn't go as expected. Not even close.

Before we headed out, I briefed the team on the Purcell and Associates building. "The layout is open plan with a small waiting area and staff cubicles in the front. The single enclosed office is at the rear. That's where we'll find the suspect."

I warned everyone that Vinnie had jammed all electronic signals and we wouldn't be able to call for help once we entered.

One of the team exclaimed, "Wow. Not even city hall or the police station has electronic security like that."

Someone else added, "You be careful. It's dangerous to go into an unknown situation without backup."

Vicki interjected, "There is even more. Zarand tried to record a conversation, but when our forensics team listened to the sound file, it was useless. In addition to blocking electronic signals, they also have ultrasonic audio jammers."

That was news to me. I thought I had him recorded breaking into the school computers. Now I see that he'd spoken freely knowing I couldn't record him. This increased the importance of the afternoon's op and warned me that I'd underestimated Mr. Purcell.

'Understatement,' prophesied a smug Fitch.

Someone asked, "Should if we be prepared for armed resistance?"

"Vinnie carries a pistol and has an AR-15 in his office," I replied.

Everyone looked nervously at Detective Yukawa.

She said, "You should suit up in your body armor just to be safe."

In response to their anxious chatter, she added, "We have a good plan. Zarand and I will enter first, and you will all stay out of sight until we secure the suspect. I don't want anyone panicking."

I clarified, "Out of sight means beyond the range of the rotating CCTV cameras mounted around the perimeter."

Vicki gave me a harsh look before continuing in a calm voice, "I don't expect any trouble. Just be easy and wait for the call."

Another team member piped in, "No problem. There's a great pâtisserie just around the corner on Higgs Road."

I reminded them that I wouldn't be able to give them the *go* signal until I exited the building.

Everyone put their hands together and Vicki said, "The future belongs to those who prepare."

The team responded with, "Always prepared!"

I parked my Mini beside Vicki's unmarked vehicle and texted Mr. Purcell. His assistant, this time with rainbow hair spikes, brought us directly to his office. "Can I get you something to drink? We have French chocolate truffles this afternoon. We get them from a wonderful pâtisserie on Higgs Road."

I was going to accept his offer, but Vicki spoke first, "No thank you. This will be a short visit."

She waited for his assistant to leave before sliding the arrest warrant across his desk, "Mr. Vincent Purcell, we are here to arrest you for unauthorized computer access per PC 502(c) and to question you as a suspect in the murder of Ms. Lucinda Salas."

As Vicki and I had discussed, I approached our suspect before he could go for the gun that we knew he had under his jacket. We needn't have been concerned. Instead of reaching for his weapon, Vinnie buried his face in his hands.

In my years on the force, I'd arrested many people. Some got angry and struck out. One suspect stabbed my arm. The scar reminded me that an aggressive response was always a possibility. Others ran. Vicki had positioned herself between Vinnie and his office door against this prospect.

Suspects rarely responded like Vinnie—hiding his face like a guilty child, practically a confession. I've learned that this reaction came from folks who never expected anyone to catch them. They felt invulnerable. They believed they were the smartest one in the room. Once an arresting officer confronted them, their fantasy burst like a bubble. They disintegrated under the weight of their hubris and impending incarceration.

I approached him slowly and spoke calmly, "Please keep your hands where I can see them. I am going to remove your gun."

He didn't move as my good arm opened his jacket and reached for his pistol. I took hold of the grip with two fingers and lifted it from his shoulder holster. I was dumbstruck by how little it weighed.

"Puppies!" I yelled. "This is a replica." I tossed it away. The plastic toy clattered on the floor. I ran to the AR-15, mounted on the wall, lit by a spotlight. "This is also fake!" I checked the tactical knife and other weapons. "All fakes!"

Vicki leaned forward and in a gentle voice said, "Can you please tell me what is going on?"

He wheezed, struggling to get his words out, "W-w-where should I start?"

"At the beginning," Vicki said with a sigh.

"W-w-when I was in kindergarten...," he began.

I opened my mouth to suggest that he didn't need to go back that far, but Vicki waved me away. I sat down regretting that I hadn't accepted the offer of chocolate truffles.

Vinnie continued. "I knew how to read before I started school. The other kids treated me like I was weird."

Vicki asked, "Were you bullied?" with more sympathy than I would have offered.

"Y-yes. Boys and girls beat me up on the playground. Kids stole my homework. They dumped sand in my lunchbox. School was a constant battle."

Fitch predictably didn't believe any of this. *'He's acting.'*

Vinnie calmed down and continued, "I didn't know where to turn. My father ignored me, and my mother told me to be tough."

Vicki encouraged him, "That must have been difficult. What did you do?"

"I hid. In middle school, I worked in the library during lunch. In high school, I forged a note to excuse myself from gym. I became invisible, a chameleon fading into the background."

He buried his face in his hands.

Vicki let him rest before asking, "Then what happened?"

He sat up and spoke clearly, "In college, I met people like me. I remember a girl who told me I had to be tough. I lashed out at her with the retort I'd always imagined shouting at my mother, 'I won't be a bully. That is not the answer!'"

Vicki reached across his desk and held his hand.

"That girl explained it to me as if I didn't know anything about people, which I didn't, 'You just need to act tough. No one will bully you if you don't look like an easy target.'"

Vinnie pulled away from Vicki, sat up straight, and flexed his muscles. "That's what I have done."

I questioned our suspect, "Are you saying that you carry a toy gun to warn people away from bullying you?"

"Yes. And until you showed up, it worked."

Vicki let me go ahead with my interrogation.

"That's an interesting story, but no one shot Ms. Salas, so the toy guns don't prove anything. And what about hacking the school computers? All that stuff I saw you do with the V P N?"

Vinnie regained his composure. "That was just an act to impress *you*. I was desperate for your help to find my son. I would never do anything like that. Besides being illegal, just think about what it would do for my business."

I pressed him. "You know we already checked your financial records. How do you explain those large out-of-state payments you receive? We verified that your legitimate business is confined to Stony."

He didn't answer.

Fitch smiled, *'We've got him,'* and pantomimed restraining him in handcuffs.

I changed the subject to keep him off balance, "If you weren't the hacker, who broke into the school's computer?"

'Good question,' said Fitch.

He had an answer for that, "I already told you. No one."

"Maybe someone out there is smarter than you."

'Nice follow-up.'

That made Vinnie smile. "When an unnamed organization back in Virginia gets stymied, they call me. I know it sounds immodest, but I *am* the smartest one in the room. They pay me in untraceable funds, as I'm sure your forensic people have told you."

"Untraceable funds could be from illegal activities." I didn't understand my next comment, but I had the momentum, "*Crypto* money probably."

I paused and remembered we were still searching for Jackson. "If you have these fancy spy connections, why didn't you ask them to find your son?"

He leaned back in his chair and his arms went limp. I was wearing him down. This is the way good detectives ran an interrogation. "I did. They couldn't get a lead. My son was too smart to be tracked electronically. They recommended I get someone local. *You.*"

My chest involuntarily puffed out. I had no idea my reputation extended beyond Stony Estancia High School.

He shook his head like we were wasting his time and he was getting tired of talking to us. He turned to Vicki. "When did Ms. Salas die?"

"Monday morning, a week ago."

"Good."

He looked embarrassed. "Not good that she was murdered, but good that we can end this silly discussion. I was out of town."

I laughed, "On a secret mission for an *unnamed organization,* I suppose. One that *will disavow any knowledge of your actions,* right?"

I added sarcastically, "I saw the movie."

"True. But just let me make a phone call."

Vicki nodded.

He picked up his landline, punched in a number, and then continued typing on the phone pad. Just like on his computer, he was the fastest typist I'd ever seen.

"Give me your secure email, please."

Vicki responded and he typed some more.

He sat back and crossed his arms. In a short while, her phone beeped. She turned to me, "Didn't you tell me our phones wouldn't work?"

Vinnie gave me a self-satisfied grin.

Vickie tapped her phone and showed me the screen. I watched a surveillance tape of Mr. Purcell walking through the airport in Washington, DC. The timestamps showed it to be the Monday morning Lucy died.

I had so many questions, but none of the answers would contradict his alibi. If nothing else, he'd proven that he had connections beyond our small village.

Fitch stated the obvious with no shame for having been so wrong, '*Um, wrong suspect.*'

Vinnie might have been smart about computers, but his tough-guy façade was clumsy and about to collapse. I felt bad for him. He was just a frightened nerd, somewhere on the autism spectrum. There was nothing illegal about play-acting as a *gangsta*. I felt sorry we were going to mess it up.

Vicki also understood his predicament. "Here's what we're going to do. Pick up your gun. We'll perp walk you out of here and after a brief interrogation, we'll release you. That should protect your image."

"Thank you."

Just then, we heard a loud crash in the front of the building. Vicki swung the office door open. We all saw the SWAT team in full riot gear, just like on Vinnie's website. They had broken through the steel entrance to Purcell and Associates.

When the squad leader saw Vicki looking aghast, he raised his black faceplate, backed away, and said in a soft voice, "It had been a long time and we thought you were in trouble, that you'd been taken hostage."

"Did someone say, hostage?"

Everyone turned to see César's camera poking its long lens through the smashed doorway.

César explained, "I followed the SWAT trucks from the pâtisserie."

Vicki took charge. She sent the SWAT team home. "Nice to see you, César. Did you bring your lovely wife?"

Leticia stepped in from the parking lot. *"Hola."* She walked past the cubicles to where Vicki stood just outside Mr. Purcell's office. Tish positioned her boom mic over Vicki's head and asked, "Do you have a statement?"

"Yes. The city regrets damaging Mr. Vincent Purcell's property and is grateful for his assistance in our search for Ms. Salas's killer."

She turned around and winked at Vinnie.

"Now if everyone can get back to work, we have a murderer to catch." We returned to Vinnie's office. When we were alone, she laughed. "That was plan B. Your secret is safe."

"Thanks. After this misunderstanding, I'm reconsidering my tough-guy masquerade. Getting arrested and having SWAT smash down my front door has opened my eyes. It might be time to end this charade."

Vinnie continued in the same gentle voice he used with his wife. "Let me know how I can aid your investigation."

The smartest guy in the room had just offered his services and I wasn't going to pass up this opportunity. "Thanks, Vinnie. We could use your support with some codebreaking."

His face broke out in a huge grin. "I can certainly help with that, and if I can't, I have friends who can."

"Great. I'll get the coded book from my car." My stomach grumbled. "Excuse me. My tummy would love some of those French truffles."

Vinnie smiled, "No problem. They'll be here when you return."

As I walked away, I could hear Vicki explaining, "He's always hungry. He has the metabolism of a teenager."

When I returned, I exchanged the blue book for a truffle. "I found this hidden in Ms. Salas's classroom."

While Detective Yukawa and I enjoyed our chocolate delicacies with tall glasses of cold milk, Vinnie flipped through the pages. "The little drawings are the phases of mitosis."

I'd already figured this out, but I was amazed that Vinnie recognized the rough sketches so quickly—Biology was far from his IT expertise.

Fitch laughed, *'He is the smartest one in this room.'*

"What about the coded letters? I think they are names," I prompted.

He absentmindedly sipped his milk and took small bites from a white chocolate truffle while he flipped through the pages.

"Could it be such a simple code?"

"So many Fs, Ss, Ts, and Us."

"Of course! Jack must be my son."

He put down his half-eaten truffle and wiped away his milk mustache with a linen napkin. "This is a simple plus-one Caesar cipher. A is coded as B, B is coded as C, and so on. The last entry just before Ms. Salas was killed—BOOJF—is Annie."

Vicki asked, "Did you see your son mentioned?"

"This KBDL—Jack—must be my son. I see his name in the log every month or so. Each time Ms. Salas annotated the entry with a prophase sketch—never anything else. A few months ago, his name stopped appearing."

I remembered what Jackson's mother had told me about him changing. I intuitively connected those two things.

'I bet those prophase drawings were the most frequent,' Fitch surmised, adding, *'and I'm the second smartest.'*

Vinnie must have been on the same wavelength as Fitch because he said, "Most of these sketches are prophase."

I finally deduced what prophase meant and moved forward. "Tell me about Annie."

"On the morning Ms. Salas died, Annie had a telophase drawing. The only other entries for Annie were three anaphase drawings about three months apart."

Vicki jumped in. "Those anaphase symbols must be for pre-natal vitamins—dispensed once a trimester. The telophase sketch—*telos* is Latin for end—was the birth."

I excitedly exclaimed, "Annie must be Ms. Salas's daughter."

Vicki cautiously advised, "That's a good guess, but let's not jump to conclusions. We have everyone's DNA so forensics can verify that one way or the other."

She flashed Vinnie a smile before turning back to me, "We're done arresting people based on your intuitions."

Undaunted, I completed the puzzle. "All those prophase drawings signified the condoms that she was so popular for."

'Jackson's name stopped appearing when Annie told him she was pregnant—at the same time money and career superseded his interest in art,' Fitch explained proudly.

I thought of Jackie Siegbahn isolated at home, worrying about her missing son. We had good news. The decoded logbook revealed that she was a grandmother and clarified Jackson's sudden interest in money—family finances.

'She'll be one happy grandma,' exclaimed Fitch before having second thoughts, *'unless she doesn't like Annie.'*

Regardless, Jackson was still missing. This wasn't the time to talk to Jackie. With her fragile mental condition, I didn't want to raise her hopes.

We were done at Purcell and Associates. I thanked Vinnie for the chocolates. Vicki told him we'd be in touch. I packed a couple of to-go truffles into my sling, and we exited the building through the damaged entryway. In the parking lot, the contractors had arrived to fix the door. I spied Tish and César across the street capturing B-roll footage of the strip mall.

We'd closed the Vinnie mystery. I raised my good arm to offer Vicki a congratulatory high-five, but her face told me she wasn't in a celebratory mood.

Her glum expression didn't discourage me. I had a plan.

Vicki said, "Why do I listen to you when you're so often wrong?"

'Here it comes,' warned Fitch.

"Our evidence was all hearsay and circumstantial. I should have known better than to act on your intuition."

Fitch, with his retrospective brilliance, seconded Vicki's criticism, *'Vinnie's one of the good guys. Why did you think you could pin the murder rap on him?'*

"Eliminating Mr. Purcell brings us one step closer to closing the case," I offered to counter these defeatists.

Vicki was not encouraged, "Before you say anymore, I'm not arresting anyone else without solid evidence. If I'd been thinking more clearly, I wouldn't have wasted time with the unfortunate Mr. Purcell. We should have waited for the DNA results. We would have known about Annie."

I didn't argue or point out that we didn't have DNA from Annie. Like Jackson, she'd gone missing before we collected those samples. Just because I was wrong about Vinnie didn't mean that my methods were flawed. Nothing works every time.

I took a positive approach. "We've removed Dr. Fowler, the reformed bully with surgeon's hands, and Vinnie Purcell, the bodybuilding, smartest guy in the room, from our suspect list. That leaves Cha Cha Bragg-Fowler, the heiress, and Mr. Kapitsa."

'It's Kapitsa,' chimed in Fitch.

I was ready to accuse the principal, but Vicki had been clear that she didn't want to hear my intuitions. I took a different approach. "You have the principal's phone. Let me know what your forensic people discover."

"Are you referring to that lost phone you found?"

I recalled our little fiction. "Yes, that one."

"Okay. I'll be reviewing the forensic evidence, especially the DNA. I told you that we'd solve this crime in the lab."

We didn't need more lab work, but Vicki didn't appear open to discussing it. I raised my good arm, palm forward, fingers splayed, signaling surrender. "I'll leave the murder to you. I'm going to find Annie, Jackson, and the child. With her head of black braids, and his short, white hair, they should be an easy couple to spot."

That was my misdirection. I intended to solve the murder. Annie and Jackson were the parents—I didn't need to wait for the DNA results. What mattered to me was that they were the last ones to see Ms. Salas alive. Whether they knew it or not, they held the key to finding Lucy's killer. I would question them and clear up all the mysteries.

I waited until Vicki drove away before I waved to César and Tish. "Annie Landau and Jackson Siegbahn were the last ones to see Ms. Salas alive. Can you help me find them?"

I omitted my *intuitions*—that Annie was Lucy's daughter, that Lucy was the midwife Dorothea Ghez, and that Jackson and Annie were the parents of a newborn. Everyone understood the need to interview murder witnesses, so, that would be enough for these reporters to track them down.

Tish looked up from her phone. "They both have social media accounts. What a cute couple—all those black braids and his white crew cut—a study in contrasts."

César said, "How about: HAVE YOU SEEN THESE TWO? THEY KNOW WHO KILLED THE STONY HIGH TEACHER."

Tish countered, "Too long. THESE STUDENTS WITNESSED A MURDER is better."

César loaded his equipment into their van. "We'll A/B test both teasers and see which works best."

As they drove away, Leticia waved and called, "We'll let you know when we find them."

My gut told me that the new parents were still in Stony Estancia. I flashed back to Annie's distress when the Ecology Club uncovered Tristeza's grave in the science garden. She had been just days away from delivering her own child. No wonder that infant's skeleton upset her.

Now she and Jackson were on their own. My chest tightened and I gasped at the thought of those frightened teenagers with a newborn. Being teenagers, they might not realize that they needed help, but they did. I had to figure out where they were hiding. That was my top priority. Lucy's killer and the cruise could wait. A methodical search would take time, but we'd locate them. All police departments are trained for this. As long as we didn't panic, we'd find the new family soon enough.

Fitch agreed, *'The two of them are doing their best to feed and comfort the child. They might be exhausted, but no one's in any danger.'*

I had time for dinner and a good night's rest. I'd delegated the detective work to the internet. STONY ESTANCIA SURFS was digitally knocking on doors to find the new parents. With all those eyeballs, how hard could it be to find a teenage couple with a new baby? Especially one as distinctive as Annie and Jackson.

When the sunny suburb woke up, people drank their morning coffee and checked the web. Jackson and Annie smiled at them from the front page of STONY ESTANCIA SURFS. I waited for the internet to do its magic.

With time on my hands, I decided on crepes for breakfast. I mixed eggs, milk, melted butter, and flour in my blender. After a few quick pulses, the batter went into the refrigerator to rest. My recipe said, PREPARE THE FILLINGS, so I went online and ordered mascarpone, crème fraîche, an assortment of berries, and powdered sugar.

I waited—for the fillings to be delivered—for the bubbles to subside so the crepes wouldn't tear—for the internet to find Annie.

I called Vicki but she replied with a text, LATER. MEETINGS ALL MORNING.

No problem. I relaxed knowing my grocery order was on its way. I was a modern, high-tech detective, crowd sourcing leads. After a good breakfast, I'd know where to find the missing children and solve the murder.

I went out on the balcony and listened to the finches while browsing STONY ESTANCIA SURFS. I scrolled past the pictures of Jackson and Annie. The Stony Estancia All-Stars had defeated the San Amano team in the girls' softball tournament. The animal center had a collection of adoptable kittens.

'Cute,' purred Fitch, 'You need one of those.'

The STONY ESTANCIA SURFS posts continued with benches installed at the Pauli Falls trailhead. The patisserie in Higgs Road was having a sale on madeleines.

I loved this sunny suburb and could get used to being an internet detective.

Unfortunately, I misjudged the situation.

ALEJANDRA: WEDNESDAY BREAKFAST

After checking STONY ESTANCIA SURFS, my secondhand plaid sofa called me for a nap. A cellphone alert flashed before I could get comfortable. It was too soon for the groceries and Vicki was in meetings, so I assumed Leticia had located Jackson. That was great news. The crepes would keep, and I was eager to talk to the last people to see Ms. Salas alive.

But it wasn't Tish, it was my video doorbell—fully operational again after I peeled off the googly eye. Brooklynn and Toby were downstairs.

'Look again.'

When I rechecked the low-res image, it wasn't Toby. No earring. She was with Charlie. It was about time. Toby wasn't her type.

I buzzed them in.

Before I could ask why they weren't in school, I noticed Charlie was upset. He looked like he might break down into tears, but Brooklynn was all business.

She pointed to the sofa. "Charlie, sit down and try to hold yourself together."

He pursed his lips and hugged himself as he collapsed into the worn cushions.

I addressed Brooklynn, "Whassup?"

"Annie's missing."

Why was Charlie distressed? I hadn't seen Annie this week, but nobody had seen Jackson for even longer—since Lucy's demise. Vinnie's secret spy agency couldn't even trace him. Why did Brooklynn say Annie was missing? Surely, the kids knew where the new parents were, and someone was already reporting their whereabouts to César and Tish.

'You're not seeing the whole picture,' said Fitch stating the obvious.

"Isn't she with Jackson?" I asked hoping to unravel this mystery.

No response.

I probed again, "If Jackson and Annie aren't together, who has the baby?"

Someone had to be with the baby, only days old.

'Unless the baby was stillborn, like Tristeza,' Fitch speculated in his unhelpful way.

Teen miscarriages were rare, but not unheard of. I braced myself for the worst.

Brooklynn shook her head, "We don't know where the baby is either. Can I start at the beginning?"

"Yes, please. From the beginning."

Brooklynn said, "This is a long story."

"No problem." I pointed to Charlie sitting on my recycled sofa. For Brooklynn's benefit, I boasted, "It's from Schrödinger's Secondhand Store, Stony's premier recycled furniture emporium—YOU CAN'T KNOW WHAT WE HAVE UNTIL YOU OBSERVE."

Brooklynn gave me a thumbs-up and joined him. She asked, "You know about the baby, right?"

Was she asking about Annie's pregnancy or the infant's death or something else?

I didn't need to disclose my ignorance because the groceries arrived. "I'll be making crepes while you tell me what happened. Take all the time you need. We can have breakfast together."

Charlie graced us with a half-smile.

I worked with a minimum of clatter while she recounted the story, "Jackson was supposed to Safe Surrender the newborn and return to school, but no one has heard from him. We don't know where he is."

The child was alive! That was a relief.

Charlie whispered, "We assumed he was depressed and had driven into the desert. He'd done that before."

"Amen," said Brooklynn. "Jackson took things hard. I saw it in his eyes when Alejandra—" She interrupted herself, "They named the girl Alejandra."

"W-w-we told them not to name her."

'They were there when Ms. Salas—Dorothea Ghez— delivered the baby. They are also witnesses.'

I shushed Fitch to let Brooklynn continue. Good detectives never interrupted witnesses.

"We wished to give the child a nice sendoff to Safe Surrender, something that was loving, but final. We wrapped her in a silk blanket and entrusted the tiny bundle to Jackson."

Charlie spoke in a monotone, "I told the infant we all loved her and gave her a blessing for her adventure ahead. Ms. Salas kissed her fingers and toes."

I noticed Brooklynn's eyes tearing as she continued the narrative, "Jackson adjusted her little knit hat, put on her cotton mittens, and kept repeating her name. We'd all agreed that it was his job to Safe Surrender the baby, but he wasn't happy about it."

Brooklynn took a deep breath and Charlie continued, "We'd done the research. The closest place was the firehouse on Higgs Road. We had a car seat from Schrödinger's and the completed forms."

Brooklynn recovered. In a slightly angry voice, she said, "Jackson should have dropped her off and returned in under an hour. The firehouse isn't that far, and it was too early for traffic."

I served everyone raspberry and blueberry crepes. While they ate ravenously, I reviewed the new facts. The infant was healthy. Lucy delivered Annie's baby with the father, Jackson, and these two friends in attendance. Shortly after the birth, the father and child disappeared. Brooklynn and Charlie expected Jackson to Safe Surrender the baby.

I volunteered my news, "I checked with that firehouse, and they haven't received an infant. Lieutenant Mutai assured me any Safe Surrender would be all over the internet. We haven't heard anything, so he still has her."

I could see the gears whirring in Brooklynn's head as she processed this information.

Charlie spoke first, "S-s-so Alejandra is with Jackson. B-b-but where are they?"

Brooklynn added, "And where is Annie?"

'Simplex sigillum veri.'

"Don't you think she joined him?" I suggested.

"M-m-maybe."

I made another round of crepes, waiting to see if they had more to say. We finished the blueberries, raspberries, and crème fraîche, so these were strawberry crepes with mascarpone. While they ate, I pondered aloud, "I've been in touch with Jackson's parents. They don't know where he is. What about Annie's?"

Brooklynn said, "When Annie was born, she was a Safe Surrender baby. That's where she got the idea."

'Um, that explains why Lucy didn't know Annie was her daughter,' interjected Fitch. *'The law protects the anonymity of the mother, so even though Lucy knew she'd had a daughter and Annie knew her birth mother was out there someplace, neither made the connection. Confidentiality was not their friend.'*

"Annie had bad luck and wasn't adopted. By kindergarten, she had resigned herself to living in the foster care system. She joked that it was her curly dark hair."

'Unfortunately, she was right,' said Fitch raising his fist in a Black Lives Matter salute.

A sad realization came over me. Ms. Salas didn't know she was delivering her granddaughter. Annie didn't know her mother was at her side during the birth.

Brooklynn continued, "In second grade, Mr. and Mrs. Landau fostered Annie."

Charlie added, "Th-th-they were nice, an older couple without any children. After they became her guardians, we expected them to adopt her, but they didn't."

A few years ago, the courts emancipated Annie when the Landaus moved to a retirement village in Arizona."

"S'cuse me. Did they know she was pregnant?"

"Of course, I called Mrs. Landau when the baby was born and told her about the Safe Surrender. She always called me her second foster daughter," Brooklynn said proudly.

"Do you think Annie and Jackson took the baby to Arizona?"

"Good guess, Mr. Detective, but, as I said, I'm close with Mrs. Landau. She's not a person who keeps secrets. Neither Annie nor Jackson is in Arizona."

"What about Annie's apartment?"

"Just her roommates," Charlie said.

"They have no clue," Brooklynn added with contempt.

I considered the anonymity provisions of the Safe Surrender Law—how different this might have turned out if Lucy and Annie had reunited.

'Focus,' Fitch chided me.

I was speaking with the last people to see Ms. Salas alive so I asked, "What happened after Jackson left?"

Brooklynn began, less upset now that we weren't talking about the newborn, "At first, everything went according to plan. Ms. Salas stayed with Annie, feeding her juice, cleaning her up—there was so much blood—and dressing her. Annie was in good spirits."

"W-w-we went to work straightening up the room. I took a bag of stuff to the dumpsters. In between housekeeping, we comforted Annie, promising her the best breakfast ever. She asked for fried chicken, waffles, grits, ham, corn fritters, and a banana smoothie." Charlie stopped talking and looked to Brooklynn.

In a soft voice, Brooklynn added, "Annie interrupted our work shouting, 'Where is he?' I looked at the clock. He'd been gone too long."

The energy drained for my narrators as they relived these disturbing events.

Brooklynn ate the last of her strawberry crepe in silence.

'She's sad about something. Alejandra died,' Fitch put his gloomy spin on the situation.

I wanted to hurry them along, but experience had taught me to let them go at their own pace.

Children laughed in the Higgs Haven playground. Someone swam laps in the pool.

Finally, Charlie resumed his recollection of that unfortunate morning. "Annie collapsed in tears when Ms. Salas said, 'We can't stay here. School is going to start.'"

Charlie shook his head before he continued, "Between sobs, Annie said, 'He doesn't love me anymore. He ran away. The Landaus ran away. Everyone runs away!' We all hugged her, but we couldn't soothe her."

This was like a trauma tag team. Charlie couldn't go on, so Brooklynn did, "Ms. Salas got an ice pop from her little fridge. Annie took a few licks and threw it on the floor. 'I want real food!' she shrieked. We abandoned our unfinished cleaning chores to take Annie home."

That memory made Brooklynn angry, "That was classic Ms. Salas denying the big issue, just like with Mr. Kapitsa. Annie sobbed all the way home, but when the sun came up, she demanded a shower, that banana smoothie, and to see her friends at school."

Annie was in my class that morning. That seemed to be so long ago. She contributed to Lucy's remembrance. Her fond recollections appeared in a different light now that I knew that Ms. Salas had just delivered her child. The memories were bittersweet knowing that they were mother and daughter.

"Sh-she didn't show up at church last Sunday and we haven't seen her since."

Fitch was strangely silent. Lucy had been alive when my star witnesses left the scene. They weren't witnesses after all. Jackson and the baby had vanished, as had Annie. Had she joined Jackson and the child?

I closed our discussion with, "César and Tish have posted pictures of Jackson and Annie on STONY ESTANCIA SURFS. You should go to school and talk with your friends. Please let me know as soon as you find them."

Two somber adolescents climbed down the stairs. I watched from the balcony as they drove away. I took a moment to enjoy the children playing, silently reminding their parents to hug them every night. Then I made another crepe.

I was eating that crepe with just powdered sugar when my phone rang. "Hello, Vicki. Thanks for returning my call."

I took a deep breath, "Forget about the cruise. Forget about everything. Let me tell you about the infant." I couldn't wait to give her my news. "The baby's name is Alejandra."

"Okay but listen. I have something important to tell you."

She wasn't interested in the name. What could be more important? "The baby has a name," I repeated. I expected her to be more excited. It told me that the parents cared. I expected to find Annie with the infant because she had named the child, her child. "The baby's name is Alejandra."

"Listen Szilard! Just shut up!"

Vicki never spoke to me like that.

'Just listen,' scolded Fitch. *'You never learn anything when your mouth is open.'*

She exhaled and spoke deliberately, pausing between words. "My lab collected as much baby blood as they could. They sent it to Stony Estancia Hospital for newborn screening."

Fitch put his hands together making an impromptu megaphone, "Bad news! Listen up for the bad news," he announced to an imaginary crowd.

I froze. "Puppies. Puppies," I whispered.

"Puppies is right," she said. "The baby...Alejandra...has low TRECs."

WTH. "What the heck?"

"TRECs are T-cell receptor excision circles but don't worry about that. She might have SCID—Severe Combined Immunodeficiency. Now you can worry."

I knew about SCID. I saw the *Bubble Boy* movie where even the mildest infection was life-threatening.

"Alejandra needs further testing immediately, and is likely to require a bone marrow transplant, which must happen within the next few days."

No problem I thought. Tish and César had already found Alejandra. I confidently checked my email, but nothing, nada. I should never have counted on the internet.

Vicki went on, "Incidentally, DNA tests have confirmed Jackie Siegbahn and Ms. Salas are the grandmothers. Those kids are the parents."

Annie had been missing for a week. Where did they get her DNA?

'Um, duh, that was her blood in that puddle on the floor,' said Fitch.

Those DNA results would have been happier news if baby Alejandra's life hadn't been in danger.

Vicki spoke rapidly, "I've taken everyone off the high school cases and assigned them to find the newborn. I authorized overtime. The clock is ticking. We put out an Amber Alert. My team is interviewing students, teachers, and Jackson's parents. Others are at the church, and we're tracking down Annie's foster parents in Arizona. The internet teams will chat with the writers that Jackson befriended in Vancouver."

She took a deep breath and sighed. "This is urgent. An infant's life is at stake. I'll even listen to Fitch."

"Fitch and I will do what we can. Something is already up on STONY ESTANCIA SURFS."

"Oh no! HIPAA protects Alejandra's medical condition. You can't tell anyone about her test results and the risk of SCID."

We had to balance the infant's life with her privacy. As with Safe Surrender, privacy was a two-edged sword. "I only told our internet reporters we were looking for Annie and Jackson as witnesses to Ms. Salas's murder. I didn't even mention the child."

"Good. That was a perfect cover story. Now is the time for your intuitive detective magic."

"Thank you. I'll let you know as soon as I find them."

"Good luck," she said before she broke the connection.

This was serious if Vicki was willing to listen to Fitch and my intuition. Fortunately, when Alejandra's life was held in the balance my gut feelings delivered.

Vicki deployed her people to cover all the bases. I scraped my blender with a silicone spatula for one final crepe. I rolled it like a taquito and dipped it into a jar of peanut butter.

The sticky treat made it impossible to talk, but I kept thinking. Where were Annie and Jackson? His friends thought he drove into the desert. She had stood up to Richie, the bully, for a handful of beads. A woman like that wasn't going to allow Jackson to endanger her child. What did she want? Where did he go?

Fitch had the breakthrough, *'Forget them. Find Alejandra.'*

He was right. By visualizing the infant, a small human wrapped in swaddling, his insight came to me. I searched for FAMILY SHELTERS NEAR ME. The internet reported 134,000,000 RESULTS. How was all this spam, clickbait, and advertising going to lead me to Alejandra? Why did I even turn to the internet?

'You're the detective. Find the clues,' Fitch encouraged me.

I wrote down the best leads ignoring the listicles, self-help advice, distant shelters, and obvious scams. So much useless information. After many phone calls, only three addresses remained. I imagined recounting this process to Vicki, "That internet will never replace human detectives."

The Stony Estancia Family Shelter was first. It was the closest—just a few miles down Higgs Road. I drove as fast as I could—the traffic lights turned red at the most inopportune times impeding my progress. Being in an ambulance with a siren and flashing lights would have been helpful.

I found the address in a residential neighborhood. A small, detached house painted pale yellow with tan trim. Like the other homes on the street, it had security bars on the windows and a video doorbell. Was it big enough to be a family shelter? Was I in the wrong place? My fingers tapped on my phone to repeat the web search—verify the address. Had my browser served up an old listing? Had they moved?

I was cursing the internet for never forgetting anything—no matter how out-of-date or obsolete—when I noticed a small plaque reading STONY ESTANCIA FAMILY SHELTER above the buzzer. This was the right place. I pressed the button and stepped back so the camera could see me, nervously hopping from foot to foot.

The doorbell said, "Can I help you?"

"I am Zarand Szilard." I held up my school ID.

The doorbell didn't respond.

"I am looking for Jackson Siegbahn, Annie Landau, and their newborn daughter."

"Sorry, I can't help you."

'Can't or won't,' Fitch snapped back.

"But I'm on an important mission. I must find the infant." I almost told the doorbell about TRECs and a life-or-death emergency but remembered Vicki's warning against disclosure.

An electronic bolt whirred, double locking the entrance. The doorbell repeated, "Sorry, I can't help you. Please leave before I call security."

I said, "Not necessary."

'Wrong approach,' critiqued Fitch, *'but this is the right place.'*

I didn't let Fitch discourage me. Shelters offered a sanctuary for victims of domestic violence. They had to be cautious. Next time, I'd give them better identification.

'And don't be so anxious. I wouldn't open the door for you either—jumping around like a cat in heat.'

I didn't waste time critiquing myself. I ran to the car, knowing how to do better the next time. Alejandra depended on me.

I checked my GPS and headed west. After who-knows-how-many red lights, I was at a nondescript storefront. This place was bigger but still didn't seem very inviting—more like a small warehouse than a home.

I took a deep cleansing breath to calm myself and entered the reception area. The receptionist's name plate said, DANA

(THEY/THEM/THEIR). In a calm voice, I said, "Good morning, Dana. I'm a teacher at Stony Estancia High School." I showed them my school ID and my driver's license.

"I am looking for a couple of students who are caring for a newborn. I showed them the pictures from the news website. Landau and Siegbahn."

I remembered that he had ditched his driver's license. "He might be using a different name."

The receptionist typed slowly on their computer, being careful to not let me see the screen. "Sorry, I can't help you."

I wasn't going to give up that easily. "I must find the infant. This is a life-or-death situation. There's an Amber Alert. You can check." I couldn't say more without violating HIPAA regulations.

They placed one hand under the counter where I assumed they had a panic button. "I am just the receptionist. The rules are firm. Someone comes in pleading life-or-death every week."

"Can I speak to your supervisor?"

They graced this with a half-smile. "Certainly. They'll be in this evening."

I was wasting time. I had one more place to check, so I said, "Thank you."

'No improvement,' chided Fitch.

I needed an even better approach. The baby could have been at either of those places, but I hadn't passed the security screening. Alejandra was dying of TRECs and SCID. I was making no progress. The last place on my list was east of Stony Estancia. San Amano.

Time was important. I wasn't going to risk the perfidy of the traffic lights again. I got on the Desert Freeway and drove into the morning sun, speeding past the rush hour traffic that blocked the other side of the highway, weaving between lanes, and hoping to avoid the CHP. Luck was with me, and I arrived without any difficulties.

That place was painted in bright colors with a playground and a basketball court. It might have been a childcare center except for the barbed wire topping the tall fence. Finally. This was what I imagined when I visualized a family shelter.

As soon as I entered the building, a security guard led me into a holding room with a small table, two chairs on either side, and what I was sure was a two-way mirror.

I sat down and waited.

After a few minutes, a young woman in a tee shirt and jeans entered. "You're Mr. Szilard, right?"

"Yes ma'am, I am," I said with my most disarming smile.

"We've been expecting you. Let me save you some time."

"Thank you." This was it. Success.

"When someone checks into our shelter, or any shelter, they write a list of acceptable visitors. You are not on any of our lists. Unless you work for law enforcement *and* have an unquestionable reason to be here, client confidentiality and safety come first."

I understood their caution. If Jackson and the child were in one of these places, I'd need to come back with Vicki in her uniform driving a black and white, preferably with a court order.

I considered disclosing Alejandra's medical condition, but with no documentation, no relation to the child, and no official reason to be there, I'd just sound crazy.

I said, "Thank you," and returned to my car, hoping the infant had enough life left to survive this bureaucracy.

"Whassup, Zarand," Vicki answered her phone. "Did you find the baby?"

"Fitch thinks so and you said you'd listen to Fitch."

"I did say that." She sounded exhausted. "What do you have?"

"The infant is at the Stony Estancia Family Shelter, but they won't talk to me."

I could hear people in the background trying to get Senior Detective Yukawa's attention. With a sigh, she asked, "Gosh, what do *you* need?"

"I need you to look official and visit the shelter. A court order would be even better."

"There's no time for a court order, but I'll look as official as I can."

"Perfect. I'll meet you at police headquarters. We can drive together."

Vicki wore her dress uniform with all the insignias and ribbons. We arrived in a black and white escorted by another one, both flashing their lights. My friend Tsui and a female officer went with her when she pressed the video doorbell. I waited in her car.

I anxiously watched her talking through the intercom. She looked very official. Would she pass their security screen? We didn't have any official authorization—only whatever courtesy that might come with the uniforms. Knowing the Stony PD, I expected they had good relations with the shelter.

While Vicki and her deputies spoke to the doorbell, I puzzled about how the yellow house with barred windows could have sufficient space for a family shelter.

Looking down the street, a security guard exited another home. He looked around before a young lady pushing a stroller joined him. He escorted her to the building where Vicki waited. When they arrived, the door opened, and they disappeared inside. That explained the size of the shelter. It included other buildings in the vicinity.

With Vicki still waiting, I opened the car door, thinking that they needed my help. If the shelter was requesting more information, I'd spoken to Brooklynn and Charlie and knew all the details. Vicki must have seen my movement because she flicked her hand signaling me to stay put. I closed the door but opened the window so I could hear what was going on.

Vicki said, "Yes, I understand. Can you tell them we're here?"

Fitch did a happy dance on the roof of the squad car, chanting, '*We found them.*'

I missed the intervening conversation.

Vicki said, "Thank you," and returned to the car. Officer Tsui and his partner departed to resume patrolling the high school.

Vicki said with a sigh, "The only person on the visitor list is Jackson's mother."

"Well, that's awkward. She doesn't leave the house."

"I know, but Vinnie brought her to the police station for her DNA test. Surely, he can bring her here."

I called Purcell and Associates on speaker. "This is Mr. Szilard. I must speak to Mr. Purcell about his son."

"Vinnie here. What do you need?" he whispered. From the background noise, I deduced he was in a meeting.

Delivering good news was my favorite part of being a detective. "We found your son, and Annie, and the child." I omitted the dire information about the newborn screening results.

"That's great," he said, sounding distracted. I expected more excitement.

"One problem," I said, ready to dive right into his wife's condition.

He didn't reply. The background noise now sounded like an argument.

I charged ahead, "The only person he'll see is your wife. Can you bring her to the Stony Estancia Family Shelter?" I didn't understand his whispered reply. I turned up my phone volume to max. "Can you repeat that?"

He said, "I'd love to, but I'm in—" He lowered his voice further. "I'm out of town. I don't know when I'll return. I must go now. Thanks for finding Jackson. You can text me your invoice."

Before I could remind him that there wasn't going to be an invoice, he broke the connection.

Vicki said, "It's up to us. You know where she lives, don't you?"

Vinnie had phoned Ms. Siegbahn before he brought me to interview her. "Sure, let me call her first. She doesn't like unexpected visitors."

Bearing in mind Jackie's condition, I didn't want to upset her. "Vickie, I'm not going to tell her about the SCID."

"I understand. Should I stop off at the station to change into civilian clothes and ditch the police car? That might make Ms. Siegbahn more comfortable. Do you think we should take your car? It is the least threatening."

I ignored the slight to my Mini and called Jackie—again on speaker. "Good morning, Ms. Siegbahn. This is Mr. Szilard. I have some news about your son. He's fine and he's in Stony."

She shrieked, "I am so happy."

Even after turning down my phone volume, I could hear her stomping her feet.

"When can I see him?"

"He's sequestered in the Stony Estancia Family Shelter."

"Why is he in a family shelter?"

I was concerned about her fragile psychological state, especially with her husband away. Regardless, Alejandra's life came first. So, I just blurted it out, "He's a father. You're a grandmother. He's with the baby."

Another shriek.

Vicki mouthed, "Should I call nine-one-one and send the EMTs to her house?"

I shook my head no.

The phone kept saying, "A baby," over and over.

Then Jackie said, "What about the mother? Who is she? Is she okay?"

"The mom is Annie, Annie Landau. She's with them."

"Oh, I know her. She's wonderful. The Landaus were so nice to foster her. They're in Arizona now. Where are the kids? When can I see them?"

Vicki repeated, "Stony Estancia Family Shelter."

Jackie spoke rapidly. "Oh, I know where it is. I used to volunteer there before the accident. Near Purcell and Associates and that great pâtisserie on Higgs Road. It's a delightful place."

She paused a moment to catch her breath. "I can see it now. Is it still that dull yellow with faded brown trim? I pushed them to paint it bright colors like the San Amano shelter. Are you there now?"

"This is Senior Detective Yukawa from the Stony PD. We're here, but they won't let us in. You're the only one on the visitor list. Would you like us to come to get you?"

"No!" she barked.

I shook my phone in frustration. So close, yet so far. I considered an alternative. We could send a note to Jackson to tell him his mother was happy about Annie and the baby. Certainly, he knew about her agoraphobia and would adjust.

Jackie continued, "Just wait. I will be there as soon as I can."

Vicki gently asked. "Are you going to call for a ride? We can send a police car to get you. Would you prefer something bigger? I can get a van."

"I can drive." She sounded insulted. "My Mini's in the garage with a full battery charge. Just wait. Don't worry about me. I'll be there."

Vicki and I high-fived. A grandchild outdid agoraphobia.

We told the doorbell that Jackson's mother was on her way.

After a brief delay, the doorbell asked, "How is she getting here?"

We explained that she knew where the shelter was and would drive her Mini down the hill.

After another delay, the doorbell replied, "They'll meet her here."

Vicki smiled and said, "Congratulation, Ms. Siegbahn and the new family are in transit."

I surveyed the neighborhood. On both sides of the street, crepe myrtle trees were getting ready to bloom. The front yards were small with neat lawns and a variety of flowers bordering the walkways. Through my open car window, I could smell jasmine and hear the bees harvesting rosemary flowers.

Vicki pointed through the windshield at a purple and blue Mini. "Look! Is that Ms. Siegbahn? She didn't waste any time." She paused a moment. "And her car matches my bathing suit."

I recognized Jackie's pale complexion. A white plait hung over her shoulder. She was wearing a dramatic red, black, and green African print and her matching fingernails curled over the steering wheel.

"Yes. That's her." I turned around searching for Annie and Jackson. Would Jackie panic if they weren't here to meet her? She'd left her safe home to see her granddaughter. What if the baby wasn't here?

I turned to Vicki, "Where're the kids?"

She pointed to a security guard holding a door open. I was overjoyed to see Annie's braids and Jackson's crew cut step out of the building. Annie was carrying her daughter. "Yes!" I cheered.

I reached across with my good arm to open the door, but Vicki grabbed it. "This isn't our reunion."

We sat in our Stony Estancia black-and-white patrol car and waited for the approaching people to recognize each other.

Jackie saw her children first. She stopped in the middle of the street, jumped out of her car, and ran to them. There was so much joyous screaming. First, she hugged Jackson and then Annie. Annie presented the baby to her.

I nodded to Vicki, "Our work here is done."

She said, "Not quite. I'm just giving them a moment. I need to tell them about the screening results."

She retrieved Jackson's IDs from her black bag, exited the car, opened the passenger door, and grabbed an infant car seat before walking over to the happy family and introducing herself. Jackson accepted his IDs with some explanation that I couldn't hear. As she talked, the group became solemn and worried. They took the car seat, and all piled into Jackie's Mini.

Vicki returned. "They are off to Stony Estancia Hospital for a complete newborn screening. I hope the TRECs were a false alarm." She closed the car windows and we drove away.

Up and down the block people were working in their gardens, walking their dogs, and cats were sunning themselves in the windows. This neighborhood was a lovely place to start a family. I imagined the Siegbahns retelling this story around the Thanksgiving table for years to come.

With Alejandra safe in the arms of her family, Lucy's murder returned to the top of my list. I asked Vicki, "How about lunch? We can strategize about the open cases."

"Not today. I'm glad Alejandra is getting the care she needs. Now, I have a lot of paperwork that was put off by the search."

She headed back to PD headquarters. When we entered the parking structure, she said in an exhausted voice, "You and your friend Brooklynn have placed me in a difficult spot."

What misdeeds had Vicki attributed to Brooklynn and me? "S'cuse me. What did we do?"

"That phone you—"

She parked in her numbered space in the for-official-use-only garage, turned off the car, and raised two fingers on each hand. *Air quotes.* "That phone you found."

Aside from pictures of Stony Estancia High School girls, I didn't expect anything else. "What was the problem with Kapitsa's phone?"

She opened her car door, stepped out, and headed for the secure entrance. I stood beside her while she inserted her identification card and the CCTV scanned us.

After we settled in her office with the door closed, she said, "The forensic techs discovered Ms. Salas's DNA on the phone. She might have been the last one to use it."

That sounded great to me. "Doesn't that connect Mr. Kapitsa with Lucy's murder? She grabbed his phone to call for help before he murdered her."

"There you go making up stories again," she said while shaking her head.

"Even if you don't like my story, we can get a warrant to search Mr. Kapitsa's office and car."

"You've been retired too long. Have you forgotten the law? The phone was stolen. We didn't have probable cause to check for DNA. The evidence is inadmissible—unauthorized search and seizure. That clue may be tantalizing—suggestive that the principal is guilty. However, we have no legal evidence to justify prosecuting him." She slapped her desk, "You can tell your friend that her larceny is letting Ms. Salas's murderer walk free."

Even though it was successful, the frantic search for Alejandra had exhausted Vicki. I didn't argue. Since we'd cleared bully Fowler and victim Vinnie, Kapitsa was my top suspect. The DNA hadn't changed anything—other than to upset Vicki.

"That's not the worst of it," she said with a sigh.

I offered her a chance to take a break. "This has been a long day. We can continue tomorrow after you've had some rest. You'll feel better in the morning." I leaned across her desk and lightly kissed her forehead before turning to leave her office.

She grabbed my wrist. "No! You need to hear this."

I stopped.

"We sent that *found* phone to our computer consultancy. They had no difficulty identifying the owner, Mr. Kapitsa."

She paused. What was coming next?

"In their process, they discovered photos of high school girls. I felt bad for those students. Kapitsa had been stalking them. I'd been stalked myself...more than once. This brought back unpleasant memories and made me angry."

I contemplated becoming judge and jury. I reached out and held her hand. "Angry enough to bend the evidence rules?"

She took a deep breath before continuing, "While everyone was looking for Alejandra, I printed out a selection of photos and went straight to the city attorney. I didn't mention how we'd acquired them, but I assured him that there were more and demanded that he do something."

I agreed with her. In memory of Lucy, the least we could do was protect those girls.

Then her face tightened and between clenched teeth, she said, "He grabbed the pictures and handed them off to an assistant. 647.6, he said."

"Good. Did he swear out a warrant to arrest Kapitsa?"

"No. He lectured me about wasting taxpayer money on misdemeanor cases he couldn't win."

"Is this the guy that campaigned on saving money?"

"Yes, that's him. I argued, but he wouldn't budge. He ranted against the state legislature, saying that the law is subjective, and each jury interprets it differently."

"Did you tell him how much Kapitsa's behavior violated those vulnerable girls?"

"Yes. I got so mad that I shared my personal story, even though I don't like to discuss it. I thought that I'd convinced him to move forward until his assistant returned. It turned out that all the pictures were of senior-year girls who are no longer minors."

I thought back to Richie, also no longer a minor. Nothing is easy once you get lawyers involved. "So, you couldn't convince him?"

She pursed her lips in disgust. "I gave him my best arguments, but he refused to empathize with those girls while blaming his reticence on the law. I got his message. He wouldn't prosecute."

'Someone should change the law to make it easier to stop these people,' Fitch demanded.

Even if the city attorney wouldn't pursue the stalking case, we were still tightening the noose around the principal's neck for murder.

'We're close,' Fitch supported our pursuit of the principal.

I left her sitting behind her desk with her head in her hands.

"One way or another we'll get him," She vowed.

Brooklynn would see this as another example of the adults letting down the students—driving her to more radical action.

I rehearsed what I'd tell Brooklynn. "Kapitsa lucked out with the harassment charges, but we'll get him for murder. His phone had Ms. Salas's DNA on it. A phone isn't a murder weapon, but you uncovered our best lead."

I picked up Chinese food for a late lunch on my way back to Higgs Haven.

When I arrived home, I stacked my takeout boxes on the dining table. Savory aromas filled my apartment. Tomorrow was Thursday, Friday was the prom, and Saturday was the cruise.

If the killer wasn't Kapitsa, we'd miss the prom and the cruise. It didn't look good, and Vicki had already returned her blue and purple bathing suit.

I wasn't discouraged. I'd promised Brooklynn and the Ecology Club that I'd do something about Mr. Kapitsa, and I would.

The only evidence was his *illegally seized* phone. It proved that he was obsessed with the young women, but evidently, it wasn't sufficient for the city to move forward. I knew he was guilty but couldn't do anything about it. *Yet.*

While I feasted on sweet and sour soup, moo shu pork, Peking duck, Szechuan shrimp, and special fried rice, I thought of those tempting boxes of mac and cheese. I checked online and my grocery store was having a sale on case lots. As I packed my leftovers away, the siren song of gooey cheese and chewy pasta called to me. I gave in to that temptation and ordered a case.

I awoke from my nap hungry. The lingering takeout aromas enticed me to stack all the boxes in the microwave and press REHEAT.

'*Why only living witnesses?*' Fitch queried, always ready to turn to the spirit world.

He was right. I must interrogate Lucy. She hadn't returned to my dreams, so I'd find another way. I called Purcell and Associates. To my surprise, Vinnie answered the call himself.

"Zarand, I've been meaning to thank you for locating Jackson. Also, my wife is a new woman chauffeuring Annie and Alejandra around town, setting up a nursery, and buying cute baby clothes."

"You're welcome," I said happy for his family. "I need to see Ms. Salas's personal emails."

"Why call me? Doesn't the PD have her laptop?"

"No. They don't know what happened to it."

"Are you asking me to break the law again? You know I'm not going to do that."

A tracking alert interrupted our phone call. YOUR PACKAGE IS ON ITS WAY. It was the case of mac and cheese. As long as I was going to break my rules, I'd cajole Vinnie to break his. I enticed him with my best story, "Vicki has a search warrant for Ms. Salas's computer. How crazy is that? We have the warrant, but nothing to search." I tried to sound lighthearted about it, but I was getting desperate. We did have that warrant but I didn't know if it covered what I was going to ask of Mr. Purcell. I didn't care.

"I don't know," Vinnie stalled.

"Those emails are important. They must be somewhere in the cloud." I pressured him. "I found your son. You owe me."

"Okay. I'm not promising anything. I'll let you know in the morning. Get some sleep."

Vinnie broke the connection before I could think of something else to request from the smartest guy in the room. I mixed the remains of the special fried rice into the sweet and sour soup and drank it down.

The Thursday-morning sun flooded my bedroom with light—another beautiful day in Stony Estancia.

'Getting close. We're getting close,' Fitch repeated like a mantra while I prepared breakfast. Somewhere in the middle of this case, Fitch had become an optimist.

My first email was from César with the subject MISSING STUDENTS. I'd already found Annie and Jackson, so I skipped this one.

The only other email to make it through my spam filter was from Purcell and Associates with no attachments. Not promising, but I opened it.

It had a link. I never opened email links. Instead, I called Vinnie.

"Morning, Zarand. I see you received my email but didn't follow the link." How did he know that? Before I could interrupt him, he continued, "You're smart to check. It's okay to follow the link."

He disconnected.

The link demanded electronic signatures confirming Vicki's search warrant. It also required me to prove I wasn't a robot and verify my identity.

After this, a report labeled SALAS EMAILS appeared.

It didn't take me long to see the pattern. I filtered the emails with the subject INVASIVE SPECIES. As Brooklyn had hinted, Ms. Salas had collected statements. The girls reported lectures about their clothes, reprimands for bare skin, and uncomfortable attention directed at their chests and legs.

Based on the attorney's response to the creepy photos, I doubted Ms. Salas had enough for the city to prosecute. Her best hope was disciplinary action by the district. However, the school administrators had contracts that would've made that difficult. Brooklynn wasn't going to be pleased.

The emails went back to the beginning of the school year. I understood why Brooklynn was frustrated. She was one of my honorary grandchildren and I hoped she wouldn't do something stupid. The long-term impact of Dr. Fowler's high-school arrests was a cautionary tale. I could still hear his frustration when he bemoaned that he was on every suspect list.

I called Vicki and told her about the emails omitting my suspicion that they might be the product of another illegal search. I urged, "Let's move forward on Mr. Kapitsa's arrest. Even if the city attorney won't pursue sexual harassment, we'll still have him for murder."

She was still unhappy enough about him to put everything together. "Opportunity—we have her DNA on his phone. We can't use that in court, but it tells us he was close enough to kill her. Motive—those emails you uncovered prove Ms. Salas had collected evidence to get him fired and sent to prison."

I stopped her to inject some reality, "Wait. Our city attorney would never prosecute him based on those emails. He's too afraid of losing a case"

"True, but Kapitsa didn't know that. That collection of emails was his motive. I'll put together an arrest warrant immediately." She lowered her voice, "And I'm not running it by that exasperating attorney. Every time I think about him, my rage increases."

Vicki was ready to move faster than I had expected—too fast for my honorary grandkids. The students were looking forward to prom. Tomorrow was the day. I didn't want to spoil it with a police raid on campus. The community treasured prom and graduation after the COVID-19 cancellations. It had once been cool to mock these traditions, but not anymore.

I put the brakes on, "Let's put off Mr. Kapitsa's arrest until after the Reuse and Reunite Prom. He's not a flight risk. I don't want to spoil the dance. They're all looking forward to it."

"Really? You were in such a rush, and now you want to delay?"

"It's only a short delay and we've already solved the case. The senior class has had enough trauma with Lucy's murder."

"Okay. The paperwork won't be complete until tomorrow anyway. I can bring it with me to the dance. Reuse and reunite? Am I supposed to wear something special?"

"You can thank Brooklynn, aka the Ecology Club. She doesn't want anyone to buy new clothes. She wants them to reuse old party clothes."

Vicki cheerfully responded, "No problem. I have my high school prom dress—black, short, shiny, and with lots of ruffles. And it still fits."

I made a note to check out Schrödinger's for something I could wear. With that decided, my thoughts returned to murder. "Has the coroner given us a cause of death?"

"Not yet, but I'm not waiting for Persey. I have enough evidence to arrest Mr. Kapitsa. This won't be another Vinnie debacle."

I hung up the phone feeling good about this. Kapitsa's arrest would deter Brooklynn from getting into trouble. However, I wondered about the cause of death. Why had the coroner had so much difficulty? How could someone die without a clear cause?

Vicki still had to complete the paperwork to arrest Mr. Kapitsa but my contribution was complete. After visiting Schrödinger's, I ordered a celebratory lunch, "Lamb souvlaki, salad, hummus, and pita."

Ms. Salas's killer? The Stony PD would arrest Kapitsa after the prom.

Vinnie's missing son? Jackson had reunited with his mother, the happy grandma.

Prom? I rented a yellow zoot suit from Schrödinger's *and* Vicki had her high school dress—black, short, shiny, and with lots of ruffles.

Cruise? We'd embark from San Pedro Saturday morning even though Vicki had returned her bathing suit.

My doorbell that had survived the fireworks announced, "Greek delivery."

I pressed the door release, and the delivery lady bounded up the stairs, two at a time. The savory aromas of garlic and onion with a hint of oregano and thyme drifted up the stairwell ahead of her. I looked forward to this meal before a week of Mexican cuisine.

"*Yassas* Zarand. Are you Greek?"

"No. You're thinking of Zorba. *Zorba the Greek* was a big movie—years ago. That was a good guess. I'm Hungarian."

Without missing a beat, she came back with, "*Szia* Zarand."

She handed me my food and I gave her a generous tip for her language efforts—Greek and Hungarian greetings—and bounding up the stairs.

I enjoyed my lunch while I finished packing. With my suitcase closed, I stretched out for a well-deserved nap.

Well-deserved or not, my phone woke me—UNKNOWN CALLER. I tapped ACCEPT, and answered with a yawn, "Whassup?"

"Mr. Szilard? I hope I'm not disturbing you. Senior Detective Yukawa told me to call."

My phone displayed two o'clock. A whiff of garlic recalled my Greek lunch. I stretched and wiped the sleep from my eyes. "It's fine. Who's this?"

"It's me. Officer Tsui. Senior Detective Yukawa assigned me to watch the high school for suspicious activity."

'*How many officers work for the Stony PD? Why do you keep running into this one?*' Fitch wondered.

"Yes Officer Tsui, we wanted to monitor Brooklynn and the Ecology Club. Is there trouble?"

"Maybe. None of my five children are teens yet. I don't know what to expect here."

Five children. That explained why I encountered him so often. He must volunteer for extra work at every chance to support his family. "So just maybe-trouble. Why call me?"

"I called Senior Detective Yukawa. She's busy...meeting with the city attorney and some judge. She said, 'Call Szilard,' and hung up."

That made sense. Despite her angry vow to go it alone, Vicki, the future Chief of Detectives, was getting her ducks lined up to arrest Kapitsa after the prom.

But what had Tsui seen?

"I'm listening. What's happening?"

Officer Tsui explained his suspicions. "Brooklynn and her friend Xuan Hua ditched the last period. Instead of going to class, they went to that science garden, where the kids are digging up the chaparral. I can't see what they're doing. They're behind a pile of brush."

That didn't sound like anything to worry about. "Thanks for the report. Don't approach them. Call me back if anything happens."

Two honor-roll girls cutting class was odd. Like the city attorney had concluded after the spaghetti-strap demonstration—good kids, senioritis, nothing to worry about. They were comparing prom dresses. Or planning a baby shower for Alejandra. Girly stuff.

I retreated to my kitchen to organize my lunch leftovers. The extra lamb went into a reusable container and the wilted salad to my compost bin. The takeout containers were compostable—not plastic. The Ecology Club's campaign against plastic was working. Brooklynn hated the stuff, claiming it all ended up in a landfill.

Less than an hour later, Tsui called again. "They're still in the science garden, but they've been joined by those two boys that hang out with them and a half-dozen others that I don't recognize."

'Um, not prom dresses or baby showers. Not girly stuff,' Fitch pointed out.

"Do you have a surveillance camera?"

"Not with me. I have one in my black and white. I signed it out for the family shelter operation and haven't had a chance to return it."

"Perfect. Take pictures of the group. Try to get all the faces without being seen."

"Yes, Sir."

Brooklynn could have been organizing something related to the dance or the newborn, but it would be best to be sure. Emotions were running high at the school. She hadn't been herself. I never expected her to cut class, organize a protest, or steal Mr. Kapitsa's phone. I didn't want her to throw her bright future away for some misbehaving principal. I considered calling her mother, but it was too soon to raise an alarm.

Fitch sneered, *'Detective Yukawa shouldn't have delayed the arrest. She should have taken Kapitsa into custody and worried about the paperwork later.'*

Fitch was right. Brooklynn was organizing another protest. If we had removed the principal, Ecology Club plans wouldn't be anything to worry about. The worst they could have done was picket the jail.

After stashing a couple of leftover pitas into my shoulder immobilizer, I rushed to confront the Ecology Club. I ran down the stairs holding onto the handrail with my left hand. The Mini's tires screeched as it turned onto Higgs Road and again at Blackett Street. I didn't want the Ecology Club to leave the science garden before I could stop them from something they would later lament.

Across the football field, Brooklynn stood with Xuan Hua and a group of students just as Tsui had reported. They were deep in discussion. I thanked my lucky stars that they were still there.

'You're welcome,' replied Fitch.

Approaching the football field, I considered that they may scatter when they saw me. I called Officer Tsui for backup. "Position yourself at one end of the field and your partner at the other but stay out of sight. If they run, try to detain Brooklynn and Xuan Hua. We don't care about the others. This situation calls for gentle persuasion. Absolutely no physical force."

"Yes, Sir. Give us a minute to get in place."

I ambled down the fifty-yard line, waving to the group. I approached close enough to hear individual voices before Brooklynn spotted me. "Mr. S., what are you doing here?"

The Ecology Club stopped talking and they all stared at me. Whatever was coming next, I was prepared. Tsui and his partner were in place.

I gave Brooklynn my friendliest open-mouth smile, "I am bringing good news."

They looked at me and back at each other, thinking, *'What's he doing here?'*

I took a deep breath and began my rehearsed speech, "The city attorney is going to arrest Mr. Kapitsa for Ms. Salas's murder. Thanks to you!"

When no one responded, I added, "All of you!"

I ignored their blank stares and carried on with an upbeat spirit, "Congratulations. His phone was the decisive clue. Brooklynn found it and the forensic techs discovered Ms. Salas's DNA on it." I purposely didn't say Brooklynn had stolen it.

The blank stares continued, so I elaborated, "That was the forensic evidence that led to his arrest. He murdered Ms. Salas so she wouldn't reveal his bad behavior."

I sought their buy-in. "Ms. Salas threatened him with those invasive-species emails you sent her."

Still, no response and I'd already said too much. This crowd had out silenced the detective.

The realization that Mr. Kapitsa murdered Ms. Salas was a shock to them. Horrified faces exhibited fear and disbelief. These children were too young to think about murder. This was the suburbs, not the big city.

Girls wearing spaghetti straps gave me an idea. I started over. "Do you realize that after that spaghetti strap stunt—"

Brooklynn interrupted, "Not a stunt! A peaceful protest. Exercising our constitutional rights."

How could I get them to consider the ramifications of another demonstration? I constructed an innocent fiction. "The city attorney didn't see it that way. He was ready to arrest all of you. Senior Detective Yukawa and I argued to stop him. Do you know what an arrest would have done to your college plans? How disappointed your parents would have been?"

That backfired. Brooklyn kicked over the stack of sagebrush and said between her clenched teeth. "My mom would have supported me." The others nodded in agreement.

I tried again. "I'm sure your moms—and your dads— would have been on your side, but the rest of the world wouldn't have ignored a police record." I told them the cautionary tale about how Dr. Fowler's high school arrests had followed him, but they didn't care.

Xuan Hua pulled my favorite trick and changed the subject. "Forget the DNA on Kapitsa's phone. What about the pictures?"

The crowd nodded in agreement.

"Don't worry about those pictures. Kapitsa will be arrested for murder. Once he's in prison, he won't bother anyone."

Brooklynn wasn't convinced. She whispered, "For a detective, I expected you to be a better listener."

'What she said,' echoed Fitch.

That stopped me. My best idea was to place the principal behind bars, but they didn't agree. I had to find out why Brooklynn had called this Ecology Club meeting.

I changed the subject. "Let's pile up this brush for Mr. Mbacke and the woodchipper."

A few students helped me restack the sage that Brooklynn had scattered. We worked together without talking.

This diversion gave me a chance to think.

Brooklynn repeated Xuan Hua's question, "What about the pictures?"

This time I just answered—no innocent fiction—no editorial—no expectations. "They found lots of pictures. However, the city attorney didn't think they were serious. He has some ideas about saving the taxpayers' money by not pursuing cases that he might lose."

Brooklynn spat out, "So Kapitsa won. The murder covered up all his abuse. He's not even going to register as a sex offender. Are you okay with that?" She raised her voice, "I'm not!"

Xuan Hua roared, "Me too! I'm not okay."

The women echoed, "Me too! Not okay."

The men joined in, "Not okay."

Now that they'd revealed their motivation, I had something I could work with. Kapitsa had abused his power. They were not going to turn the other cheek. They demanded an eye for an eye and a tooth for a tooth.

Brooklynn added, "We're sorry about Ms. Salas, but she gave us bad advice. We were patient and now he is going to get off without being called out and punished."

Xuan Hua added, "All those ladies sent their emails to Ms. Salas, and no one will hear their testimony."

One of the women in the crowd added, "And Kapitsa will be free to harass others."

I almost said, *'He's not going to harass anyone from behind bars,'* but didn't. The murder conviction was my goal, not theirs.

Brooklynn repeated, "Ms. Salas gave us bad advice."

I was hearing them, but I didn't like the way this was going. They were putting themselves ahead of Lucy. Lucy was dead. She'd missed meeting her daughter and granddaughter. That was worse than being stalked by your principal.

Fitch didn't agree, *'Evil is evil. Do not compare.'*

Xuan Hua said, "Do you know how many women he traumatized?"

I had an answer for this. "Yes, I read the emails the girls sent to Ms. Salas. There were a lot."

"A lot!" echoed Brooklynn. "You sound like Ms. Salas. 'Be patient,' she said. Now we find that 'a lot' was not enough. The courage of those ladies to write it down was not enough. Everyone thinks of us as just kids and no one cares."

I could feel their frustration and anger. Did her accusation apply to me? Had I given into the temptation to ignore them? After all, they were just kids and I had adult priorities.

No, I was better than my temptations. That case of mac and cheese was still unopened. I'd resisted that temptation and I wouldn't succumb to ignoring the Ecology Club. They could count on me.

Fitch consoled me, *'Even Ms. Salas didn't take these students seriously,'* but that wasn't much of an excuse.

Xuan Hua added, "If she hadn't been murdered, nothing would have happened."

The group stared at me, not with the anger that Brooklynn and Xuan Hua had expressed but with the pity teens felt for an adult who is too old and out of touch.

Their faces reminded me of those pictures on Mr. Kapitsa's phone. I had focused on the principal's gaze—where he pointed his camera. I had become a voyeur. Now I considered the expressions on the women's faces in those same pictures. Some were fearful, others were resigned, but most were full of disgust and ready to fight. I'd stand by them.

The city attorney might have seen Kapitsa as simply annoying, but from his victims' point of view, this wasn't something to be left unaddressed. Just because Ms. Salas was murdered was no excuse to forget what happened to these young women.

My eyes had opened. These students might have lived in a privileged suburban bubble, but they were more like the ones in Los Angeles than I realized. All these adolescents yearned for the same thing. The Stony High students had more stuff, but just like the teens in the big city, they craved agency and respect, something all young adults deserved.

These were my grandchildren, and they had grown up. I would facilitate their forays into the adult world, to enable their actions. It was time for them to leave the nest, time for them to fly.

"What can I do?" I asked. "Because if you won't listen to me, I might as well listen to you."

They looked to Brooklynn. She was the leader.

She began, "Mr. Kapitsa is going to be visited by three ghosts—the ghosts of the past, the present, and the future."

I recalled the Dickens' classic, how the ghosts transported Scrooge through space and time.

'That's kidnapping,' Fitch said in shock.

Turning the tables, I told him, 'Just shut up and listen.'

Xuan Hua added, "We'll be exchanging roles, taking the position of power. See how the bully likes that."

I asked, "How can I help?"

"We want you to do what you're good at."

Why did they need a detective?

Brooklynn set me straight. She spat out one word in the same tone she used to say *landfill*. "Misdirection."

'Innocent fictions. They figured you out, didn't they?' Fitch laughed.

Fledglings leaving the nest. I wouldn't prejudge them. "What can I do?"

Brooklynn explained. "Tonight, we're going to give Mr. Kapitsa the Ebenezer Scrooge treatment. You just need to misdirect your girlfriend, so we don't get interrupted."

"No problem."

There were high-fives all the way around.

The original Ebenezer Scrooge plan was great. However, they'd grown up with action movies. I didn't want them to take it too far—injure him, booby trap his car, or set his house on fire.

I turned to Brooklynn, "Can you assure me that he won't be injured, and you won't blow anything up or burn it down?"

She laughed, "This is Stony Estancia, not Hollywood."

With that, I enthusiastically concurred, "Let's do it."

These were my grandkids—my grown-up grandkids—my family and I'd support them and trust in their good sense.

'This is going to be good,' Fitch smiled.

After a dreamless night, I awoke relaxed and invigorated. Today was the prom, the arrest of Mr. Kapitsa, and closing of the file on Ms. Salas's murder. Tomorrow would be the cruise.

The finches welcomed another day in the sunny suburbs. STONY ESTANCIA SURFS had nothing to say about any nighttime activities. The front page reported the success of an e-waste collection event with a quote from BROOKLYN CURIE OF THE STONY HIGH ECOLOGY CLUB. I thought about how glad I was to have retired to peaceful Stony Estancia.

Chuck Berry interrupted my reverie. The computer invited me to sub for Ms. Salas. "This is a same-day job."

It seemed strange that the system had lost my suspension. That wasn't the only anomaly awaiting me.

On the way to school, I stopped at the Blackett Bakery. That's how I showed up at Stony High School on Friday morning with a box of donuts totally unprepared for what greeted me.

31. DONUTS AND CONDOMS: FRIDAY AM

As I drove past the administration building, two trucks greeted me. The gray one had the school district logo and a crew in gray work shirts, the district maintenance uniform. The bright orange one announced SCHRÖDINGER'S SECONDHAND STORE in large iridescent letters along with their motto: YOU CAN'T KNOW WHAT WE HAVE UNTIL YOU OBSERVE. The crew wore orange jumpsuits.

After parking the Mini, I walked to the administration building balancing my box of donuts. A lady in orange smiled at me and held the door open. Mrs. Wilson scowled as I signed the substitute log. "Who let you in?"

I wasn't about to let her disturb my day. "That's a lovely frock," I said complimenting her violet-and-white gingham dress. "I don't know who requested me. Check your computer. I'm here for Ms. Salas—again."

She ignored my friendly overture and after clacking on her keyboard, she threw me a key card.

I missed the catch. Before I picked it up, I opened my box and offered her a donut.

She took a plain powdered-sugar one and mumbled, "Thanks."

While picking up my key card, I caught sight of the activity around Mr. Kapitsa's office. The Schrödinger's truck was emptying it. Gone were the chocolate leather chairs with nailhead trim, the high-tech desk chair, the Persian carpet, the oil painting of the principal standing beside a greyhound—everything. The gray truck was delivering gray furniture from the district warehouse. A couple of women in gray work shirts were removing the office door.

I smiled at Mrs. Wilson and pointed to the back-and-forth parade of furniture. She frowned and tossed the last bite of her donut into the trash.

I exited through the back of the administration building into the courtyard.

The first thing I noticed was a crowd of young men and women gathered around a table. Many of the ladies were wearing those forbidden spaghetti straps. Where was Mr. Kapitsa? What happened when the ghosts visited him last night?

Someone in a Bruin-green polo was handing out donuts. Stacks of Blackett Bakery boxes covered the table. Toby and Flora from the Ecology Club collected the empties and flattened them for recycling.

I looked at my smaller box.

'You can never have too many donuts,' Fitch assured me.

I set my modest offering on a brick wall and took out a chocolate glazed one. I enjoyed the sugary treat while watching the happy students.

Fitch addressed them, *'You might as well enjoy yourselves until Kapitsa shows up with his detention slips.'*

To the side of the donut table was a smaller one with a goldfish bowl. Some of the students reached into the bowl. This appeared to be a raffle with them placing their tickets inside. Then I realized they weren't putting anything into the bowl. They were removing something. To my shock, the bowl was full of condoms.

I looked back at the man in the green polo distributing donuts and laughing with the assembled students. It was Mr. Kapitsa! Those ghosts had brought about an impressive transformation.

The buzzer sounded and everyone, including me, headed for homeroom. I greeted the students at the door handing out my modest offering of donuts and high fives. Even Richie took one. Fitch was right that there could never be too many.

Brooklynn was absent. Had something gone awry last night?

'Hospital or jail?' Fitch worried.

The students hadn't settled down when Mr. Kapitsa came on the PA system. "Brooklynn from the Ecology Club has something to say."

She wasn't in the hospital or jail. She was on the PA reviewing the Reuse and Reunite Prom. Her announcement emphasized that everyone was welcome. "Tickets available at the door. If you can't afford a ticket, the Ecology Club will pay for you."

The class responded grumbling, "What about all those people Kapitsa banned?"

Brooklynn continued, "No need to buy new clothes. Look in your closet. Checkout Schrödinger's." When she finished, she said, "Now, back to our principal," like he was her BFF.

Mr. Kapitsa made announcements about end-of-year testing and graduation plans. "Remember to order your cap and gown. You don't want to be a graduation ghost."

Without changing his tone or cadence, he continued. "We will not be enforcing the dress code for the remainder of the year."

The class whispered to each other incredulously.

Brooklynn added, "And in honor of Ms. Salas, Ms. Blume is making a fishbowl of condoms a permanent feature in the library."

Now the class went silent. I think they were in shock.

Mr. Kapitsa came back on the PA. "By way of apology—"

He paused without explaining further.

He started again, "As Brooklynn said, everyone is welcome at prom. No one is banned. I hope to see you all tonight."

'Kapitsa's attending prom? Will wonders never cease?' Fitch mused before adding, *'Do you think he has a date?'*

With that, the class broke out in cheers.

I doubt the teachers taught anything for the rest of the day.

The students never settled down. The ladies were talking about getting their hair done. "Brooklynn didn't say we couldn't fix up our hair." The men chatted about corsages and boutonnieres. "There's nothing in the rules against flowers. They're natural and compostable."

As far as Mr. Kapitsa had gone to make amends to the women of Stony Estancia High, at the end of the day, Vicki and I would still hold him accountable for murder.

When I signed out for the day, I overheard Kapitsa talking to Mrs. Wilson. "I'm going home to get my white disco suit. What are you wearing?"

"I rented a flapper costume."

Kapitsa smiled, "I can't wait to see it."

Fitch gasped, *'I can't wait to see that either. Hard to imagine Aunt Polly dressed as a flapper.'*

I was taken aback by what happened next, Kapitsa leaned down and kissed Mrs. Wilson's cheek, "Am I still picking you up for dinner?"

Fitch gasped again, *'Kapitsa and Mrs. Wilson? I'd never guessed it.'*

The principal's new cheerful persona had rubbed off on her. She broke out in the first smile I'd ever seen when she replied with a laugh, "Oh certainly. I'll have rings on my fingers and bells on my toes."

Last night had belonged to Brooklynn and the Ecology Club. Tonight, Vicki and the Stony PD would have their turn.

'This is going to be even better,' Fitch chuckled.

Would this prom deliver all that it promised? So many coming-of-age fantasies climaxed on this night. Could a single evening fulfill all those expectations?

I was beyond adolescent passions, but I had my own dream.

Vicki and I in fancy dress. Dramatic music in the background and roving spotlights. Drum roll. We reveal Mr. Kapitsa to be Lucy's killer and lead him away. Cheering crowds. Fireworks. Music fades. Cut to the heroic detectives boarding their cruise ship through a shower of confetti and balloons.

Of course, Brooklynn would never approve of confetti or balloons.

Realistically, we wouldn't have a soundtrack or cinematic lighting.

'Or fireworks. Or even cheering crowds,' Fitch added.

Even Fitch couldn't foresee the bombshells the Reuse and Reunite Prom would deliver.

Following my well-practiced routine, I released the belts and buckles on my shoulder immobilizer— shaking out some crumbs. My yellow zoot suit paired a long jacket with matching high-waisted slacks—enough material to clothe a small family. Under my jacket were a black dress shirt and a wide white tie with matching suspenders.

If I'd worn this outfit to jitterbug at the Cotton Club, I would have been a rug cutter. Unfortunately, tonight it failed the mirror test. I didn't recognize my own reflection. The suit might have been down with it in the last century, but now it was simply weird. That stranger in the mirror wasn't leaving my apartment in this bizarre costume. I kept the jacket as a nod to the prom theme, but I exchanged the baggy pants for jeans and the dress shirt for a black turtleneck. The mirror looked more like me.

I picked up Vicki in my Mini. As promised, her outfit was short, shiny, and covered with ruffles.

I gave her a low whistle. "You clean up well."

She did a little shimmy and said, "Gosh, thanks."

She accessorized with her black satchel embossed with the Stony Estancia seal, not something that she would have taken to her own prom.

"What's in there?"

"Lipstick, phone, and house keys."

"Is that all?" I joked.

She laughed, "Plus a warrant to arrest Kapitsa, handcuffs, and my PD radio."

"No gun?"

"Of course not. When the time comes, we'll have plenty of support."

I took her hand and gave her pre-op slogan, "The future belongs to those who prepare."

She responded, 'Always prepared.'

Fitch prompted, *'Tell her about his redemption.'*

"Mr. Kapitsa has changed. You should have seen his reformed behavior at school today. Handing out donuts and condoms. Revoking the dress code and all those prom bans."

Vicki said, "That's hard to believe after seeing all those leering photos."

"You would have been impressed. His eyes only looked at other eyes. It was a warm day, and the women wore summer clothes. He never gave them a glance."

She shook her head, "Unbelievable. Are you still sure we have the right guy?"

"We've done our homework. This will not be a repeat of the Vinnie debacle."

As we approached the school, Vicki asked, "How do you think the Ecology Club will decorate?"

Decorations? I pondered. Brooklynn had already spoken out against single-use clothing. What about the traditional paper streamers and plastic balloons? Would she forbid all embellishments? I was sure of one thing, "Brooklynn will prohibit anything destined for landfill."

We were early and the front parking lot was empty except for a bright orange truck—Schrödinger's Secondhand.

Vicki pointed to it. "What are they doing here?"

That truck foreshadowed one of Brooklynn's surprises.

The courtyard was ablaze with colored lights. Brooklynn had staged an *al fresco* prom—something only possible with accurate weather forecasting. There was a projector displaying STONY HIGH REUSES AND RECYCLES on the side of the theater—the tallest building on campus. I turned to Vicki, "I told you. No single-use decorations."

She said with a sigh, "I expected this to be contained in the gym or the cafeteria. I'm going to call for reinforcements."

An outdoor event could turn chaotic if the crowd scattered and became uncontrollable—so many buildings, so many alleys.

I welcomed the next surprise—food trucks parked in the courtyard. Greek. Sushi. Chinese. Pizza.

Vicki pointed in the direction of the science building, "There's our favorite—Cocina de Cetto."

I nodded, "And next to it is that great pâtisserie on Higgs Road." I took the familiar menu as a good omen. The evening was on track.

In the center of the courtyard, the Ecology Club had constructed a platform and installed an outdoor sound system.

Vicki, still worried about crowd control, suggested, "When the time comes, we'll make some harmless announcement to collect everyone around that stage."

'Your specialty—innocent fictions,' joked Fitch.

Tucked between the Sushi and Chinese trucks, I noticed Cha Cha Bragg-Fowler. She wore a dress like Vicki's, most likely from her prom. It was shorter, bright red, and covered with sequins that sparkled under the lights. It supported her claim that she was wild in her high school years. In front of her was a table of cookies.

"Good evening," I smiled, "Are these homemade?"

"Sure are," she said. The baked goods contrasted with the dress. Was she Mrs. Bragg-Fowler the cookie-baking heiress or Cha Cha the wild teenager? She turned to Vicki. "Love your dress."

Vicki did another shimmy. "Strictly here for pleasure," she lied while helping herself to a shortbread.

I tucked a couple of to-go cookies into my sling.

Vicki and I found a table near the entrance where we could watch people as they arrived.

"Look at these chairs. Not your typical rentals. They don't even match," I remarked.

"You can say the same for the tables." Vicki got a big smile. "This explains the truck. Schrödinger's supplied the rental furniture in keeping with the Ecology Club's reuse theme."

Each item had a Schrödinger's Secondhand price sticker. "And everything is for sale."

Brooklynn and the Ecology Club arrived as a group. She led her entourage around the courtyard on an inspection tour. They greeted each food truck. I suspect she was verifying that all the throwaway stuff was compostable.

Toby shook the temporary fencing blocking the corridors between buildings until Brooklynn reprimanded him in a disgusted voice, "That's enough. They're fine." He looked dejected and moved to the back of the crowd.

I pointed out the barricades to Vicki, "Do you see that? The prom isn't as open as it appeared."

"Yes. That solves my problem. I won't need reinforcements. Remind me to thank the prom committee."

The fencing was another indication that things were going our way.

"I suspect your gratitude goes to the faculty advisors who required them to prevent teenage couples from disappearing into dark alleys."

Vicki pointed to Cha Cha flirting with some teenage boys. "Some things never change. I doubt those fences are sufficient to contain teenage passions."

I recognized some of the adults, arriving separately from their progeny.

I greeted Dr. Gwendolyn Curie, MD, PhD. "Evenin' Wendy. Brooklynn has organized quite an event here."

She beamed, "I'm proud of her."

Wendy was accompanied by a lady dressed in a long black gown with leather opera gloves, a fascinator hat suitable for Ascot, and a veil that covered her shoulders. When they left, I turned to Vicki, "Who was that? Did she dress as a Victorian mourner for her prom?"

"Absolutely," Vicki said, "Don't you recognize her? That's Persey. She wore clothes like that when she went to Stony High, and everyone expected her to run for county coroner. Her campaign posters presented her in her Victorian Goth finery with her slogan, PERSEPHONE, QUEEN OF THE UNDERWORLD, FOR CORONER."

"Wow. Has she given us a cause of death yet?" I asked.

"Sadly, no. I don't understand what she's waiting for."

The one exception to the separation of parents and children was Vinnie Purcell and Jackie Siegbahn pushing the stroller under the watchful eyes of Jackson and Annie. Their entrance created quite a stir. The three women wore matching dresses of batik silk with a striking blue, orange, and green floral pattern. The prom served as a coming-out party for the new granddaughter. Fortunately, those TRECs were a false alarm, and Alejandra passed the rest of her newborn screening with flying colors.

Vicki turned to me, "There goes another of our suspects."

"Yes. Mr. Purcell had the technical expertise, but he wasn't our hacker."

Vicki said with a sigh, "Now that I see him as a doting grandfather, I can't imagine him as a murder suspect."

"Agreed. As Sherlock Holmes said, 'When you have eliminated all which is impossible, then whatever remains, however improbable, must be the truth.' That leaves us with Kapitsa."

She patted her black bag. "I have his arrest warrant here. But I just wish we had stronger evidence."

After the early arrivals had a chance to eat, the DJ raised the volume and opened the dancing with Prince—*Party Like It's 1999.*

Fitch laughed, *'They're even reusing their music.'*

The young women and men of Stony High surrounded the DJ. When she played a slow number, the adults joined in. My favorite couples were Dick the Stickman with Cha Cha, plus, being seen in public for the first time in years, Jackie dancing with her husband. I noticed he wasn't packing his toy gun tonight and suspected he'd decided to change his image.

The slide show on the wall of the theater featured the Ecology Club cleaning up the campus and working on the science garden. Other pictures included cameos from previous proms. I recognized Megan Rainwater dancing with her daughter in her arms. Photos of infant Alejandra Siegbahn and others of the deceased Ms. Salas drew the biggest responses. I smiled to myself noticing their matching eyes.

During a slow dance, live images replaced the slide show.

"Do you see anyone who could be a hacker?" I asked Vicki as the camera panned the crowd. "With the forged recommendation letters, the falsified transcripts, and the threatening notes, those hackers were our strongest lead—"

Vicki interrupted, "That's it! How can we make an arrest if we haven't identified the hackers? Surely Mr. Kapitsa isn't a hacker. No one takes him for a tech wizard."

I countered with, "Smartest-one-in-the-room Vinnie asserted that there were no hackers. I trust him. Kapitsa is our guy."

'Um, then how do you explain those letters and transcripts?' Fitch queried resuming his role as critic.

Vicki took a deep breath and exhaled. "Okay. Forget hackers. There were no hackers. I have the warrant to arrest Kapitsa in my handbag." She raised her black satchel—a parody of the tiny evening bags carried by the older women. The high school ladies rejected those little purses for pockets.

She looked around and asked, "Do you know what's missing?"

"No. I'd say the Ecology Club thought of everything." I was stymied. Nothing was missing. The prom was perfect. The students were dancing. The adults were catching up on old times. Everyone was taking advantage of the food trucks. The slide show drew sporadic oohs and aahs with occasional applause. Teachers took turns monitoring the temporary fences barricading the dark alleys.

Vicki said, "Our star, Mr. Kapitsa, has not made an appearance. I'm worried that he discovered our plan. Stony Estancia is a small town and it's impossible to keep a secret."

That was a disconcerting thought. "Do you really think he's gone into hiding?"

"I hope not," she said, patting her black case. "If he doesn't show up, I'll regret delaying his arrest for the sake of this dance."

Had Kapitsa disappeared? Was he on his way to Mexico?

Brooklynn stopped by. "Are you enjoying yourselves?"

Vicki answered, "Oh yes. You've done a fantastic job."

If anyone knew where Kapitsa was, it would be Brooklynn.

"Have you seen the principal tonight?" I asked.

"Haven't seen him," Brooklynn replied with a typical teenager's indifferent attitude.

Vicki interrogated her with a worried tone, "Did you tell him he couldn't attend?" She grinned, "Did you ban him from prom?"

Brooklynn reverted to her serious self, "Oh no. The opposite. I knew you intended to arrest him, so I demanded that he show up."

Whoops. Had she inadvertently let him know the plan?

Brooklynn searched the courtyard. "And there he is. Just arriving."

Mr. Kapitsa, in his white disco suit, wore a flamboyant satin shirt unbuttoned too far for a man his age. His face had a sheen of sweat as if he'd already been partying. He had his arm tight around Mrs. Wilson's waist. Her peach sequined flapper costume would never have passed the dress code— too short with spaghetti straps—not that anyone cared anymore. Her blond hair hung down to her shoulders in soft finger curls. A rhinestone headband held it all in place.

'Wow,' said Fitch, *'that lady is ripped.'*

I'd never seen her bare arms. It was obvious by her well-defined biceps and triceps that she put in hours at the gym. She was made up with deep red cupid's bow lips and dark eyes. If she hadn't been with Kapitsa, I wouldn't have recognized her.

When Brooklynn moved on, I asked Vicki, "Do you think he knows what you've planned?"

"Don't know. Don't care. I'm only glad he's here," she said matching Brooklynn's teenage attitude.

Fitch bounced in time to the music, *'Everyone's going to party tonight.'*

The DJ announced, "Last dance," and everyone crowded around the stage, even Mr. Kapitsa and Mrs. Wilson.

'They should enjoy their last dance together,' Fitch said sadly. He'd become sympathetic to Kapitsa after the principal's remarkable transformation.

When the music ended, Brooklyn took the microphone to thank the adults for volunteering to clean up. Around the periphery, uniformed officers stationed themselves at each section of temporary fencing. In a short while, mostly adults remained.

Vicki picked up her black satchel and approached Mr. Kapitsa flanked by Officer Tsui and his partner. The city attorney, dressed in a purple zoot suit with a matching fedora, followed Senior Detective Yukawa—a short distance behind.

I spied County Coroner Persey close to the city attorney.

'This is going to be the best,' Fitch laughed aloud.

Vicki and her deputies approached the principal. When he saw them, he stepped forward and presented his wrists, palms up, ready to be handcuffed. We had the right person this time.

Senior Detective Yukawa gently took hold of his elbow, "There's no need for cuffs. If you'll come with me, we can do this without creating a scene."

Kapitsa nodded.

Vicki continued sympathetically, "I heard about your reformed behavior."

The principal murmured, "I am so sorry. It was all an accident."

33.   CONFESSION: FRIDAY AFTER PROM

What accident was Kapitsa confessing to? Certainly, he wasn't going to attempt to explain away his harassment of the Stony High women as an accident. He must have been thinking about Lucy's death. How could Lucy's murder be an accident?

Detective Yukawa and Principal Kapitsa walked away from the crowd. Officer Tsui and his partner followed a few paces back. The city attorney and the county coroner didn't follow. News of Mr. Kapitsa's arrest spread through the crowd.

"He murdered Ms. Salas?"

"Yes. He just confessed."

The few students who were still around returned. This included Brooklynn who went to stand with her mother.

'Well done,' Fitch begrudgingly congratulated me.

We didn't get the cheering crowds and fireworks of my fantasy, but his confession was a perfect finale.

A loud crash interrupted this orderly process. Toby and Flora had collapsed a section of temporary fencing trying to sneak back from one of the dark alleys between the buildings.

'Didn't take him long to find someone else after Brooklynn dumped him,' snickered Fitch.

The two embarrassed teenagers stared at the crowd.

Flora regained her composure first. She carried a silver object—not an evening bag. "Did someone lose this?"

It was a laptop.

Toby grabbed it and held it over his head. He yelled, "Look what I found in the bushes!"

While everyone was in shock, the county coroner raised her veil and intoned in a very official voice, "No one move."

Persey opened her small bag and took out a pair of blue examination gloves. She put them on and slowly walked over to Toby and Flora. Her gloved hands gently inspected the laptop.

Vicki asked no one in particular, "Could that be Ms. Salas's?"

Brooklynn pushed through the mob, "Yes, it is. I recognize her ecology stickers."

Everyone watched as Persey continued to study the computer. "Interesting."

Vicki withdrew an evidence bag from her black case and handed it to Persey.

The county coroner whispered, "If that dark stain is blood, this might be the cause of Ms. Salas's head trauma."

Everyone waited while Persey bagged the evidence.

Senior Detective Yukawa turned to her prisoner, "We're going to find your fingerprints on that laptop, aren't we?"

Again, he held out his wrists to accept handcuffs.

In a subdued voice, he mumbled, "It was an accident."

He sighed before elaborating, "It was early. I had been walking around the deserted campus when I discovered Ms. Salas looking distraught. I put my arm around her to comfort her."

'I bet that didn't work.' Fitch predicted before adding, *'She had just delivered baby Alejandra. Jackson had disappeared with the infant. Brooklyn and Charlie had left with a distressed Annie. And Kapitsa was on her to-do list for sexual harassment.'*

Kapitsa continued, "Ms. Salas yelled, Get away from me you dirty old man."

He looked at the crowd, realizing that he had an audience for his sad confession. When he noticed Brooklynn, he took a deep breath and added, "She said a lot of other things too."

Brooklynn seemed sympathetic to Kapitsa's plight, "Yes, I can imagine."

Kapitsa stopped as if he was trying to get his story straight, "She shook her laptop at me, angrily shouting, I have enough evidence here to put you away. Then she stepped towards me, still wielding her computer."

He took a deep breath, again seeming to take time to think. Everyone moved closer to better hear what he'd say next. Everyone except Mrs. Wilson.

He whispered, "There was blood on the floor."

People gasped, so he quickly added, "That didn't have anything to do with me."

I had no idea where this story was going. My thoughts were swirling like a tornado wondering whether to believe him.

The next part came quickly. "Then it happened. She slipped—fell—and the laptop flew into the air. I tried to catch it but only managed to target it at her head. When she didn't get up, I knew she was dead."

After another pause, he finished with, "I picked up the bloody computer. It had killed her, not me. It was an accident."

We all waited for him to continue, but he just stood there with his wrists waiting for the handcuffs.

Vicki cuffed him. She calmly asked, "And what did you do next?"

He replied, "I panicked. When I reached the courtyard, I was still holding the bloody laptop. Teachers were arriving, so I threw it away."

He sighed as if he'd said everything.

I prodded him, "We found Ms. Salas's DNA on your phone. How did that happen?"

He looked shocked. "My phone? I was talking about her laptop. Don't know. The phone never left my pocket."

'He's telling the truth,' Fitch contributed to my confusion.

Vicki turned to the county coroner. "What do you say?"

Persey faced Mr. Kapitsa and pronounced in her official voice, "The trauma from that fallen laptop was not the cause of death."

At that point, we still didn't know how Lucy had died or how her DNA ended up on Mr. Kapitsa's phone.

'I told you he wasn't the right one,' Fitch taunted always happy to take credit in retrospect.

I considered the remaining mysteries. How did Lucy's DNA get on Kapitsa's phone? What was the cause of death? I knew it all fit together. I just had to see the bigger picture.

I waited for Fitch, but he had nothing.

Then it came to me.

"Take off his handcuffs," I demanded.

When I had everyone's attention, I pronounced, "The missing piece is a lowly plastic bag. When we—"

I stopped myself from mentioning Brooklynn's part in this.

"I found a lost phone—it was later identified to be Mr. Kapitsa's phone. I'm retired so I don't carry evidence bags. I looked around the administration offices for something. I found a clean plastic bag, but when I opened it, I should have known it was contaminated. It smelled sweet—floral—like Lucy's lavender shampoo."

I paused for everyone to think about lavender shampoo. "In addition to traces of Lucy's shampoo, the bag contained her DNA. That's how Kapitsa's phone got contaminated."

My audience was silent, not from understanding, but from confusion. A lost phone, a plastic bag, lavender shampoo, DNA. I'd managed to confound the mystery. At the risk of adding to the chaos, I changed the subject.

"If you allow me a slight divergence, I'll make it all clear. Several days ago, I had red spots on my arm because of my shoulder immobilizer." I patted my sling. I felt my food cache, extracted a cookie, took a bite, and chewed slowly.

I made a joke. "You know how this works. I searched the web for RED SPOTS, and I was lost for hours."

A few people laughed.

Kapitsa shook his head, undoubtedly thinking, *'Whenever there's trouble, you're in the middle of it.'*

Vicki and Persey listened intently.

"I read about fifth disease, allergies, and Christmas tree rash, but none of that mattered, because I didn't know about Lucy's DNA inside a plastic bag."

The county coroner gave me a big smile. She'd figured it out. I gave her a lead-in, "You certainly remember those tiny red spots on Ms. Salas's face? Do you want to tell everyone how she got them?"

"Petechial hemorrhages," she said triumphantly. "I had a near-impossible job. Strangling and drowning are the typical causes of suffocation. Both result in obvious indications—fluid in the lungs, neck bruises, or a fractured hyoid. A plastic bag leaves none of those clues."

She switched to her official voice, "The cause of death is asphyxiation. That plastic bag was the murder weapon."

Fitch filled in the details, *'Someone arrived shortly after Mr. Kapitsa left, found Ms. Salas on the floor dazed and confused, assisted her into the desk chair, and murdered her with that plastic bag.'*

I added the last clue, "I found the murder weapon in Mrs. Wilson's desk."

At this point, Mrs. Wilson ran from the crowd, pushing Toby and Flora aside, jumping over the collapsed fence, and disappearing into a dark alley.

Officer Tsui and his partner took off in pursuit. Vicki opened her black case with the embossed Stony Estancia seal and extracted her PD radio. "Suspect on foot. Peach dress. Stony High prom. Request air support."

The crowd was in an uproar.

"Not the principal?"

"Mrs. Wilson!"

"Hard to believe."

Shortly a helicopter appeared over the courtyard with a large searchlight. As it circled, the noise overpowered all conversation. When it dived low over a parking lot, everyone cheered.

The helicopter departed and Officer Tsui returned. His partner had Mrs. Wilson in custody, her hands cuffed behind her back.

'What about those hackers?' Fitch queried, never satisfied.

Of course, Vinnie had been right all along. There were no hackers. *Simplex sigillum veri.* Mrs. Wilson, like all office managers, had administrator access to the district's computers. You might say she was an authorized hacker. She changed the grades on Richie's transcript and forged his recommendation letter.

After Mrs. Wilson was taken away, Vicki and I watched the parents—some still wearing their fancy dress costumes, some having changed into work clothes—clean up after the prom. Someone put an oldies-but-goodies playlist on, setting their phone on a small speaker system. The parents and a few teachers took down the lights, picked up the small bits of trash from the food trucks—which had closed and driven away—and then began disassembling the stage. It felt like a fitting end. And then we watched prom just disappear.

At that point, Vicki and I decided, without speaking, to leave. She stood close to me and said, "Gosh, you did an outstanding job solving this one."

"Don't I always," I replied modestly.

She gave me a playful squeeze, "I'll meet you at embarkation tomorrow morning."

"What about your bathing suit? You returned it."

"I'm sure they sell them on the ship."

Saturday morning, on the way to the ship, I proudly donated the unopened case of mac and cheese to the local food bank. I hadn't given in to temptation. They were grateful to receive it. It was something they regularly stocked.

Once on board, the ship sold Vicki a bikini like those offered in the store next door to Purcell and Associates. They even sold me the pajamas that I'd forgotten to pack when interrupted by Brooklynn's spaghetti lunch.

That should have been the end of our adventure, but the cruise brought one more twist and solved a mystery we'd all but forgotten.

No one was murdered on the cruise. In La Paz, we snorkeled with the sea lions. In Ensenada, we rode horseback along the beach. Camels carried us across the desert outside Cabo San Lucas. In between, we had *chilaquiles* for breakfast, made-to-order tacos and burritos for lunch, and a different Mexican specialty each evening. Everything was *en su punto* and the variety put Cocina de Cetto to shame. I'd never eaten so many different flans and sweet empanadas.

All too soon we were at sea for the final day—returning to San Pedro. I had expected to nap, but instead, I read the welcome packet—describing the ship and introducing the crew.

'Better late than never,' observed Fitch.

I discovered—too late—that the casino offered a sunrise champagne breakfast and there was an urgent care clinic on the first deck. Of the most interest was the ship's captain, *Pedro Salas*. His round, smooth cheeks made him look young, but the beginning of crow's feet showed his true age.

"Say, Vicki, something tells me that our captain is Lucinda Salas's missing brother?"

She scoffed, "Another of your intuitions?" She took the packet and studied the captain—shown in his dress whites. "He could be the right age, but he seems more Black than Latin. Shouldn't he look more like Ms. Salas?"

'Ms. Salas stole his sister's identity,' declared Fitch.

I laughed. "It's easy to forget that Lucinda Salas is an alias. The teacher we know as Ms. Salas is in fact Dorothea Ghez. She and Captain Salas are not related."

In the picture, Captain Salas sported a big hospitality-industry smile, but his narrow eyes and the creases between his eyebrows told the story of a more serious demeanor. It was the perfect combination for a cruise ship captain.

Vicki read from his bio, "Captain Salas grew up in Southern California." She put down the brochure. "We have nothing planned today. Let's interrogate him."

"How are we going to find him? You can't barge into the bridge and flash your badge."

"This is the last day. We're just cruising the open sea, something safely delegated to his first mate. I expect he's mingling with the guests."

I ran a few steps to catch up with Vicki as she bolted down the passageway in search of Pedro Salas.

The ship was enormous—bigger than a mall. We visited restaurants, pools, water slides, cabanas, bars, casinos, and stores—so many stores offering jewelry, clothes, souvenirs, sundries—even luggage, electronics, and liquor.

Fitch wondered, *'Why do they sell luggage? Do people embark with their clothes in paper sacks, having forgotten to buy a suitcase?'*

Finally, we found him in the sales office.

"*Hola*, Captain Salas." We shook hands. "I'm Zarand and this is Vicki. We're from Stony Estancia."

He broke into a grin—even bigger than in the picture we'd seen. "Small world. I grew up in Stony. I went to high school there."

"I'm a substitute teacher. I know Stony High well. Go Bruins."

"Small world indeed. Is Mrs. Wilson still there?"

This wasn't the time to say that she'd be going to prison. "Sure is," I said.

Vicki had had enough small talk. "Do you have a sister Lucinda?"

Captain Salas's smile disappeared. "How do you know about my sister? She died years ago."

My intuition had been right. He was Lucinda Salas's brother. There had to be a connection between his long-dead sister and our recently murdered teacher—both Lucinda Salas.

Moving the discussion from recollections of Stony Estancia to murder was a delicate transition. We didn't want to appear to be cops.

Vicki did it perfectly by ignoring the detail that Lucy had been murdered. "Gosh, Ms. Lucinda Salas teaches Biology at the high school."

His smile returned. "Oh, that's not my sister. That's Alejandra. You want to hear a funny story?"

'Alejandra? Like Alejandra Siegbahn, Lucy's granddaughter?' Fitch puzzled.

I knew about Dorothea Ghez and Lucinda Salas, but who was Alejandra? I shared Fitch's confusion, but I let Captain Salas proceed, "Funny story? *Sí, por favor.*"

He told us of his sister's death, "She wasn't concerned by that sore throat until she started to lose her hair."

Sore throat? Hair Loss? I had no idea what he was talking about. Why didn't he start from the beginning?

Captain Salas continued the story that he'd probably told over and over, "After several specialists, many tests, and false diagnoses, the death sentence read medullary thyroid cancer."

Now I understood. His sister had cancer.

'Um, and it killed her.'

He looked around until he spied an unoccupied desk. We all sat around it, and he continued in a faint voice. "We tried everything—chemo, radiation, hormones, but she was one of the unlucky ones."

'That's not a funny story,' Fitch opined.

As if he could hear Fitch, he said. "That wasn't the funny part. You know how people donate their organs after death?"

We waited. Even if Captain Salas had an odd sense of humor, this still wasn't funny.

"Lucy donated her identity. Have you ever heard of such a thing?" He laughed. "Lucy went into hospice in Cabo San Lucas. When she died, Alejandra took her identity." Captain Salas laughed again. "My friend Alejandra went down to Mexico and never returned. My sister Lucy died in Mexico but still returned." He laughed, "Have you ever heard anything like that?"

I understood what he was saying. It was a bit funny. But who was Alejandra? Was that another alias for Dorothea Ghez?

'*Or the other way around,*' suggested Fitch.

Asking about aliases would make us sound like cops. Instead, I shared our part of the story. "We're sorry to tell you that that second Lucinda Salas was murdered."

Now nothing was funny. Tears ran down Captain Salas's smooth cheeks and his shoulders slumped. Life drained from his body. Even his hospitality-industry smile disappeared.

I could barely hear him as he whispered. "*Pobre Alejandra. Tanta tristeza.* She had such a difficult start. She had so much potential. She cared so much."

Vicki reached across the desk and took his limp hand. "Is there someplace we can go."

He looked around and snapped to attention. "Isabella, I'm taking these two guests to the captain's conference room. Please have the steward send in lunch." With that, we all marched down the passageway to a cabin with a round table, a few chairs, and a monitor showing the view from the bridge.

As soon as the door closed, he collapsed. "Tell me what happened."

I didn't know what to call her. She was in the FBI database as Dorothea Ghez, but he called her Alejandra. I decided to stick with Lucy, an alias we both knew. "Lucy was a champion for the students. She sponsored the girls' football team and the Ecology Club." I recounted the stories from the remembrance ceremony. Vicki added more praise for the murdered teacher and talked about the dispensary for condoms and prenatal vitamins.

Captain Salas listened intently. After the story of his sister's death and the murder of his friend, I'd expected we were through the worst of it. However, there was a loose end—Annie. I asked, "Did you know she had a daughter?"

Captain Salas took a deep breath and held it. He was in shock. I hadn't expected this reaction. I looked to Vicki, but she too seemed lost.

We were all rescued from the awkward silence when the steward came in to deliver lunch—tacos, burritos, rice, beans, and more sweet empanadas. The food sat untouched while the steward set the table, poured water, and finally departed.

"How do you know about *our*—" he hiccupped. "About *her* daughter?" He went quiet but then asked, "What's our daughter's name?"

'*He's Annie's father,*' Fitch explained.

Vicki also figured it out. "You're Annie's father, aren't you?"

"If Annie is Alejandra's daughter—" He interrupted himself. "If Annie is Lucy's daughter, yes." He sighed. "Let me start at the beginning."

"*Sí, por favor,*" I said.

"The night before her graduation, Alejandra and I hiked up to Pauli Falls, a favorite place. She had so many plans—college, medical school, and research. Of course, back then, none of her dreams were possible with a baby."

Vicki listened and I helped myself to a shrimp taco. It was delicious. As I savored the fresh shrimp, I recalled Megan Rainwater raising her daughter while in medical school. I now understood why this was so important to Ms. Salas. It was her teenage dream.

Captain Salas continued. "Back then my young brain didn't believe teen pregnancy led to an actual child. Our friend Jackie had lost Tristeza, her baby. We'd all buried the infant together. Between sobs at the full-moon funeral, Alejandra kept repeating, 'Shouldn't have given him a name.'"

He took a sip of water. I helped myself to a fish taco. It was even better than the shrimp, and just barely kept me from drowning in the gloom that filled the room.

Vicki took his hand. That encouraged him to continue. "That night before graduation, on a blanket, listening to the bubbling of the falls and the coyotes in the distance, she delivered our child, small, but perfect."

He took a deep breath. "I had no idea, but Alex, Alejandra, told me what to do. She tore off her shirt and bra. 'Place the baby here...Let the placenta drain into the baby...Don't worry about the cord...Don't cut it...Call nine-one-one.'"

"That must have been frightening," Vicki consoled him.

Captain Salas shook his head. "It's frightening to recall, but back then I just listened to Alex—she always knew what to do." He became calm and had a genuine smile, not the hospitality-industry one. He was remembering his Alejandra, my Lucy, the FBI's Dorothea Ghez.

Captain Salas spoke as if in a dream, "I sat next to her in the ambulance. She explained that we must forget the baby. She wouldn't let me name it. The infant was always *the baby*. We Safe Surrendered *the baby* at the firehouse on Higgs Road."

He was saying that he and his Alejandra, who later changed her name be Lucinda Salas, Safe Surrendered their child, who through the foster care system became Annie Landau.

Vicki still held his hand. "What happened next?"

"Alejandra cried all morning, missing graduation. She wouldn't stay in Stony. Too many sad memories. That same morning, we left and didn't stop until we were well south of Tijuana. I drove and she made so many vows to prevent and support teen pregnancy. Her mantra was, 'Let me be the last one.'"

He continued still lost in some distant memory, "Alejandra, my Alex, and I spent the summer on the beach. I apprenticed on a tourist boat, and she was adopted by *la abuela y partera,* the grandma and midwife. After that summer, she changed her name to Dorothea Ghez and planned her return. I never liked that name and have never used it."

He snapped out of his reverie, gulped down a full glass of water, and returned to the present. "How did you find our daughter?"

I said, "Just before Ms. Salas was murdered, she delivered a baby. As part of the murder investigation—DNA stuff—we learned that that newborn was related to her. The infant's mother was Annie Landau—Lucy's, Alejandra's daughter." I gave him a moment to appreciate the situation. "Annie is your daughter."

"*Yo soy un abuelo.* I am a grandfather," he managed to squeak out between happy sobs.

Vicki nodded, "I suppose you are."

"What is my granddaughter's name?"

"Alejandra Siegbahn," Vicki and I said together.

That brought on more joyous tears. "They named her after her grandmother, Alejandra Marconi. How sweet."

Captain Salas's Alejandra, his high school sweetheart, was Alex Marconi. Alex, the graduation ghost, was a girl, not a boy.

'Lucy is the graduation ghost.' Fitch did a happy dance. *'That's really good.'*

That night we ate at the captain's table. The cruise billed the final dinner as a Fresh Seafood Fiesta. It started with shrimp *pozole rojo*, followed by oyster *antojitos*. Before the main dishes, *baile folklorico* dancers entertained us. For the entrée we were offered a choice of grilled pork tenderloin in charred-chile *adobo*, sautéed scallops drenched with *mole negro*, or vegetarian *enchiladas verdes*. They all came with *elotes*—Mexican grilled corn. I indulged myself with the *tres sabores*—a large plate with a portion of each dish. While the staff cleared the tables for dessert, roving *mariachi* bands serenaded us. The dessert was *cinco leches* cake and espresso.

Afterward, our dinner companions left to go to the bars for a final night of dancing or to the casinos. The three of us from Stony Estancia retired to the Starlight Lounge to enjoy a farewell Agua Mala cerveza with the captain.

The new moon left the top deck in darkness.

The captain pointed to the Milky Way. "That was the display that guided Alejandra and I into Ensenada. Each time I see that band of stars I think of her and the baby we left behind."

I didn't remind him that his Alejandra had been murdered.

Vicki said, "When we disembark in San Pedro, you can come with us to Stony Estancia. I have several spare rooms. You can stay with me."

I seconded the invitation with, "I am sure Annie would love to meet her father and introduce little Alex to her grandfather."

From our location, we had a panoramic view of darkness in all directions. We were but a dot on the vast sea, but I felt a togetherness reuniting Annie with her lost father and Pedro with his new granddaughter.

EPILOGUE

The arrival in Stony Estancia of *abuelo* Pedro was a repeat of the celebration for little Alex. With no prom to bring everyone together, Jackie Siegbahn hosted a welcome party at her home. STONY ESTANCIA SURFS covered the event with stories of the graduation ghost and how Pedro Salas and Alejandra Marconi ran away to Ensenada. Also, there were many pictures of Alejandra Siegbahn with her parents, three grandparents, and numerous honorary aunt and uncles. *So many pictures.*

Annie interred her mother in Bragg Vineyard Memorial Cemetery beside her grandparents. This was the plot that Persey had purchased to keep the graduation ghost case open. The gravestone read:

ALEJANDRA "ALEX" MARCONI

AKA

DOROTHEA GHEZ

AKA

LUCINDA SALAS

OUR TEACHER

WE'LL ALWAYS REMEMBER HER

Abuelo Pedro turned to Annie, "I wish your mother was here." Annie just smiled because Fitch brought Lucy's ghost to the funeral. Lucy gave her blessing to daughter Annie and granddaughter Alejandra. When she placed spectral kisses on baby Alex's fingers and toes, the infant cooed, and the living grandparents smiled. Lucy said, *'That's it. I had planned more, but this is enough.'* Fitch said, *'You're not done. Baby Alex will need a spirit guide. Welcome to the club.'*

Brooklynn received a book contract for Ms. Salas aka Alex Marconi's biography. The working title was *Many Aliases: One woman's journey to liberation.* She hired Jackson as her editor.

Jackson and Annie took a gap year to spend time with little Alex. Afterward, they moved to Vancouver British Columbia where he enrolled in a creative writing program, and she studied anthropology.

I was reinstated as a substitute teacher, but Vicki didn't get promoted to Chief of Detectives. *Yet.*

When the story that Mrs. Wilson was the murderer went viral, students and parents came forward with their own reports. They told of threats for imagined transgressions against Mr. Kapitsa. Girls accused of flirtatious behavior. Boys blamed for spreading rumors. Her paranoia wreaked havoc throughout the school. She changed grades, lost recommendation letters, misplaced chapter tests, and adulterated exam keys with incorrect answers. She also harassed the teachers with miscalculated paychecks that were surprisingly difficult to correct.

When it all came out, I was astounded that something hadn't surfaced earlier. If someone had spoken up, Lucy might still be alive. Regrettably, each paranoid delusion and retribution was small. For years, her behavior went unreported. No one saw the pattern.

After learning of Ms. Wilson's craziness, the city attorney feared an NGI plea—not guilty by reason of insanity. Ever cautious to not waste taxpayers' money, he cut a plea deal for second-degree murder. He locked her away, saved the city money, and was reelected.

He needn't have been concerned because Vicki's detectives uncovered that she'd also murdered her husband, and possibly two roommates.

To everyone's amazement, MIT accepted Richie and he decided to leave California to major in Course 12—Earth, Atmospheric, and Planetary Science along with fellow Bruin, Brooklynn. The pair of them, thrown together as the only students from Stony Estancia, went on to start up a green tech company dedicated to saving the planet as a tribute to Ms. Salas.

At the end of the summer, I received an invitation from Jackie Siegbahn, Vincent Purcell, and Pedro Salas to the wedding of Jackson Siegbahn and Annette Landau. I recognized the address—Jackie's home in the hills. Since the birth of her granddaughter, Jackie and her expansive home had become the social center of Stony Estancia. Not surprisingly, her sculptures experienced a sharp uptick in demand.

The wedding was the social event of the summer. Brooklynn attended with her mother as her plus-one. She even purchased a new dress.

Charlie was the officiant.

The home theater played movies of Alejandra Siegbahn— Little Alex—on a loop.

Mr. Kapitsa, in a rented tuxedo, arrived alone. He sat with the Stony High teachers. Both his tux and the party rentals came from Schrödinger's Secondhand Store.

We all talked about plans for the next year and the upcoming dedication of the Ms. Lucinda Salas Memorial Science Garden where the AP Biology class had repeated Mendel's classic experiment.

The wedding cake—red velvet filled with white chocolate ganache and covered with white vanilla-bean fondant—was from that wonderful pâtisserie on Higgs Road. After it was served, the music ended, and the guests began flowing down the hill. I helped myself to a second piece of cake and walked out to the backyard to enjoy the city lights.

Vicki came up behind me, "Peaceful, isn't it?"

I swallowed my mouthful of cake. "Maybe, but Stony Estancia isn't as quiet as I expected."

She put her arm around my waist, "You can't always trust your intuition."

"You're right," I admitted. "I'm going to the animal shelter to adopt one of those cute kittens. That's all the excitement I need."

'*Or two,*' Fitch laughed.

SAVING THE PLANET

How can this book save the planet?

A book can't stop global warming, but it can set an example. Take a moment to think back on all the small ways Brooklynn and the Ecology Club supported a greener planet. Saving the planet wasn't a special event like prom, stopping a stalker, or finding a murderer. It was a way of life, a quotidian routine. Minimize trash. Renewable energy. Cloth hankies. Less consumerism. More reuse. Less plastic. Composting. Vegetarianism. Electric vehicles. Progress in the real world depends on everyone adopting a green lifestyle as a part of ordinary day-to-day life. Be like Brooklynn—do your part—lead by example.

To the Reader

Please accept the author's gratitude for finding and reading this book.

I am an independent author and appreciate how difficult it is to select my books from the flood of offerings. I am dependent on reader-to-reader recommendations.

If you enjoyed my novel and wish to support independent writers, I would appreciate any posts on social media, especially an all-important Amazon rating. A review on Goodreads also helps.

If you would like to correspond with the author or receive infrequent updates about Zarand Szilard, substitute teacher, you can send an email to Zarand.Szilard at gmail.com.

You might also be interested in the novel mentioned in chapter 20, *Darwin's Paradox: An international science mystery* by J. Oestreicher and D. R. Oestreicher. Available from most online booksellers: ISBN: 9780963175557.

Omega Cat Press books can be found at:
https://amzn.to/2SpaDMN

Thank you.

Dr. O. (the name I wrote on the whiteboard when I subbed.)

CHEERS, CREDITS, AND CITATIONS

Many people and organizations (knowingly and not) contributed to this work of fiction. Acknowledgment here does not imply an endorsement, review, or even knowledge, of this book.

Much gratitude to the San Bernardino County Museum for answering my questions about the Yuhaviatam and the (fictional) bracelet that Annie found. http://www.sbcounty.gov/museum/

Special thanks to my beta readers April and Bob, https://critters.org/, and my partner in crime, Joy, who was with me through the many rewrites. Any remaining problems belong solely to me.

Also, thanks to Jason, Samantha, Jennie, Joy, and my friends on Facebook for their review of the cover.

"*Sí, se puede*" (quoted in chapter 5) was the rallying cry of the United Farm Workers. Co-founders Dolores Huerta and César Chavez adopted the slogan during a 25-day fast in 1972.

In chapter 7, "Every murderer removed something from the scene and left something else in exchange," is a paraphrase of Locard's principle of forensic science formulated by French detective Dr. Edmond Locard (1877-1966).

"Though she be but little she is fierce" (quoted in chapter 11) is from William Shakespeare's *A Midsummer Night's Dream*, spoken by Helena in act 3, scene 2, referring to her friend Hermia.

Isaac Newton (1642-1726) and Gottfried Leibniz (1646-1716) (mentioned in chapter 12) were contemporaries who independently discovered calculus.

The idea that eyewitnesses are unreliable (referred to in chapter 13) came from Mark L. Howe & Lauren M. Knott (2015) *The fallibility of memory in judicial processes:*

Oestreicher

Lessons from the past and their modern consequences, *Memory*, 23:5, 633-656.

The idea that clearance rates are negatively impacted by DNA evidence (referred to in chapter 13) came from Schroeder, D. (2007). *DNA and homicide clearance: What's really going on?* The Journal of the Institute of Justice & International Studies, 7, 276-295.

The case of the chimeric mother's welfare difficulties (chapter 15) is fictional, but a similar case is reported in *Natural human chimeras: A review* by Kamlesh Madan published in European Journal of Medical Genetics 63 (2020) 103971.

This is *The Magical Number Seven* publication (mentioned in chapter 19): Miller, G. A. (1956). *The magical number seven, plus or minus two: Some limits on our capacity for processing information.* Psychological Review. 63 (2): 81–97.

Infants with severe combined immunodeficiency or SCID (introduced in chapter 27) appear healthy at birth but cannot fight off infections. The condition is fatal unless they receive immune-restoring treatments. Fortunately, SCID can be detected with newborn screening.

"Shelter from the Storm" (title of chapter 28) is the title of a song by Bob Dylan, released on his classic album, Blood on the Tracks, in 1975. He won the 2016 Nobel Prize in Literature.

California Penal Code 647.6 (mentioned in chapter 29), "Every person who annoys or molests any child under 18 years of age shall be punished ... Every person who, motivated by an unnatural or abnormal sexual interest in children, engages in conduct with an adult whom he or she believes to be a child under 18 years of age, ..."

"Rings on her fingers and bells on her toes," paraphrased by Mrs. Wilson (in chapter 31) is from an English nursery rhyme and has been incorporated into several 20th-century songs.

I must acknowledge these editors who believe this book and all books are about cats.

Chapter graphics
School by Mike Wirth, US from the Noun Project 54581. Pupils by David Khai, US from the Noun Project 2023631. Paid licenses.

Cover art
The cover was designed with Photopea.com, an advanced online photo editor. Ivan Kutskir is the creator of Photopea. He was born in Ukraine but lives in the Czech Republic.

ABOUT THE AUTHOR

I grew up on Long Island, NY. I attended MIT as an undergraduate. Not unlike Richie, my application was a long shot, but MIT accepted me. After graduate school in Salt Lake City (Computer Science), I worked at Silicon Valley startups. Like Mr. Szilard, when I retired, I went back to school to get my California teaching credential. As a substitute, I wrote DR. O. on the whiteboard at the start of each day. Today I live in Southern California with my wife, and often co-author, and our cats. We enjoy our grandkids, international travel (Covid-19 willing), reading, and writing.

THE SCIENTISTS

Every author must invent names. I turned to science for inspiration. These are some of the scientists whose names I borrowed. No endorsement is implied.

Luis Walter Alvarez: American physicist who won the Nobel Prize for Physics in 1968.

Hiroshi Amano: Japanese physicist who won the Nobel Prize for Physics in 2014.

Edward Victor Appleton: English physicist who won the Nobel Prize for Physics in 1947.

Niels Bohr: Danish physicist who won the Nobel Prize for Physics in 1948.

Patrick Blackett: British physicist who won the Nobel Prize for Physics in 1922.

Lawrence Bragg: Australian-born physicist who won the Nobel Prize for Physics in 1915.

Percy Williams Bridgman: American physicist who won the Nobel Prize for Physics in 1946.

Rachel Carson: American marine biologist, author, and conservationist who authored the influential book *Silent Spring* in 1962.

Ana Maria Cetto: Mexican Physicist and Deputy Director-General of the International Atomic Energy Agency (IAEA) when it won the Nobel Peace Prize in 2005.

Subrahmanyan Chandrasekhar: Indian-American astrophysicist who won the Nobel Prize for Physics in 1983.

Emmanuelle Charpentier: French professor and researcher in microbiology, genetics, and biochemistry who won the Nobel Prize for Chemistry in 2020—for the discovery of CRISPR (mentioned in chapter 16).

Marie, Pierre, and Irène Curie: Mother, father, and daughter won four Nobel Prizes.

Charles Darwin: English naturalist, geologist, and biologist. Author of *On the Origin of Species* in 1859.

Jennifer Doudna: American biochemist who won the Nobel Prize for Chemistry in 2020—for the discovery of CRISPR (mentioned in chapter 16).

Val Logsdon Fitch: American nuclear physicist who won the Nobel Prize for Physics in 1980.

William Alfred Fowler: American nuclear physicist who won the Nobel Prize for Physics in 1983.

Rosalind Franklin: English chemist and X-ray crystallographer whose work was central to the understanding of the molecular structures of DNA

Andrea Ghez: MIT class of '87. American astrophysicist who won the Nobel Prize for Physics in 2020.

Werner Heisenberg: German physicist who won the Nobel Prize for Physics in 1932.

Peter Higgs: British physicist who won the Nobel Prize for Physics in 2013

J. Hans D. Jenson: German physicist who won the Nobel Prize for Physics in 1963.

Pyotr Kapitsa: Romanian physicist who won the Nobel Prize for Physics in 1978.

Lev Landau: Azerbaijani physicist who won the Nobel Prize for Physics in 1962.

Antonie van Leeuwenhoek: Dutch businessman and scientist known as the Father of Microbiology.

Gottfried Wilhelm Leibniz: German mathematician and scientist in the 17th century.

Carl Linnaeus: Swedish botanist, zoologist, taxonomist, and physician who formalized binomial nomenclature.

Guglielmo Marconi: Italian inventor and electrical engineer who was awarded the Nobel Prize for Physics in 1909.

Cheikh Mbacke: Senegalese statistician who was awarded the Rockefeller Foundation Outstanding Achievement Award in 2003.

Gregor Mendel: Austrian monk who discovered the basic principles of heredity through experiments in his garden in the 19th century.

Barbara McClintock: American scientist and cytogeneticist won the Nobel Prize for Physiology in 1983.

Peggoty Mutai: Kenyan chemist who researched parasitic worms and neglected tropical diseases.

Isaac Newton: English mathematician and physicist in the 17th century.

Wolfgang Pauli: Austrian physicist who won the Nobel Prize for Physics in 1945.

Edward Mills Purcell: American physicist who won the Nobel Prize for Physics in 1952.

James Rainwater: American physicist who won the Nobel Prize for Physics in 1975.

Margarita Salas: Spanish scientist, medical researcher, and author in the fields of biochemistry and molecular genetics.

Erwin Schrödinger: Austrian-Irish physicist who won the Nobel Prize for Physics in 1933.

Manne and Kai Siegbahn: Father and son Swedish physicists who won the Nobel Prize for Physics in 1924 and 1981.

Leo Szilard: Hungarian-American physicist who wrote the letter that resulted in the Manhattan Project.

Daniel C. Tsui: Chinese-born American physicist who won the Nobel Prize for Physics in 1998.

Hoàng Tuy: Vietnamese applied mathematician.

Martinus J. G. Veltman: Dutch physicist who won the Nobel Prize for Physics in 1999.

John Hasbrouck Van Vleck: American physicist who won the Nobel Prize for Physics in 1977.

Eugene Wigner: Hungarian physicist who won the Nobel Prize for Physics in 1963.

Charles Thomson Rees Wilson: Scottish physicist who won the Nobel Prize for Physics in 1927.

Hideki Yukawa: Japanese physicist who won the Nobel Prize for Physics in 1949.

Pieter Zeeman: Dutch physicist who won the Nobel Prize for Physics in 1902.

Zarand Szilard #2 (The Library Club) borrows names from authors, especially those on the American Library Association's lists of Banned and Challenged Books (https://www.ala.org/advocacy/bbooks). No endorsement is implied. These two appeared in The Ecology Club.

Judy Blume: Children's author with five books on various lists: *Are You There, God? It's Me, Margaret*; *Blubber*; *Deenie*; *Forever*; *Tiger Eyes*.

Mark Twain: 19th-century American author with two books on various lists: *The Adventures of Tom Sawyer*; *The Adventures of Huckleberry Finn*.

HELP IS AVAILABLE

Information retrieved from the World Wide Web in 2022.

Suicide

US: National Suicide Prevention Lifeline: Available 24 hours. Languages: English, Spanish. 9-8-8. Suicide and Crisis Lifeline.

UK: Samaritans: Contact a Samaritan. If you need someone to talk to, we listen. We won't judge or tell you what to do. We're here 24 hours a day, 365 days a year. Call 116 123 for free.

Canada: The Canada Suicide Prevention Service. Need help? Connect with our responders now. Call 1.833.456.4566. Available 24/7/365.

Australia: You are not alone. We're here to listen. Every 30 seconds, a person in Australia reaches out to Lifeline for help. 24-hour crisis support and suicide prevention services. Call 13 11 14.

Domestic Violence

US: If you are in immediate danger, call 9-1-1. For anonymous, confidential help, 24/7, please call the National Domestic Violence Hotline at 1-800-799-7233 (SAFE) or TTY 1-800-787-3224.

UK: If you are in an emergency, please call 999. Remember, you can call us anytime. We are here for you. Call the freephone, 24-hour National Domestic Abuse Helpline, in confidence. Call 0808 2000 247.

Canada: If you are in immediate danger Call 9-1-1 (9-1-1 is not available in Nunavut). ShelterSafe.ca provides information to help connect women and their children across Canada with the nearest shelter for safety and support.

Australia: 1800RESPECT (1800 737 732) The national domestic, family, and sexual violence counselling, information, and support service for any Australian who has experienced, or is at risk of, family and domestic violence and/or sexual assault. 24 hours, 7 days a week.

www.ingramcontent.com/pod-product-compliance
Lightning Source LLC
Chambersburg PA
CBHW060543180626
46817CB00002B/700